TALES of MURDER, MYSTERY & the MACABRE

nEvermore!

Neo-Gothic Fiction Inspired by the Imagination of EDGAR ALLAN POE

Edited by

NANCY KILPATRICK
and CARO SOLES

EDGE SCIENCE FICTION AND FANTASY PUBLISHING
AN IMPRINT OF HADES PUBLICATIONS, INC.

CALGARY

nEvermore! Tales of Murder, Mystery and the Macabre

Edge Science Fiction and Fantasy Publishing
An Imprint of Hades Publications Inc.
P.O. Box 1714, Calgary, Alberta, T2P 2L7, Canada

Edited by Nancy Kilpatrick and Caro Soles

Interior design by Janice Blaine

ISBN: 978-1-77053-085-0

EDGE Science Fiction and Fantasy Publishing and Hades Publications, Inc.
acknowledges the ongoing support of the Alberta Foundation for the Arts and
the Canada Council for the Arts for our publishing programme.

Alberta   Canada Council   Conseil des arts
                 for the Arts   du Canada

Library and Archives Canada Cataloguing in Publication

CIP Data on file with the National Library of Canada

ISBN: 978-1-77053-085-0

(e-Book ISBN: 978-1-77053-086-7)

FIRST EDITION
(O-20150613)
Printed in Canada
www.edgewebsite.com

CONTENTS

DEDICATION

This work is dedicated to the master dream-weaver! Thank you, Mr. Poe, for the thrills and chills.

And to Tanith Lee who, like Poe, deserves to be remembered.

> *All that we see or seem*
> *is but a dream within a dream.*
> — from *A Dream Within a Dream* by Edgar Allan Poe

＋ ・ ＋

Introduction

IT'S BEEN NEARLY 170 YEARS since his death, yet his name is legend, and recognized world-wide. His short fiction and poetry is still read by just about every school child in the world, and aficionados of his work peruse his essays and letters. Well over 70 films and scores of TV shows or series have been directly or indirectly inspired by his work, and there have been a significant number of theatrical presentations, musical pieces and artwork inspired by the writer. All this from Edgar Allan Poe, a man who lived and died with a broken heart.

It would be an understatement to say that Poe's *oeuvre* was created while enduring the well-known tragedies of his life, a life saturated with loss, poverty and betrayal. His troubles were many and his fortunes few. He was the first American writer to try to earn a living from writing, and one of the earliest American writers of short fiction. Fame shrouded him upon his death, leaving him immortal. It is a testament to the human spirit that Poe wrote through his sad existence to bequeath to us some of the most memorable and touching fiction and poetry that has ever been written.

Edgar Allan Poe is often identified by the Gothic-style of his supernatural fiction. He is also famous as the inventor of the modern detective story. His influence spans centuries and he inspired the grandparents of genres as disparate as romance and science fiction. He wrote from the heart and soul and his fears, worries and intellect are evident throughout what his quill translated from his genius mind to paper.

We would be lesser human beings without his cherished stories and poems and for this reason we, the co-editors of *nEvermore! Tales of Murder, Mystery and the Macabre*, wanted to compile an anthology to honor him.

To that end, we invited well-known authors to spin for us Poe-like tales. Write us a mystery with supernatural leanings, like Poe did, we said. Write a supernatural story with the hint of a mystery, just as Poe constructed, we asked them. We invited writers of all stripes to pen an original Poe-like story, or to use an existing Poe story or poem as a jumping-off point. Within are original tales that possess a Poe-esque quality, and, as well, riffs on familiar Poe stories and poems, taking his fiction as a direct inspiration. Have a read and investigate what our amazing writers have created when inspired by: *The Black Cat; Annabel Lee; The Gold Bug; The Murders in the Rue Morgue; The Lighthouse; The Raven; Berenice; The Masque of the Red Death.* We begin with an enlightening essay: *A Rather Scholarly View of Edgar Allan Poe, Genre-Crosser!*

We hope you enjoy *nEvermore!* We certainly enjoyed compiling this special and unusual anthology. It has been our delight and our privilege to immerse ourselves in Poe's legacy and to celebrate this author who gave so much to so many.

— Nancy Kilpatrick, Montreal 2015
— Caro Soles, Toronto 2015

❧ · ❧

A Rather Scholarly View of Edgar Allan Poe, Genre Crosser

by Uwe Sommerlad

EDGAR ALLAN POE did not write genres; it was his idea that a collection of stories would show a great variety, and that — read together — they would in some way complement one another.

On the 1845 Poe story collection "Tales", selected not by Poe but by Evert A. Duyckinck, the author complained to a correspondent, "He... has accordingly made up the book mostly of analytic stories. But this is not *representing* my mind in its various phases— it is not giving me fair play. In writing these Tales one by one, at long intervals, I have kept the book-unity always in mind— that is, each has been composed with reference to its effect as part of *a whole*. In this view, one of my chief aims has been the widest diversity of subject, thought, and especially *tone* and manner of handling."

The horrific worked quite well with the laughter to Poe, obviously, and his first collection of stories, "Tales of the Folio Club" — had it ever seen the light of day — was intended to be framed in a grotesque satirical setting, making fun of literary critique and the publishing business. Yet it contained stories like the dyed in the wool horror tale "Metzengerstein". He had already toyed with the idea to call his stories *Arabesques* then. The collection Poe himself had edited in 1840, which was only moderately successful, he titled "Tales of the Grotesque and Arabesque", a description he probably had distilled from an essay Sir Walter Scott wrote in 1827 for the *Foreign Quarterly*

Review about the "sickliness" of E. T. A Hoffmann's stories and novels, and the German taste for the supernatural Gothic tale in general, as opposed to "the virtuous and manly" which Scott idealized in his medieval romances.

Poe, although it is uncertain whether or not he read E.T.A. Hoffmann, was rather smitten with the subversiveness of the sickly, it seems. Still, he felt he had to defend himself against charges of bad taste and the 'Germanism' in his writing. And not only in his correspondence (he wrote to one publisher, "But whether the articles of which I speak are, or are not in bad taste is little to the purpose. To be appreciated you must be read, and these things are invariably sought after with avidity.") Also, in his preface to "Tales of the Grotesque and Arabesque", he assures his readers, while addressing his critics, that he is able to write better stories than those presented in the collection: "Let us admit, for the moment, that the 'phantasy-pieces' now given are Germanic, or what not. Then Germanism is 'the vein' for the time being. Tomorrow I may be anything but German, as yesterday I was everything else. These many pieces are yet one book. My friends would be quite as wise in taxing an astronomer with too much astronomy, or an ethical author with treating too largely of morals. But the truth is that, with a single exception, there is no one of these stories in which the scholar should recognize the distinctive features of that species of pseudo-horror which we are taught to call Germanic, for no better reason than that some of the secondary names of German literature have become identified with its folly. If in many of my productions terror has been the thesis, I maintain that terror is not of Germany, but of the soul— that I have deduced this terror only from its legitimate sources, and urged it only to its legitimate results."

Those who think it necessary to defend Poe against the accusation that he was a writer of horror stories like to point out that only a part of his output can actually be counted as *Contes Cruels*, and very few are actually supernatural tales. Yet many of his satires have supernatural elements, his philosophical writings tend to be metaphysical, and his adventurous and 'analytical' stories often make use of the grotesque and the gruesome. Take the closed-room mystery "The Murders in the Rue Morgue", the first of Poe's three tales about the amateur detective Auguste Dupin. While it has all the elements of what

Poe called an analytic story, it also is one of his most grotesque and cruel tales, in which it turns out that the horrible murders were actually committed by an ape on the loose.

Madness is, of course, one recurring theme in Poe's work, as is revenge; the first an expression of his belief that 'terror is not of Germany, but of the soul', the second probably stemming from his own subconscious and the treatment he had received during his lifetime— from his foster father, from critics, from publishers and from other writers. Often Poe makes the reader an accomplice, by having the madman and/or murderer as the storyteller. Poe called the driving force, the impulse to commit murder and other atrocities 'the imp of the perverse' (also the title of one of his tales), and some of the most famous stories by him fall into that category: "The Tell-Tale Heart", "The Black Cat", "The Cask of Amontillado". None of them is supernatural, although the first two contain every element of a ghost story, where the villain is haunted by his own guilt, leading to his downfall. The difference is that there are no *ghosts* evident, only the bad conscience of the murderer. "The Fall of the House of Usher" is a supernatural tale, describing the descent of a degenerated, probably incestuous family into madness and demise.

Some amount of madness and definitely a huge portion of psychology also play a large role in Poe's work dealing with the loss of a beloved, namely "Morella" (the closest to a vampire story in his *oeuvre*), "Ligeia", "Eleonore" and "Berenice" (and quite a few of his poems, namely "The Raven"). The first three concern the possibilities of reincarnation, the last one is a *Conte Cruel* about the fear of premature burial, which is another recurring theme in Poe's stories. Poe himself had lost his mother when he was two, his foster mother Frances Allan when he was twenty, and finally his wife Virginia when he was thirty-eight— probably the only three people he was ever really devoted to, apart from his aunt Maria Clemm, who survived him and lived for another twenty-seven years, mainly because of the generosity of Poe's friends, admirers and colleagues, including Charles Dickens and Henry Wadsworth Longfellow.

In the adventurous sea yarn "MS Found in A Bottle" — a warm-up for Poe's only novel, *A Narrative of Arthur Gordon Pym of Nantucket* — the supernatural appears in the shape of a ghost ship. Although the hair of the protagonist in Poe's second sea story, "A Descent into the Maelström" turns white because of the terror he faces, he saves his skin by analytical evaluation of his situation. Another adventure story, "The Gold-Bug", first describes a treasure hunt but then delves into the analytic when a secret message has to be deciphered.

Poe, especially in his early writings, was much influenced by Lord Byron's doomed heroes and probably by E.T.A. Hoffmann, who made use of the doppelganger theme, later utilized to great effect in Poe's "William Wilson". One of Poe's tales, "The Pit and the Pendulum", obviously took its inspiration from the similarly-themed "The Iron Shroud" published twelve years earlier by William Mudford. Poe makes the fundamental idea completely his own, though, and gives it a fresh spin.

✦ · ✦

The reception of Poe during his lifetime was mixed. He never made a larger sum out of his writing than the $100.00 he won in a *Philadelphia Dollar Newspaper* writing contest in 1843 with his "The Gold-Bug". Despite the huge popularity of this story, and of his 1845 poem "The Raven", his books did not sell well, and his larger fame lay more within his work as a fearless, strident, often acerbic critic than as a poet or a writer of fiction.

In a rather strange turn, he made the Reverend Rufus W. Griswold his literary executor. Griswold, a mediocre writer more than once criticized by Poe, quickly took revenge on his 'tormentor' by publishing first an obituary (signed as *Ludwig*), which was initially printed in the *New York Tribune* and then re-printed in newspapers and magazines around North America. It began: "Edgar Allan Poe is dead. He died in Baltimore the day before yesterday. This announcement will startle many, but few will be grieved by it. The poet was known, personally or by reputation, in all this country; he had readers in England, and in several of the states of Continental Europe; but he had few or no friends; and the regrets for his death will be suggested principally by the consideration that in him literary art has lost one of its most brilliant but erratic stars."

Whatever was written after this much lengthier biographical obituary and the notoriously-inaccurate "Memoir of the Author" biography, also by Griswold, published the year after Poe's death (in the third of the four-volume "The Works of the Late Edgar Allan Poe" Griswold edited, now known as "The

Griswold Edition"), nothing could change the public's perception of Poe. But Griswold, who had poisoned the water for about a century, still throws a long shadow. He painted Poe as arrogant, irascible, unfriendly, envious, selfish, vulgar, a cynic, a Godless man and a miser, and worse: "...there seemed to him no moral susceptibility; and... little or nothing of the true point of honour". Even Griswold didn't deny Poe's genius. He did deny him, though, the human qualities to deserve it. Those writers coming to Poe's aid could not undo the damage of Griswold's opprobrious, hypocritical writing. One commented that Griswold obviously misunderstood the meaning of 'literary executor' by taking an axe to Poe.

Although Poe was heavily damaged by Griswold — who even rewrote passages in a few of Poe's letters to put himself in a better light and to stain Poe even more — his work survived unharmed. It's hard to think of a history of literature without including Edgar Allan Poe. While he was inspired by few, he, in turn, influenced almost every field of writing that came after him — another sign that his writing wasn't received only as 'genre literature'.

Mark Twain's satires, for example, owe quite a bit to those of Poe, one — "The Invalid's Story" — being a parody of Poe's "A Descent into the Maelström". There are more than just traces of "William Wilson" in "The Facts Concerning the Recent Carnival of Crime in Connecticut" and a good dose of "The Gold-Bug" in "The Adventures of Tom Sawyer". Alan Gribben points out that "A Narrative of Arthur Gordon Pym of Nantucket" obviously impressed Twain immensely, and that its influence can be traced in both "Life on the Mississippi", and his masterpiece "The Adventures of Huckleberry Finn". Supposedly Twain, who once quipped about Poe that "to me his prose is unreadable" always kept Poe's prose in his pocket when he was young.

Another great American novel, Herman Melville's "Moby-Dick", also is much influenced by "Pym", as well as by "MS. Found in a Bottle".

Ambrose "Bitter" Bierce — also walking in the footsteps of Poe — made his own explorations into the macabre, which led to him being compared to Poe all the time, despite the fact that Bierce developed a much more cynical view on the world than his predecessor — who was fundamentally a moral writer, despite everything Griswold said about him — ever had. Like every writer of *Contes Cruels,* including Poe, Bierce was stigmatized as 'morbid'.

This sometimes called an *unhealthy* influence of Poe was not limited to America. Charles Baudelaire, who during his lifetime also struggled with poverty, idolized Poe and translated him into French. From the fertile soil of Poe's imagination grew Baudelaire's own "Les Fleurs du Mal", which in turn made a huge impression on Rimbaud and Mallarmé. Baudelaire now is described as an important representative of literary surrealism— another strange fruit from Poe's roots.

Probably France's greatest admirer of Poe — at least the most commercially successful — was Jules Verne. The 'analytical' Poe, his interest in the scientific beliefs of his time and their probable development and outcome as well as his fascination with the forces of nature, inspired Verne's *Voyages Extraordinaires*. The airship from Poe's "The Balloon Hoax" and "Mellonta Tauta", the moon flight from his "The Unparalleled Adventure of One Hans Pfaall" grew roots in Verne's work, making *Robur the Conqueror* a king of the skies and the Baltimore Gun Club explorers of space. Again, *A Narrative of Arthur Gordon Pym of Nantucket* set high sails. The cannibalization of a shipmate in Verne's 1875 "Le Chancellor: Journal du passager J. R. Kazallon" owes a debt to Poe's only novel, and "Le Sphinx des glaces", published in 1897, is a straight sequel to *Pym*. And his grotesque short stories mirror the satires of Poe. Verne went on to inspire not only many writers — like Ray Bradbury — but also explorers and scientists, from Norwegian polar explorer Fridtjof Nansen to German-American aerospace engineer Wernher von Braun, becoming not the inventor of the so-called science fiction novel, but regarded as its godfather.

In Britain, the writers who were influenced by the power of Poe make quite an impressive line-up. Robert Louis Stevenson— would *Treasure Island* have been written without "The Gold-Bug"? Is *The Strange Case of Dr. Jekyll and Mr. Hyde* imaginable without Poe's explorations into the human mind? Stevenson loathed Poe the man, but admired his literary skills as well as his "important contribution to morbid psychology".

The early tales of Herbert George Wells show the footprints of his predecessor; experts in English literature point out connections to Poe's work in the short story "The Star" and in the novels *Days of the Comet* and *The Island of Dr. Moreau*.

The vengeful feline in Bram Stoker's "The Squaw" is quite obviously of the same ilk as Poe's "The Black Cat", while the giant rat in Stoker's "The Judge's House" and the red horse in Poe's "Metzengerstein" share their malevolent influence on the two protagonists.

Joseph Conrad always praised Poe's authenticity of descriptions of the sea and spiked his own works with references to his writings, including his masterpiece *Heart of Darkness*. That Conrad's 1913 short story "The Inn of the Two Witches" borrows directly from Poe's "The Pit and the Pendulum" — as Jeffrey Meyers wrote in his Poe biography — is somewhat doubtful though. Conrad's tale is more of a re-telling of Wilkie Collins' 1852 story "A Terribly Strange Bed" — which in turn might well have been influenced by the moving walls in Poe's yarn.

That people could reenact events of the past, as in Poe's "A Tale of the Ragged Mountains", became quite a common plot device in the works of Henry Rider Haggard. Rudyard Kipling wrote that "My own personal debt to Poe is a heavy one," most likely referring to his own supernatural tales and poetry.

With his essay "The Poetic Principle" — praising art for art's sake and denying that "every poem... should inculcate a moral," — Poe opened the door to Oscar Wilde, who went on to phrase something similar, if more radical, in the preface to his novel *The Picture of Dorian Gray*: "There is no such thing as a moral or an immoral book. Books are well written, or badly written. That is all." *Dorian Gray*, brilliantly written, is an offspring of Poe's story "The Oval Portrait", with a difference; while Poe's artist puts so much of the life of his subject into his painting that the subject withers and dies the moment the portrait is finished, in Wilde's novel the painting does not reabsorb the subject's life force, but lives on the evil it commits. The finale brings us straight back to the end of Poe's "William Wilson".

The Victorian writer who never stopped bowing to the memory of Poe was Sir Arthur Conan Doyle. His story "The New Catacomb" is a variation of "The Cask of Amontillado", and there are more than just traces of Poe in many of his stories. His main tribute, though, was the creation of Sherlock Holmes and Dr. Watson, taking the lead from where Poe left off Auguste Dupin and his nameless friend and making the genre Poe had invented — the detective story — completely his own. Doyle wrote in his book "Through the Magic Door": "Poe is, to my mind, the supreme original short-story writer of all time.... If every man who receives a cheque for a story which owes its springs to Poe were to pay a tithe to a monument for the master, he would have a pyramid as big as that of Cheops."

Poe, the horror writer. Poe, the poet. Poe, the critic. Poe, the inventor of the detective story. A major force in the development of the science fiction genre. A master of the Gothics. The godfather of psychological thrills. The obstetrician of symbolism. A jester. A philosopher.

Did Poe write in genres? No, he did not. He did not care to be slotted. He was a major force in his time, never afraid to cross a border on well-trimmed grounds or to explore unknown regions in literature. Poe shaped the future. He was adored by Thomas Mann. He left imprints in the work of James Joyce. He made Howard Phillips Lovecraft a high priest in his temple. His disciples are impossible to count, impossible to trace, but you find him in the morbidity of Hanns Heinz Ewers, in the dark world inside the head of Robert Bloch, and in the investigations of Douglas Preston and Lincoln Child. He's on the surface of Ray Bradbury's Mars and hidden in the charms of Neil Gaiman's poetic prose. One could almost say his offspring rule the world of literature. Today we can identify and acknowledge the presence of Edgar Allan Poe, who came like a thief in the night and to this day holds illimitable dominion over all.

Poe, the genius. He probably would like that honorific. Let us build a pyramid to him, or two.

＊ · ＊

THE GOLD BUG CONUNDRUM

by Chelsea Quinn Yarbro

Chelsea Quinn Yarbro says: "The second of two required English courses when I was in college was devoted to American literature; the professor earnestly believed that all fiction was based on some actuality that was either the writer's personal experience, or something he had heard or read. From Hawthorne to Hemmingway, we spent the semester scrounging through biographies to find some justification for his theory. I did my semester paper on Poe, and it has returned to haunt me."

✦ · ✦

IT WAS AN OLD HOUSE, a relic of the Gilded Age, abandoned almost forty years ago after a sixth powerful hurricane had plowed right through the area, pulling off huge sections of the old roof, shattering windows, demolishing most of the central chimneys, spilling bricks in all directions, and stripping the east side of the structure of shingles and 1880s gingerbread. Since it was ravaged, trees and lower-growing plants had made inroads on their reclamation of what remained of the place, repossessing it for the island; an odor of decomposing wood, plants, mortar, and excrement hung over it in an all-but-visible haze.

For the last half hour of their drive to the enormous house, Jeff Milton and Peregrine Rudolph had been discussing *Moby Dick*, and the historical incident upon which it was based. "Melville didn't need to have an actual event to tell the story," Milton had declared for the third time as they rounded a particularly steep curve in the poorly graded road.

"But he knew about it. People talked about it," Rudolph had insisted, clinging to the steering wheel. "He used that to add credibility to his work."

"That's likely, yes. But the book's not reportage— it's a novel: you know, a made-up story," Milton had responded adamantly.

"Yes, it is, but it's rooted in fact. Melville didn't imagine it, not completely. He used a real situation to build on."

"God, Rudi, why is it you can't stand that it's *fiction?* Why does every good story have to be based on something before you'll accept it?"

"No, of course not," said Rudolph. "But it happens more often than you think that actualities contribute to stories, and that increases the believability of the story. And you know it."

"You may be right, but I still wouldn't discount the imagination. You use your games all the time." Milton had been more annoyed than he wanted to admit; Rudolph often had that effect on him.

"But based on reality," Rudolph maintained.

"Does that include your *Enemy Stars* game? All those peculiar beings you came up with. It's pretty out there, even for a science fiction game, or don't you think so?"

When Rudolph had not answered, Milton had fallen silent, and waited to arrive at the old, so-called summer cottage — fifteen bedrooms, two dining rooms, a breakfast room, a parlor, a sitting room, a ballroom, a library, and all the other necessities required by the seriously wealthy — that had been built well over a century ago.

"We're here," Rudolph said, turning toward his brother-in-law as he pulled in to the sand-scoured expanse of what had long ago been one of three tennis courts, about one hundred feet from the battered front door that was partially visible through a heavy screen of tropical plants.

Milton had been uneasy for most of their hour journey along the dusty, graveled road, becoming more and more apprehensive the farther they got from Sainte Gertrude, the nearest town, and now that they had arrived, he asked, "Rudi, whatever possessed you to buy this God-awful place?"

Peregrine Rudolph chuckled as he unfastened his seatbelt. "Location, location, location," said as he opened the door and stepped out onto the littered swath of sand, grinning like a ten-year-old rather than the nearly forty he was. He gestured toward the gentle slope that led down to the wide swath of beach and the outrageously blue Caribbean. "Look at this spot, Jeff. Just look at it. It's beautiful— or don't you agree?"

"Oh, the view is nice, I'll give you that," said Milton, then turned to regard the disintegrating structure behind them. "But the house, Rudi. It's horrible."

"It can be fixed," Rudolph said blithely.

"But why? It's a ruin," Milton declared. "That house is only standing because the trees are holding it up. Rudi, think about it, please."

"Yeah, okay, it's pretty far gone. But consider the potential. Once this estate is restored, the view alone will spur business, don't you think?"

"You still want to make it a spa resort? Now that you're actually here, don't you see how impossible that is?" Milton asked, incredulity making his voice high and quarrelsome.

"Certainly I want to make the resort. Expensive, exclusive, and luxurious: world-class chefs, grand dining, celebrity entertainers, two swimming pools, hot tubs, the tennis courts, jogging trails, saunas, maybe a small casino, the whole experience," said Rudolph, his smile widening. "If we put in the cabins as we have them in the initial designs, we can accommodate up to two hundred guests, and a staff of three hundred."

"You plan to have people come through Sainte Gertrude, or will you bring them in from Esplanade?" Milton asked, his question verging on complaint; the central city of the island was little more than a slightly larger versions of Sainte Gertrude.

"I've submitted a proposal for building a new road from Sainte Gertrude; the harbor can accommodate cruise ships if we enlarge the waterfront and dredge out a channel."

"That will cost a fortune," Milton exclaimed.

"Then it's lucky that I have a fortune," Rudolph said. "We should be able to come up with a route from the docks to this place that won't disrupt the town too much, and won't upset the arriving guests." Rudolph took a long breath. "That's assuming that we have the right approach to the potential patrons. We need to be thinking about its snob appeal."

"That's a lot of supposition," Milton said. "And now I understand why you've played your cards so close to the vest with Caroline. You made it sound like the house was largely undamaged, and that there were cabins in place already, didn't you? Did you think she wouldn't figure it out? She'll have a fit when she sees this." Milton got out of the Land Rover, and frowned as his hiking boots sank a short way into the matted vegetable detritus underfoot.

"I gather you're planning to tell her," said Rudolph, some of his geniality fading.

"I'll have to," said Milton, doing all he could to sound reasonable. "She's my sister, and she depends on me, *especially* in regards to you. She'll pester me with questions, and you know it. To repeat: whatever possessed you?"

"I can afford it, if that's what's troubling you. This is a good project for me; you said so when I broached it with you. So did she," said Rudolph at his most placating. "Look, I appreciate my wife's concerns, which is why I asked her to come along with us, but she decided not to. She sent you in her stead: I understand that. But I'm glad to have you along, Jeff, no matter how sour your mood."

"She was afraid of what she'd find here. And looking around, I can't say I blame her. Jesus!" Milton made an abrupt gesture toward what little remained of the roof of the house. "What a wreck. I can't believe you know what you're getting into."

"Shit, Jeff, this is her idea as much as mine. I've got to spend my money on something, and I'm already giving to nine charities, endowing chairs at three universities, supporting twelve third-world schools, and a symphony orchestra. It's not that I'm not proud of my philanthropy, but I need some other kind of activity. This is just for me. It's a great opportunity." He came around the front of the Land Rover, stretching his arms over his head; the mid-afternoon sun was warm but not oppressive, the breeze carrying the aroma of blooming flowers as well as the smell of decay. "Caroline always complains that I spend too much time in my head, developing more computer games, tied to my computer room, and not paying any attention to the rest of the world— she's right. I have let myself get obsessive about more game development. So now I'm taking her advice, and finding something new to *obsess about*— her words."

"To put it differently, she thinks you need a hobby," said Milton. "Why this massive house restoration? It's overwhelming, and it could be more trouble than anything you can imagine, and that's crediting your imagination for being as vivid as it is. Why not do something in New England or Santa Cruz or Santa Fe — you have offices near those places — instead of the Caribbean? Why open a resort? Particularly in this... place? Wouldn't taking up fishing be better? Or sailing? Or bowling, for that matter? You're supposed to relax."

"They're boring, not relaxing. This won't be. Caroline knows how easily bored I can be." Rudolph took his rucksack out of the car and slung it over his shoulder. "And she's right about that, as well, of course. I can't think of anything more unlike designing computer games than restoring this old house. I've given this a lot of thought, and I have some basic figures on costs."

"Don't tell me yet, Rudi; I'm not sitting down," said Milton.

Rudolph smiled. "It's expensive to do it, but I've got it covered— I've told you, Jeff. And you agreed that I have a lot of disposable income."

"You do— but this looks like it could take all you have, and more."

"And when *The Outer Reaches* is released next year, I'll have more. If the HBO deal goes as well as we all expect, a lot more. The first opinion groups are very enthusiastic. Every teen-age geek in the world will want to see the series, and to buy the game after the movie's released."

"If you happen to develop a game about restoring old buildings, you can just plow the profits into this house, as well," said Milton with a hint of disapproval.

"I won't have to do that, but my accountants might recommend it, so I'm working out a Plan B. This ain't gonna be cheap, getting this estate in shape, but it's nothing I can't handle, unless the computer game industry collapses, and the way they've figured it, I'll have a healthy tax write-off on the restoration, and making the resort into its own profitable venture. I've already got some basic bids on the job— all US companies with branches in these islands." He grinned at Milton. "I researched the original plans, and all the information I could find about Gold Bug."

Milton groaned. "That's it, isn't it? Location be damned— it's the name. You and your Poe fixation. I still don't understand how a technophile like you can be hung up on Poe."

Rudolph was used to wrangling with Milton, and so he resisted the urge to snap. "That's part of the attraction here; it's what got me started thinking about this place; you've got to admit that the name is provocative— the builder let it be known that he financed it through treasure he found on this very site, and that intrigued me," he allowed, and started toward the front door, taking a flashlight from the capacious lower pocket in his jacket. "I don't know what we might find inside. You ought to be prepared."

"Squatters, probably, or rats and snakes," said Milton, reluctantly following Rudolph toward the wide covered porch that fronted the door, all partially concealed by encroaching undergrowth. "You'll have a real job protecting the site."

"I don't think so— most of the people hereabouts avoid the place. The people in Sainte Gertrude say that dangerous spirits guard it."

"Oh, shit," said Milton. "You *are* going to turn all that into another game, aren't you? With malign ghosts and every kind of nasty critter you can think of."

"Okay— the basic script has crossed my mind, but that happens often, and only about a third of those scripts turn into games. But this place is tempting in its own right. Might as well get a little extra for my efforts, right? An exclusive resort that has more potential than just a haunted house for a setting. It could have possibilities to open up a new sub-genre. We'll see how I feel when the job here is finished." Rudolph pushed aside a huge fan of tropical leaves and went to the stairs up to the wide, covered porch, taking care to test each step before actually putting his full weight on it; the planks groaned as Rudolph walked. He reached the broad veranda, and made his way gingerly toward the door, which was incongruously closed although only a few fragments of colored glass were left in the large, oval window set in its center.

"Pirates, too?" Milton waved away a flotilla of small, flying insects that had appeared around his head like a buzzing halo. "Your pirate game was your first big success. I can see you using pirates again."

"Or monsters," Rudolph answered, peering into the interior of the house. "There's more variety in monsters."

"Poe-monsters?" Milton asked, sounding worn out; he was growing tired of Rudolph's obsession with Poe.

"Lovecraft, more likely." Rudolph made an effort to remove the bits of glass without cutting himself. "You know, tentacled horrors shambling out of the sea, eldritch gods, that sort of thing."

"So you've started on it already?" Milton shook his head in dismay.

"Not started, Jeff, just trying out some ideas." He sighed. "As I've told you, I'll get this place restored before I turn my attention to a new game, no matter what that game is, if there is a game," Rudolph said, and focused his gaze on the entry hall. "It's a mess in there."

"Is it locked?" Milton asked, not quite sarcastically. "I'm not going to climb through that medallion window in the door."

"I doubt you'll have to; I have the keys to the house, just in case; I got them from the mayor of Sainte Gertrude." Rudolph reached for the door-latch, but drew back as a large spider made its way down the doorframe toward the pitted brass. Slowly Rudolph shrugged the rucksack off his shoulder and donned one of the canvas gloves he kept in the left-side bellows-pocket on his jacket. "We'll probably have more of these creepy-crawlies inside the house. I've been told there're bats in the upper floors." He sounded calm, but the high pitch of his voice revealed his nervousness.

"You sure you want to go in?" Milton asked as he came to the foot of the stairs.

"Not entirely, but it's something I have to do; I own it, and I need to make a report to the architects and engineers; you don't have to join me if you don't want to. I'll give you the keys to the Rover, and you can take a nap," Rudolph said, grasping the latch as he spoke; it groaned as the ancient mechanism moved. "We'll have to do something about this door."

"Among other things," Milton agreed dryly, making his way up the stairs in a sign of capitulation. "You'd do better to raze it and start over from scratch."

The hinges protested more loudly than the latch, setting off a flurry of scuttles and flappings inside the old house, and from one of the trees near the house, a bird screeched. At least, Rudolph thought, it sounded like a bird. Or it could have been a metal-on-metal screech. He picked up his rucksack before he shoved the door more fully open, and went tentatively into the large entry hall to the broken rubble of the collapsed domed ceiling. There was a big, broken chandelier lying in pieces amid swaths of shards of stained glass and dead leaves; the odor of mold was intense. Rudolph turned back to Milton. "You coming?" His first step crunched, and Rudolph shuddered at the sound, and the texture under his boot.

"I guess I have to," said Milton, and stepped into the entry hall. He stared up at the vacant hole where the dome had been. "Holy shit."

"You can say that again. I knew there was a lot of debris in this place, but this is more than I anticipated. The floor looks like it's been mulched." He paused and coughed against the dusty air, then winced as he watched a small, longitudinally striped snake wind away from where he was standing. "Be on the lookout for wildlife." He kicked some of the detritus aside. "I can't figure out where to begin, but that's not my job. The engineers will sort it out."

"What do you see your job as being, then?" Milton wanted to know. He looked about with increasing consternation.

"To restore this place to its original glory, of course. To make it everything it was when it was built. And make it better. All the steam-punkers will be slavering by the time I'm done." Rudolph squinted up toward where the dome had been. "I think I'll have to send the plans for the dome to one of those reconstruction companies in L. A.; we have the originals to work from; they have the artists to manage the stained glass, and the architects to figure out how to make it secure. We'll need the right kind of footing and anchorage so that it can stand up through the next big hurricane." Rudolph was regaining his composure.

"Is the staircase safe?" Milton asked, casting a wary eye on the grand sweep of it, circling the oval entry hall twice in its climb to the third floor; many treads were missing, a few of the risers were gone, and only three sections of the broken banister remained.

"I wouldn't think so. I'll skip going upstairs for now." Rudolph turned toward the parlor on the right. "The window-frames are intact in here. That's something."

"No glass in them," Milton pointed out. "This is the leeward side, isn't it?"

"Looks like it," said Rudolph, taking stock of his surroundings a bit more analytically than he had when he first caught sight of the place. "The window-frames are gone on the windward."

"Do you have any official report on the damage?" Milton asked.

"From the hurricane-before-last, I do. That one was a Five, as you will recall. The most recent barely made it to Four, and the house hasn't been assessed in terms of rebuilding; there's too much prior damage. That's because it's unoccupied— I'm going to have to find someone to be caretaker while the restoration is going on," said Rudolph, looking around; he set down his rucksack beside the newel-post at the foot of the staircase. "The main dining room's behind this parlor, and the breakfast room is behind that; the kitchen is on the left. According to the old plans, it's twenty-seven feet by thirty-four feet. Good sized for the time, but it will need to be enlarged when the house is rebuilt."

"What are you planning to do about electricity?" Milton inquired as he took his flashlight and turned it on. "Or will you go in for authentic gas-lighting?" He did not apologize for his critical tone. "Or maybe kerosene lamps?"

"Oh, all solar. With a gas generator for back-up, just in case. Doesn't any of this challenge appeal to you?" Rudolph kept his eye on the floor as he made for the parlor. "There's supposed to be most of a native-stone fireplace in here. The top's gone, but the body of it is said to be intact." He paused as he tested a bowed part of the under-planking and decided to walk around it. "There're two cellars, as well."

"You're not planning to go down there, are you?" Milton was alarmed. "Come on, Rudi. Give me your word that you won't try anything like that."

"Can't do it. Jeff. I may have to see what kind of shape the foundation is in, if the stairs down are safe enough to use. I'll have to put that in my report."

Rudolph made his way farther into the parlor: it had been a large room, twenty-nine by forty-one feet, made to accommodate two or three dozen people at a time; the fireplace, composed of oval river stone, was half-way along the far wall. "It's in better shape than I thought it would be."

Milton stood just inside the double-doorway, his flashlight poking its bright finger into the assortment of shadows that gathered in the corners of the parlor. "The ceiling's sagging," he remarked.

"There were two chandeliers in here, up to the 1960s, and a grand piano until the late 1930s," said Rudolph as he approached the fireplace, his remote tone indicating that he was not paying much attention to his brother-in-law. "Most of the furniture was left when the last owners abandoned the place. Framed pictures, too. The mayor said they were stolen many years ago."

"And you trust him?" Milton asked.

"This resort is going to bring needed money and jobs into Sainte Gertrude— he's not about to endanger that. The people in the village will be happy to have this place operating again. So, yes, I trust him to know where his best interests lie." He was in front of the fireplace now, and inspecting it closely. He looked at the pile of fallen stone on the floor of the fireplace, and nodded a kind of approval. "This is really in very good shape, considering."

"Glad you think so," Milton said, making no excuse for his sarcasm.

Rudolph carefully leaned forward and thrust his head into the fireplace's open maw, turning his head to look up into the ruined chimney. "Most of the flue's clear, but there is a tree-branch pushing through the top of the chimney," he told Milton, and went on with his investigation of the flue. "There's supposed to be a damper in here somewhere."

"What does that matter?" Milton asked, and noticed another snake winding its way through the entry hall. "How long do you plan to stay in here?"

"As long as it takes," said Rudolph.

Milton was losing all patience with Rudolph. "You are aware that it'll be dark in four hours. We can't remain here after dark, can we?"

"Yes; you're right. I'm sorry about that. If we could have gotten here earlier, we'd have more time to do this properly before nightfall, but with the storm stalled off of Florida… I can't blame the pilot for waiting until the weather improved; we're in the Bermuda Triangle, remember." Rudolph reached up and tugged at a wedge of rusted iron he saw sticking out from the stones. The wedge clattered down, bringing a small shower of football sized stones with it; Rudolph withdrew quickly and took a step back from the fireplace. "Not here," he said more to himself than to Milton.

"Are you looking for something in the chimney?" Milton demanded. "Why not look down rabbit holes while you're at it?"

"More hoping than looking," said Rudolph.

"Because…?" Milton pursued, aware that he was beginning to pry the whole story out of Rudolph.

"There's supposed to be a chest with something valuable hidden in one of the fireplaces in this house. I'd kind of like to find it." Rudolph patted the front of his jacket to rid it of dust. "If the chest really exists, it might have something… valuable in it."

"And what would that be?" Milton asked as he watched Rudolph come back across the parlor to the entry hall. "Pirate treasure?"

"Maybe."

"Oh, God, don't tell me," said Milton, flinging up one hand as if to divorce himself from the whole project. "It's that Poe connection, isn't it? Fuck it!" He flung up his hand again. "I give up. I swear I give up!"

"Maybe it's something else; I'd like to find out, wouldn't you? Come on, Jeff." said Rudolph, treading through the entry hall toward the opposite door. "The ballroom's on the other side. Let's have a look at it."

But Milton blocked his way. "It's that damned story, isn't it? You're trying to prove it was true, the way you tried with—"

"So what if it is?" Rudolph challenged him. "It's my money. If it turns out I'm right, and *The Gold Bug* was based on real events — like *Moby Dick* — I could do something useful for the history of American literature, at the very least, and I could have the fun of the publicity from it to make the game I develop into a best-seller."

"It's *crazy*, Rudi." Milton was almost pleading now. "This is a potential financial catastrophe. You know it, and I know it, and Caroline knows it."

"You *don't* know that, not for sure; no one does," said Rudolph. "And I can afford—"

"Would you *please* stop saying you can afford it!" Milton stood in front of him, his flashlight raised like a weapon. "Never mind your romantic notions: how can you expect your wife to go along with this ridiculous scheme of yours?"

"I expect it because she's gone along with all the rest of my … um … ridiculous schemes, and hasn't regretted it yet," Rudolph said calmly. "Now, Jeff, do get out of my way. There are three other fireplaces I want to examine before the night closes in."

"The Good Lord between me and idiots," whispered Milton as he stepped aside. "You do understand that I think you're nuts."

"You've thought that since Caroline and I met in middle school," said Rudolph, and went on into the ballroom, taking care to walk on the portions of the floor that were not cracked or broken.

Milton could not deny it. "She took a big chance on you."

Rudolph chuckled. "So far, so good."

The ballroom had once had an array of tall, narrow windows down the longest wall in the room, an impressive forty-six feet long by thirty-six feet wide; the frames remained in less than half of them, and there were low-growing plants intruding through the vacancies. There had been an elevated platform at the far end of the room where small orchestras had played that was now cracked and broken. The floor had a number of gaping holes in it, and half of the ceiling had fallen at least four decades ago. Rudolph aimed his flashlight around the room in a cursory survey; the beam stopped at the fireplace at the far end of the room, opposite the demolished platform, and was greeted by the sound of small creatures in retreat.

From his place just inside the ballroom door, Milton watched Rudolph with increasing unease. He had long ago accepted that his brother-in-law was eccentric, but this struck him as being beyond the bounds of the acceptable. He found himself thinking of that movie with Peter O'Toole, *The Ruling Class,* as being more applicable to Peregrine Rudolph than he wanted to admit. What on earth would he tell Caroline about this present adventure, and how could he account for his inability to dampen Rudolph's ambitions for this wreckage.

This fireplace had once been tile-clad, but most of those tiles were gone, exposing the bricks beneath. There were filmy curtains of spider-webs in the hearth, many extending up into the chimney itself, and four large arachnids squatted in them, patiently awaiting the arrival of their dinners. Rudolph batted at the webs with his flashlight, and stepped on the one spider that had run toward him; the other spiders had retreated up into the flue.

"Hey, Rudi, be careful. Some of those things might be poisonous," Milton warned from the door.

"Yeah. I'll watch out," said Rudolph as he squinted up into the chimney; he got out of the fireplace quickly. "If there was anything hidden in there, it's gone now," he said, and picked his way back to the entry hall. "Spiders give me the creeps."

"No kidding," said Milton. He reached for his handkerchief from his inner pocket and wiped the sweat from his face, telling himself that heat and not nerves was the cause for it. "There're plenty of them about. And snakes."

"As well as beetles and other bugs. The mayor told me to be on the look-out for centipedes."

There was a screech and the sound of flapping wings; a hooked-beak bird with black-and-blue wings went up and out through the hole at the top of the entry hall.

"Jesus!" Milton exclaimed. "What was that?"

"A bird. There are supposedly a number of them roosting inside this house," said Rudolph. "I understand that they help keep down the mice and rats."

"Wonderful," said Milton at his most sardonic.

"How about we have a look at the kitchen?" Rudolph suggested as he picked up his rucksack. "I need to see what kind of space we have in there."

"You're going to do it no matter what I say," Milton told him.

"I am. But you can stay here if you'd prefer." Rudolph slipped the rucksack over his shoulders and started toward a near-by corridor. "It's this way."

Milton hesitated, but then followed, saying, "Just in case you need help."

A tangle of vines clogged the kitchen windows, a number of roots protruding into the spacious room like a gathering of enormous worms. The ceiling was spotted with mold, and there were large patches of damp along the exposed beams. Open shelves sagged on their brackets, some of the wood rotten or eaten by beetles. There had been two large stoves in the room at one time, but they had been carried away for scrap three decades ago, and now only the brick footings that had held them remained. Three large sinks, their basins cracked and the faucets and other hardware long gone, stood against the right-hand wall. The concrete floor was pitted and cracked in places, silent testament to the damage wrought by water. A five-inch-long mantis clung to the outside of the open hearth where sides of beef and entire hogs had been turned on spits in the hey-day of the house.

Rudolph was smiling as he looked over the kitchen. "They had five chefs here in 1915, and a staff of eight," he said. He nodded toward a door hanging precariously on one hinge. "That's the pantry, I think."

"And what did they store in there?— whole rhinos?"

"Stop it, Jeff," said Rudolph calmly. "I know you disapprove, but will you at least stop being so snarky?"

Milton was taken aback. "I thought I was protecting you."

"Because Caroline asked you to?" Rudolph went to the places where two large preparation tables had once stood. "Can't you see even a suggestion of what I see? Doesn't any of this excite you?"

"Bluntly, no, except in my desire to leave." Milton folded his arms and stared at the places in the wall where pipes and cabinetry had been cut away.

"I'm not stopping you," said Rudolph. "I'll be out when I'm done." He reached into his jacket pocket and pulled out the keys to the Land Rover, which he tossed to Milton. "Go on then. There's material for sandwiches in the cooler, and beer as well as water."

"Good of you." He tucked the keys into the lower pocket of his cargo pants, taking care to button it closed. "But Caroline would have my head if I left you in this... derelict of a house."

"What were you going to call it?" Rudolph asked as he started toward the fireplace. "A calamity?"

"More like a catastrophe. But I've called it that already, and it didn't faze you," said Milton, trying to guess what else his capricious brother-in-law might decide to do.

Reaching the fireplace, Rudolph took what remained of the spit from the rusted supports that stood in the gaping opening. "It looks almost Medieval, doesn't it? They could have cooked for Plantagenets in here rather than for Carnegies and Wainwrights, couldn't they?" he asked as he started poking up into the darkness of the chimney. He swung his flashlight around to aid his investigation of the fire-blackened bricks. "I don't see..." Then his tone changed. "There's some kind of chest up there. You see?"

"Not from here," said Milton, refusing to move.

"Well, take my word for it. There's something..." He thrust the spit upward and was rewarded with a shower of mud and dried leaves.

"Hey! Rudi!" Milton cried out in alarm. "Don't!"

Rudolph remained where he was, still using the spit to dislodge the object that had caught his attention. "It's okay, Jeff. I won't—" He stepped out of the fireplace.

Half a dozen bricks fell with a brattle and a thud accompanied by a distressed squawking from a bird nesting farther up the chimney.

"That was close," Rudolph said merrily, and bent down to pull something from the rubble. He had to tug it out with both hands. "I hope nothing got broken," he said as he stumbled back, turning toward Milton to show what he had in his arms. "It's a chest."

Milton was suddenly afraid, although he had no idea why. "Put it back."

Rudolph laughed. "I can't, even if I wanted to. The rest of the chimney could come down on me." He carried the chest — a large, black one banded with iron and padlocked — to the most intact of the sinks, and set it down with care. "The padlock is rusty. So are the iron straps around it. I don't know if we can get it open." His demeanor indicated his dejection.

"What about the keys the mayor gave you?" Milton asked.

"The lock is rusted. A key won't open it. We need bolt-cutters, or a metal-saw, but that's no guarantee that the lock will open." He sighed his frustration.

"Then leave it there; it's probably nothing in any case," Milton suggested at once. "Honest to God, Rudi, you shouldn't mess with it."

Rudolph was not listening. "It had to have been put up there after the fireplace was being used for cooking; it would have been incinerated otherwise. That means one of the last families to live here must have done it, and knew what was being saved."

"Why hide pirate treasure— unless they wanted to start a legend about the place?" Milton folded his arms and stubbornly remained where he was.

"Don't be cynical, Jeff," Rudolph recommended. "They didn't need to do that; there were already a lot of tales about the house."

The wind sprang up, heralding the fading of the day, and the chimney moaned; Milton shuddered. "I'm surprised the chest is still here. I would have thought someone would have found it before now."

"They didn't have the advantage of the letter Matthew Horner sent before he left here," said Rudolph, enjoying the confusion that overcame his brother-in-law.

"Matthew Horner?" Milton asked. "Who is he and what does he have to do with this place?"

"He was the last caretaker who lived here. He departed in 1939 to work for the British during World War II. He informed his sister in 1944 that he had put the chest into a chimney—"

"And didn't bother to mention which chimney?" Milton shook his head. "Isn't that a little... inconvenient?"

"I doubt he intended that she should come and find it. Most of the letter was concerned with closing up most of this house and the grounds. He did a whole paragraph on Holland covers." He saw the blank expression in Milton's eyes, and said, "Those sheets that go over furniture when a house is going to be empty."

"Oh. Yeah." Milton felt out of his depth. "How did you happen to find that letter? Do you know it's authentic?"

"It is. I got it from Matthew Horner's sister." He pulled futilely at the padlock. "She was twelve years younger than he was."

"And how did you happen to find out about her?" Milton asked, not at all sure he wanted to know.

"It was my sophomore project, the spring before I dropped out of college. I wanted to do my paper on Poe's sources—"

"Oh, God. I remember," said Milton, recalling how obsessed Rudolph had been.

"—and my professor suggested I check out archives and other sources at the library. I found out that Myra Davis — Matthew Horner's sister — was still alive and living near Toronto, so I wrote to her and she answered me, saying I could read the letter and make a copy of it. At her death, all her brother's papers, as well as her own, were going to her alma mater — Wake Forest — which is where I assume the letter is now. She died eight years ago, in her late nineties; she was pretty frail, but her mind was still sharp. We kept in touch in a desultory way for a number of years. She wanted to know about my work."

"So you looking for this place isn't a recent whim," said Milton, not surprised now that he heard the back-story.

"Hardly." He smiled briefly.

"Did the letter mention what is in the chest?" Milton inquired. "Yes."

Their silence was interrupted by another howl from the chimneys, an eerie harmony that ended in more protests from birds

"Well?" Milton waited, and then said, more forcefully. "What is it?"

Rudolph ran his hand over the chest, almost in a caress. "If we're lucky, there's a skull in here. And it's reasonably intact."

"A skull," Milton repeated as if he did not know the word.

"Yeah," said Rudolph, then launched into an explanation. "You know, how in *The Gold Bug*, a skull is used to find the proper direction to the treasure?"

"I vaguely remember," said Milton, who had not read the story since high school.

"And the deviation from one eye socket to the other was more than six or seven degrees?" Rudolph went on, expecting no answer. "That got me to thinking: human eyes focus forward, and so the deviation of focus should not be more than a couple of inches, otherwise binocular vision won't work. The lines of sight are next to each other, and parallel. Right?"

"Yeah. Okay. The degree of deviation is wrong." In spite of himself, Milton was becoming interested. "And your point is..."

"With a deviation of six or seven degrees, what kind of skull was... is it?" Rudolph stared at the chest, then looked toward his brother-in-law. "Think of what this could mean to the development of this estate. Think of the publicity."

"But what if it's just a narrative device that Poe added to the tale? Even you will allow that story-tellers will embroider facts to make for better fiction. Are you sure that the name of this place wasn't after-the-fact?" Milton stared at the ruin around him. "You know, a name to give the place a touch of the mysterious?"

"It's possible," said Rudolph as if he did not believe a word of it. "But this island was once a haven for pirates and other adventurers."

"Like a lot of Caribbean islands," said Milton, listening to the tree branches thrashing in the rising wind batter at what remained of the house. "And there are estates that are as fancifully named as this one."

"According to Matthew Horner, the original owner, who had the house built in the first place, he chose this location because it was the place where the actual discoveries were made that are recounted in Poe's story. There had been a treasure recovered from this spot." There was a stubbornness in Rudolph's stance that did not encourage dispute.

"Let me guess: you want to put the skull on display here, and recount the whole preposterous tale." He shook his head. "Why not donate it to the Smithsonian instead, and give up this resort scheme of yours."

"The Smithsonian would probably hide it away in one of their warehouses, and take decades to authenticate it. Same thing with most universities." He touched the chest again. "This deserves better than that."

"If it really is a non-human skull," Milton reminded him. "There's no reason to suppose it's all true."

"We'll probably have to take it with us," Rudolph said contemplatively.

"Oh, no," Milton declared. "I'm not getting into any vehicle with that thing."

Rudolph turned to stare at Milton in amazement. "Shit. I never realized that you're so superstitious, Jeff. Whatever kind of skull is in here—"

"Assuming for the minute that there *is* a skull in that chest," Milton interjected.

"Yes; assuming that. You're imbuing it with destructive properties—"

Milton raised his voice. "Have you looked at this house? I may be superstitious, but you've got to admit, that chest hasn't done well here."

Rudolph laughed aloud. "You're being blockheaded, Jeff. This skull — and I suspect it must be — has historical value, and I would like to see it restored to the public." He reached to take the chest from the sink, but another gust of wind, stronger and longer-lasting than the previous ones had been, brought more rubble down the chimney to clatter atop the bricks and dust that had already accumulated there. "The weather seems to be on your side."

Now thoroughly spooked, Milton began to back out of the kitchen, almost blundering into a break in the concrete flooring. "We need to get out of here, Rudi. And you should leave that chest." He steadied himself. "It isn't safe here."

"I agree," said Rudolph. "Like any neglected structure, this one is dangerous." He remained by the sink. "If this were a little smaller," he went on, stroking the chest, "I could probably fit it in my rucksack, but that isn't going to work." He aimed his flashlight's beam at the pantry. "If I put it in there, we could come back in the morning with a hand-cart and pick it up."

"*You* can come back tomorrow," Milton corrected him. "I'm not getting into the Land Rover with that box. Like you said, this is the Bermuda Triangle."

"Whose imagination is running away with him now?" Rudolph goaded. "But you're right: the road is not easy to drive, and it will be dark before we get back to Sainte Gertrude." He lifted the chest out of the sink and carried it as if it were a living infant and not an iron-bound wooden chest to the pantry, where he put it on the floor under a hanging bin that had once contained rice. As he emerged from the pantry, there was a distant grumble of thunder.

Milton had already reached the entry hall when a new display of lightning lit up the gathering clouds moving in on the island. He could not keep from yelping at the flash. "Rudi!" he shouted. "It's going to pour! We've got to get out of here.

Hurry up!" He heard the panic in his voice, and that only frightened him more.

Rudolph appeared in the corridor that led to the kitchen. "Calm down. These storms happen here regularly."

"Maybe," said Milton, panting a little, "but I still don't want to be on that road when it opens up."

The broken chimneys were beginning to croon with wind, a counterpoint to the thunder.

"It'll pass soon enough," Rudolph said. "If we have to pull over and wait it out, we will." He came up to Milton. "You can stay in Sainte Gertrude tomorrow."

"You can't come back here alone," Milton cried out. "Don't come here ever again."

"Jeff, calm down," Rudolph urged as he went to open the door. "I think you'd better recline the seat in the Rover. Let me attend to the driving. We'll talk about what happens tomorrow in the morning." He slung his rucksack over his shoulder and reached for the brass latch on the front door, and never saw the lightning that struck the house, setting it afire, as the thunder roared overhead.

✦ · ✦

STREET OF THE DEAD HOUSE

by Robert Lopresti

Robert Lopresti says: "*The Murders in the Rue Morgue* is the first detective story, and one I have always loved. A few years ago a radio quiz show asked panelists to pair detectives with their arch-enemies. Poe's Dupin came up and I was amused that they treated the ape (completely off-screen in Poe's story) as the equivalent of Professor Moriarty. At that moment the idea for my tale hit me so hard I almost fell over."

+ · +

WHAT AM I? That is the question.

I sit in this cage, waiting for them to come stare at me, mimic me as I once mimicked them, perhaps poke me with sticks, and as they wonder what I am, so do I.

I don't think Mama had any doubts about what she was. I don't think she could even think the question. That is the gift and the punishment Professor gave me.

+ · +

I remember Mama, a little. We were happy and life was simple, so simple. Food was all around us, dangers were few, and there was nothing we needed. When I was scared or hungry Mama would pick me up and cradle me to her furry breast.

I was never cold. It was always warm where we lived, not this place, called *Paris* or *France*. Goujon cannot talk about anything without giving it two names. Sometimes he calls me an *Ourang-Outang,* and sometimes an *ape.*

Mama called us nothing, for she could not speak like people, or sign as I have learned to do. That did not bother her. She was always happy, until she died.

The hunters came in the morning, firing guns and shouting. Mama picked me up and ran. She made it into the trees but there was another hunter waiting in front of her. He made a noise as if he were playing a game, but this was no game. He fired his gun and Mama fell from the tree. I landed on top of her but she was already dead.

My life has made no sense since then.

I remember the first time I saw Professor. He tilted his head when he looked at me and spoke. We were in his house. The smell of the hunters was finally gone.

He gave me food and tried to be kind but I was afraid. The food tasted wrong and soon I got sleepy, but not the kind of sleepy I knew with Mama.

I know now something in the food made me sleep. Things were confused after that and I would wake up with pain in my head.

He did things to my head. Each time I woke the room looked different, *clearer,* somehow. And one day when Professor spoke I understood some of his noises.

"Ah, Jupiter. You are with me again. And you are grasping my words, aren't you? The chemicals are working just as I predicted."

He held out a piece of fruit. "Are you hungry, Jupiter?"

I was. I reached for it.

He pulled it away and moved his other hand. "Do this, Jupiter. It means *orange.* Tell me you want an orange."

After a few more tries I understood. I copied his hand and he gave me the orange.

That was my first lesson. That was my first surrender.

❖ · ❖

Many more sleeps, many more words, many more pains in the head.

Soon I knew enough gestures to ask Professor questions.

Where is Mama?

"Dead. Hunters killed her. When I heard they brought back a baby I bought you from them."

Do you have a mama?

"I did, Jupiter. Everyone does. I will show you a picture of mine. I grew up in a place called Lyon. It is far from here, and full of men like me."

Where is your mama?

"She died when I was young."

Killed by hunters?

"No, Jupiter. She got sick. Not sick like you did last month. Much worse."

Where did you live?

"With my papa. Oh dear. A papa is something like a mama. You had one too but *Ourang-Outang* papas don't live with their children. I don't know why. My papa was a baker. That means he made bread, like I eat with my meals."

I tried bread once. It had no taste.

Did your papa die?

"Yes, but that was much later. There was an accident, he was hit by a wagon. You've seen pictures of wagons." His face changed again. "I had to go to the morgue to fetch him. I knew then I would leave Lyon, because it made me so sad."

What is that?

"What is... oh, morgue? It is a house where they put the dead."

Did they put my mama there?

"No, Jupiter. Only men."

Why?

"Well." He scratched his head. "I think it is because men think that only they have souls."

What is that?

Professor waved his arms. "I was afraid you would ask! I know nothing about souls. We would need a priest to explain that— and don't bother asking me what a priest is, because I can't explain that either. Let's say a soul is what makes men different from animals."

A soul lets you speak?

More head scratching. "I'll have to think about that one, Jupiter."

＊ · ＊

I lived in the middle of the house, where there were trees to make nests in. It was surrounded by white walls, and Professor lived on the other side of the walls. There were some windows, spaces in the walls with bars, through which I could see into his rooms. There were also bars on the top of my part of the house.

One day Professor came to me, excited. "We are to have a visitor, Jupiter! A man who speaks French."

What is that?

"The words I speak, that I have been teaching you. Men from different places use different sounds, and French is how they speak where I was born. Most men here speak English, or Dutch, or Malay."

He made the playing noise. "So many ways to talk, Jupiter. But until now none here have spoken as I do."

Is that why they are afraid of me? Because they cannot speak to me?

His face changed. "Why do you say they are afraid?"

I can smell it on your helpers. The men who clean and cook.

"Have any of them bothered you, Jupiter?"

No. But they peek in my room when you are not there. Some of them speak but I do not know what they say. And when I tried to sign back they did not understand.

Professor got quiet. "I am sorry they are afraid of you, Jupiter. Men fear what they don't understand. Perhaps I should have let my helpers visit you, but I didn't want to confuse you with many kinds of words."

He stood up. "We will see how things go with the sailor, yes? Maybe we can find more friends for you."

What is that?

"What, friend?"

No.

"Hmm. Then… Sailor? A sailor is a man who travels on boats. I have shown you pictures of boats, yes? We need a sign for sailor, I see."

Boat man.

His face changed. "Very good, Jupiter. You are getting better and better at thinking of signs."

I want to see the sailor.

❖ · ❖

I smelled him as soon as he came into the house. The sailor smelled like the fish Professor sometimes eats, and like the smoke some of the helpers smell of.

I heard them while they ate.

"So, where are you from, Monsieur Goujon? Is that a Norman accent?"

"It is, Professor. I was born near Caen, but I have lived most of my life with my uncle near Paris. That is actually why I am here in Borneo. He asked me to supervise a load of precious cargo so I left my ship and will take another back."

"Excellent. I trust you will visit me often while you are here. It is a rare treat to chat with someone who speaks the mother tongue."

"How can I resist such a charming host? Not to mention this wonderful food."

It didn't smell wonderful to me. Mostly bread and burnt meat.

"I am amazed that you can survive here in this primitive land. Pirates, natives, opposing armies... and yet here you sit in this beautiful villa! How do you do it?"

"Ah well, it is a little miracle, I suppose. The English assume I am a French spy, and would root me out if they could, but this end of the island is run by the Dutch and the Dyaks, and they have no desire to lose the only physician in their territory.

"When I first reached Borneo some of the Malay pirates tried to take me as their personal physician, but I told them I couldn't work that way. If they wanted my services they would have to set me free— and they did! I suspect they feared I could make them sick as well as heal them. But they come by cover of darkness, when they need me."

"Professor, if I am not being rude, may I ask what a scholar like yourself is doing out in the wilderness? It amazed me to hear about you."

"Hmm." Professor's voice got quieter. "What *did* you hear, exactly?"

The sailor made the playing noise. "Oh, you know what the locals are like. The natives are pagans and the Dutch aren't much better. They say that you have turned animals into servants!"

"I suppose that is better than if they thought I turned my servants into animals." They made the playing sound. "In fact, my friend, they are closer to the truth than you might imagine. But they are far away, too."

"Really? I am fascinated! Please explain."

"Very well. I should tell you I was trained as a doctor in France. I found myself working in a rural area and, alas, there were many feeble-minded people there."

"Very sad, but I have heard that that condition runs in families."

"It does. And often a healthy member of such a clan will produce feeble-minded offspring, even though both parents seemed completely normal."

"Perhaps the family is cursed by God."

"I know nothing of curses, my friend. As a natural philosopher I can only deal with *this* world. But my breakthrough came when a fever struck our village and, alas, killed a number of small children, both the normal and the feeble-minded."

"Death makes no distinctions, I know."

"Very true. But it occurred to me that I had a great opportunity here that for the sake of all mankind I could not let slip away. As you know, what we call the mind is contained here, in the skull."

"The brain, yes. I saw one once, when a man was killed by an explosion."

"Ah. Then you understand that there is nothing magical about the brain. It is just a pile of meat, one might say. And yet all art and literature and wisdom spring from it, yes? So I decided to see if there was a difference between the healthy and feeble-minded brains."

I heard nothing for a moment. When the sailor spoke he sounded different. "You cut open dead children? Is that *legal?*"

"No. Autopsies, for that is the word, are not legal in France. But they should be or how can medicine advance? My so-called crime was discovered and I had to flee the country. How I wound up in Borneo is a long story. But the important thing is what I learned. The feeble-minded brain looked different; there were variations in shape. It did not smell like a normal brain, and I became convinced that there were chemical differences. I thought, perhaps, it might be possible to improve the little ones."

"Surely you have not been experimenting on living children, Professor!"

"No, my friend. Not even on feeble-minded ones, although I hope I will get the chance to do so. Out here I was able to try my ideas out on apes. Have you seen them?"

"I have, here and in Africa."

"And what do you think of them?"

"I hardly know. They seem like a joke the devil played on mankind. A satire."

"Hmm. I think they are more likely a rough draft, if I may call it that. The Bible tells us God made animals before man, after all. I have worked on almost a dozen of them over the years, trying to improve their brains."

"With what goal, professor? To turn them into men?"

"No, my friend. That would be neither possible nor moral. But if I can improve their ability to think, imagine what I can do for the feeble-minded children!"

I heard a chair scrape back. "That is the most fantastic scheme I have ever heard! Has there been any success?"

"Ah! There has indeed. The latest subject has been a marvel. Come with me, my friend, and you can meet my greatest triumph. He lives in my courtyard."

I heard them coming so I backed away from the door.

The sailor was big, higher and wider than Professor or his servants. He had fur all around his face, and where there wasn't fur his skin was red.

He stared at me, eyes and mouth wide.

"Jupiter, this is my guest, Goujon. Goujon, let me introduce you to Jupiter."

I am happy to meet you.

"What is it doing?" said Goujon, quietly. I smelled his fear.

"The gestures? That is how Jupiter speaks. You will notice I sign while I speak to him. What is it, Jupiter?"

Is he the sailor?

"Yes, the boat man. Boat man. You see, Goujon, he invented this combination of signs to mean *sailor* when he heard you were coming."

"This is amazing, Professor! I wouldn't have believed it possible. How long have you had him?"

"I purchased him almost three years ago. He was a baby and hunters had killed his mother. He is by far the brightest and most trainable subject I have been lucky enough to encounter."

Goujon said more and I got angry. He backed up, toward the door.

"What is it?" Professor asked me. "What is the problem?"

Can not understand.

"Oh. The sailor has an accent. He learned to speak far from my home. I am sorry, Goujon. Jupiter gets frustrated when he can't understand what is said to him."

The sailor looked at me. His face changed. "You know what? So do I."

Professor made the playing sound. "Ah, very good!"

"Could you teach me to sign, Professor? I would like to speak with your amazing friend."

+ · +

It was exciting to be teaching instead of learning.

The sailor came every day. He would say a word and I would show him the sign, then he would copy it.

Professor sat and watched. He helped when I could not understand, or when there was a word there was no sign for.

"Gold," said Goujon.

What is that?

"Ah!" Professor said. "It's a metal, Jupiter, like iron, but yellow and heavier. It shines. How about this for a sign? *Yellow metal.*"

"You leave out the most important thing about gold, Professor," said Goujon. "It is valuable."

What is that?

"Valuable? You can get things with it. Here." Professor pulled flat metal things from his pocket and handed them to me. "These are coins. Here's a sign for coin, yes? I give these to the fruit man and he gives me fruit. Then he can give them to, say, the fish man, and get a fish."

Are they gold?

"No, Jupiter. Gold coins are very valuable. That means you would have to trade a lot to get them."

"Or trade something very valuable," said Goujon.

+ · +

One day the sailor told us he would be leaving soon. A boat had come that would take him and the things his uncle wanted away. After that he kept coming over, but not for lessons. I heard him and Professor talking. They sounded angry.

"You can find another one. My God! With the money he would fetch in France you could hire armies to hunt the deep woods for them."

"What do you think he is, a circus act? This is a great experiment. My greatest! I may never find another I can train so well. And when he starts to decline I will examine his brain and see how my chemicals altered it. Then I can apply what I learned to the children—"

"That's another thing. Do you think anyone, *any* civilized country would let you cut up people the way you have done with that thing in there? That is madness."

"Get out of my house! You are not welcome here! Go back to France, or to the devil!"

After a few minutes Professor came into my room. "How are you, my friend?"

Well. Where is the sailor?

"Ah. He is gone. He is going home. I am sorry he couldn't come to say goodbye to you. Did you like him, Jupiter?"

I liked teaching him.

＊ · ＊

Two sleeps later and I woke, hearing screams and smelling blood.

I screamed too.

I left my nest and climbed to the top of the tallest tree. I heard more screams. Professor's helpers were running away from the house.

The door opened and the sailor ran in. "Jupiter! Where are you? Come down!"

I stayed in the branches.

"Jupiter! The hunters are here! The professor says I must take you away or they will kill you. Hurry!"

I came down and followed him out of the house, the first time I was outside since I was a baby.

There was a cart at the door with many men. I screamed and tried to back away but Goujon was behind me. "It's all right, Jupiter. They are my friends. They will help us get away from the hunters. Climb into the cart."

I did, but Goujon did not. The door closed and I saw that the walls were bars, like the top of my room. I screamed.

"Shut the brute up!" said one of Goujon's friends.

"Let him prattle. Go!"

I could smell animals I had only had hints of before. Those must be horses, I thought. Professor had shown me pictures of horses pulling carts.

And then there were so many smells and sights that nothing made sense.

＊ · ＊

There were many sleeps on the boat. I was never out of the box of bars and I was too sick to eat. No one came except Goujon.

"How are you, Jupiter?"

Sick. Where is this?

"We are going to France. That is where the Professor was born."

Where is Professor?
"He died. The hunters killed him."
Is he in the dead house?
"The dead house? I suppose he is. But don't worry. You will be safe from the hunters in France. There are many people there who will want to see you. No one has ever seen an *Ourang-Outang* who could talk before! They will pay a fortune."
What is that?

＊・＊

Goujon called the place where we lived a *barn* and a *house*. It did not look like the Professor's house. It was dark and cold and there were no trees to sleep in.

Trees wouldn't have mattered because he did not let me out of the box.

Two sleeps after we arrived Goujon came in, excited. "Good news, Jupiter! Some professors from the university want to meet you."

Professor is dead.

"Yes, yes, but these are other men like him. You will sign for them and they will want you to come live with them in a beautiful house full of trees and fruit and people. You will be famous, Jupiter!"

What is that?

As usual, he didn't answer.

I heard the professors arrive. I was excited to meet them. Perhaps they would be my friends like Professor was.

But I heard Goujon talking on the way up the stairs. "The man who trained him was mad, gentlemen, quite mad. He wanted to experiment on children! I don't pretend to understand what he did to this poor beast. The scars on his head have healed. But we had to stop the professor before he engaged in more such crimes. I'm afraid he fought to the death."

Then I knew how Professor died.

Goujon entered the room with two other men. They had white hair like Professor and one wore circles that made his eyes look big. They stared at me.

"He can't speak, gentlemen," said Goujon. "You will have to learn the signs he uses, but it is not hard. Even I can do it. Jupiter!" He started signing. "Here are two new friends for you. Say hello."

I looked at them.

"Come, Jupiter," said Goujon. "Show them the sign for your name. Or for sailor! You created that yourself. Boat man! Remember?"

I hooted.

"He's a fine specimen," said the man with the circles. "The *Jardin des Plantes* would be pleased to have him, but not at the price you are asking."

"He's not a zoo animal," said Goujon. "He can talk! Or sign, anyway. Ask him about life in Borneo."

The younger man came closer to my box. "Oh, why not? We've come this far. Jupiter, my name is Pierre. Are you hungry?"

I said nothing. I did nothing. Soon they left.

Goujon was angry. "What was that for, you brute? They would have taken good care of you!"

You killed Professor.

He backed away. "How—? Oh. You heard what I told them. I didn't mean that, Jupiter. It was just… just… Well, they wouldn't have understood about the hunters."

You killed Professor.

He made the playing sound. "I'm afraid your evidence would not hold up in a court, even if you knew what a court was. You don't want to set a quarrel with me, Jupiter. The sooner you cooperate, the sooner you can live with someone you prefer."

I will not help you.

"No? We will see about that."

He took the lamp and left.

Two sleeps passed. I had no food. No one cleaned my box.

On the third morning Goujon came in with a basket of fruit. "Are you ready to be sensible, Jupiter?"

You killed Professor. I will not help you.

He waved his arms. "If you starve to death it won't help anyone! The professor is dead, Jupiter. What do you want?"

Home.

"Where do you think that is, exactly? You think you can go back to the professor's house and live there again? Will the Dyaks bring you food and clean up your mess? You could never survive in the forests. In the name of the good god, let me help you."

What is that?

He didn't answer. He took the food away.

The next morning Goujon came back with more fruit. "Don't eat so fast. You'll get sick."

When I was done he said. "All right. You want to go back to Borneo, do you? Very well. It will take money."

What is that?

"Money? The professor told you about that the first time I met you. Remember? Gold coins?"

Why do I need them?

"Because the captain — the big boat man — won't take you to Borneo without them. Now, my uncle keeps an eye on all the important things that happen here in Paris, and he knows of a caper that is perfect for us."

What is that?

✦ · ✦

Goujon said his uncle knew of an old woman, a fortune-teller, who was going to buy a shop. I didn't know what most of those words meant but Goujon just waved a hand.

"Never mind. All that matters is this: On Friday she will have a big bag full of gold coins in her house. If we get them there will be enough to send you back to your Malayan hellhole and for me to live here for many years."

He told me that the woman was a mama and her child lived with her, but the child was grown. They lived on the fourth floor of a house.

"My uncle says there is no way to get into the building but through a window on the fourth floor that can be entered from the yard; I have seen it and you could do it easily." He made the playing sound. "Easy as climbing a tree."

That night he let me out of the cage. We went outside where he had a closed wagon waiting. Two horses pulled it. The man in front was so frightened I could barely smell the horses.

"Come inside, Jupiter," said Goujon.

I didn't want to. It was dark and small and the air was cold.

"If you run away, you will never get home. Do you understand that? You can't get home except by boat and only I know which boats go there."

I will go.

Goujon turned to the driver. "Rue Morgue. Jupiter, what's wrong? Calm down."

Why are we going to the dead house?

"The dead... the morgue? No, morgue is just the name of the street. We won't be going to the morgue at all. Just calm down and get in the carriage. Please."

We travelled through the place Goujon called Paris, although sometimes he called it France. The windows were shuttered but I could hear and smell. It was like the boat ride; too much to remember.

The house where the woman lived was not the dead house. Goujon told me the dead house was far away and I shouldn't think about it.

This house was bigger than the professor's had been.

"The door is always locked."

What is that?

"Locked? Closed so no one can get in. Like your cage or your room back in the Professor's house in Borneo." He led me to a yard at the rear of the building. "Look at the windows on the top floor. The woman lives there with her daughter. Could you get in?"

I looked up at it and felt happy. I had never been able to climb so high.

I can.

"Are you sure, Jupiter?"

I can. Now.

Goujon put a hand on my arm. "Not now. She will not have the coins until the end of the week. Let's go back home."

I pulled my arm away. *Practice.*

"Practice? That makes sense. But not here." He leaned out of the box and spoke to the man who helped the horses.

"We will go to an empty building I know. You can climb there without being seen."

We went. The building was not as tall as the one where the woman lived, but it was still wonderfully high. I stretched out my arms and began to pull myself up the outer walls.

I felt my heart beating. I had done nothing like this in my life. I had only climbed the trees and walls in Professor's house. I never wanted to stop. I swung from one piece of wall to another. Swung again and caught a window with my leg. I could have gone on forever.

Goujon yelled. "Jupiter! We have to get going! It will be morning soon."

I wanted to ignore him. He said we were going home, but where was home? The cage?

"Jupiter! There's no food here. If you don't come with me you will never get back to Borneo!"

He was right. I climbed to the top once more and then rushed all the way to the street beside him.

Goujon's face changed. "You liked that, didn't you?"

Yes.

"It was very cruel of that professor to keep you locked up like that. Jupiter, what's wrong?"

I never thought Professor was cruel to lock me up. Why didn't he let me climb the trees outside his house?

I got in the wagon. When we went into the house Goujon said: "I won't ask you to get in that cage again, Jupiter. We have to trust each other, yes?"

Yes.

◆ · ◆

Each night Goujon took me out to practice at a different empty building.

"That metal tree is a lightning rod, Jupiter. There is one on the roof of the fortune-teller's house, near the chimney. It is much higher. Can you climb it? Yes? Very good!"

I enjoyed the practice so much I did not want it to end, but on the third night Goujon said, "I think you are ready, Jupiter. Tomorrow the old woman will buy another house. So tonight we must move, eh?"

Yes.

I didn't know why the old woman wanted another house. But I was sure she didn't need it as much as I needed to go home.

When the carriage arrived, the street was empty and silent. I could hear that no one moved inside. I could smell how nervous Goujon was.

"Ready, Jupiter?" he whispered. "Excellent, excellent. I will be down here waiting. I'm sure the women are asleep by now."

I climbed the tall lightning rod. It was easy. The shutter was open against the wall. I grabbed it with both hands and swung across to the open window. That was easy too.

Inside the room was one bed, the kind Goujon sleeps on, the head against the window. I squeezed through the window and landed on the bed.

The old woman sat in a chair beside the bed, a metal box full of papers on the table beside her, and she slept. Her eyes were closed, and she growled.

I crept to her. The bags of gold coins Goujon described were lying on the table beside her. I tried to pull one but there were strings on it, and they were wrapped around her wrist.

She growled again. What could I do?

I went back to the bed and stuck my head out the window. I tried to sign my problem, but Goujon didn't understand. Finally he climbed up the pole, badly, and reached the top.

I crawled out the window, hanging onto the sill, and when our heads were as close together as they could get he looked up and me and whispered, "What's wrong?"

Woman asleep. Bags tied to hand.

Goujon took one hand off the pole and almost fell. He pulled something from his pocket and held it up to me. "Razor. You know how to open it?"

Yes. I had seen him shave.

I reached down to take it. I opened the razor and made sure I knew how to hold it. Then I crept back to the woman. I took hold of the first string and started cutting. The woman kept growling.

I caught the bag so it didn't make a sound. I put it on the floor. Then I started to cut the other string.

I heard a door close. A young woman had come in. Her back was to me and she was doing something to the door.

What could I do?

She turned and saw me. She screamed.

The old woman woke. She saw me and screamed.

Now I was scared. I wanted to scream too.

Before I could back away the old woman hit me in the face. Then she grabbed me by my fur. I tried to push her away but the razor caught her in the throat. Her eyes went wide and blood squirted out poured down.

I smelled blood. I was scared. I dropped the razor and jumped back. The old woman fell to the floor.

The daughter screamed louder than ever.

Outside from below the window, I heard Goujon shouting, "My God! You devil! What have you done?"

The daughter would not be quiet. I put a hand over her mouth. She bit me.

I put my hands on her throat. I made her quiet. She fell down.

"Get out of there, Jupiter! Take the coins and come!"

I was scared. I had never done anything so bad before.

I tried to pick up the old woman by her fur but pieces of it came out. I grabbed her by the middle and rushed up the bed to the window. I held the woman outside so Goujon could see her. Maybe Goujon could help her?

His eyes went wide. "What have you done?" he yelled, frightening me. I lost my grip and the old woman fell out the window to the yard below.

"My God! What have you done?" Goujon slid down the lightning rod. He ran from the yard. I heard the carriage with the horses pull away.

I lifted the daughter and looked for a place to hide her. The door was locked. I didn't want to throw her out the window.

There was no fire in the fireplace. I hid her in there.

I heard people running up the stairs, banging on the door.

I left the coins on the floor and climbed out the window, and it slammed shut behind me. I climbed up to the roof.

I kept going from roof to roof until I could not hear the screams, or smell the blood.

＋ · ＋

Before the sun rose I found a forest. There were many trees and a grassy place with a path where people walked. I climbed into a tree and hid.

I had not meant to hurt anyone, but I think those two women were dead. I had killed them like the hunters killed Mama. Like Goujon killed Professor.

Professor whipped me once for hurting one of his helpers. This was worse. What would happen now?

I stayed in the tree all day. People walked by on the path but they never saw me. I don't think they were looking for me.

After dark I went down and searched for food. I found a place where there had been many kinds of food and carts. I found bins where old food was piled and found fruit I could eat. Then I went back to the trees and made a nest.

That's how I lived for many sleeps.

＋ · ＋

The food was bad. It was making me sick. Professor could make me better but he was dead. Goujon killed him but maybe he did it to help me.

One night I knew I couldn't stay there anymore. I climbed down and followed the smells back to the place where Goujon lived.

The door would not open but I knew what to do. I climbed in a window on the top floor. Goujon was in a bed growling like the old woman had done.

That made me sad.

I touched him on the arm. He woke with a jerk and sat up. He was afraid.

"Jupiter! Is that you?"

I touched his hand.

Goujon leapt out of the other side of the bed. "Wait, just wait." He lit a lamp.

"It is you! I thought you were lost forever. Where have you been?"

Food and water.

"Of course! Where are my manners? Come with me."

I ate. He drank something that smelled spoiled.

I told him what happened.

"What an amazing adventure, Jupiter. I never would have thought you could survive for so long in this city. I am glad to have you back."

Are the women in the dead house?

"Yes. You know you killed them, don't you?"

I didn't mean to.

"Yes. But I doubt anyone else would believe it." He put down his glass. "Listen, Jupiter. There was one man clever enough to realize that only an animal like you could have broken into that house. A strange fellow named Auguste Dupin who lives in a ruined house with his boyfriend, I suppose. You should see the place! Nothing but moldy furniture and books, hundreds of books.

"This Dupin is both a genius and a fool, I think. He tricked me, convinced me that he found you, but he wasn't clever enough to realize that you are an animal who *thinks*. And that's the point, Jupiter. Do you know what they do to murderers in France?"

What is that?

"A murderer? Someone who kills people, like you did. They kill murderers; chop off their heads. Do you want them to chop off your head, Jupiter?"

My hands trembled as I signed *no*.

"And I don't want them to cut off mine, either. Understand me, Jupiter. If you are a mere animal then you are not a murderer. But if you are smart enough to help me *steal* then you are smart enough to *kill*, and they will kill you for it. Do you understand, Jupiter?"

No.

He sighed. "If they see you signing they will know how smart you are. Then I will be killed as a thief and you as a murderer. But if you don't sign, if you can keep from ever letting anyone see you do it, then they will think you are just a brute, and neither of us will be punished. What do you say, Jupiter? Can you keep the secret?"

Could I? Could I pretend to be as empty and silent as the horses and the dogs?

"Jupiter?"

I didn't answer. I have never answered.

* · *

Goujon had no money to send me home. I understood. This is my punishment.

He couldn't sell me as a talking beast but he sold me to the *Jardin des Plantes*. There are many animals here.

I live in a box of bars in a big house that is always cold. That is my punishment, too.

There are other apes, but they don't like me. The Professor made me different and they can tell. So I live in another building, alone.

Goujon came once and talked to me. I didn't answer.

He thinks I am afraid. He thinks I pretend to be an empty beast because they will kill me if they find out I can think.

I am not afraid. But after I killed those women I knew I had to decide.

What am I?

Professor tried to turn me into a man. I am not a man. I will not be part of a man.

So I must be a beast. I have decided.

Beasts do not speak. Beasts do not sign.

Yesterday there were a lot of excited men in front of my cage. They were all facing one man, who was pointing at me and talking. I couldn't understand what they were saying until one of them called him by name: *Dupin.*

That was the man Goujon told me about, the one smart enough to realize an *Ourang-Outang* killed the women, but not smart enough to know that I was also smart.

Now he was telling everyone how he figured out that it was me and the men were telling him how clever he was.

He looked at me and I thought: if I sign now and he is so clever he will know that I am signing, even if he cannot understand the words. Would he tell everyone or would he be ashamed that he was mistaken?

My fingers itched to sign: *You are the fool.*

But I am a beast. Beasts are silent. I let him pass me, still thinking that I cannot think.

There are more people outside my box now. They yell at me and make the playing sound. I do nothing.

They look at me and I look back. I look back.

✦ · ✦

NAOMI

by Christopher Rice

Christopher Rice says: "I was told the premise of Poe's *The Tell Tale Heart* when I was a child and it's been lodged in my consciousness since then. I'm a guilt-prone person and I've never encountered a better literary metaphor for guilt, remorse or regret. But reading it as an adult, I was taken by how the story also makes a devastating statement about obsession in general."

+ · +

THEY'RE SAYING IT WAS her ringtone that killed her; the kids I've talked to, the ones who were still friends with my niece when she strolled into the middle of rush hour traffic on Interstate 5. According to the story they've told me, a few weeks before her suicide, Naomi changed the ringtone on her Galaxy Note from a chirping bird to a few bars from some bubble gum pop song that was all about dancing with hot boys during the summertime. When the jocks in her class heard it for the first time, when her phone went off during Chemistry class one afternoon and everyone realized the bouncy little dance beat was coming from the book bag of the same *freak* who'd showed up first day of sophomore year in eye-shadow and a spaghetti-strap halter top, demanding to be called Naomi even though she'd spent the first fifteen years of her life as Nathan, that was it. After that day, those fuckers never gave my niece a break.

Such is the power of music, I guess. The makeup and girl's clothing could be dismissed as a silly costume, unworthy of their contempt. But a shitty pop song? That was way over the line, *dude*. It's a lesson I'll remember. Maybe I'll share it with my kids if I ever adopt any. Tell the world the soundtrack to your daydreams and the world just might do you in over it.

They chased Naomi down hallways after that, surrounded her in gyrating groups, hips rocking, arms swinging as they sang the lyrics of the offending song in high lisping voices, punctuating now and then by slamming her into banks of lockers with their stomachs and their open palms.

Heart beat, my feet, moving to the mu-ooo-sic.
Summertime, so fine, is everybody groo-oovin?

When I played the whole song through the first time, which required me to watch it's god-awful music video on You Tube — swimming pools, beach balls, three bad (and probably gay) male dancers awkwardly gyrating around a tiny pop starlet with fried hair and Lady GaGa makeup — I literally put my head in my hands and said, "This song, Naomi? You turned yourself into a pin cushion for assholes over this shitty song?" I was trying for a little gallows humor, but given that I ended up crying at my laptop, it seems my technique could use some work.

At Cathedral Beach High, fags were off their radar these days, a big change from the years I'd spent at the same school, pretending the fact I was willing to skip lunch three days a week for the chance to gobble Randy Gregson's cock behind the bleachers was just some kind of phase. (Insert joke about protein diets here. *Har har har.*) It was the *trannies* who were up at bat now. You didn't call them that anymore, of course. Not if you lived in my neighborhood, at least. But that lesson hadn't filtered down to my alma mater, because there were boatloads of students there willing to call my niece that very thing all day, every day, even on her way from school, and on Facebook, and on Twitter, and on her own phone if they managed to somehow get her number. (Fun fact you find out after your niece kills herself; Naomi had been forced to change her phone number four times in the past three months.)

When my niece wasn't being tormented by the kids at school, my own sister had taken to locking her in a closet for hours while she shredded all the dresses Naomi had managed to borrow from sympathetic friends.

Fitting that my sister's the one locked up now, I guess, even though locked up isn't exactly the right term for it. Institutionalized is closer, maybe. Truth is I checked her into a drug rehab where they've put her under suicide watch, but the press has translated this as "hospitalized for emotional distress after her uhm, er... *daughter's* gruesome death". But if you know my sister at all, you know this is just the latest stop on her decades long tour of Southern California rehabs; the fact that Naomi's death inspired this latest visit to *12-Stepia* is kinda beside the point. What matters — to me, at least — is that Callie's being watched. That she doesn't have access to a computer. That she can't go online and obsess, as I've been doing, over Naomi's suicide note, which went viral a day after her death, which was how I found out about the dress-shredding and the discipline-by-closet, neither of which Callie has denied. She's too busy sobbing. Not grief-stricken, regret-filled sobs like you'd expect of a mother who'd just lost her child; rather, the kind of wound-licking, self-obsessed, how-could-my-life — *my life, my life, my liiiiiiiife* — have-come-to this sobs my sister's been expert at since we were kids.

Mr. Franklin, did you do enough to help your niece?

This is the first question the reporters shout at me when they catch me on the front lawn. It's been a week since my niece was torn to pieces by an eighteen-wheeler, a Mack truck and a mini-van full of carpool kids. (Allegedly, it all happened too fast for any of the eyewitnesses to give a statement as vivid as my nightmares of that moment, nightmares in which Naomi spins from grill to grill like a frenzied Salsa dancer switching partners in the blink of an eye.) The flock of camera-toting vultures perched outside my sister's townhouse is a lot smaller now than it was in the beginning, right after Naomi started trending on Facebook and Twitter. Trending by the name she chose for herself, thank God. But I didn't say anything to them then and I'm sure as hell not saying anything now, not in the middle of this clusterfuck, not since the other kids started dying. Let them say what they want about a family refusing to grieve. There has been no official statement from the family, which I intend to be the official statement about this family.

I'm surprised the reporters have reverted back to their old scripts. The day before, all they wanted to know was if I thought there was a connection between Naomi and the other deaths.

There've been two now, but the real headline-grabber was Jimmy Murdoch's fatal swan dive onto the jagged rocks that line the cove. The golden boy football star, a guy who'd probably spent most of his free time banging cheerleaders and making secret visits to his dad's doctor friends to get treated for curable STD's, had opted to take his last leap in full view of a bunch of tourists taking pictures of the seals lounging on the beach nearby. There are at least seven different, variously gruesome camera phone videos of that horrible moment floating around the Internet now and I've managed to avoid all of them, mostly by changing the channel as soon as a news anchor starts in with some version of the words, "What you are about to see is very disturbing. But it asks the question, Is there *a plague of teen suicides* affecting a small Southern Calif—?"

At least the other kid, Arthur Lu, chose to die in peace. They'd found him in his father's BMW, parked on the side of the same access road Naomi had walked to reach her final destination. The cops are tight-lipped as to the exact cause of death, but rumor has it he cut his own throat with a kitchen knife. Maybe cut himself up in other, more survivable ways first, but that part sounded like more Internet bullshit.

One of the San Diego news stations has taken to showing a digital map including both the spot where Arthur Lu parked his father's car for the last time and the section of 1-5 where Naomi was torn asunder. Like they thought viewers at home would be able to discern some pattern to the bloodshed from the ripples of surrounding foothills, or the number of yards between the access road and the freeway's western guardrail. My sidewalk-hogging friends have been asking me about connections too, in hopes the bitter fag uncle from West Hollywood will snap and give some expletive-laden sound byte that might feed the narrative they've already put together, that Jimmy and Arthur had been two of Naomi's many bullies, that they'd offed themselves out of guilt.

I haven't given the reporters a damn thing. I'd been to school with guys like Jimmy Murdoch and Arthur Lu. I knew damn well guys like that didn't kill themselves. Kids like Jimmy and Arthur saw the world in two dimensions; everything they wanted and everyone who was in the way, and like most of the kids in Cathedral Beach, their parents' money insulated them from even the idea of consequences. But I'd kept all this to myself, so now my reporter friends were back to square one, trying to provoke me with talk of my dead niece.

Did you do enough to help Naomi, Mr. Franklin?

To which I don't say, *At least you stopped calling her Nathan, you fucking prick.*

But the answer's no, of course. The answer will always, for the rest of my entire fucking life, be *no*. True, I'd stayed up some nights with her until two in the morning, chatting with her on Facebook while she asked me increasingly personal questions about my body and my sexual urges. I'd pull back slightly when the questions got too inappropriate, assuming that she was looking for a father figure and didn't know how to go about getting one in a healthy way, or maybe she was just stoned or a little drunk or both. But now I can see what Naomi was after, confirmation that we were not the same, she and I. I was gay; she'd been born in the wrong body. Once my answers to her prying questions made this clear, she'd pulled away on her own. Stupidly, I had assumed she'd gone looking for help from someone else, and I had also, just as stupidly, assumed my sister's stories about being clean and sober for three years now were the truth. Meanwhile, Naomi had done the worst thing a kid in her position could do; she'd gone to school.

What would you say to Naomi if she were alive now, Mr. Franklin?

They're trying. They really are, these assholes, but they've lost their initial spunk. They don't even try to block my path as I go for the driver's side door of my Prius. The assault is in their phrasing, and I wonder if they know I'm headed out of town and these questions are their last ditch effort to get something from me.

I'm surprised, however, that not a single vulture in the flock asks me what's inside the cardboard box I've just carried down the front walk in both arms; the one I'm now setting carefully on the passenger seat, the one that contains all the personal items of Naomi's the police took from her room so they could confirm her death was truly a suicide; a slender laptop, two diaries they pried the locks off of, scratching the sides of the puffy pink covers in the process, and her Galaxy Note, which after a week in a police storage locker still has a surprising amount of juice.

I'm almost to the freeway when I realize what leaving town will mean. I can either take a snaky, forty-five minute route north up the coast, or I can get on I-5 and end up speeding right through the spot where Naomi was killed. There's only one freeway entrance and exit for Cathedral Beach and that's exactly how the town likes it. Maybe the original city planners would have allowed for more if they could have hung a sign over each that screamed *NO NON-DOMESTIC LATINOS ALLOWED*, or, *NO TRANNIES WHATSOFUCKINGEVER AND ALL FAGGOTS BETTER BE DECORATING HOUSES HERE.*

This realization short-circuits my brain. Suddenly I've pulled over into the parking lot of the big Hilton where I used to work as a banquet waiter during my first year of college. But there's no employee reunion happening at the valet stand. Instead, I'm hunched over my steering wheel, sobbing my guts out, a snotty, desperate eruption to rival my sister's breakdown of the day before, and the day before, and the day before that.

Heart beat, my feet, moving to the music
Summertime, so fine, is everybody groovin'?

For a second, I think I've turned the radio on by mistake, like maybe I knocked the dial with one arm or something; that's how clearly I can hear the lyrics of that stupid song, the same song that drew a target on my niece's back. But the radio's display is dark. But if I am hearing it, I'm hearing it from some other place, some place that feels buried deep in my... my *neck*. As crazy as it sounds, that's exactly how it feels, like the song is coming from the very top of my spine and it's playing every bone in my skull.

I'm cracking up, that's all. I've slept an average of three hours a night for a week now. I need my own apartment, my own bed, maybe some quick, meaningless sex with a stranger I snare online, a guy who peppers me with the kind of fast, nasty dirty talk I crave. Instead, I part the flaps of the cardboard box with one hand, reach in and take out the slightly chipped Galaxy Note. The police gave it back to me two days ago and ever since then, the display's shown a half-full battery. The cops were also generous enough to give me Naomi's passcode, probably because the girl had received forty-five voicemails after her death. It was hell on earth, but I listened to each one. Some of them were hang-ups, but most were tearful goodbye messages and they made my throat feel like a thin tube of sandpaper. I managed to contact most of the kids who left them, and that's how I'd found out about the bullies and the fateful ringtone.

"You fucking killed her, you know that?" I say before it hits me that I'm talking to a phone. "You know that, *phone*?"

Heart beat, my feet, moving to the music
Summertime, so fine, is everybody groovin'?

When I hear it this time, I remember why I took the phone out of the box in the first place. To see if it was the ringtone I'd heard just a moment before in the middle of my breakdown. But there's no evidence of any new calls; not now, not a few minutes ago. Just the time and date, both accurate, and that little battery icon at the top right hand corner of the screen, half-full with the same sacred green light that gave life to all of Naomi's text messages and e-mails over the past few years.

How many secrets did she share with this thing? How many times did she take refuge in its contents in an attempt to beam herself up and away from the hatred closing in around her every day?

"You're staying here, phone. I've got a Xanax prescription in my future when I get home, but *you* are staying *here.*"

Just a few moments before, I felt like I was salvaging the last pure fragments of Naomi from the town that had killed her. Now it seems ghoulish and perverse, this large box with only three personal items sliding around inside of it. It's probably a smart move, taking her two dairies instead of leaving them in my sister's empty house while reporters still linger outside. But the phone, the same phone she left behind so it would upload her suicide note to all her social media accounts at almost the exact time of her death? Why not just ask the cops for her bloody clothes and every last tendril of whatever jewelry she was wearing at the moment of impact and impact and impact?

Just north of town, the coastline bends slightly to the west and from atop the high bluffs there's a lookout point that gives you a sweeping view back towards the cove and the line of low rounded hills to the south, their westward flanks strung with mansions that stare out at the glittering Pacific. As a child it was one of Naomi's favorite spots, and up until recently we'd still go there during my rare visits home. Back then, Nathan would watch the paragliders take off and land, and I would watch Nathan pull dandelions from the grass on either side of his stretched-out legs with a series of prim, delicate movements that made me think he'd be a drag queen someday, whereupon I'd let him stay in my guest bedroom while his mother came to terms with it all. Neither one of us would ever have the courage to sail out over the perilous drop ourselves, just as Nathan would never summon the courage to ask me to call her Naomi.

Today's a weekday so I'm not surprised to find the lookout abandoned. But I'm still relieved. I don't want any reporters sneaking footage of me burying my niece's phone near the edge

of a cliff. I park in the empty lot and then get out, Naomi's
phone in hand. I'm searching the trunk of my car for anything
that might double for a small gardening shovel, something
capable of digging a shallow hole to drop the phone in, when
I see his reflection in the glass panel of the open trunk door.
There's something wrong about his silhouette; he's either a
hunchback or he's bending forward so far he's about to hit
the asphalt face first. When I turn, I see for the first time he's
gripping a crowbar in his right hand. There are matching floes
of dried blood painting either side of his jaw. I've never seen
the guy before, but even though he's wild-eyed and bloodied
and looks like he hasn't showered in a day, I recognize his type
instantly. Seventeen, at the most, with more muscle than any
teenager should have. The same type of jock as Jimmy Murdoch
and Arthur Wu. And he's got a crowbar.

And his lips, so bloodied and chapped they looks like he's
been sucking on an exhaust pipe, are moving, and in between
the throaty groans he's making with a regular, spastic-sounding
rhythm, I can make out these words he's muttering.

"...myfeetmovingtothemusicsummertimesofineiseverybodygroovin..."

But even as the song lyrics pour from him in a hypnotized-
sounding frenzy, he's lifting his free hand in the air in front of
him. It looks like it takes all the energy's he's got just to extend
one finger in the direction of the phone in my right hand. The
same thing that happened to me in the Hilton parking lot is
happening to him now, only a different version of it. A times-ten,
nuclear-powered version of it that's made him shit his pants,
maybe more than once, from the stench of him.

He opens his mouth wide, lips curling, blood-stained tongue
visible. Is he gulping for air? No. He's fighting. Fighting with
all his might to give voice to something besides the song lyrics
somehow tearing through his brain.

"Giiiiiiive.... me....."

It's the best he can do, but I know damn well what's he's
trying to say. He wants the phone in my hand; he wants to get
at the source of the impossible transmission that's turned him
into a bloody, shit-stained wreck. He's one of them, the assholes that chased Naomi down the hallway, followed her home
from school, shouted slurs at her from the lowered windows

of their parent's luxury cars. Whoever he is, he's just like Jimmy Murdoch and Arthur Wu and if I just do nothing, if I just stand there, he'll probably end up just like they did.

He's such a mess, I'm stunned by his next move, that he's even capable of it. But in the last few seconds before he takes a swing at me, I've been distracted by his ears, or what's left of them, because it looks as if he's gouged them out, possibly with one end of the crow bar that's now arcing through the air towards my face. I hit the asphalt, the phone clutched in my right hand, just as the crow bar smashes down into the trunk's door. I'm still trying to get my bearings back by the time I'm on my feet again, running, my feet hitting grass and hard-packed earth. I'm headed straight for the cliff's edge and when I glance back, I see the kid chasing me, crowbar raised high over one shoulder as he runs with the loping gait of something half-man, half monster.

He's a crazed beast, for sure, but his brain is way too scrambled for him to become the predator he's desperate to be in this moment. There was more than enough time to get off another few whacks with the crowbar before I took off. But he couldn't manage it, and now he's lost valuable time. Now I'm running him straight to the edge of the cliff, Naomi's phone still clutched in my hand. Now I'm dropping at the last possible second and rolling to one side, literally inches from the cliff's edge, so close a few of the rocks jutting out from the very top of the cliff face fall away from me as I roll past them.

The kid runs straight out over the drop, crowbar raised high in one arm, dropping straight down, with no time to look back and get a last glimpse of the guy who just duped him.

✦ · ✦

His name was Pete Scott and it took the cops three days to find him. They'd located his car by the time I got back to West Hollywood, the Mercedes he'd used to follow me up to the lookout, but the beach below was narrow and isolated and the tide ended up carrying him a way's up shore. Nobody saw the two of us together, and I'm guessing the earth was packed too hard for our pursuit to leave behind any telltale footprints. Or maybe they did, and the cops will be on my doorstep any minute now.

I'm pretty Zen about the whole thing, not because I'm foolish enough to believe that whatever force still inhabits Naomi's phone will somehow reach out and save me from the long arm of the law. My confidence has more to do with the fact that the cops in Cathedral Beach have been kept busy by more events at home.

The phone's still there, you see. I buried it. After my would-be killer plunged to his death, I made a beeline for the nearest Home Depot and brought a proper garden shovel. I figured it wasn't safe for me to go back to the lookout, so I drove down to the cove instead. The beach is broad and roomy there, and on weekends it's covered with tourists and locals, Naomi's bullies among them. There were so many of them, you see. From everything her friends had told me, I knew that Jimmy Murdoch and Arthur Wu and Peter Scott were just the beginning, and if one thing was clear, Naomi's sassy little ringtone had some serious reach.

So I found a spot in the sand a few feet from the sidewalk that separated the parking lot from the beach, a good distance from where I guessed the surf line would be even at high tide, and that's where I buried my niece's phone. It's a great location, really, right in the middle of town. Better yet, as the phone's glowing face disappeared under the sand, I could see it still had half a battery's worth of juice left.

I figured there were a lot of people left who were about to hear Naomi's favorite song. Now that I'm home and watching the news again, I can see that I was right.

✦ · ✦

FINDING ULALUME

by Lisa Morton

Lisa Morton says: "When I was invited into this anthology, I knew instantly what Poe piece I wanted to riff on: The poem *Ulalume* is the only work by Poe that makes any possible reference to Halloween, and even that reference is oblique (*For we knew not the month was October,/And we marked not the night of the year—/Ah, night of all nights in the year!*). And I love the poem!"

+ · +

WHEN THE MESSAGE CAME, it was simple enough:

SCSSAR Team needed. Please proceed ASAP to end of County Route 24. There were GPS coordinates after that.

It was the fourth Search and Rescue I'd been called for since I'd volunteered two months back. A lot of folks got lost up in the mountains— hikers took a wrong turn, maybe a bad tumble into a ravine, and it was our job to save them.

But this time I wasn't going to the mountains. I knew damned well what was at the end of Route 24:

Weir Forest.

As a child, it has been forbidden territory. My grandmother, who we all called Grams, lived at the edge of the place, and sometimes my parents would drop the two of us — my sister Anna and I — off for the weekend with her, loaded down with warnings about children who'd disappeared in the black, pathless interior of the woods. At night, as the silhouettes of the trees grew below the starlight, Grams told us stories about how things got worse the farther in you went: First, there were ghosts; then ghouls, half-demons who craved the taste of human flesh.

But there was something in the very heart of the woods, something too terrible to even speak of. When Grams mentioned that last, awful thing, she dropped her voice to a whisper, which was sure to produce a shiver in us. It was near Lake Auber. No one knew what it was exactly, because to know it would be to die.

Anna was a year older than me, and an elegant tomboy; she wore boys' jeans and flannel shirts, but kept her hair long and pulled back, and moved with an uncanny grace. She was as brave as any of my male friends, and so of course she and I challenged each other to enter the woods. We'd tell Grams we were taking our bikes into town to get ice cream or batteries, but we'd ride a half-mile down the county road, turn left onto the dirt trail that led through the cypresses and crab-apples, pedal to the end of the road and then look into the dense brush that picked up where the road ended. Through the mass of brambles and vines and rotting logs, shadows formed a patchwork with squares of dusty sunlight. Things flickered, skittered. We didn't know *what* things.

We never went beyond the end of the road, into the brush. There didn't seem to be anywhere to go— no obvious trail, not even openings to pass through.

"Go in," I might dare Anna.

"I'd get scratched up in there."

"Chicken."

Anna would turn and sneer at me. "If you go in first and keep the thorns away, I'll go in."

I didn't, of course. After a few minutes, we'd get back on our bikes and ride fast into town, feeling proud of how close we'd come to mystery, to danger.

Once, we'd been there later in the day, as the sun crouched down behind the trees. We were standing, smelling the mulch, watching the pollen swirl in the last rays of light, when something *big* crashed through the branches. We both stepped back involuntarily, gripped our bikes' handlebars tightly, preparing to flee should whatever it was — *a ghost* — come roaring out of the woods, but after a few seconds we heard a few smaller sounds, as if the creature that had neared the border of Weir Forest were retreating again.

"Whatever that was, it was big," Anna said, her eyes wide when she looked at me.

"What do you think it was?"

Anna shrugged. "A bear, maybe…"

I don't think either of us really believed it was a bear.

✦ · ✦

Anna went missing two years later.

She'd just turned thirteen, and the way the jeans and flannel shirts looked on her made boys consider her with something other than preadolescent disdain. When Anna hadn't reappeared after a few days, some of those boys even fell under suspicion. Police interviewed them; they stammered and squirmed, but none of them knew anything about Anna.

They asked me, too. I told them I didn't know.

I didn't tell them what I really thought: That Weir Forest had taken Anna. She'd finally gone in there, alone, and it had kept her like a possessive lover.

They found some threads on a blackberry bush on the rim of the forest. The threads might have been from Anna's shirt. It was the only clue they ever had.

After Anna's disappearance, my parents kept me from visiting Grams again. I only saw her when she visited us. When she died, in her house, I hadn't seen her for nearly a year. She'd been dead for a week before her mailman asked the sheriff to check.

I grew up after that, went to college, got a degree I would never turn into a career, took a job in a chain drugstore I would never manage. I was one more millennial burdened with student loans and no real future, a smart phone in my pocket that interested me more than my friends-in-the-flesh. I lived in my parents' house (the same room I'd grown up in, next to Anna's old bedroom on the second floor), and on Saturday nights I drank alone. I drank alone and thought of those who'd vanished from my life. Or those who'd never appeared in it at all, who'd left me alone and unfulfilled, whose names I didn't know but who I missed with terrible longing.

One of my few joys was simply being outside. The most useful skills I'd learned at college were from friends who taught me how to hike and camp. Just before graduation, one of my friends had told me about how much he'd enjoyed being a volunteer in his home town search and rescue team, so I signed up when I came back from college. By the end of my fifth week, I'd been involved with finding a runaway kid who was hiding out in a cave on Mount Yaanek, I'd rescued a family dog from a bear trap, and I'd tracked down a grandfather with Alzheimer's who'd wandered away from home one night. It was mid-day when I located Grandpa Henry, so the poor old guy had spent the long October night there, turning this way and that, with no idea where he was or why he was there. When I spotted him, he was standing beneath the shade of a sycamore, facing the trunk, chattering. I made out part of it before he knew I was there. "...they're all here, I seen 'em but goddamnit I can't remember the names, but I knowed *every goddamn one of 'em*, and—"

I said, softly, trying not to frighten him, "Henry?"

He stopped muttering and turned to me. Squinting, he asked, "Who are you? Are you alive?"

I would normally have laughed at the absurdity of the question, but here, on the perimeter of Weir Forest, it didn't seem so funny. "Yes, I am. I'm with a search and rescue team that's been looking for you, Henry. Your family is very worried about you."

"My family? Hell, they're all dead."

"No, sir, they're not. They're fine, and they're waiting for you..." Henry, at least, was docile and let me lead him back to his home, but he muttered the whole way and occasionally glanced back over his shoulder, as if expecting to see something following him out of the woods. One of the last intelligible things he said before I left him was, "Tell them to stop laughing... they laughed all goddamn night..."

That'd been last week, before Halloween.

Today, I'd been scheduled to work, selling plastic bags full of bubble-gum eyeballs and flame-retardant masks, but when the SCSSAR text came through, I called into the store sick. There were other team members who could take this one, but I knew where Route 24 led.

Weir Forest.

It took me thirty minutes to reach the destination. After I turned onto County Road 24, civilization thinned out— houses gave way to isolated farms to abandoned shacks to nothing human. It was the end of October, and even though the tree branches were barren, their leaves already fallen and crisp, the brush around the sides of the road was so thick that it was impossible to see more than a few yards in. I passed no other cars in either direction, saw no one walking or biking. Soon the trees met over the road, creating a shadowed, organic tunnel, blocking out the gray skies.

I rounded a final curve, and saw two other cars already parked before a metal barrier with a sign reading *ROAD ENDS*. I parked and walked up to two of the county sheriffs, Sam and the tall Asian one who was still new— Cheng. They turned and smiled at me and Sam gave me a mock salute. "'Morning. You're the first to arrive."

"What've we got?"

Sheriff Sam gestured at the car parked beyond his sheriff's cruiser, near the barricade at the end of the road. It was a big black SUV that looked like it had just rolled off the lot. One of the doors was open; there was no one inside.

"That SUV belongs to a company called Durand Enterprises— sound familiar?"

"As in… Mark Durand?"

Sam nodded, a cynical half-smile curling his mouth up on one side. "The same."

Mark Durand… everyone around here knew that name. He was a tech billionaire who'd decided to move his company headquarters to our little county, and the influx of hundreds of jobs had cheered some but left others anxious. Then, last month, Durand had made a deal with the state to lease a huge chunk of unincorporated land— which was most of Weir Forest. There'd been a few attempts to turn it into a national park in the past, but they'd all failed. The area had no landmarks, no renowned monuments or natural beauty; there was Lake Auber, at the region's heart, but it was surrounded by marshland and largely inaccessible. The state was only too glad to let Durand take Weir Forest off its hands.

Sam nodded at the black SUV. "Durand wants to start developments out here, so he sent a surveying crew — three guys and their equipment — out here yesterday. Then, when they didn't come home last night, we sent one of our guys out to check, and sure enough— there's the van, but no sign of the three. Their equipment's gone, too, so we figured they made their way out into the forest and, being city folk, just got turned around."

I shrugged. "If they're surveyors with equipment, you'd expect them to be able to find their way out again, wouldn't you?"

Sam took a swig from his travel mug (emblazoned with the logo of a local golf course) and peered into the trees. "Maybe. It's Weir Forest," he said, as if that explained everything.

The new sheriff, Cheng, said, "Oh, right— it's supposed to be full of ghosts or something, right?"

Nobody answered. Sam and I looked away. Cheng hadn't grown up around here, but we had. We'd heard tales of Weir's ghoul-haunted woodland for as long as we could remember.

I turned to look back, gesturing at the empty road behind us. "The others are coming, right?"

Sam glanced at his phone. "Got affirmatives from eight of you, and Bill Morse should get here soon."

Bill Morse was the only one of us civilians who'd undergone actual SAR training, so he usually took lead on these operations. But this time I didn't want to wait. This time it was Weir Forest.

I tried to sound casual as I said, "I'm just going to go scope out the immediate area a little."

"Fine. Just don't go too far. It's darker than a dog's ass in there."

I heard Cheng offer up some comeback about wondering how Sam knew so much about dogs' asses, but I was already pulling on my pack's shoulder straps and heading for the woods.

I stepped off the asphalt (badly cracked where it ran up against the forest), around the metal barricade with the *ROAD ENDS* sign, and let my eyes adjust— it was as if I'd entered an unlit structure. There was only one clearing in the brush, the closest thing to a trail leading away from the road, and I walked to it. Pausing, I peered along its length; it entered the forest, but seemed to be an actual animal track of some kind, the easiest way in. If three surveyors had decided to inspect Weir Forest, they would've had to come this way.

I walked maybe a hundred yards along the path, which veered between winter-drained trees and deadfalls as thorns and twigs clawed at me. At one area where the trail broadened slightly and moved over a rotting log, I pulled out a Maglite and knelt to inspect.

There was a shoe imprint in the mushy top of the log, its treads almost clear enough to name the brand.

So they *had* come this way.

I pulled out my cell phone, intending to send a text back to Sam to let him know what I'd found, but I had no reception. That seemed odd; my reception had still been fine when I'd parked, and I hadn't come that far.

I knew I should go back now. I should let everyone know I'd found some sign of the missing persons.

I should. But I didn't.

Because Weir Forest was before me, and it was time to accept its challenge. Its mysteries pulled on me; they always had, just as they'd pulled on Anna. But I wasn't Anna. I wasn't a teenager, alone and unprepared.

So I stepped over the marked log and set off into the murkier depths of Weir.

I walked on, although at some point I began using my Mag just to find the path before me. What time was it? It was the last day of the month but the withered branches entwined above me should have allowed in more light, yet it remained dank, dismal, and I moved slowly. I stopped at one point, saw my breath exit in a thick puff. When had the temperature dropped? I zipped my down jacket all the way to the neck, shrugged out of my pack, and removed a water bottle. As I took a long swallow, my gulping sounded amplified, and it took me a few seconds to realize why: I hadn't heard another sound for a while. Normally a forest like this was full of bird sounds, leaves crunching as animals dashed through them, wind soughing in high branches.

But Weir was completely silent.

I recapped the bottle, stowed it, shouldered my pack, and decided I was anxious enough now to go back. Entering Weir had been a mistake.

Turning around, I pushed back down the path, away from the decaying heart of Weir. I walked, my breath in vapors. The woods grew no warmer, no brighter. It all looked the same, but none of it looked familiar. I walked. Sweat turned to a layer of damp chill. I walked.

And went nowhere.

I tried my cell phone again. I tried scaling a tree for a better view, but the bark repelled me. I searched the thick organic carpet of the forest floor for traces of my own footprints, but there were none. I hadn't come this way.

I was lost.

As that realization sank in, I stopped, dropped my pack, squatted down to think. What time was it? I was reaching for my phone when I saw something in the trees nearby, a whiteness that shone against the dark gray tree-shapes.

I rose slowly and moved to the side, where I could see it better. It was a person, another human being. I nearly choked in relief, started to run forward, to call it— but my voice froze in my throat when my Maglite swung up and settled on the face.

It was Anna. My sister, Anna. She was still thirteen, still dressed in the sweatshirt and denim skirt she'd worn the day she vanished.

"Anna?" I staggered forward. She didn't move or speak, just looked at me.

"Anna?"

I smelled something dead then. The force of the stench hit me like a blow, and I turned aside for a second, coughing. When I turned back, Anna was gone.

First there were ghosts...

"Anna," I said, and gave in to the frigid tears that spread down my cheeks.

✳ · ✳

After some time — as even the vague light of the forest faded and full night came on — I found matches in my pack, gathered material, and lit a fire. I hoped Bill Morse had his SAR team looking for me. Maybe they'd already found the surveyors, and would find me soon. Maybe a fire would help.

Its warmth did little to dispel the chill, but the orange glow was welcome after the silver daylight. I was leaning forward to warm my hands, contemplating eating a protein bar, when I heard it:

Laughter. High-pitched, distant, tittering, but clearly laughter.

I almost put the fire out, but whatever had made that sound could probably find me in the dark. Besides, I wanted to see *it*, and my Maglite was dying.

I waited, feeding more stripped branches into the flames.

The laughter came again, closer, and from multiple throats.

The ghoul-haunted woodland.

They appeared, edging forward out of the darkness into the circle of pumpkin-colored light. Three of them, ashen-colored, bare-skinned, with crimson eyes and jagged teeth. Adrenaline coursed through me. My hand instinctively sought a burning branch to use as a fiery weapon, but they kept their distance, leering. After a few seconds, one of them beckoned me, gesturing behind, into the woods. They wanted me to follow them.

I debated. If I didn't, they could well turn on me, tear me to shreds in seconds. Or they might abandon me here, to die alone, to join my sister in a frozen afterlife. But what would they show me if I followed them?

The truth was I wanted to know. I thought it might be a secret revealed, a question answered.

I picked up the longest, thickest branch from my fire, one with a flickering end that would make an effective torch. I hefted it, stood, and moved toward them. They tittered and leapt off into the night-black woods.

The ghouls kept up a quick pace and I stumbled more than once, but tried to be careful of the flame, tried to hold it up and keep it going.

At last I saw the fire glint off something before me. I pushed past a final stand of brush that tore through my jeans and gloves, leaving sharp, throbbing scratches, and then I saw where we'd come: Water. Lake Auber. The heart of Weir.

I gazed across its expanse, the flat ebon surface reflecting only my faint light, and then I heard my monstrous guides utter their grotesque amusement again. I turned, moved toward them, holding out the torch, feeling the ground beneath me change from sodden mash of leafy detritus to sucking, damp shore—

And then I saw the three surveyors… or what was left of them, because the ghouls had already feasted. Limbs were reduced to bones with a few bloody shreds; clothing, which was apparently not to the ghouls' taste, hung in tatters or littered the ground. The remains had been stacked in a pile, a pyramid shape with three severed heads on top. The eye sockets were all hollow, the orbs sucked out.

I retched. Leaning over the tarn, I convulsed, producing only a thin string that sizzled as it hit Auber's surface. I panted, wiped the back of my hand (which had lost its glove some unknown time ago), and tried to straighten up. My eyes were drawn back to that hideous collage before me, to the ridiculous thought that Weir would never be charted, never be neatly divided into squares on a map, to be flattened and paved and populated.

One of the ghouls touched me. I leapt back, crying out, nearly lost my balance on the soggy ground, but then saw that the creature merely wanted to direct my attention away from the gore-covered pile. I followed its pointing finger, and saw something near the shore of Auber, something that glinted without need of starlight or moon's glow.

It was a stone edifice, a marble square with columns and metal gate.

A tomb.

As I neared it, I saw a word carved into the front, a name. I stepped closer until I could read the name by the ethereal light:

Ulalume.

And then it was as if I fell headlong into a tunnel, a passage through lives and centuries, a backward, descending spiral. I rushed past other versions of me — a 1960s soldier, a 1920s dance girl, an 1890s Victorian matron — back, back, down, until I came to the bottom and the beginning. To Ulalume, who I'd once loved and lost and buried here, on another night such as this so long ago. Ulalume, who appeared now before the tomb, who had seized the surveyors and given them to the ghouls as a sacrifice on this night, to bring me here. Ulalume, whose loss I now understood I'd felt throughout my life, even though I couldn't put a name to that loss. Ulalume, whose hand was cold fog in mine, but strong enough to pull me toward the black waters of the Auber. Ulalume, who I would join now, at last, united forever here in the ghoul-haunted woodland of Weir.

My beloved. My Ulalume. My destiny.

Ulalume, found at last.

✦ · ✦

OBSESSION WITH THE
BLOODSTAINED DOOR

by Rick Chiantaretto

Rick Chiantaretto says: "I was first introduced to Edgar Allan Poe around Halloween in junior high school. My eighth grade teacher thought I should move on from Roald Dahl's *The Witches*, and decided it was time for me to read something more mature, something I could *really* call horror. The emotional connection I had with Poe's whimsical sense of darkness made me an instant fan. I loved the classics, of course (*The Raven*, *The Pit and the Pendulum*, *The Murders in the Rue Morgue*), but found my favorite story, *The Cask of Amontillado*, when I purchased a copy of Edgar Allan Poe's complete works. After reading it, I realized I had a personal story to tell about inescapable walls and tombs of my own making. Fifteen years later, *Obsession with the Blood Stained Door* became one of the most symbolic and intimate works I'd ever written. It exposes readers to parts of my mind that I'm still afraid to admit exist."

◆ · ◆

IF I THOUGHT ABOUT IT long enough, I could tell you how long I've been here, but after thinking as much as I have, the exact number grows less and less significant. All that matters is that it's been a very long time.

I used to ride my bicycle by this place when I was a child. I didn't call it a house back then, because in reality it had always been much more than that. A palace perhaps? Mansion? Estate?

Castle? I suppose I could sum it up by telling you that it was a large residence with seemingly no caretakers.

Can you see why the child I was, who had to pass by this place every day, would be intrigued?

The rusted gate and large oak trees sagged under the weight of age but looked to me like stately soldiers guarding a playground. The fallen leaves along the sidewalks created a golden walkway to a place that rose out of the mists of perfection. I could be a king there.

The exact age that I found myself strolling up the lengthy lane beyond the rusty gate is also of no consequence— all that matters is that I *did* walk up the lane. I remember it had been a very warm day sometime in the fall, and the leaves from the giant oaks made a pleasant crunching sound as I curiously surveyed my surroundings. Large black birds perched on the branches seemed to watch my every move. Their incessant peering grew more disturbing with time.

From the road the house looked large, but when I stood at the foot of it, staring up at the stretching spires, it became monstrous. Without even passing through the heavily aged door I was engulfed; every which way I looked, all I saw was brick and mortar. The view was broken only by leafy ivy that parasitically forced its way into the crevices. As I reached toward the doorknob, I heard drafts being pulled through the gaps in the door. That was an eerie sound. Like breathing.

I felt the corrosion of the rusty doorknob on my hand. The knob turned with a little effort. The latch softly clicked, a sound followed by a rousing whoosh as trapped air escaped. The door swung open far enough for my anticipation to grow.

I entered a large vestibule decorated with flowing tapestries, which had once been colorful, but were now dimmed by decades of dust. I promised myself that once I was done exploring, I would return here and give them a thorough cleaning. But I did not return. I got lost. In all the time I've been in here, I have yet to find that room again, and I cannot find my way out.

Logic would dictate that the house was larger than my boy's mind conjectured, but I am no longer a boy; conjecturing on the nature of the house is now irrelevant. I am unsure of exactly *where* I am.

The first hour alone with the grand staircases and rooms that spoke of royalty had been a childhood fantasy come to life. My footsteps and boyish chuckles echoed throughout the halls.

If I listen closely I can still hear them echo, as if they will echo eternally, although they have grown fainter; ghostly. The house parrots my cries for help too; they sound even more menacing mingled with the boyish laughter.

It hadn't taken long for the demeanor of the house to overwhelm me with fear, especially as the sun began to set and moonlight spilled through the barred windows and thread-bare curtains. Shadows were cast that spilled into one another, each quivering with a sense of preternatural life.

But what first caught the fierceness of my growing alarm was a suit of armor. I screamed at the metallic human, sure it was possessed by the moonlight that reflected off its sword and shield. That scream became the first ghastly echo to plague me. As I ran from the suit of armor, I buried myself deeper in the maze.

It was then that I found the door.

My feet pounded heavily on the hardwood floor as I ran from room to room. Once fear had hold of my mind, everything morphed into an enemy: bedposts and bureaux, tapestries and ornamented bell-pulls— they all drove me to run faster, inadvertently leading me deeper into the house. Rooms turned into hallways, hallways to stairwells, and stairwells to hidden passages. I raced to the first closed door, reaching for the doorknob in front of me, turned in my terror, and knocked my head harshly against the wood.

I woke hours later; the sun had pushed the shadows back far enough to warm my face. I was on the floor at the end of a corridor, lying at the base of the door. I had not seen a door like this except in antique shops and cartoons. It was painted white, and the ornamental coffering made it glimmer like snow under sunlight. When I regained my footing I tried (this time much more carefully) to turn the ancient knob.

Locked.

The ceramic oval knob was intricately fashioned with running pink and green floral designs. Above it, I could see through the antique keyhole, although as my youthful eye pressed against it, all I could make out on the other side was darkness.

No other door in the house had been locked.

Even now, with my young self gone, I have yet to discover another locked door. Naturally, this has weighed significantly on my mind for some time. Besides the fact that the door was locked, it seemed to be the only place in the house that felt familiar to me. For no matter which direction I have taken, still, the route always leads to that damned door!

Perhaps you think, well, isn't it different doors that all look the same, and that are all locked? You wonder how I can claim there are no other locked doors in the house and yet, having been so lost for so long, never having found another locked door, how can you question the validity of my statement?

Do you honestly believe, over all this time, that I haven't attempted to mark my path? I know it's the same door because there is a stain where my battered head had spilled blood the first time I ran into it!

Pshaw! Here I am pretending there *is* a *you* when I don't know who *you* are. I don't even know if you have the thoughts I imagine you having.

Surely it's easier for me to pretend to have a conversation with myself and address my own concerns, for I'm certain that all of this will be lost to misunderstanding anyway. If there is a *you*, rest assured that I'm not crazy. At least, I wasn't when I entered this house. If I have gone mad since, it's certainly not from loneliness, but from an unexplained desire to get beyond that blasted door!

Trapped as I have been, I began to imagine exactly what could be behind that door. An exit, perhaps? Oh, if only it were just an exit. It would be glorious to see the sun without the dyes of unbreakable stained glass. But I'm certain that whatever lies beyond the shadows of that door will be more glorious still; it is a door behind which surely lies all glory and wisdom. Neither hunger nor thirst, nor any earthly or heavenly desire for anything or anyone could compare to my lust for whatever is behind that door!

It was during one of these fits, while I sat in front of the door contemplating what wonders the room beyond must contain, that I discovered the mirror. I spent days sitting cross legged in the hallway that led to the door, staring, willing the door to open. Finally, when my eyes were fatigued enough for sleep, I set off in search of a bedroom, knowing full well that after I had rested, I would again return to sit before the door and marvel at its magnificence.

Today, when I turned, my eye caught movement. I had not seen movement in so long that the faint flicker sent chills down my spine. I spun around to catch nothing more than a view of myself. The mirror sat opposite the door, oval and ornately framed, like the doorknob.

It was odd, seeing myself stare back at me. I didn't recognize that years had passed. All that allowed me to be certain that another man did not stand by my side obscuring my boyish reflection was that when I moved, so did the reflection. The years have been kind to me, I thought. The roundness of my childhood cheeks had been pulled back, flattened by a stately jaw. My eyes were gentle, even though set deep, darkened beneath from exhaustion.

All this time I had been so preoccupied with the door that I hadn't taken notice that I was naked. As I processed my image in the mirror, my mind returned to the clothes of my youth; those I had worn upon entering the house wouldn't have fit for long.

I saw myself and was intrigued. I studied the round firmness of my chest and the bluish veins that seemed to be traced onto my arms with blue crayon. My sleek midsection flexed in harmony as I twisted and I became fascinated by every small muscle that I could bend and contract. The hair on my head, though unkempt, was the color of cherry wood charred by fire, and my leg muscles trembled violently when I stomped my feet upon the floor.

I held up my hands and studied the palms, tracing the indented lines with my fingers, only to study them again with the help of the mirror's reflection. My lips, the color of blood against my pale skin, were pulled over white teeth in a broad smile. I realized the smile came from the sensation of moving my fingertips gently along my bare flesh. Oh, the sensation that is touch! I wanted to feel every inch of myself!

I looked deep into my brown eyes and thought I could see a light shining from within the darkened pupils. It was in this moment that I saw who I was. To see myself, truly for the first time, having lived in oblivion for so long, focused solely on a door—

I gasped. I almost felt guilty. In the moment I discovered myself, I had forgotten completely about the door.

I saw my eyes flicker toward the door in the mirror's reflection and was filled with a dizzying sensation that a normal person would probably identify as joy. There, in the mirror's deep reflection, was the door... standing open.

My eyes burned. I wept and let out a breath of air I didn't remember inhaling. My feet were already running toward the door though my eyes still stared, unbelieving, at the reflection. A feeling of relief and accomplishment washed over me, but as I turned toward the door at the end of the hall with the bloodstain, I was horrified to find it was still closed.

I grasped the handle and pulled. Confusion furrowed my brow. I turned toward the mirror again and could plainly see the door wide open. I could see my reflection standing next to the open door, but when I turned away from that mirror image, there was nothing but a door with an ornate knob securely fastened.

I glanced at the mirror one final time; the face in the reflection had twisted in fury. I picked up a small chair in the hallway, and hurled it viciously at the mirror. I cannot begin to express the felicity I felt as I heard the glass shatter into thousands of shards.

Suddenly, something caught my attention. It wasn't something I saw or felt, but what I heard: glass sharply cracking, pieces hitting the floor with a tinkling sound. Then, a thud, like something heavy hitting the floor.

I trained my ears to the echo I knew would carry throughout the house, listening for the crash to be repeated. Amidst my boyhood laughter and my fearful screams, the echo was clear: the smashing of glass, the cracking, the tinkling, the thud.

Could I be sure the thud wasn't my own heart pounding in my chest?

Moonlight spilled unevenly over the broken glass, reflecting light around the room in thousands of beams. As I slowly made my way toward the mirror, one of the pieces refracted a different kind of light. This light wasn't as piercing as the other, but duller, dirtier, metallic.

My steps were slow, my breathing irregular, but the object became more defined. It was so small that I was standing directly over it before I realized it was a key. Intricate, floral, antique, with a piece of red ribbon tied through the loop.

I had no doubt it would fit the door. I was so certain of this that I had the key in my hand and in the lock before I remembered picking it up.

I stood with one hand on the key, the other on the knob. My quest's end was in sight. There was nothing, nothing I wanted more than to discover what was beyond the door. Yet, I felt a sense of completion, of wholeness that had been so long in coming— I dared not rush the sensation.

Sensation. Realization dawned as the sun I could see starting to spill through the stained glass windows. My image in the mirror had burned itself into my memory. I recognized the fire in my eyes as my soul, my true self. I acknowledged that it wasn't until I found myself, my truth, that I was able to identify what I most earnestly desired.

I twisted the key. The lock clicked, and the knob turned freely in my hand.

I opened the door and stepped into the waiting darkness. I'd never felt so afraid, so enticed, and so repelled by a decision that was entirely mine to make. This felt final but I was ready, consequences be damned.

Staying would be hell. I knew what was there for me in the house. I wouldn't lose myself again.

It was time to move on.

✦ · ✦

THE LIGHTHOUSE

by Barbara Fradkin

Barbara Fradkin says: "The Lighthouse is inspired by Edgar Allen Poe's controversial story of the same name. It was begun shortly before his death and apparently unfinished, generating much speculation about possible endings. Its spare style and elusive ending left plenty of room for my imagination, and the lighthouse is a perfect metaphor. Not only does it symbolize both loneliness and hope; it connects with my ancestral roots."

✦ · ✦

NOVEMBER 2, 1942

Quirpon Island, Newfoundland. Temp 32.1° Wind NE 20 knots. This is worse than I imagined. It's dark as pitch up here on the head, and out on the open sea, winter is gathering force. I'm so lonely I talk to the birds. The last steamship has gone, leaving us with supplies that have to last until May, and soon the pack ice will form in the strait.

Three months gone since I got up here, and I've got nothing to show for it but this diary. Hardly a word written of my radio play! It's going to be a murder mystery set back home in Goose Cove, complete with blood-curdling screams and spooky sound effects. I had pictured myself with lots of time on my hands, up on this remote island that juts out into the North Atlantic like it's reaching for the edge of the earth itself. Pictured myself with nothing to do but write.

I knew Uncle Nat wasn't much of a conversationalist. A quarter century spent manning the lighthouse with nothing but gannets and gulls for company will do that to a man. 'Not a fit place for a woman or children,' he'd grumble whenever anyone back in Goose Cove pushed him on the subject. Truth to tell, he'd be happier without any assistant, but maintaining the lantern and the foghorn is a two-man job, so when his last assistant went off to war, my mother volunteered me.

She said it was because I was big and strong enough to carry the heavy loads up and down the cliff from the boat and to climb the hundred steps up the lighthouse tower. But I think she figured two sons serving King and country in the fields of France were sacrifice enough for one mother. She'd lost a brother and half a dozen cousins in the Battle of the Somme last time around. 'War's not for you, Sammy,' she said. Sammy— even though I'm eighteen years old. Sammy had been her brother's name. 'You live in the clouds with your stories,' she said, 'not down here on earth where the German bullets will be hunting for you.'

But my stories haven't followed me up here. I've stood on the rocky head of the island with my pen in my hand, the wind flattening my clothes and the salt spray stinging my eyes. I've called and called, but nothing comes. Nothing but loneliness. Strange, that. In Goose Cove you're never alone, no matter where you try to hide. There's always a cousin or an aunt finding you with a 'Hey, Sammy, where y' to, b'y?' and settling in for a chat like they've got no place else to be.

I stand on the lighthouse gallery now and look out into the darkness. These days, ships are just black smudges on an even blacker sea, no more than a dull sheen of metal in the passing light. But tonight the sweep of the lantern reveals nothing beyond the limestone, lichen, and tuckamore scrub of the head. Like my characters, everything that tries to grow here is twisted and shrunk. I even long for Uncle Nat's company, for his cheap pipe smoke and his toneless whistling that fills the silences between us.

But he's gone down the island to the new radar station again. Ever since the fly boys arrived in September with their tents and towers and cables, Uncle Nat has been a new man. He makes the two-hour hike down there at least once a week with a bottle of screech and a kit full of stories about the Great War. When he came back from the war, my mother says, he wouldn't say a word about it. 'Nothing to say,' he'd snarl. I guess he just had to have the right audience.

And a common enemy. Jerry. These days the coast of Newfoundland is crawling with U-boats. Like sharks, they circle in the deep, sniffing out their prey and planning more deadly strikes, like the ones near Bell Island two months ago. Not just naval ships but also merchant supply ships, and last month even a passenger ferry. 'No honor,' Uncle Nat roars, foaming at the mouth like a mad dog with each new strike. He's puffed up with pride that the new radar station is going to stop the bastards in their tracks. The story is that it's just a weather station, but that's fooling nobody.

Where there was once a lonely lighthouse on the windswept island to act as a beacon to passing ships, there will soon be a radar station to guard the entire Strait of Belle Isle. Uncle Nat is back in the war and proud of it. I hear his whistling now as he walks back up the coastal path. His feet know every crag and crevice, but it's black as sin out and the rocks are slick from the spray of the whipping sea. Until he bangs open the door, I hold my breath.

November 3, 1942

Temp 28.3°. Wind N 40 knots. Blustery and cold. A busy day. Repairs needed to the clockwork of the lantern and Uncle Nat wasn't up to it. 'A touch of the flu,' he said, but a touch of screech is more likely. He doesn't go down to the radar camp tonight but retires to his bed right after his shift, leaving me alone in the lighthouse, surrounded by the darkness and the snap of the flag in the wind. A shutter has come loose on our house and it bangs. I try to think about my radio play, but all I can think of is the shutter banging and the yawning blackness outside. Characters, where are you hiding? Talk to me. Someone talk to me.

November 4, 1942

In the middle of the day, while I'm trying to sleep, I have a brainstorm! The radio play takes place not in my cozy little village where everybody knows everybody, but right here on this barren slab of rock. Where a lone man holds a solitary vigil over the seas. Where nothing but a single sweep of light stands between safety and dark death.

I get out of bed in a fever of excitement and start to write. Opening scene voice-over. 'A brave lighthouse keeper stands alone in the tower, staring out into the night. Listening.' Sound effect of wind howling and shutter banging. The distant bellow of a foghorn.

I sit awhile, chewing my pencil. What next? What does he hear? A scream of fear? A cry for help?

November 5, 1942

Temp. 35° Wind NW 6 knots. Clear and calm. Tonight Uncle Nat was feeling better, so he headed back down to the radar camp after his shift. The station is almost built but it won't be operational until after Christmas. Can't be soon enough for Uncle Nat, who imagines U-boat periscopes every time he looks out to sea. Newfoundland is nothing but a string of lighthouses and villages, but it's the first line of defense for the North American continent. U-boats are prowling all around it waiting for their next kill. Uncle Nat takes his rifle from the Great War with him wherever he goes, firing out over the ocean at every rogue wave he sees. I'm sure if he had a cannon, he'd be aiming it out to sea as well.

Left alone, I look at the first three lines of my play. I need a story. Some characters. A man alone against the sea won't go far. Something needs to happen. A ship lost in the fog? Or maybe it's a U-boat, sunk, leaving a single lifeboat washed up on shore. Sound effects of surf, of groans as the keeper drags the survivor to safety. I try to imagine the words they exchange, but my mind is a blank. Am I even forgetting how to talk?

I power up my shortwave radio just to hear a real human voice before I start imagining one. The radio hisses and spits out a few words, but all I catch is 'bombs', 'harbor' and 'bonfire' before the voice is swallowed up. What bombs? Is Newfoundland being blown to smithereens while I'm stuck out in the beyond? I twirl the dials in vain, clutching at sounds. It gets me thinking; can I make a mystery that takes place over shortwave? One man connected to the world only through invisible fragments of a sound wave?

November 6, 1942

I'm listening at the lighthouse door. It's two in the morning and Uncle Nat isn't back yet. He always sticks his head in to get my report before retiring to bed, but tonight there is no sound of clomping boots, no whistling. The air is dead still and heavy with dew. Not a good sign. I look anxiously out to sea, which glistens like molten tar under the starless sky. There is a sliver of crescent moon in the west, but a wall of fog is rolling in from the east, swallowing sea and sky.

Uncle Nat had better come quickly. A faint sound of singing drifts on the still air, and I wonder if they're having a bonfire down at the radar station. Bonfire Night is forbidden now, of course — no point in telling the Jerries where we all are — but memories of home and happier times creep up on you. I picture the soldiers huddled around a little flame at the center of the camp, far from spying ocean eyes. The thought brings a lump to my throat. Uncle Nat says I'm too young to go down to the camp, even though Uncle Sammy was younger than me when he died.

The solitude is worst at two in the morning, so I busy myself with my duties. First I check the ship-to-shore wireless for nearby ships. Even the rat-a-tat of Morse code would be welcome company on a night like this, but there's no one out there. Since the U-boat attack on the passenger ferry, everyone is spooked. Next I get the furnace going for the foghorn and polish up all the lenses on the lantern.

As the night crawls on, I start falling asleep over my note-book. The foghorn's wail drifts into my half-sleep, washing over the lifeboat and the survivor in my dream. When I wake again, it's near morning. There are no bursts of laughter, no whistling coming up the path, nothing but the mournful wail of the foghorn. The silence is suffocating. The fog has wrapped the tower in an icy, wet shroud that seeps through the very walls.

Then, through the silence, I hear a distant rumble. I get up to peer out the window, but stare into a void. When I climb the tower to the gallery, it is like stepping into the clouds. Fog swirls in the beam of light from the lantern, but I can see nothing beyond, not even a glimmer of pink across the eastern sky. Uncle Nat should be waking soon to take his shift.

As I climb down, I hear a soft splash from down the cove. Fear shoots up my spine. Uncle Nat? Or just a wave whipped up by my over-active imagination? I hold my breath, straining to hear through the rush and hiss of the surf. Nothing. I feel my footing along the short path and knock on our cabin door.

"Uncle Nat," I whisper, as if speaking more loudly will bring a hail of bullets from an unseen enemy lurking in the fog.

There is no answer. No grunts or snores. Alarmed, I step inside. The little cabin is empty. Uncle Nat has not returned. I stand in the dense, choking stillness, my blood roaring in my ears. Uncle Nat could have misplaced a footstep in the fog or slipped on the icy path and plunged to the sea below. He could be lying near death, unable to move or even to cry out.

I am alone on the cape, sole keeper of the lighthouse. Even if I could navigate the cliffs in the fog, I can't leave my duties. The lighthouse is the only beacon of light for ships on the dark and treacherous sea.

I breathe to calm my racing heart. Maybe Uncle Nat is just hunkered down in the radar camp to wait out the fog. When it lifts, he'll come whistling up the path as if he'd just done his patrol of the point. Saying 'What's all the fuss, b'y?'

I shake my head at my own foolish thoughts. My mother always said I had too much imagination for my own good, and got too many fanciful ideas from the radio dramas I listen to. I turn and go back to the lighthouse. Just as I set my hand on the door, two muffled pops pierce the mist, like the sound of hunters in the woods. Uncle Nat, shooting at U-boats again? Firecracker from the bonfire? Or something more deadly.

I stand in the darkness, my hand on the heavy cast iron door handle. My scalp prickles as I listen, but the sounds never come again. 'Foolishness!', I hear my mother say as I go inside.

Later November 6, 1942
10 o'clock. Temp. 37°, Wind 0. I am still on duty. The fog is a pale gauze now in the morning light. There is still no trace of Uncle Nat. I've stopped being mad at him; I just want him to walk through that lighthouse door, safe and sound. The lighthouse is cold and I think about the cozy warmth of my bed. I stoke the fire, refill the lanterns, and rewind the clockwork yet again, my arms aching.

My duties done, I have time to check out the path as far as the cliffs that skirt the landing cove. That's the most treacherous part of the path from the radar station. As I walk, the fog lifts just enough for me to see the damp, scoured rock that flanks the path. Boulders loom up out of nowhere, startling me. As I get near the cove, I tune my ears to each new sound. The rush of a bird's wings, or the sad howl of the foghorn that helps me mark my time. Soon another sound reaches my ears— a soft, rhythmic bumping like a piece of driftwood against the shore.

I stand at the top of the cliff above the cove and peer down into the white abyss. I can't see the ocean, so I start down the stairs, each foot feeling its way on the slick treads. Halfway down, the smudged outline of our wharf and boat begins to form. The boat, a sturdy thirty-five footer, is hauled up on skids for the coming winter.

The bumping grows louder. I creep down another few steps, and slowly a ghost boat emerges from the mist, banging against the wharf in the ocean swell. I stumble down the last few steps and stare at her in disbelief. She's a little rubber dinghy equipped with nothing but a pair of oars and a bailing can.

Just like my dream, I think. Is she real? She's too small to stay afloat for long in the open sea. Where did she come from?

I reach out to touch her, and she rocks. I shake the foolish notions from my head. She probably broke loose from the radar camp wharf down the island and washed up here all on her own. Or perhaps Uncle Nat took her to make a sea journey along the coast rather than trying the hazardous cliff-top walk in the fog.

Full of hope, I rush back up to the lighthouse, slipping and stumbling over the icy ground. I am panting by the time I reach the tower.

It's deserted.

I tour the perimeter of the headland, squinting into the mist and calling Uncle Nat's name. The sea tosses his name back to me, unheard.

I don't know what else to do. I am too tired even to think. Uncle Nat has been missing from his post for more than twelve hours. I power up the shortwave radio, but all I get are growls and hisses. I send out a message anyway, hoping that someone, somewhere, will hear my call for help. The Americans listen to everything, but Uncle Nat says they wouldn't concern themselves with a missing lighthouse keeper. U-boats, enemy aircraft, and enemy communications are all that matter in their war.

Time ticks on, but no one replies. Even the Morse Code transmitter is silent. It's as if I live in a world forgotten. I think of all the shipwrecks on the rocks below, and the ghosts of the dead and lost. I even imagine I can hear them call.

By the time darkness falls again, I'm in such a state I can barely hold this pen. But I must keep my duties. Wait out the fog. When the weather clears, help will come, from the soldiers at the radar station or the naval ships off the coast. But I must keep...

November 7, 1942

A sound wakes me. I jerk my head up, blinking and confused. It's dark, and so cold in the lighthouse that I can see my breath. The fire is stone cold ash. The lantern is out, the foghorn silent.

In a panic, I race to rewind the clocks and refill the lantern. How long has it been out? Have any ships foundered on the rocks below? Or taken a wrong heading through the straits? I throw open the door to the lighthouse and stand in the doorway, searching and listening. The night is quiet, but overhead the sky is strewn with stars. The fog has lifted! Help will come.

I go back inside to light the fire, throwing on junks of wood until orange flames fill the box. Only once the roaring dies down do I hear a faint scraping sound. I get up and go closer to the door. The sound is hollow and muffled, like footsteps dragging along the path. Up the lighthouse steps. A gasp of air. *Finally*, I think, letting out a breath I barely knew I was holding. I am about to rush out to greet him when there is a knock at the door. Soft, like someone not sure of his welcome. Once. Twice. Then a faint call, almost swallowed by the thunder of the sea.

"Help."

I freeze. A shiver races through me. Uncle Nat would not knock. He would not beg. He's a powerful, stubborn man, more likely to swat away a helping hand with an impatient grunt.

Maybe I'm dreaming. Or imagining again.

The doorknob begins to turn. Startled, I yank open the door. A man is slumped against the tower wall, dripping sea water, disheveled, and red-faced from the cold. His blond hair is plastered to his hatless head. All this I see before I register the German naval jacket wrapped around his body and the rifle drooping from his hand.

He lifts his eyes with an effort. "Please," he says through chattering teeth. "I am cold."

He speaks English like a proper Englishman on the radio rather than a Newfoundlander.

He looks like me, with the same blue eyes and blotches of acne on his unshaven cheeks. He smells of diesel oil, smoke, and gunpowder. His rifle looks just like Uncle Nat's antique, more likely to blow off his own hand than anything else. I don't know which of us is more scared.

"I will not hurt you," he says when I don't speak. "I do not want to hurt anyone. But..." He hooks his rifle under his arm and holds up his hands in a plea. "May I sit beside the fire for awhile?"

I can't bring myself to close the door in his face. I just stand there staring at him, trying to figure out what to do.

"I understand you are afraid," he says.

"I'm not afraid. But I don't know..." I want to reach out and touch him, to see if he's real. His rifle looks like a cast-off from the last war.

"I am not your enemy. Look." He leans his rifle against the wall and peels off his leather coat, which he tosses to the ground. Next, his Luger and his uniform — the shirt, belt, and trousers — all dumped in a heap on the ground, until he stands in the doorway in his skivvies. There's hardly a spare pound on him, and he's shivering.

"You see? I am nobody," he says. "My name is Karl."

My mother didn't raise me to leave a man naked and shivering on the doorstep, even in my dreams, so I finally invite him in. I offer him a blanket and a seat by the fire while I climb the tower to the gallery. Using the spy glass, I search as far as I can see, but the sea is empty, rippling silver and black under the crescent moon. No dark hulks of ships, no lurking submarines.

I don't know what I expected — a bullet in the back, maybe — but when I climb back down, I find him reading my radio play. "You are a writer," he says with a smile.

Caught off guard, I snatch up my notebook and diary and shove them into my pocket. "It passes the time."

"I am sorry. I mean no trouble. I miss books. I miss so much!"

He stares at the Morse Code transmitter for a second then his gaze shifts to the shortwave radio set in the corner, and he gestures. "I had a radio almost like this at home before the war. I used to listen to jazz music from America until Hitler forbid it."

His voice is liquid honey, like Laurence Olivier in a British radio play. I feel myself sinking into it.

He leans closer to examine the radio. "Can you get American jazz on this?"

I almost say 'yes' but stop myself just in time. Instead, I wave my hand at the radio, as if it has no importance. "I can't get much of anything on her these days. Sometimes local music or news, but mostly she just hisses at me."

"Too bad." His voice trembles. "I miss my trumpet."

"You play trumpet?"

"Just in a small band, at private clubs. Do you play music?"

"The mouth organ, but you don't want to hear me try."

He smiles weakly as he runs his fingers over the knobs. "Could we—?"

"There's no reception, because of the fog." I move towards the door. "Come on then. I'll fix you some tea and soup in the cabin."

He turns from the radio reluctantly. "Thank you," he whispers. "Some dry clothes too, if you can spare them?"

He follows me out the door and down the short path to the lightkeeper's house. Silently he accepts the clothes I offer and, while he dresses, I build a blazing fire that will heat up the little kitchen in no time.

He doesn't speak again until I hand him a cup of tea. His hands shake so badly he can scarcely drink. My work pants and sweater fit perfectly. "You look like a proper Newfoundlander now," I joke, hoping to cheer him up.

"You are here alone?" he asks.

I want to tell him about Uncle Nat being missing, but stop myself. "Oh no, there are two of us. Plus the men in the rad— village down the island."

He nods. "You are lucky. It is very peaceful here. No killing, no fear."

The despair drips from his voice, so I don't tell him there's plenty of fear here too. "Is that your boat in the cove?"

"I became lost. I was lucky to find the cove, but I have been wandering around for hours in the fog. I thought I was surely going to die."

My mind seems to float above the scene. I'm dreaming my own radio play! A man alone on the cape, with an enemy ghost from the last war sitting in my kitchen sharing tea! But he seems so real. Just a young man who misses his home and is scared he's going to die. He has brought his rifle inside with him, as if he is hanging on to that smidgen of fear.

"Where were you going?" I ask.

He waved a weary hand. "Anywhere. To America, I hope." He pauses. "What's your name?"

"Sam."

"Sam." He gives a sad nod, as if it's just the right name. "I am running away, Sam."

"Deserting?"

He flinches. "It is not how you think. I love my country, and it is for my county that I walk away. In her name, terrible deeds are being done— to anyone who is different. You do not want to know."

My soup is hot now and he spoons it up eagerly. "I am six months on the *Unterseeboot,* and home feels very far away. My country is wandering in the darkness, Sam. No, it *is* the darkness. Torpedo the innocent, drown the children. I saw your lighthouse from the U-boat and it was like a sign, calling out to the lost. I had to come."

He is speaking in riddles, rambling, probably too cold to think straight. I don't know what he's talking about, but I can tell he's had enough of war. Maybe six months inside the dungeon of a submarine will do that to any man. But that doesn't help me know if he's real.

The soup has steadied his hand, and soon his gaze drifts to the map on my wall. He stands on wobbly legs and props himself against the wall to study it.

"We are here?" he asks, tapping his finger on the cape.

I don't answer. How I wish Uncle Nat was here! My brain is dead tired, and mind tricks and enemy soldiers are way beyond what he taught me.

"This is an island?" Karl traces down the island to the narrow strait that separates us from the mainland. "And I go across here to get to America? Is it very far to swim?"

"Much too far, and much too cold."

He sighs and returns to the map. "This... village you talk about. It is where?"

Being top secret, the radar station is not on the map, but when I say nothing, he taps the middle of the island where it is. "It is here?"

I feel a small chill of doubt. "They won't help you."

He looks at me with his sad blue eyes. "Please, Sam. I am one man, not the German army. I will give no trouble to anyone. I want to go to America. To New York, to play in a jazz band like Benny Goodman. Please, show me how I can leave."

His eyes look far away and he even smiles a little. I know that look. He's a dreamer who creates stories in his head, just like me. And like me, he's caught in a war beyond himself. "You'll never make it," I say softly. "There's no roads from here."

"Then I will walk. I would rather die than go back."

The whole idea is crazy. There are two hundred miles of rock and bush between him and the closest railway station. With winter coming, he will die of cold and starvation. I shake my head against the fog of fatigue. I know I should send a message on my shortwave, because he is too young to die. But part of me can hear my mother's voice. 'You're talking to a ghost, Sammy my son!'.

"Cross the strait here in your boat," I tell him. "There's a village on the coast there, and other villages along the way. If you can get down to the railroad here at Deer Lake, you have a chance of reaching the mainland."

Karl is studying the map again. His hands are steady now and his eyes narrow, as if he's trying to keep the whole map in his head. "Thank you, Sam. If you let me sleep for a few hours, I will go."

I'm falling asleep on my feet myself. My head throbs, and my arms and legs quiver with fatigue. I need time to sort things out and decide what to do. I gesture to the kitchen daybed. "I have to get back to the lighthouse, but you can sleep there as long as you need to."

He looks at me, blinking as if he's trying to read my thoughts. I hope my confusion doesn't show on my face. For a long moment he just looks. Then he nods and lies down on the bed. He turns to the wall, cradling his rifle the way Uncle Nat does, as if it is a lifeline, and pulls the rough blanket up around his ears. Before I even have my boots on, he is fast asleep.

I watch over him for a moment, listening to him whimper in his sleep. His breathing sounds real enough, and I wonder whether I should take the rifle from his hand.

But in the end, I leave him be.

November 8, 1942

1 a.m. I'm wide awake! Scribbling down my radio play as fast as I can. Ghosts and fog and little dinghies that bump in the night, all inside the lonely lightkeeper's mind.

I hear footsteps outside. A soft knock at the door. I look up in surprise, and see the doorknob begin to turn...

✦ · ✦

THE MASQUES
OF AMANDA LLADO

by Thomas S. Roche

Thomas S. Roche says: "*The Cask of Amontillado* scares the hell out of me. It appears to break the rule that main characters need clear motivation. That would make a retelling easy as pie if Poe hadn't already shocked us. I couldn't flout Montressor's obscure motive without contravening Poe's intent. But, I discovered that for certain horrific crimes, character motivation can be derived from an implied rapport between narrator and narratee. Which scares the hell out of me."

＋ · ＋

"DAMN IT," FORD SAID, punching buttons on his phone. "I can't get a signal down here." He put the thing away and gazed at the long rows of padlocked sheet metal doors.

"This place is sick," he said. "How long have you had a storage locker here?"

"A long time," I said. "Twenty years. You might say it's been in the family."

"And there's *another* basement below this one?"

"Mine's in the third basement, yes. Sorry, there's no elevator. You're not too cold, are you?"

"I should talk to Luke about buying this place," Ford mused, ignoring my question. "Turn it into apartments or something. Down here could be one kick-ass party space." Without warning, a violent shudder ran through him. He crossed his arms, clutched his biceps, and rubbed vigorously. "Put some heaters in, though." The bells on Ford's jester's cap jingled, part of his costume. "How much further, bro?"

"Just down this long hallway," I said, gritting my teeth at the sound, once again, of that hated one-syllable appellation. "Really, it's not all that far... *bro.*"

The word felt like shit in my mouth. This man was far from a 'brother.' He wasn't even a friend. He was my ex-boss, the young beneficiary of management idiocy in the local tech boom that valued the concepts of youth and 'innovation' without knowing what those things meant.

As such, Ford Donato was my mortal enemy.

"Hey, speaking of Luke," he asked, "have you seen him? He moved out of his place on Fourteenth Street, I guess. No one's heard from him."

I shrugged. "I barely knew Luke. I doubt he even remembers me."

"Aw, we all remember you, bro. You were the older guy with the beard. But, like, not like a cool beard, just a beard. I wish Luke would text me, if he's got a new cell or something. I thought for sure he'd be here. I mean, it's his party, right? *Musi.fy*'s his baby, bro."

"Indeed it is," I said tightly. I'd guessed that Ford kept calling me 'bro' because in the nine months since he'd laid me off, he'd forgotten my name. At this, I did not take offense. I saw *opportunity.*

We who wander, invisible, through the streets of a long-dying city; we walk with impunity. Thus may we act!

To be fair, there had been a lot of layoffs that day. Ford Donato and Luke Casey, respectively CMO and CEO of *Musi. fy*, had run ragged a baker's dozen of underpaid music writers recruited from the underemployed survivors of the close of the *Weekly* a few years ago. Working insane hours in preparation for *Musi.fy*'s launch, we'd produced more than 20,000 capsule reviews. Carefully keyworded, these were intended to capture online traffic for the soon-to-launch online music portal that promised its users they'd *'Never hear the same song twice... unless you want to!'*

Gone, too, was the startup's venture capital, squandered not on our meager salaries, but on lavish 'pre-launch parties' for Ford, Luke, and their friends.

When *Musi.fy* had imploded three days before launch, and I and my twelve colleagues were cashiered with two weeks' severance and a murmured promise from Ford that we'd 'get a chance to work for him again', when he launched the new pet-food retailer he claimed to 'have some feelers out about'.

That had been nine months before. Tonight, I'd encountered Ford at the Camp *Musi.fy* post-Burn wind-down, to which I'd somehow scored an invitation despite having been, apparently, long forgotten by Ford. In fact, as I discovered, *Musi.fy* itself now existed *only* as a Burning Man camp.

Ford had been drinking a forty-ounce bottle of fortified wine 'ironically', I'm sure.

"Damn!" he chortled. "They really stuck you in the ass-end of nowhere!" Ford showed a propensity for *Schadenfreude* that seemed to be endemic with the city's new crop of twenty-something dot-com executives. Their wealth was a landfall they'd convinced themselves they had earned by being so 'awesome'. The misfortunes of others, such men often delight in.

I forced a chuckle.

"Yes," I said. "When I got this unit, I was a bit short on money. I'd been evicted. At the time, this unit — right there, it's just down those next stairs, a ways — it was the cheapest they had. There's no elevator. It was more space than I needed… but, then, when I closed down the record store three years ago…"

"Oh, yeah!" said Ford. "I forgot you owned a record store, bro. What was it called?"

"*Montresor Music*," I said. "Twenty-fourth Street and Guerrero."

"Yeah! Did it have a gecko on the sign, or something?"

"Yes, yes, you have a very good memory," I lied.

In fact, the *Montresor Music* sign had featured a snake, biting an ankle as it was crushed. Fifteen years ago, when I'd opened *Montresor*, the device had appealed to my sense of fatalist justice. I thought it the duty of the oppressed to destroy their oppressors, even to the point of self-destruction.

In the years since, I'd revised my thinking.

Ford said, "Didn't it have some words in Greek or some shit?"

"Latin," I said. "*Nemo me impune lacessit.*"

"I remember that sign," Ford said, his breath misting before his thin lips. "What does it mean, again?"

"Buy music here," I lied.

Ford nodded. "Cool sign, bro. I remember it. I used to go to hit this cool bar near there." He guffawed. "I think I puked in your storefront once, bro. How much further?"

"Just down these stairs at the end of the next hallway," I said mildly. "Then, just a bit further."

"You're sure it's there in your storage locker? That Amanda Llado album?"

"It's Llado," I said sharply, correcting his pronunciation for what felt like the hundredth time, but was actually only the second— I had let it slide before tonight. Nonetheless, I began to lose my temper. "It's Spanish. The initial double-L isn't pronounced like an 'L,' it's pronounced as a—"

"I've always heard it said 'Llado,' bro," Ford said, repeating his sin. "I think it's Llado. But you're sure you've got it?"

"You're shivering!" I said. "Let's go back to the party. We can find Luke, and we'll get you a jacket, and—"

"Bro, forget Luke. Luke's a good guy, don't get me wrong. But he doesn't know Amanda Llado from Neneh Cherry. I'll be fine. Let's keep moving."

"Just down these stairs," I smiled.

Ford's bells jingled as he picked up the pace, racing ahead of me toward the stairs.

I took pleasure in following at a discrete pace, faking a bit of a limp.

"Sorry," I said. "The cold does things to my joints. I'm getting old."

"You're not that old," Ford said. "What are you, fifty?"

"Forty-two," I said through gritted teeth. "You flatter me, boy. It often pleases me to think I might someday possess the wisdom of my elders."

"So you were around in the nineties and shit?"

"I most certainly was," I said.

"Did you see her?"

"Who?" I asked innocently.

"Amanda Llado."

"Oh, yes," I said. "I knew her."

"Bro, you *knew her*? You knew Amanda Llado?"

"Yes. Quite well. *Too* well, in fact. She was a very sad woman…"

"No shit!" said Ford. "Were you friends?"

"Of a fashion," I said mysteriously. "I won't say we were fond of each other, but—"

"Dude, did you bang her?"

I covered my disgust for Ford with a strained smile.

"Every time we got a few minutes alone," I said dryly.

"Was she a total freak in the sack?" He sneered. "I bet she was into some—."

"Ow!" I barked, clutching my knee and stumbling against the roll-up door of Unit B2-112. The cheap sheet metal issued a gargantuan rattling sound, so loud it made Ford jump. "This cold! It's killing my joints. We should go back to the party. You can get your jacket, I'll take some ibuprofen, and we can find Luke—"

"Screw Luke!" growled Ford. "He can't tell Amanda Llado from Frankie Valli." Ford sneered. "You know what Luke told me?"

"What?" I asked innocently.

"Luke thinks *Dead in Baltimore* is better than *Born in Boston*!"

"It has been said. I'm fond of both, myself."

"Dude, *Born in Boston* is the shit! *Baltimore* is okay, but... shit, a band's first album is *always* better." He waved his hand in disgust. "Let's just hurry, okay?"

"My thoughts exactly," I purred.

Ford shivered and hurried down the stairs.

I had been wise to conjure the specter of Luke Casey. Ford's music-fan rivalry with his best friend and employer had been annoyingly evident during the nine months we'd all worked at *Musi.fy*. Luke and Ford frequently tried to one-up each other about everything, from juggling techniques to the proper old-school mustache wax, but most notably about music. They'd spent many billable hours having loud arguments in the halls about obscure indie bands from Philadelphia and Akron and Chapel Hill. They generally did this while the rest of us worked, or tried to.

In the world of the dot-com startup, I believe this phenomenon is unremarkable. At *Musi.fy* specifically, the company's officers tended to occupy themselves doing extremely annoying things whenever the rank-and-file music writers like me were working.

Over the course of their loud hallway debates, it became clear that both men had a weakness. They both loved the aforementioned early-nineties post-punk folksinger, Amanda Llado.

I, myself, once had a bit of an acquaintance with the esteemed Ms. Llado. During my tenure at *Musi.fy*, I had listened intently whenever Ford and Luke vigorously debated the various merits of her two released albums. I listened still more intently when they speculated on what might have happened to her when she disappeared from the music scene.

Amanda Llado had been a seventeen-year-old Boston run-away transplanted to this very city, rumor had it, by that most romantic of methods— the upthrust thumb. She'd arrived here in 1990 with nothing but a seven-string guitar and a change of underwear. She'd found a local crash pad and set out to play her songs at local coffee shops for small change.

Amanda quickly captivated the local music scene with her ethereal voice, dark and sensual lyrics, and youthful good looks, not to mention her dissonant guitar playing. The latter was owed to her fondness for 'alternate tunings', most notably the tri-tone or 'Devil's Interval' that had so troubled Debussy in the 1890s.

Amanda Llado could make an acoustic guitar scream like the damned.

The unsettling sound of Amanda Llado's deliberately inharmonious chords, haunting voice and disturbing lyrics set her apart from other local musicians. Her songs drew inspiration from Poe and peyote, Baudelaire and barbiturates, Rimbaud and Robitussin. She appeared to speak Medieval Latin, or at least performed an approximation sufficient to convince her audience. Her dark style appealed to fans of punk, goth, folk, and even alt-country. But her occult influences and drug references appealed to a still-broader audience of rootless cosmopolitans. At the time, their numbers seemed legion.

Amanda Llado became the toast of the town.

Her first release, 1993's *Born in Boston*, had long been forgotten in the indie music scene proper, but was still celebrated by a small but die-hard group of fans who often prided themselves on a love of the obscure. More controversial among Llado's few remaining fans was her 1994 album, *Dead in Baltimore*. It contained Amanda's only 'hit', *I'm Not Drunk!* It had reached #87 on the charts at AltCollege.com in the fall of 1994, providing a brief bounty for *Snakebite Records*, if not for Amanda herself. For this, *I'm Not Drunk!* and *Dead in Baltimore* remained the target of sneering disdain from self-important dilettantes like Ford.

Such a man is familiar to me. Ford was far from the first. Desperate to quiet his demons of deepening self-doubt, he believes the only good song is the song none but himself has heard.

I must say, I tend to agree with him.

I was there, in those days, in the warm coffee shops and cold lofts of the old city, then, the town that once was, a bastion of The Arts. That was long before the skyrocketing rents of the tech boom took it away.

I was there, watching as if from a distance while Amanda
Llado's haunting performances captivated the crowd. I searched
for beauty in her pale face. I looked for meaning in her complex
lyrics and sought salve to my wounds in her discordant notes.
I found none. I found only hatred.

But, oh, I knew her well.

I knew Amanda Llado better than Ford or Luke Casey or any
glib hipster could ever pretend to know her through her music.

I had heard Amanda's third album, 1995's *The Masques of
Amanda Llado*, teased via promo singles for local college radio
stations, but never released. According to music industry legend,
the first printing of 5,000 discs was already in the *Snakebite
Records* warehouse when every last disc — and the artist herself — disappeared.

Neither she nor the CDs have been seen since. Only one
man heard the finished recording, and he wasn't talking. I had
written capsule music reviews — many hundreds of them —
but not for that album.

Masques sometimes showed up as a title on torrent sites—
always as cover for some insidious virus loaded by Russian
hackers. Mostly, though, Amanda Llado and her lost album
were forgotten. The prior two were only remembered by a
small cadre of fans, some of whom — as Ford Donato and Luke
Casey demonstrated — were total douchebags.

As for the artist herself, she remained an open question. For
some years, Amanda Llado sightings were occasionally reported
on music message boards. Claims were made: Supposedly,
Amanda was now in Menlo Park living in sin with a millionaire,
or employed in a live-in Nevada brothel, or telling fortunes as
Madame Rue Morgue in a trailer park in Nebraska, veiled to
hide her identity. Some even said she'd become a man.

I'd heard all these speculations and more. I heard them
repeated by Ford and Luke when I worked at *Musi.fy* during
their lively debates. They'd also argued about which of the
black-and-white nudes of Amanda from the interior CD book-
lets were the hottest, and — less often — what caused her
disappearance.

For neither question will a satisfactory answer ever be found.

The former is merely a matter of opinion. Myself, I find all
of those photos grotesque.

For the latter question, no single answer is sufficient.

Drugs... alcohol... manic depression... they all were but part of the truth.

I knew, and know, the story— but, you know that, don't you?

You, who know all too well the darkness of my soul, must already know I did not join the debate on Amanda Llado the first time I heard her name uttered by two postmodern frat boys. I chose to bide my time. I made preparations. I saw the layoffs coming. I used part of my meager salary to prepare, sparing no expense. What I purchased would need to stand the test of time... eternity, hopefully.

When I'd received my invitation to the *Musi.fy* party, I knew Ford would be there.

I knew a secret that Ford did not; it would prove his undoing. Ford would sprawl, still and decayed, before he ever knew the full story of Amanda Llado.

No man but me would walk the earth knowing that story; I had sworn that long ago. I swore that before I opened *Montresor Music*. I swore it before I closed *Snakebite Records*.

◆ · ◆

Ford's shivering had lessened by the time we reached Unit B3-120. We were three levels below the street. The overhead lights clicked off as I fitted my key into the padlock and we were plunged into inky blackness.

"What the fuck?" Ford barked. "Whoa! Dude, it's dark!"

"They're on timers," I said. "I guess we took longer than I thought to get down here." I twisted the key; the padlock clicked open; I removed it and put it in the pocket of my cargo pants.

I said innocently to the dark: "I thought for sure twenty minutes would be enough!"

"Looks like you were wrong, bro!" Ford attempted one of his annoying chortles, trying to hide the obvious trembling in his voice. "You don't, um, have a flashlight, do you?"

"I'll see, but... help me open the roll-up door first."

"Where?"

I grabbed his hand in the darkness and felt Ford jump. I put his hand on the handle of the sheet metal door.

"Straight up," I said. "One—two—go!"

The tortured scream of metal-on-metal nearly deafened us both as the door rolled up. It was sweet music to my ears.

I fished a small flashlight from my pocket, clicked it on and aimed the light into the storage space. Ten feet by twenty seemed like it would be more than enough when I first rented this space. But it was getting crowded in there.

Stacked to the ceiling were boxes of CDs. Little space remained. Nonetheless, I'd left a narrow gap between the stack of file boxes marked *SOUL/FUNK* and the ones marked *HORROR SOUNDTRACKS*. The back wall of the storage space was just barely visible. I swept the flashlight across the wall briefly, illuminating a box marked *AMANDA LLADO*.

"There it is!" Ford cried excitedly.

I groaned and clutched my leg, dropping the flashlight.

I said: "Ow! This damned cold… it's supposed to be climate-controlled down here!" I tried to bend over to pick up the flashlight and grabbed my back, groaning.

I collapsed on my ass at the edge of the locker, panting. The light from my flashlight reflected off the silver sheet metal, casting ominous shadows everywhere.

I gestured toward the back of the storage locker and said, "I can't climb with this cold. You go. It's straight back, there, along the rear wall."

"No problem," Ford said. He bent down to retrieve the flashlight. His hands were shaking. "Um, where?"

"Right back there," I said. "There's a box marked —"

"Yeah! I see it! Luke is going to be so jealous!"

Ford climbed into the narrow crawlspace I'd left between boxes.

The light of the flash disappeared.

I moved with practiced grace, near-silent, slithering into the narrow tunnel formed by the boxes of CDs. I knew the way all too well; I'd practiced it thousands of times in my dreams.

And once in reality.

"Hey!" Ford said. "Cool skeleton! Whoa, and cool manacles, dude! That shit is sick. You know Suzi Inryo, Japanese girl, horn-rimmed glasses, used to work with us at *Musi.fy*? She bought a pair just like that at Folsom Street. Total freak! She and I had a date three weeks pre-launch, and she was all, like— uh?"

It was Ford, not his erstwhile conquest, who was all, like, 'Uh?' The presumably X-rated anecdote never came, because Ford was staring slack-jawed at the ceiling-high stack of boxes.

"Dude, what the fuck? All these boxes say 'Amanda Llado'!"

Ford was almost shouting, thinking I remained at the door of the storage locker. In fact, I was right behind him

The jester's costume he wore had tapered pants, tight to the hem. I found his foot in the darkness with one hand, the open shackle with the other. The heavy chain was bolted not to the sheet metal wall, but to the cement floor. The manacles came as a pair, as such things tend to. Ironclad Leathers charges an arm and a leg, but it's worth it.

My prey was distracted. He swayed with shock as he played the light up and down the stacks of boxes that framed what remained of Luke Casey's corpse.

It dawned on Ford that it wasn't a Halloween skeleton. Even so, he remained clueless for crucial seconds.

The manacle circled Ford's ankle. The barrel lock clicked shut. I withdrew.

Luke's skeleton, decayed to the bone, sat half-upright on a stack of CD boxes bearing labels straight from the printer: *SHIP TO: SNAKEBITE RECORDS. AMANDA LLADO: MASQUES OF AMANDA—*

There were 5,000 discs in those boxes, stacked to the ceiling.

"Very fuckin' funny," Ford said, rattling the chain now attached to his ankle. "You shackled me, bro!" He snickered: "That's what Suzi Inryo said on our date! Don't get me wrong, bro, you're cool, but I'm not into you like that."

His shackled ankle dismissed as a joke, Ford turned his light back to the stack of boxes and asked: "How did you get so many of these? They're probably worth a fortune!"

"Probably," I said, crawling back over the boxes.

"And who did you kill?" Ford asked drunkenly. "It's okay, bro. I'm cool. I won't tell the cops. I had this buddy once who ran this stop sign when we were on mescaline, and … uh … what the fuck? Bro? *Bro?*"

I paused at the mouth of the storage locker. Ford pointed the light at me. The little flashlight half-blinded me, but I didn't need eyes to taste my revenge. Beyond the glare, I saw a beauty I'd never found in the esteemed Ms. Amanda Llado.

Ford's face was twisted in horror. That brought a smile to my face.

"Oh, fuck. Bro?" he asked meekly.

"Call me Amanda," I said brightly. "Amanda Llado."

Ford's horror turned into a rare kind of shock: The surprise of sudden recognition.

"Amanda?"

"It's been a long time," I said, stroking my beard. "I feel some secrets ought to stay buried. Like some overpaid business executives. Rest in peace, Ford."

I started pulling the roll-up door down. Again, there came the scream of metal. And another scream.

Ford howled: "Bro! I mean... Amanda. Wait, Amanda? Amanda Llado?"

"Llado!" I shouted back at him through the sheet metal, emphasizing the initial double-L. "Amanda fucking Llado! It's fucking Spanish! You're from California, God damn it!"

I took a deep breath. Damn my temper! I calmed myself and said: "Some call testosterone the root of all evil, *bro*. I call it breakfast!" I laughed. "The two are not mutually exclusive..."

"Amanda!" Ford screamed. "For fuck's sake!"

At that, I howled as well. I laughed so hard it brought tears to my eyes.

"Yes," I said. "For the sake of all the fucks I don't give!"

I slammed down the roll-up door and secured the padlock, then started up the stairs at a good clip.

Ford's screams of terror could be heard for a time, echoing throughout the sub-sub-basement of 16th Street Storage, but, like all dead dreams, the remnants of the *Montresor Music* and *Snakebite Records* inventory remain buried with the decaying inventory of a hundred other dead small businesses and their dreams.

And who knows? Perhaps there are more than two dot-com executives down there.

＋ · ＋

For some weeks after I buried him, I took the stairs down and listened to Ford's plaintive screams. As I had with Luke Casey, I patiently waited as the screams choked to groans, then to moans, to hacking coughs, plaintive whimpers, gurgling sounds... and then, *nothing*.

For some weeks after Ford made his last sound, I returned to hear the sweet silence. I would sometimes sit outside the very storage locker, contemplating the 5,000 discs deep inside. So many songs, but... just silence.

Years ago, after I'd sobered up, I'd done a similar thing. I used to go to the coffee shops and clubs I'd once played as Amanda

Llado. I would sit in the half-light, bearded and unrecognized, and take pleasure in the faux-angst of others.

After some years of that, I thought I'd like running a record shop. Indeed I had. There was temptation to exhume Amanda Llado, I'll admit, on disc if not in person. But temptation faded as the past decayed in the memories of others. I found a pleasure in their growing silence. Some secrets are buried forever, which is as it should be.

I found that there wasn't much money in selling used records, but *Montresor Music* did keep me busy. A man's mind can turn to terrible things if he doesn't keep busy. A man can have nightmares. Instead, I lived my dream of happy obscurity.

But the tech boom seemed to have it out for the dreams of small men. In such times, it becomes our obligation to think terrible thoughts, indeed.

It has been many years now since I saw my revenge carried through. The basement at 16th Street Self-Storage remains undisturbed, the resting place of many a small business. The units remain occupied, paid for by auto-drafts. They entomb the dreams of a thousand émigrés still harboring dreams of returning to the city 'when things settle down'.

Each year, those dreams are strangled anew by skyrocketing rents and a booming supply of high-end tech startups squandering venture capital. New startups open daily, paying six figures to young 'entrepreneurs' who pay $4.90 for a latte, drop the dime in the tip jar and step over the homeless man out front who might or might not have expired in the night.

But some of us still walk in shadows, holding bright dreams and dark fears for what's left of the arts in our city.

Every now and then, one of us disappears, the way Amanda Llado did. Rumors swirl for a time, but before long, all are forgotten. To some of us, vanishing is the only dream left worth a damn.

Ford and his bro still molder in the sub-sub-basement of 16th Street Storage. In the seemingly endless cycle of boom-and-bust that defines the economic life of the city, what are two more of the vanished?

In pace requiescat!

And I mean that *ironically*, bro!

+ · +

ATARGATIS

by Robert Bose

Robert Bose says: "There is a wonderful secluded dive spot on the Saanich Peninsula, north of Victoria, British Columbia. When you surface around a rocky point, you are under a jagged cliff with an old crumbling manse looming out of the forest high above. The accompanying sense of *insufferable gloom* always makes me think about of the *House of Usher*."

◆ · ◆

MY GREAT GRANDFATHER was dead. There was no doubt about that. His mortal remains lay in quiet repose under half a dozen surplus military blankets, faded and threadbare, from an age where such things were handmade and treasured. His pale blue eyes were still open, staring at me in a distant glazed sort of way. He looked surprised, if that makes any sense, as he had known the end was near for some time. We had spoken of it each day as I stayed at his side in the crumbling manse he called Ascalon.

His last word to his great granddaughter was "Atargatis!" It was a curious word. I turned it over in my mind and spoke it aloud, mangling the pronunciation from the way he cringed. I said it again, this time trying to mimic his tone and inflection, and that brought a hint of a smile and a small nod. The word meant nothing to me at that particular moment, yet felt familiar and intimate.

He gripped my hand tightly and pulled me close. I smelled the sea, deep upon him, and knew a kind of fear I'd never experienced before. It was as if the hand of death was reaching from the watery depths and that I would be taken as well. I tried to pull away, but his grasp was absolute, holding me in one final embrace. It wasn't until he gave a small sigh and went slack that the grip relented. The old man was dead.

Something cold bounced against my chest as I backed away and sat in the folding wooden chair I'd spent so much time in of late. A locket on a thin chain hung from my neck. My now-deceased forebear had placed it there at the last, while he clung to my quaking form. I pulled it from beneath my shirt and examined the locket with interest. It was fashioned from a ruddy form of brass and caught the candlelight in a way that gave it a layered appearance. A faint embossing displayed a coiled snake-like creature, worn to the point of being nearly unrecognizable. A tiny clasp indicated an interior compartment. My fumbling fingers were not delicate enough to engage it but the tip of a nearby pen proved its master. I'd expected a picture, a memento of my long-missing great grandmother, or at least some other lost love, but it held a key.

It was a clever key, of the same unusual form of red brass that comprised the locket, the bow in the shape of a curving fish tail with a short thick stem and three jagged teeth. Foreign letters, or perhaps glyphs, adorned the stem on two sides, meaningless but intriguing. I replaced it in its cavity for later consideration, confident that time would reveal its mysteries.

❖ · ❖

Ascalon itself stood tucked within a quiet cove in Lands End on the peninsula. It arose from the battered shoreline, a stone and wooden monument now moss covered and falling to the ravages of storms and time. Even in a dilapidated state it far exceeded my humble apartment in neighboring Victoria, so the decision to move in was made without debate.

Before long I set about putting my great grandfather's affairs in order. His files were slim and well organized, and his Last Will and Testament a simple document without the complications that a hundred year old man might have accrued. This proved an easy task as I was his only living descendant, all others having perished over the years. My inheritance included the landholding, the manse and its contents, and funds sufficient to maintain the household in perpetuity. I considered leaving my part-time job as a bookkeeper for a local winery, but kept it as an excuse to avoid the stuffy solitude.

I wasn't alone for very long. The old man's library was extensive and singular. For insurance purposes I had it assessed and the brokerage sent over a young professor of naval history from the University of Victoria. His name was Dale. He had been an acquaintance of my great grandfather and was excited to dive into the prestigious yet disorganized collection. Intelligent and charming, he spent his days cataloging it and I was heartened to hear an excited exclamation whenever he came across a treasure of particular distinction.

Winter came and went. The constant drizzle gave way to sunshine, lush greenery and abundant flowers. Each morning, before my late ten-o'clock commute, I would sit on the flagstone terrace and watch the mist dissipate under the warm rays to reveal a spectacular view of the Channel and Salt Spring Island. These days, I thought to myself, had become the best of my short life.

Dale came out onto the deck holding a small volume. "I found something that might be of special interest." With professional care he opened the book to a page marked with an old string bookmark. "You mentioned you had never seen a picture of your great grandmother. Well, I found one." The image was a simple pencil drawing, but clear and precise, with the word 'Star' written underneath. He held it up next to my face. "You look just like her."

"I was named for her as well."

"There was something I was meaning to ask. You once mentioned a tragedy concerning your parents. I hate to dredge up bad memories, but I'm curious."

"They were lost at sea when I was a baby. I was raised by my great grandfather."

"What about your grandparents?"

"Drowned in the 70's. They were caught in a terrible storm sailing across the channel."

"How dreadful. In all my research I haven't come across a mention of any of them. Old Gabriel, I mean your great grandfather, didn't write about them. Not a single word in any of his correspondences at all."

"He didn't like to talk about it. When I inquired he would just shake his head and say something like 'love is a trap for the weak'. He pretty much forbade me dating. Said he was the only man I needed in my life. I had to move out to get away from him. I didn't think he would let me go, but in the end he just didn't have the strength to fight me."

Dale looked uncomfortable.

"I have something I wanted to ask you as well." I ran into the house and returned with the locket. "Have you found anything in his library that mentions this? There's a strange key inside."

He took it from my hand. As we touched there was a spark and we both jumped. We grinned at each other as if we were children. I found I was becoming quite fond of my resident scholar.

He seized upon an old trick to better reveal the faded image. With a sheet of parchment paper and a soft pencil he made a rubbing. When it was complete I realized my guess had been correct all those months ago. It was a sea serpent, one with the face of a woman. A woman with cruel eyes and a hint of a fanged smile. "I've seen this before." Dale said. "Long ago. It might even have been at one of Gabriel's lectures. It's a representation of an ancient Syrian sea goddess. I believe her name was Atargatis."

Atargatis. He pronounced it the same way the old man had. "That was the last word my great grandfather said to me. I always meant to find out more about it."

"It's an ominous name in near east naval circles. She was said to haunt the Mediterranean and drag sailors to a watery grave. A devil mermaid with a long mane of copper colored hair. Beautiful, I imagine, just like you."

I blushed, flattered, and ran my hand through my own red hair. "Sounds like a frightful character."

"So the stories say."

I went to bed thinking of Dale, old ships, mermaids, and the sea. A great storm rolled in as I lay staring out the window. Lightning flashed and wind rattled the shutters. My dreams soon matched it in equal measure, dreadful and chaotic. I awoke to a wailing sound, eerie though not unpleasant, echoing from across the water. If I strained, I could make out a woman's voice. Then I woke again. A dream within a dream?

* · *

I snuck up behind my new love and wrapped my arms around his shoulders as he pored through a dusty tome. "You called?"

He bent his head back to kiss my cheek. "Star, could I see that key again? I found a mention in the personal journal Gabriel

kept while Captain of the HMS Epervier. I just want to make
certain."

"Of course." I extracted it from the locket and handed it over.

"Yes, yes, this is it. Listen to this passage."

*September 12th, 1943. My crew and I found a number of intriguing
items within the hold of the captured smuggling vessel Azira. The
smugglers had set out from Latakia and were bound for the German
port of Bremen with a cargo of occultish items they hoped to sell to
the Nazi's. The primary piece of the collection was a red brass door
adorned with an image of a fanged mermaid. One of the smugglers
had the matching key which took the form of a fish shaped with three
sharp teeth. He claimed the runes along the shaft indicated that the
door could only be opened by a twice broken heart.*

"This would be perfect material for a book," he said. "If
you don't mind, that is?"

"That would be fantastic." I hugged him tighter.

He flipped forward to another marked page. "The story
continues in a later entry."

*December 23rd, 1943. All of the artifacts were turned over to
the Admiralty but for the door and the key. I cannot give them up.
In Alexandria I had gone to the trouble of having a duplicate set
fashioned. I doubt they will fool the experts for long, but the artificer
worked centuries-old brass pots and urns to form the reproductions.
My research has determined that the door once occupied a special place
in King Solomon's Temple and that the representation that stares
out at me is that of the sea goddess Atargatis. I have hidden the door
and the key within my cabin aboard the Epervier until the war ends.*

"My great grandfather seemed to have had a lot of secrets."

Dale pointed to the bookshelves. "There are hundreds of
books. I found this one, and another by Aleister Crowley, of
all people, stashed beneath a sea chest in his closet. It might
take awhile to learn the whole story here."

"Take all the time in the world, love." I kissed him again
and he went back to work.

+ · +

A soft hand shook me awake, a song nibbling at the edge of my
consciousness. Moonlight cast long shadows across the bedroom
floor and I felt full of lust and fire. Dale was staring at me.

"You were singing in your sleep. It was... a bit scary. Are
you okay?"

"Yes, just a strange dream." I showed him my teeth and pounced on him, pinning him to the bed. "Now let me show you something really scary!" I bit him, hard, and though he protested, he didn't struggle all that much.

◆ · ◆

The next day was cold and miserable. I needed to smell the sea and feel the wind on my face so I made some hot tea and sat on the upper patio under the canvas awning. The channel was calm and watching the play of the water was meditative. A small dive buoy, anchored a short ways offshore, caught my eye. I had never seen anyone diving there before. After a few minutes two heads bobbed to the surface and made their way to the public dock that jutted out from behind the rugged headland just east of my property. Intrigued, I made my way down the stone steps, wandered along the walkway beside the house and caught them as they trundled their gear up the overgrown access road through the wooded area next door.

"Excuse me. I didn't realize there was a dive spot in my backyard."

The taller of the two gentlemen plopped his gear bag onto the ground and flipped his oxygen tank off his shoulder. "Yes ma'am, we came across a description in an out-of-print guide-book and thought we'd check it out."

"There's supposed to be a stone ruin down there, possibly part of an old dock," said the short, bearded man, "but all we found was a large piece of metal half buried in the mud."

"Part of a ship?" I asked.

The taller man shook his head. "I don't think so. It was a large discolored rectangular brass plate with odd markings. Hard to say exactly. We took pictures so maybe someone back at the shop will recognize it."

A brass plate? That couldn't be a coincidence. "How fascinating. I don't suppose I could bother you for a copy of the pictures?"

They said they could do better than that and showed me the images on the camera's screen. Each was dark and murky but I could make out a square-edged panel protruding from the mud. They assured me they could improve the quality once they downloaded the raw footage. I gave them my email address and wished them a good day.

That night I dreamt of an ocean where waves were flowing red hair, shimmering in the light of twin suns. There was no song, just a pause, as if that world was holding its breath, waiting.

+ · +

The pictures were in my inbox when I awoke. When the first image popped up I knew. I knew! I woke up Dale. "You have to see this."

He rubbed his bleary eyes and leaned back as I rammed the laptop into his face. "Hold on..." He groped for his glasses and took the computer from my shaking hands. He magnified the photo and panned over it. "That's a red brass door."

"Yes, a door, like the one in great grandfather's book. It's hard to see with all the overgrowth, but that etching matches my locket."

"I wonder how it came to be down there? The HMS Epervier sank off the coast of Spain in 1944 shortly after those original journal entries. From the sounds of it, he barely escaped with his life."

"More secrets. This is so exciting!"

Dale pulled in some favors at the University and got the door raised from the sea floor. In service of his book he had it placed in an outbuilding where he and his grad students could clean and restore it. They worked for weeks removing the accumulated sediment and sea life. The door proved to be in amazing condition, considering, and day by day it came back to life. Each night, after the students had gone home, I checked their progress. Dale would find me there tracing the engravings and singing softly to myself.

"It should be done tomorrow. Then we can pack it up and ship it to the University. Life can get back to normal."

He looked concerned when I frowned at him.

"I want to keep it."

"We've discussed this before. The province won't let you as it wasn't found on your property."

"If you love me, you'd find a way."

He looked exasperated. "I love you more than anything, but it is best placed in a museum and studied."

We went to bed. Our lovemaking that night was fierce, wild even, and left him drained, faded, and more than a little damaged.

+ · +

The brass door glowed under the beam of my flashlight and the fierce countenance glared out at me. It was like looking in a mirror before my morning coffee. I put the key in the lock. It slipped in as if the keyhole hadn't been clogged by sediment for decades. A jolt went through me and everything became clear. Yes, this was the way.

"Stop!" Dale stood in the doorway. He was wearing only his torn anchor-print pajamas and I could see the scratches I'd left on him earlier. I smiled and showed him my fangs.

"You don't want to do that. You really don't want to open that door." He gave me a hard stare. It reminded me of the old man.

"But I do. I've been waiting forever for this."

He sighed in a resigned sort of way. I could see tears in his eyes.

I traced the reproduction of my face on the door. "I lived four lifetimes for that bastard. Lived and died. I still don't know what sorcery he used to bind me and muddle my memory, but that doesn't matter now."

"Star, you don't have to do this." He choked back a small sob. "Don't forget that I love you."

"You're right. I did forget something." In a heartbeat I was behind him. I whispered in his ear as my coils crushed his body. "A heart broken two ways." With an answering snap, the key turned and the door opened. The light of the twin suns, radiant and ancient beyond measure, flooded into the room.

Bright Ascalon. Not the fading old world sea port she had once menaced, nor the crumbling stone ruin the old man had built as a prison, but the world of endless emerald seas and floating ivory palaces.

Leaving the key in the lock, she passed through the yawning portal, content to swim and bask until the day *Atargatis* was again whispered by some desperate and lonely soul.

◆ · ◆

The Ravens
of Consequence

by Carol Weekes and Michael Kelly

Carol Weekes and Michael Kelly say: "We love ravens and crows. They elicit melancholy. Our novel, *Ouroboros*, upholds them. Birds watch from distances, ubiquitous. We share Poe's Gothic, morbid sensibility. Poe's *The Gold Bug, The Mystery of Marie Roget*, the seminal *The Tell-Tale Heart*, and *The Raven* influenced us. Moody, Gothic, with lonely mysteriousness is what we set out to achieve. Poe-like, without being a simple *pastiche*. It's fun to play in Poe's world: dreams whose edges fray and dance like dark wings."

✦ · ✦

I SET OUT ON MY walk with my usual fervor, savoring the crispness of the wind, a thin veil of wood smoke hovering about, lending a typical lonely feel to autumn. I love to stroll, especially through the nearby woods and fields. It clears my mind, puts me in touch with the seasons, and keeps me sane. Takes my mind off things I'd rather not remember, although memory is something that evades me at times. It has happened intermittently for a few years now. I'll get fleeting images in my mind like computer pop-ups. They feel almost familiar, then when I try to capture the depiction, the thought shuts down. Sometimes, I wake up at night screaming. On other nights, I've found myself outdoors, in my backyard mostly, clad in boxers and a t-shirt, sleepwalking. It happened once in the winter last year, resulting in hypothermia. I haven't gone to see a doctor about it. I'm afraid of the potential diagnosis.

My house contains fragmental memories of things not quite concrete that tells me I should be concerned about something urgent, but I can't place the feelings.

Today, I need to walk. The day is melancholy and clings to me like damp coils of neediness, branches hurling purple veins along the ground. So I dress and head into the field again. There was a time, back when I was married, that my wife, Gillian,

there was no Gillian

would walk with me through the woods; we'd hold hands, her long, delicate fingers interlaced with mine, the feel of her rings cool against my skin. I'd feel the delicate pulse of her heartbeat through her fingers, the comforting staccato of her love clasped between warm palms.

I linked my dog, Molly, to her leash and shut the door behind me. Molly enjoys our excursions. She's part German shepherd, part Malamute and her coat sustains her well in cold weather. Today she stands with her snout skyward, absorbing the concoction of fragrances brought in along this morning's frosty wind: the wood smoke, a fungal growth of damp leaves pressing into the ground, and a distant scent of softening pumpkins. A squirrel chirrs, disturbed by our presence. We watch it bound into an apple tree where it positions itself near the top, chastising us. Halloween is two days behind us. Early November sun is weak and translucent like Jasmine tea. A delicate veneer of ice creates a tissue-paper coating along the tops of puddles. I fight the urge to crunch through them like a school kid.

"Let's go, girl," I tell Molly. When we reach the solitude of our destination, I'll disengage her leash and allow her free-roam in order to work off her energy. I feel called by the woods, so we go, the dog happy and innocent, me driven by some darker, inner urging that gnaws at me like a mouse to a scrap of bone.

❖ · ❖

We arrive at the field and nearby woods within minutes. It's quiet here; so quiet that you become aware of your heartbeat and the inhalation and exhalation of your breath. Farmland occupies the west, endless corn and soy fields that have since been harvested. Sagging barns, some near collapse, dot the horizon. To the east, the woodland now mostly robbed of leaves from recent rain and storms; they run for hectares. Hunters set up stations for taking deer, wild turkey, and geese. Today, no one is around.

I relish the solitude as Molly skirts the circumference of the trees, nose ploughing a path through the undergrowth, searching for voles or field mice to chase. She raises her head and ice crystals, sparkling like sequins, dot the end of her nose. Then she stops, alert, rigid, the way she does when she detects noise from a passer-by.

"Deer?" I ask, although I know that Molly can't answer me. Her body language will show me what comes next. Molly emits a low growl. Hair along her neck and shoulders rises, forming matted bristles.

"What's got you going, girl?" I freeze too, my gut tightening. I see no one, unless a hunter is hidden behind some makeshift camouflage; some deadfall of branches and evergreen bough, rifle cocked, ready.

"Hello?" I venture, moving to pull Molly back to my side, but before I can leash her she springs into the woods, breaking through low brush. Branches snap and pop in her wake. She's on a mission, nose to the ground, sniffing.

"Molly!" Of all bloody things... it won't be easy to follow her through this section. I periodically lose sight of her, although I can hear her progress. Finally, I catch up to her in a small clearing ringed by pine trees. I am covered in milkweed silk and burrs.

"For God's sake, dog, what the heck do you think...?" I stop speaking and look past Molly. She stands over something on the ground. It is white, pale, and coated in a film of ice.

"Move over." I nudge Molly out of the way with my knee, and use the toe of my boot to scatter leaves and branches away from whatever has caught her attention. I start. It looks like finger bones of an adult hand. Suddenly, everything about the day intensifies; the smells, the hard, cold feel of the ground, the powerful beating of my heart that now thud-thuds in each ear. I can feel the heartbeat in the carotid artery like a tapping, insistent finger. A raven screams and casts a shadow along the ground as it flies over us, making me jump. I squat down and take a closer look at this thing in the leaves, its digits the color of rain-washed chalk left out on a sidewalk.

I recall some of the names of the bones from my eleventh grade biology class. This looks like an index or middle finger— it contains the metacarpal, as well as the proximal, middle, and distal phalanges; the various bits between knuckles. Chunks of grey sinew and cartilage still hold the bone fragments together. The flesh has long gone. And on the middle phalange sits a tiny band of tarnished silver, loose like a ring-toss prize now that the life-force that had once sustained it in place has since rotted away. It's fine like a woman's ring.

I try to think about how a section of bone dispersed into the soil can worm its way to the surface like this. It almost seems to wave at me as the wind gusts hard, pushing the erect digit. Worse, what drew the dog to it from such a distance back? Decomposition had long since ceased. I've read that dogs can smell the dead for miles. The idea of it makes the hair stand up along my neck.

I squat and examine it more closely, reluctant to touch it. The ring bears the pattern of a bear, an Inuit design from the clean, round lines.

My vision blackens; I waver, but don't fall. Molly looks at me, as if requesting permission to investigate further. I shut my eyes and reach out to steady myself against a nearby tree.

"It is not a human finger. It isn't a finger at all. It must be a stump of wood that just looks like bone. You'll open your eyes and it'll be gone." So often, this is how life has been lately.

I open my eyes, staring ahead, then down; the finger is still there, a macabre pointer. The ring makes me think of Gillian.

who?

I remind myself there was no Gillian. There were no children. Just me and the dog, Molly, and most times, there's just me.

A screech rends the air into parts. I look up. The fat, black raven, wings outstretched, is silhouetted against a thin wedge of grey sky. A raucous caw and the dark bird swoops down, inches from us, and snatches the digit deftly. It lifts off over the woods, its shadow coursing the ground. The white thing dangles from its beak, ring catching dull light in a momentary prism. Molly barks, trembles with excitement, but holds her ground. I leash her now, just in case. I don't want her bolting off into the underbrush after the bird.

"It's okay, girl." My heart thumps like a wild thing. I stare at the ground, kicking away twigs and leaves. No trace remains, human or otherwise.

"I think I'm going crazy," I whisper. Moll pricks her ears to alert. "Never mind me," I tell her. "C'mon." I wonder if brain tumors can create this kind of preliminary symptom, the imagining of garish things, although I haven't experienced headaches. Sighing, I lead Molly into the woods. We follow a dirt path, its lighting gloomy. I know that it will lead into the heart of the woods where the deer gather as snow falls, hidden between cedars. Older trees form a jagged canopy above shorter growth, scrub brush low and digging at the shoulders of my coat. Few people traverse this way because it's off the conventional paths. Moving into these denser trees always excites me. A sharp tang of pine and forest decay tinges my nostrils. The miasma is aromatic and somewhat reminiscent. I think of Christmas, then discard the thought because that's not where I've smelled this before. Before long, I dismiss the sighting of the finger as just another unpleasantness of my recent hallucinations.

Another ten feet in and we reach a small clearing where an aged tree dominates within its acquired circumference of ground. I see a nest at its base, nothing unusual; nests fall, caught by winds, forgotten and lonely. Only problem is that the nest has two ravens in it and they are foreign to it — large, shiny, and obsidian — pecking away at something, ripping strips of raw meat from some unfortunate creature, and swallowing the scraps. I see a flash of red fur.

I am put in mind of Gillian—
there was no Gillian
—gone now. And an image of twins sitting in highchairs, red-faced and shrieking, tiny spoons clutched in miniscule fists, pounding the trays as patient Gillian tried to get them to feed on the watery gruel. At times, these dispersing memories, as frail as cheese cloth, feel too close for comfort, like trying to recall scraps of a dream as wakefulness takes over. It is a sense of *déjà-vu*, of having known these mystery people some-how, intimately. Sometimes, on certain nights when wind drifts through pines, I think I hear these twins. It sounds like ravens crying— *crawww crawwww*.

These two birds look at me, quizzical, then return their attention to their meal. I take a step toward the nest, to try and get a better look at what they have in there, wondering if one of them is the one just departed with the finger. They are unperturbed by my or Molly's presence. Closer, I stoop and peer into the nest. It is a large vestige of shelter made of twisted branch, mosses, and curled leaves. It sits in a Y-division of the oak where two, barnacled roots fan outwards. What I see makes me reel back, my free hand coming up to my mouth. My other hand releases Molly's leash.

"Oh," I gasp, and lean forward to lose my breakfast.

They feed on the limp body of a red squirrel, but that isn't what slaps my concentration to full attention. The birds stand on the remains of a human hand, one with four digits, minus the index finger. It looks like a broken, alabaster rake; two of its fingernails contain fragments of red polish. I know who the finger belongs to, even if I cannot place a face or a name to it. The missing finger isn't there, suggesting that a group of these birds have digested some the hand bones and perhaps other parts of a person.

"Where the hell did you get that?" The birds regard me, then take flight. Inside the nest, along with the hand I find a selection of objects. Ravens collect anything attractive, don't they? A piece of weathered fabric that may have once been crimson, but that had turned a sordid brown in the passing of seasons; a dog tag with the code 2134A pounded into the center of its surface, and below that 'Municipality of Russell'.

Unable to help myself, especially now with both avian thieves watching me from distant branches, I reach in and grasp the tag. As it rolls back, I note something shiny pushed into a coil of branches, something reed-like. I grasp it and force it out of the nest-weave. It is a child's feeding spoon, the kind you used to get for free in the mail from the infant formula companies whenever you purchased some of their products.

An infant, red-faced, screeching, tiny fist clenched around the handle, bangs the spoon on the tray of the highchair.

"She does not exist! They do not!" I scream, making the birds lift, sending a spray of rusted needles and remaining leaves down onto Molly and me. Molly casts herself back onto her haunches and howls.

2134A. Municipality of Russell.

I live in Russell. I was born here, grew up here, went to high school and graduated here. I dated here; got my heart broken in this town, found a job, saved a down payment for a house from the bank account I keep only blocks from where I stand. I got married and divorced in this town, had kids (*no you didn't*) in Russell. I've always walked in these woods. I know every street, back alley, riverbank, stream, gulley, and path in and around the town. I've owned Molly for four years. I am a lonely man, solitary, almost hermetic.

"Come here, Molly." I received her dog tag in the mail from the municipal office just last week. I pay for it out of my annual property taxes. I'd lost her other one last year while walking her in these woods. It had been winter and I'd had her pulling a toboggan behind her. I'd gone out to find a Christmas tree. The day had been bitter with ice pellets, and they hadn't wanted to go... the memory evades me again as soon as I try to hone in on it.

Molly obeys and trots over to stand beside me. This year's tag, metallic blue instead of green reads 2134A. It is a dog owner registration number issued with the first arrival of a pet.

"Your tag is in a raven's nest," I tell Molly. "Why?"

I return my attention to the spoon. It makes me think of a trowel, and once again a memory tries to form, then blots out. I use both of my hands to tear the nest apart, ripping the branches from stem to stem and hurling it from me. The birds watch, impassive. Molly whines.

"What is your problem?" I snap at her. "What's bothering you?" My head pounds with a persistent ache.

Molly inches forward to sniff at the ruined nest, and then proceeds to paw at the ground near the tree's base. She ignores the squirrel carrion for something more pressing. The base of this tree is thick-rooted and lichen-coated. Chunks of soft ground roam between its divides. I don't want to see what Molly's after; I feel the same trepidation about her interest in this tree as I feel about visiting the doctor and asking him about why I find myself outdoors at night, walking half naked through the fields, or why I awake in my bed, drenched in sweat and reaching through the dark for something that's never there.

"Molly!" I scream. She stops digging and cowers in my temper. My temper feels like molten lead, concentrating in the center of my skull and creating another pang of familiar headache. The headache always occurs in the same place; left hemisphere, frontal lobe. Something dark, hymnal, threatening, inches closer to my heart; it wants to tap against me like a finger, insistent on staying. My arms ache. My hands bunch into tight fists. I wonder about the condition of that organ in my chest? I lie in bed at night, also wondering if disease or death can creep up on you, hiding most symptoms until it knows it has you —then displays its symptoms across an x-ray screen, or blood test printout like wares tossed across a carnival table.

"Don't dig." I haul Molly back to me. She strains at the leash, whining, her tail wagging, but her eyes sad.

"Let's go." I force her away, wanting to get home. The walk has been ruined by this sensation of 'something' about to give. Let the ravens have the hand. It's not my business to extract the bones and carry them back to town; take them to the local police and say 'Here, look at what I found during my walk today'. There'd be too many questions.

As we hurry back through the woods, my headache increases and my heart pounds. It feels like a bone fragment with a yellowed fingernail in my mind, pushing hard against the soft meat of my brain, prying, digging, going for something deep inside my head. I sense it's close and I don't want to know. I don't. As we reach the lip of the forest and head into the field, a dark bird flies overhead again. It cries, and as it does, it releases something that whistles toward me. The finger bone, ring still attached, slams into my temple, tearing a scratch across my skin before the bone descends into the ground like a flagpole.

"Shit!" I scream, and kick at the bone. It breaks into segments that land in the damp grass. I stomp on them, pushing them deep into soil again, dancing, mad, heels of boots pounding, pounding, pounding. The proximal phalange cracks under my foot and the ring flattens. Molly shrieks and darts from me. In the distance, other dogs join in, their howls echoing through the frozen air like the cries of startled toddlers. I force Molly home. She keeps trying to turn back to the field again, tail between her legs, her eyes dark orbs that probe mine as we hurry.

※ · ※

Memories are not tangible things, but they represent actual moments in time and real people or places. When I arrive home with Molly, I throw the door shut and lock it. I examine my temple in the mirror. The scratch is two inches long and jagged, ending near the top of my left cheek. I rinse it with hydrogen peroxide, squeezing my eyes shut as fresh pain moves through the cut. Some of the pain deflects into my mind, settling into the annoying left hemisphere where the headache has increased, and down my left arm, into my heart. I feel my pulse hiccup, creating a drum beat that make the veins in my neck bulge. Molly sits near the front door, head on paws and longing for the other side of the frame.

"You're not going back there," I tell her. I know she'll return to the bones and try to bring them here. Molly gives a low growl, then trots away from the front door and lies down beside the couch, curling into a foetal position on her dog bed.

"Good, girl," I say, and go into the kitchen to make a cup of green tea. My hands shake as I pour the water into the mug. Even its heat can't warm me up. I bump the temperature gauge in the thermostat up another two degrees. Usually the walks help clear my head. But the headaches appear to be getting worse, not better. I've had them for about four years now. The same amount of time I've had Molly. Four years. That's when Gillian
   who?
left me after bringing the children to her parents first. She'd come back one more time to gather her things and deposit a lawyer's letter on the kitchen table, just a hint over four years ago. Lonely men and their dogs. Man's best friend, indeed.

Recently, I went to the doctor to see about the headaches. He blamed it on stress. That was his diagnosis. Asked how long I'd had the headaches, and if I could figure out the stressor or trigger. I chuckled. As if I knew what caused the headaches. I told the good doctor that I didn't know. Couldn't remember a thing.
   Gillian.
   Who?
I take the tea back into the living room, curl on the couch, and wrap my hands around the porcelain mug for comfort. I sip the tea, glance up at the mahogany mantle piece on the far wall. Knick-knacks, figurines and framed photos sit atop it. I stare at the photos. My headache begins again, screwdriver-like, right into the temple. In the largest photo a young woman, a beautiful brunette, smiles back at me. She is standing on a dirt trail in a sun-streaked clearing, surrounded by strands of ghost-white birch trees. Her eyes are bright and alive. Beside this picture is another, slightly smaller. Two young children, a boy and a girl, sit cross-legged on a beige carpet, a swatch of wooden sticks — the kind used for ice cream treats — piled between them. The children are constructing something from the sticks. They have stopped their play and looked up at the camera sullenly, as if the photographer has interrupted them. Both children are pale with obsidian hair and dark, glittering eyes like angry gemstones. The children put me in mind of the

ravens. It seems they are building a nest with those wooden sticks. But the photos are not mine. They came with the purchased frame, and I liked them enough to keep them. I was going to frame pictures of Molly and me, but this way I can have a family without all the work.

My head vibrates, spins like a blender, stabs. I bend over, grab my temples in my hands until the moment passes. Molly raises her head, gives a low growl. I sip my tea, ignoring her. I place the mug down, close my eyes to rest, and wake to a dark room. I shake my head. Molly sits attentively in front of me, her eyes locked on mine.

I stand, go to the back door. Molly follows. I open the door and Molly scoots out to do her business in the gathering gloom. I close the door. Molly will be fine in the fenced yard for a short while. I stare out at the darkening yard, watch Molly sprint to the far corner. She likes to dig in the same spot, creating a deeper and deeper crevice in the soil. In fact, Molly has dug two shallow ruts in the yard. A pair of distinct depressions. Two dark hollows in the cold earth.

The room spins. I lean against the refrigerator to steady myself. I turn, open the freezer door and dig around behind the frozen cuts of beef and pork until I find the package wrapped tightly with plastic grocery bags. I take the package, walk to the front door, slip on my long coat with the deep pockets, place the package in a pocket, grab my keys and exit the house.

It's misty outside. Water droplets catch in the glare of sodium vapor streetlights. I skirt the streetlights and keep to the shadows, head toward the park and, beyond that, the woods, leaving Molly behind. I hear her howl at this injustice and I walk faster. At the edge of the woods, along the moonlit path, I fish the frozen package from my pocket.

I unwrap the tightly wound plastic and pull the hand from the bag. I hold it gently. A lover's touch. A brief memory floods me again, clearer this time and, even more briefly, the scant feel of old love. I walk through the woods, holding hands with this secret delicacy, and it was almost like all those years ago, with Gillian, her fingers clasped in mine. I can take these walks whenever I want, however I want. I don't see the ravens coming until they're upon me, as the night is dark, foggy, cold. I feel the beak of one sink deep into my left temple, penetrating the flesh, cracking the skull. My knees buckle. The other raven drops remnants of the broken nest at my feet as my knees hit the ground and the night fades out around me. Those sticks, so much like the ones in the photograph. I hit the ground, (yet somehow hear Molly howl from the distance), and lie flat, feeling the frozen hand still clasping mine. Blood oozes from the brain injury, deep enough to stun me and leave me lying in the dangerously cooling night, out here in the edge of the woods.

"Gillian," I whisper and I think I feel the frozen hand squeeze my fingers a little. Gillian...

Who?

✦ · ✦

ANNABEL LEE

by Nancy Holder

Nancy Holder says: "I love Edgar Allan Poe with a love that is more than love, and as soon as I heard about *nEvermore!*, I asked to write a story based on my darling's very last poem. My living darling, Mark, suggested I use Annabel Lee's point of view. Perfect! And never done, as far as we could tell. Here is my result. Note: snippets of other poems by EAP are sprinkled throughout my story."

+ · +

I was a child and he was a child,
In this kingdom by the sea,
But we loved with a love that was more than love—
  —Quoth I, Annabel Lee

OUR KINGDOM WAS LUMINOUS once, and fruitful. Time and tide have worn us down; on the cliff, my family seat leans over the precipice as if pondering that final leap. Weary decay is our architecture, our battlements and parapets weep tears of moss and slime. All die quickly, too young. Thus he and I had freedoms that children in other realms do not; my nurse had many charges to look after, at least at first— my three older brothers. Two were taken by the Red Death and the youngest was so disfigured that he ended his own life. The sea was his crypt, although his name was carved into the stones of our tomb.

As mine has been.

In the kingdom, there are so few children— even fewer unblemished. My family's blood runs true: we are tall and slim, dark and pale. But in his youth he was stocky and apple-cheeked;

his hair shone like a halo. I would tell myself years later that this was evidence of foreign blood — counted a rare and valuable thing — but among the squat cottages and shops, such fair looks were not unusual. They have been described at court as *common as the common folk who bear them*. They were new to me as I, of course, had never ventured among such people, and so he utterly mesmerized me when we met upon the quay. He was gathering seaweed for his mam; I was musing, daydreaming, as lonely only-children often do.

We were barely toddlers and perhaps the waters did rush too close, too strong that first time when he grabbed both my arms and dragged me back, and he kissed me. Lips to cheek; his green eyes were like the sea glass washed upon the beach. I had never been kissed by anyone but my nurse, and she would have suffered a long and painful death had it been known. Plagues and wasting diseases stole from us common kindnesses and expressions of affection, and perhaps that is why love beguiled me so.

A chance encounter became a series of rendezvous, though one might term them *assignations*. Of a moonlit night, hidden, we strolled the beaches, my long velvet skirts trailing over bleached bones and driftwood. In the kingdom, the custom of the poor is to consign those children who did not, or could not, or would not live long to the churning tides. The ground is poisoned enough. Neighboring lands have protested our sea burials, fearing that we will distort those patterns of life in the same way in which somehow, we have distorted our own.

My nurse learned our secret, of course. With my brothers dead, her attentions centered on me, the only surviving child of the noblest family in the kingdom (with truer blood even than of those who wear the crown, even to this day.) As I confessed the many hours we had spent in each other's company, her emotions shifted across her gaunt features like shards in a kaleidoscope— joy for me, then terror, perhaps envy, and a stern reminder that someday, I must put aside selfish indulgence and do what was best for my family, and for the kingdom. We cannot marry within; our stock is too depleted. Grafting dying vine to dying vine yields nothing, not even the sourest of pomegranates. She opened the cameo locket that bore raven-black strands of my mother's hair.

"She died in her childbed. Make it a good death," she exhorted me.

But we were young then, so young. We had no thought of dynasties, and believed our love so ethereal that we would forever eschew the physical. We rarely touched in those early days. The brush of fingers, delicate as angels' wings, caused such sensations that we would both have to sit down. An oblong, smooth rock served as our divan and we would breathe in the ocean air, he settling my long, jet shawl around my shoulders, I drawing his ivory lap robe over our limbs. He would gather seashells in the green velvet basket wherein I provisioned us from my family's larder: smoked fish from our nets and bread from afar; absinthe and amontillado from a cloaked man Uncle Otranto visited every fortnight.

I have many kinsmen. My father is Rodrigo; my uncles are Udolfo, Otranto, and Polidoro; my oldest cousin is Prospero. They melt into shadows; they trail along the cobbles in whispering boots, stilettos flashing silent in the crimson slashes of their capes. My family has been feared and envied for generations, and of course our favor is more precious than unblemished apples, or pears, or grapes. Though our fortune has dwindled, our influence has not. There are many who would bend a knee or pen a poem, feigning soft feelings in a heart that is brimming over with malice and avarice.

We are courted.

I was courted. For while our kingdom is cursed, it is also enchanted, and our seashells do not echo the sea.

They whisper to us.

"He loves thee," murmured the shells he held up to my ear. *"Thou art the most beautiful maiden he has ever beheld. His heart is thine. His life is thine."*

"She loves thee," declared the ones I put against his. Or he told me that they said. He recited to me the lovely pronouncements and promises that issued from *my* shells.

We were enthralled. How could we not be? We had no one but each other. Our besotted gazes spoke of hunger for union, for the flesh... and I trembled with fear but with joy as well. By then I knew of the ways of man and maid. We had never gone beyond chaste kisses, but as we grew up, I sensed a sea change within him. Within *us*.

My nurse attempted to speak of these things with me, but I did not allow it. Though she has sworn a hundred million times that she did not go to my father, soon he and my uncles began to discuss suitors for me. They fought, and I overheard

my Uncle Otranto railing that our title should not be purchased,
no matter how mortifying our circumstances, no, not even if we
came to ruin. We are a proud race, a gently bred family, and if
we must die out, then we would do so with our honor intact.

I revealed all of this to my love, and his desperation was terrible to see. He became my shadow, my daemon, my Ruthven;
if I walked with my nurse along the cliff, he hovered behind; if
I chanced out of the castle to view the daily catch from the sea,
he materialized out of the fog. At night, upon my balcony, he
appeared, when no one could possibly climb the wet, oozing
wall of my tower, a hundred feet high in the clouds. He swore
that a sympathetic servant had let him in, which struck terror
into my heart: if my kinsmen should discover him, it would
be that slow death for which we are infamous.

He haunted me like a phantom, a ghost, a spectre, and I
began to wonder if he could work magic. If perhaps he had
enchanted me with a love spell.

Lute songs and flute melodies sang to me on the wind; a
poem appeared beneath my pillow, surrounded by crushed
rose petals. Titled *A Bridal Ballad*, it told the story of a woman
who had forsaken her true love for another, and caused his
untimely death.

Then came another:

> *My love, she sleeps! Oh, may her sleep,*
> *As it is lasting, so be deep!*
> *Soft may the worms about her creep!*
> *Far in the forest, dim and old,*
> *For her may some tall vault unfold—*
> *Some vault that oft hath flung its black*
> *And winged panels fluttering back,*
> *Triumphant, o'er the crested palls*
> *Of her grand family funerals—*

That one frightened me, and when I met him at our rendezvous point on the beach, I told him so. He embraced me and
begged forgiveness, then pleaded with me to place into my
pockets all the whispering seashells he had gathered for me.
This he would do as well; then we would rush into the sea
together, weighted down by words of true love, and so die,
breathless, in one another's arms. I took his ferocity for inflamed

heartache, and matched it with my own. We kissed as never we had before, and held each other. Our emotions became a rising tide, and I confess it now: the sword of Desire dangled above my virtue, held there only by strands of hair— those of my dear mother, vouchsafed in my locket; she would surely wail her despair in heaven if I succumbed!

"Be satisfied tonight that I give you my vow," I begged him. "I pledge myself to you, truly."

Like a madman, he half-carried, half-dragged me to our oblong rock-divan, and threw me back upon it. I was stunned, and breathless. He reached for the embroidered bodice of my gown. I screamed into his ear but it did nothing to stop him.

He would have despoiled me had the waters not dredged up a poor changeling child, thrown into the sea but not yet drowned, mewling and keening for its life. It was left beside our rock divan— a horror, unfinished, and certain to die, but I scrambled from beneath him and gathered the child up against my breast. I began to run and stumble through the sand; I fled into a long shadow for refuge. He hung back, cringing, and I took advantage and climbed the hilly path, the tiny monstrum in my arms.

The shadow was my nurse, with a heavy cloak for me at the top of the cliff, and her face mirrored the tumult in my soul; but as I pressed the babe upon her, she refused to touch it. Then she began to grab for it and I sensed she would hurl it into the sea. I held it tightly, though even now I have no idea what possessed me: I am an aristocrat, and pity is not in my nature. Still, I began to weep and shriek, and my nurse bade me silent lest my father and uncles hear me. I had been sorely compromised, and she did not want my disheveled appearance nor mad devotion to the doomed babe to add weight to a brewing *scandale* attached to my name.

Lightning struck and rain assaulted us as she conveyed me to my rooms. The babe was hidden in my cloak, and the watch did not challenge us. I was Rodrigo's daughter, and the *chatelaine* of his estate.

Upon entrance into my sleeping chamber, I started in horror: what appeared to be a black casket sized for an infant lay upon the lace and satin of my bedclothes. She hurried to it and opened it. It was not a coffin, or if it was, it had been refurbished for another purpose: it was filled with papers and as she laid them out upon my bed like a dozen tiny corpses, she told me that with the aid of the nameless cloaked man, my uncle Otranto and my cousin Prospero had stolen the casket from his family's cottage. It belonged to him. These papers were his poems and drafts of several letters, one of them to me, a copy of which I had never received.

"Read them," she told me, but I shook my head. On instinct, I dreaded the sight of them. I clung to the child, who was shuddering, and its lids flickered shut.

"Read them," she said again.

The babe panted. Its chest fluttered.

"Care for this little one and I will," I replied.

Disgust clouded her features. "That is not a *little one*. That is nothing."

I remained silent, though by that time, I, too, was shuddering. With obvious revulsion, she took the half-dead child from me and muttered, "It wants milk."

There is very little milk in our kingdom, but I had some in my private larder. As she picked up the pitcher, I crossed to the pile of parchment.

"From the one on top to the one on the bottom," she instructed me. "They are in order, oldest to newest."

First there were poems in a childish hand, so very pretty and sweet from our childhood; and then the passion of early youth:

For her this rhyme is penned, whose luminous eyes,
brightly expressive as the twins of Leda

But over time the verses curdled:

And all I loved, I loved alone.

Then, in the drafts of the letter to me, the horrible, torturous truth came out: he was the instrument of a terrible plot hatched by his family: they sought to ruin me so that I must either be married off to him or my family blackmailed for money. Fool, fools, had they no idea that we lived on less than tradesmen? That our only hope was a wealthy match, and that it must be with someone who lived beyond our borders? It is true that due to our status we could arrange a dispensation to marry within, but did he believe that our sovereign would allow the sullying of the aristocracy with a commoner such as he? Even our blood, which flows in the veins of His Majesty's bitterest rivals, must be kept pure. It is the only hope for the kingdom.

I must, and I shall do it, he had written to me in one of his many drafts. *But after I shall make you happy, such that you shall forgive me. I swear I shall.*

None of that had ever reached my eyes until that night.

I wept for hours into the bitter wine that my nurse brought to soothe me; all warmth left my body and I shook with cold despite fresh woolens and heavy furs all around me. My head pounded and my teeth ached. My nurse's arms came around me and she murmured into my ear, "I tried to warn you, poppet. My dark, dear fairy girl, all is as I have feared these long years. I am so sorry."

Then she said, "The... *babe*... has died. I shall get rid of it."

So my misplaced pity had forced it to linger, rather than sink into the waters and be done with it. When she left the room, I crawled to my collection of seashells and placed the first one to my ear:

He loves thee.

"He loves me not," I whispered back.

A second one: *His heart is thine.*

"He loves me not."

And a third: *His life is thine.*

I was undone, utterly, and could not stop weeping until my tears froze on my cheeks, or so it seemed; when my kinsmen came into my room, they threw all the shells on the floor and crushed them beneath their boot heels. My floor became as the beach, sandy and cluttered. They pulled out stilettos, daggers.

I could not fight them.

I could not fight them.

✦ · ✦

The bells. The bells, bells, bells,
All the bells of the kingdom,
sobbing, toiling, grieving.
For me.

I was borne on my bier to our tomb amid salt and sand and ocean swells; weeping willows hung down in dismay. Bells that tinkled on the harnesses of the horses; bells in the churches and chapels, announcing my death. His Majesty ordered deep mourning, but the cloaked man informed my kinsman that the king was holding a ball behind the gates of the palace. His jesters wore caps and bells. It was a cause for his rejoicing: Our direct line was dead. My cousin was the last hope for continuing our house, and he was caught in the grip of a wasting disease.

✦ · ✦

Now the bells are silent.

The pavanes have all been danced, the mourners have dried their tears.

I am waiting.

Moons have waxed and waned.

And I wait.

If he does not come, then it was all true.

It was his handwriting; I know it. But the shells whisper true, or so we have always heard. His life came from our kingdom, both poisonous and sustaining; was the same to be said of his love?

Poisonous and sustaining?

Reading his words, I felt I should die.

Lying in frozen estate day after day after day, I feel I will die, thus entombed.

For I wait in my sepulcher. My name has been carved, and I am as cold as the grave. My flesh is marble and ice.

He wrote:

My love, she sleeps! Oh, may her sleep,
As it is lasting, so be deep!

Did he wish me dead? That I would die so that he would not dishonor me? Is that why he begged me to fill my pockets with shells, then pushed me back to land... pushed me onto my back and grabbed the bodice of my gown...

If he does not come...

The bells...

"No bells are tolling," my nurse tells me.

"It is the baby crying," I reply.

But it is she who is crying.

✦ · ✦

I see the moonlight on the wall.

And then the shadow.

My heart quickens in the utter darkness of the sepulcher and I hear the boots on the marble floor: My father, Uncle Otranto, Uncle Udolfo, Uncle Polidoro. Cousin Prospero. Moonlight finds them through the grated window: their daggers and stilettos are drawn.

His life is thine, the seashell told me.

"He is coming," my nurse says. "At last."

Her voice is raised in excitement, but she has aged terribly during the months I have been hidden from view. The long hours I have been 'dead.'

Of course the casket was returned to his home that very night, before he could notice that it was missing. My kinsmen had been alerted by my nurse that he was with me, on the beach, and ran to the village to steal it. They saw nothing of my dishonor, she had promised me. But my father can scarcely look at me and my cousin can scarcely *stop* looking. His eyes take liberties; he treats me like a fallen woman. A whore.

I do not know how they got the casket back into his home; that night, I had looked at the papers for an eternity of hours— the full lifetime of the misbegotten creature I held to my breast. But they assured me that they did replace them, and he remained ignorant of the theft. They have lain in wait to kill him and all his kinsmen with impunity. They will wipe his name from the face of the earth.

If I opened my mouth and called to him, I could save him. That he is coming means that he is grieving.

That he loved me.

My Cousin Prospero leans over me. I am resting on my bier, a gauze sheet covering me like a bridal veil. I am pretending to be dead. In case he has a spy, my death can be confirmed.

When I was with him, I had never felt so alive.

I see the flash of steel and I wonder at the length of the rest of my life. My cousin lifts the sheet and the window glow frames his eyes. There are wrinkles at the corners. He is smiling.

"Slow or quick?" he asks me. "We accord you that right."

In my mind's eye I view the sea, and his green-glass eyes, his halo of hair. I see us together, he in his worsteds and woolens, I in velvet and gold braid. The shells do not lie; they cannot.

I never received the letter from him. And I wonder now how my kinsmen knew of the casket, and accomplished its return without arousing suspicion. If their cloaked man had penned forgeries in his hand. If all of this had been a mummer's pageant to force us apart.

"Cousin?" he murmurs. "Slow or quick?"

We loved with a love that was more than love —

I lie here because of that. Because of a love that transcends our dying kingdom. They have promised me that once justice is done, a wealthy merchant across the water awaits my hand. He has seen my miniature, and has been told only that my death has been feigned to release me from a lesser match in favor of his. He cares not. He has promised that the family seat will be restored. It is a brilliant match for us.

I think of the misshapen babe who washed up into my arms. Who saved my honor when the man I believed loved me would have taken it.

"Someone comes to the door of our tomb. It is he," my father whispers in the darkness. He grunts. "His arms are laden with roses. How could a beggar like him acquire roses? He is kneeling. His head is bowed. It is a perfect time to strike."

He does love me. He loves me still.

"Cousin?" My cousin prompts. He is holding a seashell to his ear.

"What does it tell you?" I whisper to him.

He snorts in derision. "That his heart is thine."

And I am of this place, this kingdom by the sea. My family's roots are steeped in poison, and I am free of pity.

If his heart is mine, then I will not break it.

I close my eyes to freeze the tears.

"Make it quick," I command.

That way, he will not know.

♦ · ♦

DINNER WITH MAMALOU

by J. Madison Davis

J. Madison Davis says: "The stories of Poe are lush, humid bayous where secrets are obscured by the tendrils of his language, and fatality lurks behind every leaf. The proud flowering of living things is exposed as vanity. They fall, rot, and perfume the air with decay. His stories are the revelation of this truth to the unaware. His characters are forced to face death and recognize its absolute power."

+ · +

THE FETID WATER STRETCHED to the horizon, thick as crude oil, moving only when a water moccasin slithered off an island to hunt for food. Many of the islands were little more than hummocks of root and moss, gathered at the base of a cypress or two, barely keeping the trees from yielding to the weight of their tortured trunks and the drapery of Spanish moss hanging like wet and rotting sweaters from the branches. Occasionally, a shack appeared beyond a crude bridge or in the distance on a mud island.

Who would want to live in such a place? Wilson asked himself. They were crunching down a road that doubled as a levee, raised sometime in the 1930s, paved with what looked like crushed oyster shells. The humidity penetrated the long black limo, oozing through the air conditioning system, filling the rear compartment with a syrupy perfume of rotting vegetation. Wilson thought he saw movement. Was that vague shape a log or an alligator?

Garrett, the CEO of Makadam Energy, abruptly interrupted Wilson's gazing out the window by wagging a finger in his face. "Just so we understand each other: if you ever put me in a situation like this, you'll end up living with whatsizname in a cardboard box!"

"Yes, sir," said Wilson. He glanced at Selwyn Fernbach, the corporation counsel, in the seat beside him. No question: Wilson understood. When millions are on the line, you don't get a second chance.

'Whatsizname,' Wilson's former boss, had backed Garrett into a corner. Garrett preferred to look down from his throne rather than out from a corner.

"This is a lemon situation," ventured Wilson, "but I'm sure you'll make lemonade out of it."

Garrett raised one eyebrow and lowered his bulldog head to scrutinize his new public relations chief. *Another unmitigated idiot*, his expression said. The thick finger jabbed again. "I pay you jackasses to scoop up after the dog. *I* do not clean up after the dog."

"If Mrs. Bertrand favors our offer we may not even have to go to court." said Fernbach. "Building a community center and a school will be a lot cheaper than settling."

"Hoops for the hicks," said Garrett. "It isn't our fault. Poor kids get sick. I don't see why we have to pay anything."

"I tell you," said Fernbach, "Atchison, Beaujour, and Mayhew will venue-shop the suit and find a backwoods jury that will set us back millions. We can beat this eventually, but—."

"But it will take years," said Garrett. "And bazillions of billable hours and years of bad publicity that will interfere with the drilling leases and crucify our share price."

Fernbach picked at imaginary lint on his pant leg. "We have prepared talking points."

Garrett rolled his eyes.

Nudged by Fernbach, Wilson put on his reading glasses and opened a folder. "Louisa May Bertrand is at least in her 70s, probably 80s, maybe 90s. They were careless registering births back then. The local joke is that she's as old as the bayou. She married a few times and had at least seven children, four of which died over the years. Her first husband that we know of was killed in Korea. Her third died in 2000 of diabetes complications, septicemia."

"Diabetes!" said Garrett. "The food, no doubt."

"She is known as 'Mamalou' throughout the area and has attended every service in the St. Germain parish, including weddings and funerals, for at least thirty years, some say fifty. She brings food, of course."

"It's got 'healing power, supping together,'" sneered Fernbach. "That's what she said. The media just loves her."

Garrett looked at Wilson. "And they hate us. Maybe I should have hired *her*."

"She is like an unofficial grandmother for the swamp community. No one wins a vote in this parish without her endorsement," said Wilson.

Fernbach snorted. "The governor washes her feet so the senators can kiss them and the congressman lick them."

"What's your name?" asked Garrett. "Never mind. The former Whatsizname should have taken care of this, that's the point. Instead, in my name, he agrees to a homey supper between me and Mama Voodoo— at *her* house. So I have to go hat in hand—."

"Mr. Garrett," said Wilson sincerely, "you are the kind of man who can turn this publicity on its head. This Mamalou may be known for her *étouffée*, but you are the master of the deal."

"Win the witch over," said Fernbach, "and our exposure will be limited. The shares will sail."

"I got it, Selwyn." He ground his teeth and sat back in his seat. "Just look at this godforsaken hunk of cottonmouth paradise! You'd think they'd be happy to sell us the whole place for a dollar and move to the projects."

"It's not like we don't pay them royalties," said Wilson.

The crushed seashell road had now deteriorated into no more than a wagon track of packed earth. Leaves brushed the windows and slapped the sun roof, as if the vegetation were closing in, ready to snap shut like a Venus fly trap.

Wilson broke into a cold sweat. The air was thickening. It was becoming difficult to breathe. He closed his eyes to control his panic, but he could hear the *shishing* of the leaves against his window and squirmed at the tightening in his chest. Abruptly, however, the noise ended. He opened his eyes to see Garrett scowling at him.

The berm had widened out and the road was dry enough to raise a plume of dust behind them. They were coming on to an island. The road swept left, and they soon passed two news vans parked at a broad clearing's entrance. Across the circular space was the St. Germain parish church, a low white building with a galvanized roof and a red plywood cross decorated with blinking Christmas lights.

If these people have electricity, thought Wilson, *maybe they have air conditioning.*

A row of women stood on the wraparound porch wearing ornate hats festooned with long, bright feathers, carnelian brooches, and multicolored ribbons. "I think we're underdressed," said Fernbach.

"Shut up," said Garrett. "We love *everything*. Got that?"

Beside and behind the women were skinny men in black suits, several with white hair, and, on the far ends of the porch, girls in pink and yellow dresses and boys in suits that mirrored their fathers'. An elderly black priest wore the blood-colored robes of Pentecost and limped down the stairs toward the car, smiling a broad mouthful of the brightest white.

Mamalou had to be the woman whose side he had left. A wizened woman, barely taller than some of the boys on the porch, she wore a turban of the same satiny peach material as her choir robe and held a white Bible in her left hand and a twisted cane in her right. Across her bosom hung a silver chain holding six large black crosses, one for each of the cancer victims.

"Show time!" said Garrett, assuming a smile he wore only in public.

Without waiting for the chauffeur, he popped open the door and thrust his hand toward the priest. "Father Robert! So glad to meet you. I've heard nothing but good about you!"

The father opened his mouth, but before he had 'thank' out, Garrett had pumped his hand and charged toward the church, leaving Wilson and Fernbach to exchange pleasantries with the minister.

Garrett brushed aside a local news cameraman who didn't back up fast enough. "And you must be Mrs. Bertrand! Gosh, what a pleasure it is to meet you! I'm so glad we have the opportunity to meet in person!"

"And I am so glad to see you, Mr. Eugene Garrett!" she said. She lifted her hem and clattered down the wooden stair, reaching the bottom before Garrett got there, spreading her arms wide.

Garrett, who had extended his hand while glancing back to see that the camera caught this, turned and was startled by her sweeping his hand wide with her Bible and flinging her twig-like arms around his midsection.

"You call me Mamalou. Everybody calls me Mamalou."

Mamalou crushed her head against his chest, as if trying to listen to his heart. Garrett's eyes widened, but Mamalou held him tight.

"Oh, Lord," she said to the sky, "this is a good day you have made!"

Amen!'s and Hallelujah!'s resonated from the porch.

Garrett pulled away and straightened his suit. "Glad to meet you, Mamalou," he managed to sputter as she moved on to clasp Wilson, then Fernbach, in similar bear hugs.

Garrett recomposed himself and spoke over her head toward the cameras and the people on the porch. "We're here to listen, Mamalou, and straighten things up. Makadam Energy has nothing to hide. Misinformation and misunderstanding is what this controversy is about. We believe in communities. We believe in people."

"All things rest in the Lord," said Mamalou. "That's what I believe."

Garrett hesitated then said, "Amen, Mamalou. Amen. Now if I could just talk to you about some of the falsehoods that have accrued around the tragic—." He turned slightly towards the news camera.

"No, no, no," said Mamalou. "We're not going to talk on the television. I invited you for supper, and supper it is going to be."

"And we are totally looking forward to that! Your cooking is legendary. Legendary!"

People on the porch nodded. Some said "Yessir!" and "That's true."

"When people break bread together, as our Lord did, God is present," Mamalou said. "His righteousness and judgment abides."

Amens erupted from the porch.

Garrett nodded seriously. "You're as wise as your reputation, Mamalou."

"Follow me," she snapped.

She strode surprisingly fast toward the back of the church, her robe flying. Garrett scurried after her. Fernbach and Wilson looked at each and followed behind, stumbling on the uneven road surface. Despite the speed with which this ancient woman ambled down the lane, she suddenly erupted in a loud, full-throated hymn. *"Guide me, O Thou great Jehovah, pilgrim through this barren land. I am weak, but You are mighty. Hold me with your powerful hand."*

The vegetation on the side of the path sagged in the heat. Garrett, who had charged forward like a race walker, began to huff. Sweat burned in Wilson's eyes. Fernbach faded to the rear. They crossed a wooden bridge and entered dense undergrowth, but the shade gave no relief.

"Where the hell are we going?" muttered Wilson to himself.

"Bread of heaven, bread of heaven," she sang, *"feed me now and evermore."*

Garrett loosened his tie and dropped back alongside Wilson, panting. "We... love... every country-fried... *everything*," he whispered. Stoking up new energy from his furnace of perpetual anger, he marched forward with renewed determination toward the billowing Mamalou, who was now past a couple of verses.

Abruptly, Mamalou stopped, turned toward them, and belted out the last line. *"I will ever si-yi-ying to You!"*

Birds scattered from the treetops. She laughed, stretching out her arm toward a footpath opening to her right. "That hymn is just the right length! Down here's my home, gentlemen."

Garrett stopped and bent, resting his hands on his thighs. "What are you boys doing?" he panted. "Dawdling like that."

"Yes, sir," gasped Wilson.

At the end of the footpath was a building shaped much like the church, a curl of smoke rising from the chimney. The white paint looked fresh. Flowery curtains shifted restlessly against the window screens. A weary bloodhound in front of the screen door raised himself and sniffed the air before flopping back down to sleep.

"Welcome, gentlemen," said Mamalou. "I got crawfish *étouffée*, cornbread, and gator gumbo. Let me slip the cornbread in the oven." She stepped over the dog and into the house.

"Did she say 'gator'?" said Fernbach. Wilson shuddered.

Garrett gritted his teeth and muttered. "I don't care if it is alligator droppings. We're going to love it. *Love it!*"

By the time they warily stepped over the bloodhound and into the house, Mamalou had lost her robe and turban, revealing a simple yellow dress, and was tying on an apron with the same flowery design as the curtains. She adjusted the necklace with the six crosses. "You gentlemen look parched. Can I get you a drink?"

"A beer would be sensational," said Wilson.

Even the swamp birds stopped singing. "Don't you mean 'sinsational'?" said Mamalou sternly.

"Goodness," said Wilson. "I meant to say root beer. I don't drink alcohol myself."

"Not under this roof," said Mamalou. "Sweet tea is what I offer. Goes best with the food, you know. With a sprig of mint for special guests, and you gentlemen are special."

"Perfect!" said Garrett.

"I was just thinking of that good Southern sweet tea," said Fernbach.

She opened the refrigerator and took out a big sweaty pitcher with ice floating in it. She filled four big tumblers. Wilson hated sweet tea, especially this sweet, but it went down cold and that's all that mattered.

"The mint is a nice touch," said Garrett. "It's things like that make a cook into a chef."

She rubbed one of the black crosses between her thumb and forefinger. "Tommy Hébert used to pick mint for me. Poor boy. Died screaming for his mama, you know." She plucked out a sprig from a bowl on the counter and chewed it.

"A shame," said Garrett. "You just can't explain why the Lord takes an innocent child."

"Glioblastoma," said Fernbach.

"That isn't what I meant," snapped Garrett.

"Actually," said Mamalou, "I believe Tommy had a medulloblastoma. Ray Solomon and Cindy Hébert had glioblastomas." She didn't hesitate in pronouncing the words.

"What terrible luck," said Garrett. "These cancer clusters, as they are called, are totally without scientific explanation."

"When children die, you got to suspect evil," said Mamalou.

"Well, yes," said Garratt. "That's why we're here, of course. The suspicion. I didn't really want to get to this right away, but believe you me, sincerely Mamalou, if I thought in any way that my company had the slightest thing to do with even one child's death, well, I couldn't sleep at night. It's just too horrible to contemplate."

Garrett had tears in his eyes. Just like that. Wilson was impressed.

Mamalou sympathetically placed a hand on Garrett's shoulder. "Ungodly. But people hereabouts, they've heard about the fracking chemicals, and they noticed that it was just a year or so after that the children started getting sick. So they've been putting two and two together, you see."

"And they've come up with five," said Garrett patiently, "according to the best scientific and medical minds we could afford. What happens with hydraulic fracturing is way, way down in the earth. Even if the chemicals were dangerous, they couldn't get into your water. And they aren't dangerous, Mamalou. Those enviro-terrorists, they just hate us, see? They want us all turning vegan and living like it's the Middle Ages, so they say everything is dangerous. The science is on our side, Mamalou."

Fernbach leaned forward. "And we will prove it in court if this suit continues."

Garrett's eyes narrowed. *Shut up. This is my show.*

"Well," said Mamalou as she walked toward the oven, "Mr. Beaujour told us strictly not to sign anything or talk legal matters unless he is here." She dropped down the oven door. "Anyway, the cornbread is looking just right!"

"Why, it smells heavenly!" said Garrett, smacking his hands together.

All Wilson could smell was the rotting vegetation in the swamp, but he nodded with Fernbach, and they both made happy uh-huhs. "Can we help in any way?" asked Garrett.

"Now, gentlemen, you're my guests!" With a big metal spoon, she dipped a fist-sized wad of rice onto a plate and then smothered it with *étouffée*. She carefully put the plate in front of Fernbach and went for another.

"You know, though," she said, "they tell me you put acids in that fluid."

Garrett spread both hands. "There you go! It's the kind of thing they like to scare people with. We use acetic acid as a buffer. Do you know what that is, Mamalou?"

"Vinegar, isn't it?" she said.

Garrett blinked. "I see you've done your homework. Why it's no more dangerous—."

"But there's also hydrochloric acid or muriatic acid," she said. Wilson noticed, as with the cancers, she had no problem with the words. She placed a large plate of *étouffée* in front of Wilson, who used his fork to pick out a piece of crawdad shell.

"It's a low concentration," said Garrett. "It basically makes it easier to crush the rock down there and get that good natural gas. It dissolves harmlessly."

"And what about this stuff polyacrylamide? I believe it's sometimes called PAM?"

Garrett looked like he was dodging baseballs thrown at his head. "Oh, that. Yes, well, it reduces friction." Recovering a little, he added, "And it's totally harmless. It's like grease on the skillet there. It's way down in the earth. Way down."

As she continued to set out the food, Mamalou flipped chemical names off her tongue like names in a Grimm's fairy tale: tetramethyl ammonium chloride, zirconium oxide, methanol, ammonium bisulfate, gluteraldehyde, peroxydisulfates. For each one, Garrett said either it was harmless or that it was in small concentrations, and anyway it all stayed 'way down.'

When she finally placed the cornbread wrapped in a checkered cloth, Garret was saying, "And potassium hydroxide's used in hand soap, so you know it can't be that toxic." He tried to change the topic. "Oh my! This sure looks wonderful, Mamalou."

"Thank you. Oh, and how about ethylene glycol? Isn't that antifreeze?"

"You certainly know your chemistry, Mamalou," Garret said grimly. "I hadn't heard you'd gone to college."

"College?" she laughed. "People are my college. Reading's my college." She saw Wilson lift his fork.

"Ah ah!" said Mamalou. "Grace first! Oh, and one more, if I might. Why do you need ethylene glycol in Louisiana?"

"It's not for antifreeze. It's for iron control— keeps the flow going," said Garrett. "No more harm to you than if it's in your car. No harm at all."

"I am learning so much!" she said, shaking her head. Her leathery face crinkled in a smile. "And understand so little."

"You've impressed me," said Garrett, barely controlling his irritation. "Fernbach, you're the lawyer. Say grace."

Fernbach blinked, his eyes begging Garrett to let him off the hook. There was no mercy in Garrett's sneer.

"Uh, thou great Jehovah, uh, thank us for the blessings of this wonderful food prepared by Mrs. Bertrand, uh, you know, Mamalou. Uh, we know you guided her hand, so doubly thank you. Amen."

"And lead us to a righteous outcome," said Mamalou.

"Oh, amen. Amen!" said Wilson. "Those poor children."

"That we had nothing to do with," added Fernbach.

Garrett hefted a great gob of *étouffée* at the end of his fork and stuffed it into his mouth. He was smiling, chewing. Then the chewing stopped. He blinked. As on an old-fashioned thermometer, a line of red appeared at the bulge of his Adam's apple and rolled up his neck and cheeks and to his forehead which instantly sprouted beads of sweat. His nostrils flared, his eyes bulged, and his lips trembled as he tried to form words.

My God! thought Wilson, *she poisoned him!*

But she was taking a second mouthful herself, smiling and watching Garrett gather his strength to swallow. He grabbed for his iced tea and gulped half the glass.

"Whew," he said. "That's, ah, kind of hot."

"Oh," said Mamalou sympathetically. "It's those Creole spices. They too much?"

Garrett mopped his brow with his napkin and drank another mouthful. "Spicy! I like spicy. We all like spicy, don't we?"

Fernbach and Wilson looked at each other and then at the red rice on their forks.

"Well, go on. What are you—" Garrett coughed, "—waiting for?"

At first, as Wilson's mouth closed, the *étouffée* landed pasty, like ordinary rice, then suddenly it was as if the sun exploded. Everything went white. He gripped the edge of the chair, tried to speak, and couldn't. Fernbach squirmed as if he were trying to avoid leaping to his feet. The sweet tea momentarily cooled Wilson's mouth, but the cinder that was his tongue soon flared up again, and he swished more tea around his mouth.

"It's delicious!" Garrett shouted with determination.

Fernbach and Wilson nodded, grunted, and tried to smile.

"Praise the Lord! There's plenty of it," Mamalou said, and placidly continued to eat.

They switched to the gumbo with its rubbery chunks of alligator meat, but it only seemed less spicy because their tongues were numb. Garrett, his nose now running, signaled them to eat up when Mamalou went to the cupboard for *filé*.

They fell on the cornbread, hoping it might subdue some of the unremitting fire. Wilson held a salty chunk of it in his mouth for some time before swallowing, but his tongue still glowed like an ember. Garrett was as red faced as a man hiking Death Valley. Fernbach went more toward uneven pink and red splotches on his forehead and neck.

"Delicious, oh yeah," Garrett gasped determinedly. "My wife would love the recipe."

Wilson pictured Garrett's trophy wife trying to figure out a spatula. He almost laughed, but the pain in his throat made him cough instead.

"Now how am I going to give you my recipe when you won't give me your exact recipe?" said Mamalou. She downed another huge spoon of *étouffée*.

Garrett laughed. "Well, I don't expect you to be cooking up a batch of fracking fluid."

"Well," — she swallowed and mopped her mouth with a napkin — "it seems like if you want to convince me it had nothing to do with the sickness in those children, you wouldn't be afraid to tell me exactly what's in it."

"You ran down a long list of chemicals, Mamalou. I explained what is available in public knowledge, and how they are all safe. But I can't reveal the exact mixture, or my competitors might gain an advantage. Imagine if you were running a restaurant—."

"God, I feel dizzy," said Fernbach. "How much hot sauce was in there?"

"Maybe a little less than the usual for you gentlemen," said Mamalou. She scooped up a big spoon of the gumbo. "I can't say exactly, but I can guarantee it is safe."

Wilson blinked. Watching her eat seemed to reignite the fire in his throat and belly. All three of them suddenly looked at each other and then at her and then at their food.

"Safe?" said Garrett. "What do you mean by that?"

She looked at him and grinned. "I mean it is safe. Safe as every chemical in that frack juice. Nobody ever got cancer from pepper sauce. You like me to get you some more?"

"No," said Garrett, "I'm st-stuffed. Izh very filling."

Wilson squinted. Garrett seemed to have been drinking. In fact, he himself felt like three martinis on an empty stomach. Fernbach looked unsteady, too. His first thought was that she'd put pot in the food to make them look like idiots in front of the news cameras. Sure. That made sense. Didn't it? The gumbo *filé* maybe. There were tiny green bits in the *étouffée* that he'd assumed were thyme. They looked like thyme. Were they?

"We've got to go," said Garrett.

"But you haven't had dessert!" said Mamalou. "We got a molasses chess pie! My specialty. Little Beau Richard, bless his soul, it was the only thing the boy could eat after doing the chemotherapy. He suffered, that boy did, even more than the others."

"We've got to go," repeated Garrett. He gripped the edge of the table struggling to recover his strength by marshaling his legendary anger.

"Well, if you must," she said, pushing back her chair. "But I'm packing up some food to go. It's way too much for me."

"Don't go to any trouble," said Wilson. "I couldn't—."

"We appreciate it very much," said Garrett. "This has been one of the most pleasant meals I have ever experienced." His head wobbled slightly. "You certainly live up to your reputation, Mamalou."

"I do the best I can," she said.

Fernbach lurched to his feet holding his belly. "I—I need air," he said, and staggered to the door.

She glanced at him and quickly dipped quart-sized plastic containers with the gumbo and *étouffée*, one for each man, and wrapped separate packages of cornbread. She lowered all of it into a shopping sack with handles. "You watch that last step off the porch. Breaking bread always helps make things right, praise God, though it can't bring the children back."

Wilson fought down his nausea with every shred of will. He couldn't look at Garrett without feeling he would lose it.

Garrett, pale and unsteady, had sweated out his bravado. All he could manage was, "Good-bye, ma'am."

Mamalou shoved the bag of food into Wilson's hands, he nodded at her without speaking and staggered through the door after Fernbach, who was lurching along the bank. Wilson felt like he was walking through gelatin. The car— he had to get to the car. The path ahead of him was swinging from side to side like a rope bridge over a windy ravine.

Glancing behind him, he saw Fernbach bend over and slowly drop into the vegetation on the bank. Only his arm was visible from the elbow, flailing weakly. Wilson spun completely around to find Garrett. He could hear him retching and then moaning long and slow. For a moment, Wilson thought it was the old hound baying.

He blinked at the fetid water. He lost his grip on the bag of food and the containers rolled like dice on the dirt. The sun grew bigger, bigger, blinding him. Its heat and brightness consumed the earth and burned off his legs.

He was on his back, looking into the canopy of the trees. No, he thought. *No!* The light dimmed and a shadow fell across him. Mamalou stood over him, blocking the light. "The food!" he croaked. "You poisoned us."

Mamalou laughed. "Naw, naw. You saw me eating right with you, didn'tcha? I ain't messing up Mamalou's food with no poison. I got pride in my cooking, Lord forgive the pride."

"You did!" He strained to roll over and crawl away, but he couldn't do more than wiggle. He was a beetle impaled on a pin, a fly in a web. "Please," he begged. "Please. Don't feed me to the alligators. Please."

Mamalou cackled. "You got a nasty imagination, Mr. Wilson. You'd be too sweet for them. Ethylene glycol, I read that's got a real sweet taste. Y'all seemed to like it in that tea. I should have had some myself, since it's just one of those harmless chemicals you pumped into the ground. But, you know, I'm not altogether confident it would agree with a gator's digestion. I wouldn't do that to them. They ain't done nothing to deserve that, now have they? Nothing, not a gator, not a sixteen-foot cottonmouth, deserves to suffer. And they are Satan's spawn, they say. Not like God's innocent children."

When she walked away, the sun blinded him again. Then darkness rose like a tide of hot tar from every horizon, and Wilson felt himself burning, burning, his screams choked as his senses faded.

As if from a great distance, the last thing he heard was Mamalou's calm voice. *"Lift up Thyself, thou judge of the earth,"* she said to God, *"render a reward to the proud."*

+ · +

THE DEAVE LANE

by Michael Jecks

Michael Jecks says: "When I was asked to think of a story in the style of Edgar Allen Poe, I was immediately struck with thoughts of *The Pit and the Pendulum*, but when I reread *Tales of Mystery and Imagination*, I was struck more by the breadth of his writing. He was not a mere purveyor of horror, but a writer of thoughtful, highly creative atmospheric stories. Here, in Dartmoor, Deave Lane is noted as a strangely haunting location. I hope that in this story I have brought a little of its atmosphere to these pages."

❖ · ❖

I KNOW MANY PEOPLE who say that in their nightmares they find themselves falling into an unfathomable depth. They topple forwards or are sucked backwards, but the result is the same: they feel themselves whirling down and down, until they waken, sweating and panic-stricken. Some think that if they continue to fall, they will die, that their dream is actually a little death, and only waking can save them.

Falling is not a dream I've ever suffered from. No, when I've had a nightmare, it's always been the same. A hideous event that replays itself in every perfect detail. It is so precise, I can see it now if I close my eyes.

I am asleep and wake to utter, impenetrable darkness. It is as if I have been blinded. There are no shades of grey or brown, only an absolute lack of light of any sort that leaves me bewildered. When there is no light, even knowing which way is up, which is down, is impossible. With all sensory awareness eradicated, it is like being dead.

But my bewilderment does not last for long. It soon turns to terror. When I reach out with trembling hands, I find obstructions on all sides. Above my head, behind me, before me, to both sides, all is cold and hard. I feel the panic rising to choke me as I realize that I can never escape. I am locked in a stone coffin!

My nightmare has always been that: being buried alive.

This nightmare has been enough to direct the whole course of my life.

In university I had little idea what career I should seek, and when a friend persuaded me to join her in the archaeological group it was like a light coming on. I never looked back. I was fascinated: utterly beguiled by people long dead, by their lives, their deaths and their burials. Here, I hoped, I might one day make sense of my fear. I specialized in the bronze age and those who were buried in stone tombs.

After graduation I was lucky to get a post with the Royal Albert Memorial Museum in Exeter, and that's why I was one of the first on the spot when they made the discovery at the triple row on Cosdon Beacon.

I wish to God I had never heard of the place.

✦ · ✦

It started because of a metal detectorist.

He wasn't allowed up there. Dartmoor is protected. Parts are listed as being of special scientific interest, while others are classified as special for their wildlife. All of it is privately owned and permissions are not granted for weekend rambles with metal detectors, but Mr. Storey ignored all that and took his Christmas present on an illegal hunt hoping to find a cache of gold.

What he found was a corpse.

I drove to Throwleigh, the nearest village, pulled on my boots, and set off up the hill.

It was a cool day in winter. The breeze that blew from the top of the moor felt as though it was cutting through my thick coat and layers of wool and skin and freezing my bones. My teeth were chattering before I was halfway to the top, and when I got there, the wind turned brutal. I'm skinny, and I always feel the cold; I had to keep my shoulders hunched and hands thrust into my pockets to stop myself from shivering uncontrollably.

At the top of the triple row there was quite a huddle of people. A woman police officer, a doctor, three walkers with backpacks who looked seriously pissed off that they were late for their meander over the moors, and a sulking, scrawny little

man with a grey, smoker's complexion and narrow, undernour-
ished face. He had dark, suspicious little eyes when he looked
at me as I approached the policewoman.

"I'm Amanda Wilcocks, from RAMM," I introduced myself.

"Good. Cheryl Seymour. Thanks for coming so quickly." She
had a pleasant, round face that looked better suited to smiling
than her current worried frown. "How much do you know?"

"Only that someone's been mucking about with a metal detector and found a body."

"Yes. I wish he'd been testing it on the military range. He
might have blown himself up and saved us a lot of trouble,"
she said with a weak smile. "So, he was up here running his toy
over the stone row."

I was looking at it as she spoke. There are lots of stone rows
on the moors. Most are single or double rows, which means
that many stones are set in a long line, or pairs of stones are set
equidistantly so that they look like irregular railway tracks. More
rare are triple rows; they have been found in only a few places.

The three rows stood at the bottom of the western slope of
the Beacon. From here the land rose steeply to the third highest
peak of the moors. To my left, the land dropped away slightly,
then leveled, thick with grasses and little white stems towards
the inviting plains of Throwleigh Common. I could imagine
many seeing that and hurtling themselves over it with abandon. It would be their last mistake, for what looked like thick
grasses was really a thin crust of vegetation covering the infamous Raybarrow Pool, a deadly peat bog.

The triple row stood like a jagged wall warning the unwary to
halt here. A tumbledown boundary erected so many thousands
of years ago, no one really knew its purpose.

"Where did he find it?" I asked.

These stone rows, some thought, had been set up as grave
markers. Often at their north-westernmost end there were burial
mounds, with the lines of stones set out to mark, perhaps, the
importance of the ruler who was buried there. Some, and I was
one, thought that perhaps there was a religious significance as
well.

"Up here," Cheryl said. She led the way up past the triple row,
past the old cist and along a narrow track to the south towards
Raybarrow itself, to a scrape of darkness in the black, peaty soil.

I crouched at the edge. In the depths of winter, when the
wind howls over the grasses, sheep kick and dig until they have

a shallow shelter. In this scrape, a trowel had cut and delved, and a little way down into the peat a dark-colored hand had been exposed.

The flesh was a bit dried, but not as leathery as some I had seen. "His detector found this?"

"That's what he said. He got a signal when he dug down."

"I see."

Cheryl leaned closer. She had been eating garlic recently. "Does it look like an old body to you?"

I wanted to laugh. "I've seen some corpses thousands of years old, from the bronze age, unearthed from peat bogs in Scandinavia, but never one this close to the surface. I'd expect the flesh to be more leathery than this."

As I spoke, I touched the dark skin of the hand. It certainly didn't feel ancient. Apart from the hideous coldness, which made the hairs on the back of my neck rise, there was nothing to make me think this body was more than a few days old.

"God, look at his nails!" I blurted, without thinking. A spasm of revulsion clenched my stomach. All the nails were either broken and partially ripped off, as though he had been desperately scrabbling at something hard. I closed my eyes and turned away.

"So, what do we need to do now?" Cheryl asked. She looked nervous and a little pale.

"*If* he's bronze age, he may have a cist around him," I said.

"A what?"

"A burial site: they're called *kistvaens*, from *cist*, Celtic for box, and *maen*, or stone. They would build tombs with large, flat stones as sides. The body and all its valuables would go inside, then they'd put a capstone over the top and cover it all with soil and grass."

"Valuables? Do you mean there could be gold or something in there? Is that what set off his detector?"

"Not likely. What we consider valuable in the archaeological field are arrowheads, bone beads, that sort of thing. If this was a bronze age burial, most of his belongings would have rotted or been eaten away by the acidic peat."

She looked relieved. "Oh, good. I wouldn't want to think I'd have to stay up here all night. This place gives me the heebie jeebies."

I left them to it. Digging up the body would take a while, especially if there was a capstone to remove— that would require heavy lifting. And while I should perhaps have hung around to watch and check for artifacts, for once the excitement of the discovery didn't work its charm on me. Usually, when there's a potential find, I'm impossible to live with. The excitement makes me thrill in every fiber. Not here. I was struck with a feeling of gloom and... well, I can only call it a foreboding. I had a dread of something, but no idea what that *something* might be.

I had booked a room at The Wonson for the night, a small pub on the outskirts of Throwleigh. Roughly seven hundred years old, it had granite and cob walls and a thatched roof. I dumped my bags in the room converted from a barn and, since it was a clear afternoon, decided to go for a walk.

I headed off towards the moors and soon found myself in rough, boggy land.

The road was the only solid ground. When I found a track, it was soggy and sodden, with scatterings of lichen-encrusted granite and mica-infused sand. The water was as brown as stewed tea, stained by the peat, and every so often I experienced that unpleasant feeling of getting my feet soaked as I placed my boots in the wrong spot. Eventually, I scrambled and slipped up through thick peat and bogs, several times narrowly avoiding getting sucked down by stepping in the streams. After a good twenty minutes, I found myself on a roadway again.

I glanced at my watch and realized it was already past five o'clock. It would soon be getting dark, and I stared back the way I had come, thinking, *there must be a shorter path back!* Ahead the road turned eastwards, and I reckoned that should be more direct.

I set off with resolution and luckily met a couple of walkers, who consulted their maps and then very kindly led me to a little lane.

"This will take you back," the man said, pointing to Deave Lane on the map.

Seeing how grim and dark the lane looked, I felt anxious, but it was late and I had no idea how else to get to the pub. I was desperate to get back and have a bath.

At first the lane was quite open and I laughed at the thought that I should feel nervous. There was a lovely old thatched cottage on my left, and the lane followed the edge of the garden. Then, as trees overgrew the path, it became a little darker. The way was enormously muddy, and on either side there were tall stone walls, with bushes and even trees sprouting above their tops. These reached out over the path, their black, straggling twigs and branches meeting above my head, squeaking and creaking, as if grasping down at me. But I was a scientist, and I pushed such thoughts away.

I must have walked a good half mile, when I found myself at a dog-leg.

I stopped.

It was astonishing. I was struck by an absolute reluctance to advance. Something, I felt, was blocking my path. It was an unutterably — I can think of no word other than — *evil* presence. The sense of horror was so palpable that I could scarcely breathe. I could almost swear that there was someone or something there.

I could not go back. I had to carry on and reach the Wonson, somehow. I moved towards a gate, walking carefully along the extreme right side of the lane until I suddenly felt a lightening of my spirits. With a heart that was hammering painfully, I threw caution to the winds and pelted up the lane. It was only a matter of a few hundred yards, and all the way the path improved, the branches clutching overhead thinned and were left behind, and at last I found myself on a roadway, cursing my superstition and foolishness. By the time I reached the pub, I was almost able to pretend to be calm. But I needed a drink!

After a quick bath I made my way to the bar. It was small, with one room that was little more than a parlor, and a second, slightly smaller room. Both had tables and chairs set out, and I walked through and sat on a settle with a large glass of red wine.

Not long after, I heard voices and the first of the evening's locals arrived. Two youths who looked like schoolboys strode in, all muscles and testosterone, and stared at me as though they had never seen a blonde before. They walked to the bar, one slightly taller, with the chiseled jaw of a Hollywood actor. The other was heavier built, his tee shirt almost ripped at the biceps, like Bruce Banner halfway to becoming The Hulk.

Every woman knows that feeling, when a guy's looking at her, and she feels her clothes are suddenly transparent. I pulled my jacket closer about me.

Soon afterwards I was glad when Cheryl and the doctor I had seen at the site came in. Cheryl sat beside me, and I shifted along the bench until there was space for her. The doctor, who introduced himself as Dr. Westerham, bought drinks and sat across from me.

He looked to be in his early sixties, with sun-burned skin, pale blue eyes and grizzled hair. There was an aura of confidence about him, but not arrogance.

"We've managed to exhume the body," he said, "and although I would be unwilling to form any definite conclusions, I—"

"He isn't from the Stone Age," Cheryl interrupted.

"Bronze. If he's the same period as the triple row," I said automatically.

"Do you think they grew designer beards and had their hair fashionably short?" she said.

"What?"

"Or wore jeans and trainers? It was probably his watch set off the detector."

I shivered. This, then, was the reason for my nervousness earlier. I had felt that something was wrong. "The poor man. Is there any indication who he was?"

"Not yet. We'll have to go through a full autopsy and check DNA and dental records, I expect," Dr. Westerham said.

"He was murdered, though," I guessed. The thought made my stomach feel hollow. To die was sad, but to be murdered and buried miles from home seemed vile.

"I doubt he buried himself," Cheryl said. "I'll have to report it, and tomorrow we'll have men crawling all over the place."

"I doubt many will want to go up there for the night," the doctor said. "Most say it's spooky."

"All the locals are nervous about the cemetery."

"The what?" I asked, almost spitting wine.

"A fanciful name, but it's what everyone about here calls it," the doctor said with a tight smile. "The cemetery has all sorts of legends tied to it. Rumors that there are dark lines passing through it and—"

"Dark lines? What do you mean?"

He gave a self-deprecating moue and shrugged. "Please do not laugh, but I occasionally dabble in superstitious arts. In the occult, I suppose you could call it."

I imagine he saw my expression, because his eyes suddenly became hooded, and as he glanced at Cheryl and me, he leaned back in his seat, as though to create space between us.

"You know of dowsing for water? It's known the world over, and it's been proved to be accurate to a degree unequalled by any mechanical or electronic device. Dowsing has been used since ancient times to find water. There is an action between the dowser and the thing he seeks."

He was talking to two women. I bit. "Are you saying women can't dowse?"

"Women are very good at it," he said coolly. "But not only for water. That's just one aspect of dowsing. In the past, Queen Elizabeth I hired German dowsers to work with her miners to find coal and ores. It's because of them that the country developed so swiftly during the industrial revolution. No, dowsing will work well for men or women to search for things, but more interesting is dowsing for energy, for ley lines."

Cheryl looked bemused. "Lines of energy."

"Yes. They have been shown to encircle the earth. Several pass through Dartmoor."

"So that's what you called a dark line?" I asked.

"No. Those are good, healthy lines. But there are others, the black lines, which reflect other energies. Negative energies. The path taken by a murderer who killed his children and ends at the tree where he committed suicide; the route followed by the man who slaughtered his neighbors; the lane traveled by a woman who killed her daughter and buried her on the moors. All are black lines, marked by negative energy."

"And you can dowse for them?" I asked.

"You can dowse for anything you like," he said with an odd tone of voice that grated. "You are linked to the earth by dowsing."

He sounded patronizing. I decided I didn't like him.

"And there's one of these black lines up there?" I said.

"Yes. It's well known. Perhaps that is one of the reasons why the place was given such a grim name. Or it was the fact that the area has that unpleasant look about it."

I shuddered. The thought of the body being buried and left up there on the moors was horrible. I had a flash of my recurring dream. I tasted mould and felt the damp in the cist. The overwhelming weight of the darkness pressed in on me as I clawed at the stones, heedless of the pain as my nails were torn away. It was an injection of horror. I swigged wine quickly.

"Why should there be a black line up there?" I asked when my voice felt steady enough.

"Who can say? Perhaps it was a place of ritual killings. No one knows what the ancients did to appease their gods, nor what arts they learned. They were so much closer to nature.

I imagine they knew more about energies than we do." The doctor sipped his beer. "I've followed the line. It starts not far from here, in the Deave Lane." He waved a hand, not seeing my shudder. "The whole lane is black, as though it's haunted. I've dowsed it all. There is immense energy there."

"What, you mean a line starts down here and continues to the cemetery?" I said.

"Absolutely," he said quietly.

"It'd be black magic," a voice said.

I looked up to see *The Hulk* watching us.

"Pardon?"

"There were plenty of witches and others practicing black magic up 'till recent times," he went on. "You go up Belstone, you fall over 'em everywhere. Round here, I'll bet many would go up on the moors and sacrifice to the demons."

I wanted to laugh, but there was no reciprocal humor in his eyes as he stared at Cheryl, then the doctor and then me, before making his way to the bar.

+ · +

Soon after that, Cheryl left.

"Do you like Dartmoor?" Dr. Westerham asked.

"I enjoy walking."

"The moors are lovely at this time of year, but they can be treacherous."

"Oh, I've walked moors often enough."

"You should walk the moors at night. It's a different world then, under the moon."

"I'd like that." But not tonight, I added to myself.

"There is something special about the moors at night," he continued, "lighted by a silver silkiness. It seems almost as though you have slipped into another dimension."

"You really are quite a pagan, aren't you?" I laughed. "Dowsing, walking by moonlight into other dimensions..."

I had been joking, but his face was suddenly twisted with suspicion. Abruptly he rose and, without speaking, left the pub.

I was confused, and oddly humiliated. I felt the eyes of everyone in the room on me, staring accusingly. When I dared shoot a look around, I caught *The Hulk* leering. He unsettled me.

A little later, I overheard *The Hulk* and his friend talking in an undertone, discussing whether they could buy me a drink.

The thought of being chatted up by farm boys with beery breath decided me. Before the pair could draw lots for the pleasure, I left.

I lay on my bed staring at the ceiling. I can walk into a house and discern an atmosphere in a moment, and tonight I had a feeling that something was not right. There was an unsettling heaviness in the air that hadn't been there before, and it left me convinced that I would fall into my dream again if I slept. I didn't want that.

I kept wondering about the man buried on the moors. His ravaged fingernails spoke of a horrible death. A spasm of dread, almost a physical pain, forced me to get up. I locked the door, but I still wasn't easy in my mind. I felt oppressed. The air was heavy with menace. I couldn't stay the night!

With sudden resolve, I decided to go. I threw everything into my rucksack, paid the bill and went out to the car. I tossed in the bag and put the key in the ignition, but nothing happened when I turned it. I tried again, but there was no answering roar from the engine.

"You leaving?"

I looked up to see *The Hulk's* friend. He smiled, but all I saw was a baring of teeth.

"Looks like your battery's dead," he said.

I ignored him and walked back into the bar to ask for help, but there was nothing anyone could do until morning.

"Is there a taxi?"

"None that comes all this way," the woman at the bar said. "You'd best wait 'till morning."

"I want a lift to a bus stop or station," I stated.

"Sit down, then. I'll see what I can do," she said.

I sat and waited pensively with a glass of red. Suddenly the door opened and Cheryl came in, breathless. She looked around the bar, and then beckoned me urgently. Bemused, I picked up my glass and went to join her, but she took the wine from me and put it on a table, then pulled me outside.

"What is it?" I asked, but she put her finger to her lips. Only when we had walked some yards away from the pub and were in the road did she speak.

"You have to go— now! I think the murdered man was killed by Doctor Westerham. He's always been a little peculiar. I think you said something that's made him suspicious of you. You have to get away. Right now."

"My car won't start!"

"Then walk!" she said harshly. "Don't you understand what I'm saying? I've just heard the dead man was a journalist investigating a cult of pagans around here. The doctor was questioned and then the journalist disappeared. You see? If you stay here, he'll kill you and bury your body on the moors."

I felt panic strike me like a hammer. "Can you drive me?"

"I can't. I'm on my way to arrest Westerham. Go up the road to Deave Lane and take that. He can't drive down that, it's too rough. Just go, and be quick!"

She was determined, and after arguing for a few minutes more, panic took over. I ran all the way to the Lane, and as I stood contemplating it, reluctant to enter, I heard an engine approaching. I bolted, running up the muddy track. Headlights swung towards the lane. I spun around and had to shield my eyes from the glare. The car was following me!

Turning back, I fled up the track, hoping I would meet someone. I slipped in the mud and spatters hit my face as I raced along.

The powerful headlights cast my shadow in front of me so I could hardly see where to place my feet. The car was gaining on me! I stumbled, my breath ragged, hardly aware of the tree branches enclosing that hellish lane. The stone walls on either side were too tall, too overgrown for me to climb them. The only way was forward. The engine behind me growled louder and louder. I was already terrified, and that fear grew as I approached the dog's leg.

And then I reached it. I couldn't go on. A gate had been opened on my left, and it reached across the lane. The gate was lighted as the headlights came nearer, and I hesitated before bolting into the field. As I paused, the car stopped, the headlights aimed at me.

"Hello."

Westerham wasn't in the car, he was in front of me! He carried a long shepherd's crook, and as I tried to dart past him, it flashed out and caught my ankle. In an instant I was down. My head hit the ground, leaving me stunned.

It was hard to keep my eyes open. My vision came and went, and I heard voices. Then a figure passed in front of the car's lights, and I wondered if I was going mad. It was Cheryl.

They dragged me across the field and past a copse of trees. I saw a group of stones in amongst the undergrowth. It was a cist. They lifted me and placed me inside. Sobbing weakly, I was so petrified with terror and the pain in my head wouldn't let me think.

"Cheryl," I managed, "help me!"

She smiled and looked at the doctor. "She still doesn't realize, does she?"

"Realize what?" I said.

"You're our sacrifice. You've checked out of the pub, and tomorrow your car will be found in Exeter. It'll be thought you tried to get home, but you were mugged and hidden somewhere. And all the while you'll be here. A sacrifice."

There was a loud rattling of a chain, a terrifying sound, then the crunch as the capstone was dropped into place above me.

They murmured incantations that sounded like prayers, but I wasn't paying attention to the words. As my head cleared, I shrieked and screamed, begged and pleaded to be released, but their laughter exploded and then faded as they walked away. I heard the engine start and the car slowly drive away.

My nightmare was just beginning.

✦ · ✦

I must have passed out for a while, but I came to with a convulsive jerk. In the pitch blackness, I shook from the cold. I wrapped my arms about my torso, trying to force some warmth into my body, but that made no difference.

Unable to see anything, I investigated my prison by touch, running my hands over the walls and roof.

My coffin was two yards square, formed of roughly-hewn granite stones, each buried in the ground with only two feet or so jutting upwards. Over these *walls*, three long slabs, one smaller, two more than two feet wide, had been placed. Somehow Cheryl and the doctor had managed to move one of the largest and then replace it when I was inside. I spent an age struggling to move even one of them: I crouched on all fours and tried to push up, but nothing shifted; I lay on my back and braced my legs, but I could get no purchase.

I tried to dig around the base of the walls, scrabbling as best I could, and at first my fingers encountering soft, moldy soil. But when I had scraped this away, I found a solid base. The cist had been paved with more granite creating a floor. I had a biro in my pocket and using this, I tested the ground at each wall with the pen. There would be no escape.

Waves of despair washed over me. I curled into a ball. I would never free myself. This cist would be my tomb. In misery I imagined how my parents would react. The idea that they would never know what happened to me was enough to send me into choking desperation. In my mind I could see my mother's face, her tears, I could see her growing haggard as she wondered how I had died and where my remains lay. Her faith and religion were important to her. Not having a grave to mourn would be torture. My father had always idolized me. He was so proud of every petty achievement of mine, and he would despair at not being able to help me.

Suddenly, a blinding rage came over me. I swore in the most filthy language I could utter. I screamed with fury, clenched fists beating the walls of the coffin as though I could shatter the rock with my bare hands.

It was a kind of madness, and in a way it was a blessing. It vanquished a sense of time, and even made me stop shivering from the cold. I felt infused with a heat of passion and began to consider my chamber again. I had no doubt that Cheryl and the doctor would be back again before too long. It would be dawn soon, and surely they would come to make sure that I was still trapped. I had to work out an escape.

I began testing the walls again, pushing them with my feet, seeing whether any would move, but nothing happened, no matter how hard I kicked or shoved. But I was determined that I wouldn't give in. I wouldn't submit. I screamed until my voice was hoarse, but I suspect that inside that stone cocoon, set inside the woods far from the road, even if someone had been walking along the moors, my cries would have been all but smothered.

It was then, as my hope was shriveling and my resolution ebbing, that I heard an engine again.

The sound sent a fresh chill through me. A fist was slowly squeezing my heart. Cheryl or the doctor or both were returning. Maybe it was only to gloat. More likely, they were impatient and would kill me instead of waiting for me to die.

I would sell my life dearly! I had my biro, and gripped it tightly. I would stab Cheryl in the neck or the face, away from any protection she might be wearing. At the least I would blind her!

The noise grew louder. A large engine, a diesel. Not the police car, then. Perhaps the doctor had brought his car.

It was so close now, I could hear its wheels crunching on the cold ground near my cist. And then it was still, and a different sound. A whining, and then a clinking, rattling above over my head. Chilly fear rippled through my body. The hairs at the back of my neck rose and I crawled into a corner at the foot of the coffin.

With an enormous groan, one of the big slabs above me rose into the air. It shifted to the side and then, with a thunderous crash, fell to the ground.

"Miss? Miss?"

I heard *The Hulk's* voice, anxious, nervous and somehow very young, and I felt a rush of anger, certain that he was with them. I gripped my pen firmly, ready to stab him.

"Quick, you have to come out!"

There was a note of conviction that I could not ignore. I was soon out, in the cab of his tractor, and we were bucketing along the lane towards Throwleigh, where he left his tractor, and drove me in his car to Exeter.

＊ · ＊

The rest is common knowledge now. How the little group of acolytes had followed Doctor Westerham and Cheryl, how they took strangers and incarcerated them in the cist they had made, and disposed of the bodies on the moors. It's estimated that twenty people, one or more each year, had been killed. Always in the same manner: leaving them in their stone coffin until the cold and starvation had killed them off.

Cheryl was never to pay for her crimes. She committed suicide, hanging herself before the police went to arrest her. Dr. Westerham was caught and, based on psychiatric reports, installed in a mental institution, where he still is.

And me? A psychiatrist predicted that after an experience like mine, the recurring dream would stop. He told me that having lived through the reality, the dream's impact would dissipate.

That did not happen. To this day, I wake nightly and am compelled to reach out all around me to make sure that I am not buried alive. Even in broad daylight, I can feel those stone walls surrounding me.

I was buried for only a few hours, but I'll never be released.

＊ · ＊

133

by Richard Christian Matheson

Richard Christian Matheson says: "Resurrection escorts second chances; often things perverse. It is a perfect metaphor for true costs. Considering serial murders, I have long felt capital punishment too kind a response to numbing lists of victims. I thought about Poe's *Ligeia* as the grieving heart of a husband, to bleak effect, brings his dead wife back. And this story came to me."

❖ · ❖

Paralytic trickles into arm. Frantic limbs strapped-down.

"How long?" The grieving man, eyes sunken.

"Three minutes." The Warden.

"Is he suffering?"

"Yes."

Gurney creaks. Black hood dreaed-soaked.

The man watches. Remembers his wife; red pieces left of her.

Heart monitor a frenzy.

The Warden checks watch. "Drugs go in a sequence. Sodium pentobarbital first... it's the anesthetic."

Chemicals slither; smother.

"Pancuronium Bromide next: causes muscle paralysis."

Spasms; wet asphyxiation.

"Potassium Chloride last: stops the heart."

Bestial cries. The hooded mouth gasps sick panic.

The sunken eyes savor.

Ghastly noises crawl. The head slumps.

The Warden checks watch. "He's paralyzed."

The grieving man steps closer. Mouth watering. Slowly lifts the leather hood. Stares into the prisoner's pleading eyes, the last face she saw as she was slashed apart. The purple, bloated tongue tries to speak. The man half-smiles. Listens to the agonized death rattle; a sweet melody.

"...FUCK YOU!" he screams, weeping as he's escorted out.

Drool creeks onto chest; death syrup.

* · *

The Warden nods to the Doctor.

The wet hood is lowered. Syringe re-filled. The needle slides into flesh, orange chemical swept into inert luges of vein, dead heart. Ventricles constrict, shocked, blood throbbing through waking ducts. The prisoner suddenly convulses and moans, body jerking wildly, coming back to life.

The Warden gestures to the Guard. Five people enter; wordless, ashen. Weeping mother, stoic father, shattered grandparents, stricken brother. They stare at the black-hooded form, frantic against restraints. Remember detectives describing what he did to her.

"We'll add something special to this one," the Warden tells them.

Strychnine slips into arm; ant poison.

He thrashes, begs for someone to make it stop. The Gurney shakes furiously. He shrieks louder; chemicals a grease-fire. Lungs desperately heave, sucking panicked air through thick hood. The family's features tic with pleasure. His mouth froths onto shirt.

He gradually stills.

The family moves to his anguished body. Lift puke-stenched hood. His eyes wide, see their loathing. Bleak joy fills them. He tries to apologize, words a blurred wail. They curse him, spit in his face. His wracked flesh shudders, slowly dies.

As they leaves, the Warden sits. Thinks about the one-hundred and thirty-three victims the prisoner met along the way. Tortured. Raped. Limbs cut-off, some while still alive. The ruined lives of everyone who loved them. He carefully crosses the name of the one-hundredth family from the list. Nods to the doctor.

As the orange fluid is injected, the prisoner writhes back to life, the Warden ignoring his tortured screams.

"Thirty-three to go," he tells the Guard. "Bring in the next family."

✦ · ✦

AFTERLIFE

by William F. Nolan, Jason V. Brock, and Sunni K. Brock

William F. Nolan, Jason V. Brock and Sunni K. Brock say: "*Afterlife* was partially based on Poe's *Eureka: A Prose Poem*, which inspired the idea that Poe could become trapped in the physical space of his own letters. We wanted to tie in text that could have been written by Poe, and also fold in some of the mysterious circumstances surrounding his death and the strange characters involved in his estate. And, of course, we wanted to explore a possible explanation for the Poe Toaster while escorting the reader on a visit to historical Poe sites."

✦ · ✦

"The boundaries which divide Life from Death
are at best shadowy and vague.
Who shall say where the one ends,
and where the other begins?"

✦ · ✦

I.

"I JUST DON'T SEE ANYTHING really, well, *unique*... Not for *my* client, anyway," Enid Blake said, wrinkling her nose at the tray of old medical instruments and preserved tissue samples.

A small, compact woman with light-brown hair in a messy, asymmetrical crop, she was dressed in black leggings and a yellowed vintage knot sweater, blending well with the musty stacks of books and curiosities in the small shop.

"Well, honey, what are they into?" asked the effeminate clerk, a man in his mid-fifties, thin and gaunt, tortoiseshell-rimmed glasses reflecting the gauzy late afternoon sunlight as it lanced down from a leaded glass window.

"I really don't know. He was a referral— at least I think it's a 'he.' Some sort of filmmaker/rock star that used to hang around H. R. Giger, you know— part of that 'Giger Gang' thing. Wants to remain anonymous. That's why I'm here." Enid sighed. "I know he likes horror."

"Mmmm, don't we all?" The clerk gingerly replaced the tray under the glass counter and locked it. "Over there is the rare horror book collection." He motioned to the far corner of the store, past still more artifacts crammed into the tight confines of the place— a suit of armor, shrunken heads, rows of specimens floating dreamily in yellow liquid.

Enid made her way around the makeshift aisles. "*How* rare?"

"Some hand bound stuff, a few untitled tomes. We estimate some date around the 1700s." He peered at her over the top of his glasses. "Just be careful. They're fragile."

Reaching the bookshelf, she ran a thin black-nailed finger along the tattered spines. Many were so worn she could not read the titles. Randomly, Enid angled a book forward to examine the cover. When she did, a pamphlet next to it slipped out; in her clumsy effort to catch it, she managed to knock three or four books to the wooden floor in a noisy clatter. Dust and the faint whiff of decaying glue rose up from the calamitous pile.

Dropping to her knees in shock, she resisted the urge to scoop up the chapbook, afraid she might inflict further damage on the aged volumes. "Damn it!" Enid gently picked up the top book, which was no worse for wear, carefully closing it; the others did not fare as well. Reaching for some of the loose pages that splayed haphazardly from the broken covers, she noticed they contained a few handwritten notes— scrawlings of strange symbols around an illustration of a mysterious 'head'. Perhaps it was a phrenology figure, or a cryptic astrological diagram, only darker, more bizarre than any she had seen before.

"Oh, *my*," the little clerk said, rushing over in a mock panic. "Now I'll have to have the glue-sniffing Bible binder come in and repair them! Oh, how I *dread* that man. I presume I can have the bill sent to *you*?" He fanned his face with a well-manicured hand.

"Don't get your panties in a bunch, dear. I'll take them. Throw in a little for your trouble. My client can afford it." Enid rose to face him. "Just put them back together and pack them up as best you can. I'll take the rest of the books on that shelf, too."

II.

"It's good to see you, Enid. How was The Big Apple?" Professor Ingels stood, grinning warmly as Enid reached his table in the little coffee shop.

Enid, flushed from the cold Boston air, removed her gloves and wrapped her arms around his neck, giving him a peck on the cheek. "Wonderful! I watched the ball drop and did some shopping. I'm glad to be back, though."

Dalton Ingels was a handsome man: erudite, distinguished, and more than a little quirky. She secretly wished they could go beyond just friends, but he was enigmatic. Though they continued to meet and talk years after she had graduated, she had no idea if he was married, involved, or even interested. Every time she tried to broach the topic, he dodged it artfully. Still, he always exuded affection and indulged her when she needed to vent.

"Your usual *chai*, I assume?" the plump blonde waitress asked, looking at Enid, then turned to the Professor. "Americano, vanilla, non-fat?"

"Yes, please," they responded in unison.

The waitress nodded and headed off towards the counter. Professor Ingels grabbed Enid's hand. "So what can I do you for?"

As much as she wanted to, Enid knew better than to express her real feelings via innuendo. Last time she tried that, the Professor recalled the mating rituals of flatworms, dulling her hope of breaking through his platonic veneer. "Well, I found something, and I want you to take a look at it. It's been really bothering me."

"Must be pretty horrible." He gave her a little wink.

"I don't know quite what to make of it." She opened her purse and pulled out an envelope. "I just... well, please say what you think."

He took it and pulled out a yellowed paper. "This looks pretty old. One of your clients find it?"

"No, I found it. I just keep thinking about it."

"Hmm..." The Professor carefully unfolded the document. He scanned the handwritten lines. "Poe, eh? The signature..."

"Could it really be... Edgar Allan Poe?" Enid was anxious to know if she had stumbled onto an unknown Poe letter.

Professor Ingels glanced at her from beneath his shaggy brows, then read aloud:

My Dearest,

I fear this may be my last missive. The most heinous and bitter remarks of the specter now assail my very being.

There is something in this pulp that removes my literal essence even as it compels me to write...

It drains my character as dark exhausts light.

It is as though writing and breathing are entwined with life and death.

[illegible] *fate is now with* [illegible]

"Where did you get this?" Professor Ingels asked. By his tone, Enid could tell that he thought it might be genuine.

"I bought some old books in the Village for a client. I was cataloging them when I found this inside one."

"What kind of books? Have you told anyone else?" The Professor was getting excited.

"Well, no. I mean, I wanted to see what you thought first. It was in an antique volume about mysticism. Strange thing— there were other handwritten notes in the book, but the handwriting didn't match this letter at all. Anyway, the book is going to my client along with the others. Just the kind of thing that will bring in good money. But this letter, I'm not about to let go of it... not yet, anyway."

The waitress returned with their drinks. Professor Ingels tentatively sipped at the hot coffee while Enid fanned the steam from her tea, taking a deep breath of the spice.

"I'm not an expert on Poe, but it reminds me..." The Professor leaned forward. "Tell you what. Come by my office next week. There's something you should see."

III.

"Thank you so much for agreeing to meet with me. And for suggesting this place. It seems so appropriate." Enid was nervous standing in front of the Edgar Allan Poe National Historic site in Philadelphia.

The other woman, dressed head-to-toe in black and a bit older than Enid, smiled kindly at her. "I always love visiting it. I hope you didn't come all the way to Philly just to talk to me."

"Well, I did have some other business. Trying to track down a child's coffin, preferably Amish, for a client that needs a new bookshelf." Enid took a chance that her new acquaintance, Diane Fitzpatrick, had a penchant for the macabre as well.

"*Darker Home and Gardens?*" Diane raised her eyebrows.

Enid giggled. "Sort of."

"Do you have time to stay here in Philly a little while? You should really see my place." Diane held the door open and the two ventured in.

"I'd love to… and if you don't mind, maybe we can look at my 'item' there after the tour of the Poe house, away from prying eyes."

"You got it. Only my cat and my bird will be snooping."

They both laughed.

IV.

"Diane, your house is *amazing!*" Everywhere Enid looked, the little cottage was filled with oddities. The place was dark, spooky; walls covered with tapestries, shelves of old books, bottles and vials, some containing human teeth. On one table perched a collection of grungy daguerreotype photographs — *memento mori* — with snippets of hair and clothing attached; lace seemed to be everywhere.

Diane sat on a Victorian loveseat, sipping tea from a dainty China cup, a cat balled up next to her. "It's a lifetime of treasures, Enid. I thought you would appreciate my tastes."

"Oh, I do, I do." Enid was glad that Professor Ingels had setup this connection. Diane was quickly becoming a friend, and quite possibly a new client to boot. "I thought you said you had a bird."

"Yes, yes. Eddie. His name is Eddie."

At the sound of his name, Eddie came half-hopping, half-flying down the hallway and alit on the coffee table.

"A *crow?*" Enid was shocked and delighted.

"A *raven!* Right, Eddie?" Diane looked at the big black bird. He made a low grumbling noise and ruffled his scruffy throat feathers.

"Of course! What was I thinking?" Enid laughed, then bit her lip.

"Diane, you have to see this. I need to know what you think of it." She pulled the letter from her case, now protected by plastic, and held it out.

Diane carefully looked over the yellowed paper. Eddie bobbed impatiently. The cat yawned.

Diane ran a finger over the plastic as if touching the letter. "When I wrote to Professor Ingels years ago, he replied that the library had no other fragments like mine." She glanced at Enid. "Are you looking for a buyer?"

"I'm not sure what I'm looking for, not yet. Can I see your fragment? I've only viewed the photocopy Professor Ingels showed me."

"Sure, of course." Diane shooed the bird off the table, got up from her seat, and disappeared into a darker corner of the cottage. Eddie jumped up onto the loveseat and pulled the cat's tail with his beak. The cat hissed and swatted at him. The raven's head bobbed up and down, wings outstretched, cawing excitedly.

"Eddie, stop teasing the cat!" Diane yelled, hurrying back into the living room.

The raven clacked his beak cheekily, responding with a throaty: "Nevermore!"

Diane shook her finger at the bird as he postured and strutted on the davenport. "That's right, Eddie. Nevermore should you pull the cat's tail!"

He replied with a metallic click of his beak which made Enid think of alien laughter. "Nevermore!" he cawed in gleeful antagonism. Diane rolled her eyes as Enid burst out laughing at the bird's antics.

"You are such a little showoff, Mr. Eddie Fitzpatrick!" Diane scolded. The raven's head bobbed up and down in delight.

At last Diane presented a sheet of plastic to Enid. One side was an envelope, the other a torn scrap of crumpled paper adorned with shaky black script:

[illegible] *is of utmost* [illegible]
this quill has become my nemesis.
It forces my hand to its unyielding will.
I fear your loving betrothed will exist merely as the script on this paper should the accursed spell remain unbroken. [illegible]
Why has this happened to us? Is there no respite? No release from that terrible man, Mr. [illegible]

Enid felt a chill. Something about this piece was so similar in tone to the one she had discovered. "What does it mean?"

Diane picked up Enid's letter from the table and held it next to hers for comparison. The paper, the ink, the handwriting all matched.

"They belong together," Diane confirmed. "Written maybe days, hours apart."

Enid frowned. "I guess I should be excited about this find, but I just feel weird about it. You're right. The pieces *belong together*. But, I really don't want to sell. It just seems wrong."

"Forgive me. I didn't mean—"

"No, Diane. I'm the one who should apologize. I sell things like children's coffins for Pete's sake! Why this one letter would bother me is stupid."

"Look, you're not stupid. If it's any consolation, I feel something, too. If you don't have to be back in Boston right away, why don't you stay here tonight? Let's have some wine and relax. Maybe we can figure out what old Edgar was trying to communicate."

Diane's reassurance calmed Enid; she welcomed her newfound friendship. "I'd love to. Meeting you has been the best part of this whole thing."

V.

Enid sat up abruptly in bed. She heard it again: footsteps, moaning.

She tried to talk, but felt paralyzed. She faced the moonlit window, its lacy curtains glowing in the darkness of the guest room.

A figure appeared— wavering, transparent. She could hardly believe it: *Poe?*

Looking at her with large, sad eyes, the apparition moaned softly, before uttering a single word: "*Release.*" Then, the ghost crouched, spectral hands desperately reaching to the dresser where the letter fragments now lay together.

Enid, still frozen in disbelief, fainted back onto her pillows.

VI.

"I don't think it's crazy, Enid. Maybe it was just a dream, or maybe you were really visited by an apparition. Either way, it's obvious that you need to figure out why it's bothering you." Diane took another sip of her tea, then tore off a corner of her toast to give to Eddie.

"Maybe stress is finally catching up with me." Enid scowled. She sprinkled nutmeg into her mug. "I can't shake the feeling, though. It's like he's trapped and wants out."

"Trapped, how?" Diane looked confused.

"Well, I know it sounds weird, but trapped… in those *letters!*" Eddie returned her excitement with an enthusiastic caw.

Diane's smile was cryptic. "Enid, I have an idea."

VII.

"This way, ladies." Mr. Pratt, the gaunt, sharp-featured library archivist, led them into a special-collections room. "Here, we have preserved many important items pertaining to Poe, including some documents regarding the mysterious circumstances of his death. I believe these will be of interest. Excuse me, I have a staff meeting, but any of our librarians should be able to help you if you have questions."

The lanky man disappeared through a white-paned entranceway.

"Diane, this was a great idea coming to Baltimore," Enid said, regarding the treasures before them.

"Well, I don't know what we're going to find, or what's going to happen if we *do*. I mean, we can't just *steal* any of these." Diane looked up and noticed Enid already across the room, staring at a chunk of wood mounted in a display protected by glass.

"Look! It's a piece of his coffin. *Wow*." Enid held her hand up as if to feel for any presence emanating from the relic.

"Darn it, you jumped ahead! I was looking forward to showing that to you."

Enid laughed. "This is exciting, isn't it?"

"Yes, it is! But we've got more places to hit. Also, I've arranged a special treat for later tonight, so we need to do our research and get out of here before the other buildings close."

"Okay, okay." Enid pulled out her notebook. "Let's get to it."

VIII.

"Another round of margaritas?" the bartender asked.

Enid nodded. Diane finished off the last of the guacamole with a broken tortilla chip. "Yes, please."

"I'll have a whiskey. Edgar style." Their new arrival, an older man with salt-and-pepper hair, called to the barkeep as he removed his gloves and sat at an adjoining stool.

"You got it, Jim." The bartender rushed off.

"We were wondering if you were going to make it!" Diane leaned over to give the man a kiss on the cheek. "Enid, this is Jim. He's an expert on Poe's time in Baltimore. Runs a tour."

"Nice to meet you, Jim." Enid held out her hand.

He returned her gesture with a firm but gentle shake. "Likewise."

"Enid here's a 'Horse' virgin. Never been to the saloon." Diane raised an eyebrow.

"Ah yes, 'The Horse You Came In On' — the longest running drinking establishment in the United States. What do you think?" Jim grinned at Enid, gesturing at the room.

"I can't believe this is really the last place Poe was seen... I'm sure Diane told you about my... curiosity?"

"Indeed." Jim hailed the bartender. "Hey, Mike, we'll take 'em upstairs."

The barkeep acknowledged him by holding a door open.

"Ladies, after you." Jim motioned them on.

IX.

Lightheaded from the many drinks, Enid was mesmerized by Jim's tales of Poe's final days.

Diane occasionally offered a question or comment to bolster the dialogue. "So what about Rufus Griswold? Do you think he had anything to do with his death?"

"Well, Griswold certainly had it out for old Eddie. But most of his damage was done after the fact, as far as we can tell." Jim responded confidently. "That obituary was stinging. He damaged Poe's reputation further... and became Poe's executor, if you can imagine that!... He did have some unknown papers of Poe's. They were found by Charles Leland when Griswold died."

"A self-proclaimed *wizard*..." Diane wiggled her fingers at Enid.

"Leland was reportedly the first to get to the contents of Griswold's desk when he died. Found a bunch of letters. Said he even found forgeries that Griswold had created to besmirch Poe." Jim made a pen motion to illustrate the point.

"And?" Enid was sitting on the edge of her seat.

"Well, I'm not sure they were forged. At least, not *all* of them." Jim sat back and took a swig of his whiskey.

"What happened to them? Where are they?" Enid demanded.

"Burned," Diane injected. "He threw them on the fire to protect Poe."

"That's what Leland claimed." Jim ran his finger around the rim of his half-empty glass. "But, there's something else."

"What, you're holding out on me?" Diane teased.

He returned her light-hearted gaze with a grim expression. "Not holding out, just... uncertain. Did you bring the documents?"

Both women nodded. They each brought out their respective fragments of the letters and showed them to Jim. He examined them carefully before pulling out a loupe to study the swirls and loops of the handwriting. "Decidedly Poe."

Jim regarded Diane for a long moment. "You never told me about this before, Diane—"

She laughed, nervous. "Well, I thought you'd think it was crazy!"

He nodded, understanding. "It's not crazy. There is a legend..." He paused, looking to the window before he continued. "It's about Poe... It says that he was cursed by Griswold. Tormented, yes, but actually *cursed*, too—"

"Griswold?" Diane asked. "But I thought Leland was—"

"Yes," Jim replied, holding his hand up in a gesture of silence. "But some theorize that both had studied the dark arts and later had a dispute. The gist is they both disliked Poe, but after falling out... As they say: 'The enemy of my enemy is my friend', right?" Jim took a swallow of his drink. "Later Leland wanted to destroy *Griswold*. Old Eddie's legacy became a pawn."

Reaching into the inner pocket of his jacket, he produced an envelope, one not covered with protective plastic. "This has been passed down since my great-great grandfather, who was the barkeep here."

Enid took the worn packet from Jim.

"Go ahead, open it." Jim leaned forward.

Carefully, Enid removed the brittle paper, unfolded it and read silently, Diane reading over her shoulder."What? I don't—"

"I can't tell you for sure that Poe wrote it. I only know that it was reportedly found in 1849, right in front of him when he was passed out here, in this bar." Jim was somber, almost whispering.

[illegible] *sorcery. I have learned that* [illegible] *is stealing my papers — papers that I — and I alone — must retrieve and destroy or* [illegible] *and* [illegible]

"Let me see." Diane gently took the note from Enid's hands. "Geez, Jim, it's just a bunch of wavy lines after this first part."

"I need to use the restroom." Enid stood, her mind reeling.

"Down that hall." Jim pointed. "On the right."

X.

The cool moist air of the washroom calmed Enid's nerves and brought some sobriety. "Jesus," she muttered to herself. She got up, pulled up her leggings and flushed.

At the sink, she looked into the mirror while waiting for the water to warm. "God, bags under my eyes." She washed and dried her hands, then turned the ancient doorknob.

Down the hall, she saw the light spilling into the hallway where her companions were undoubtedly still discussing the fragments of letters. As she took a step forward, the bookshelf to the left creaked, and she thought she heard a voice.

Enid froze. *This is no time to get spooked.* Just as she decided to move, something appeared in front of her. She watched again as the wispy figure of Edgar Allan Poe, better defined, presented itself. Without touching it, the spirit removed a book from the shelf and opened it; once more Enid heard the word: "*Release.*" A ghostly finger pointed to the text.

She leaned forward and read:

In the original Unity of the First Thing
lies the Secondary Cause of All Things,
with the germ of their Inevitable Annihilation.

Enid collapsed into a well of soothing darkness.

XI.

After the bar closed, the women decided to continue on to the final stop on Diane's tour of Poe's Baltimore. A full moon loomed ominously in the black velvet sky.

"Sorry about leaving Jim like that, Enid, but I just knew we had to come here." Diane's breath fogged in the cold winter chill as they walked through the mist-shrouded cemetery. "Are you feeling okay now?"

"A little too much to drink, that's all," Enid replied, rubbing her arms through a heavy coat, trying to forget about what had happened in the bar. "I've always wanted to see this place. And the fresh air is clearing my head. Oh, is that it, up there?" She pointed to a tall marker just ahead. Fog swirled around them as they walked.

"Yep, that's the one."

Enid approached the monument over the grave and lay an envelope containing the letter fragments against it: hers, Diane's, the scribbled note from Jim. She bowed her head respectfully for a moment. An owl hooted in the distance. Finally, Enid stepped back. After a few minutes, the two women looked at one another and giggled. Turning from the grave, they walked away, arms linked; at last, Diane offered: "Perhaps we can still catch up with Jim."

As they were about to leave the grounds, Enid stopped suddenly. A cloaked figure with a lantern approached from the shadows, roiling the eerie fog. The moonlight cast long shadows throughout the cemetery, adding to the ghostly ambiance of the mysterious individual. Enid and Diane sheltered behind a decaying old sculpture of death and the maiden, watching as the figure passed.

Slowly the figure walked to Poe's gravesite. After a brief pause, the person lay three roses and a half-empty bottle of cognac on the shrine over Poe's resting place. One thin hand reached out and appeared to touch the letters as the other moved to the hood of the cloak; in the warm flicker of the lantern, the hands seemed unnaturally thin to Enid, cadaverous.

Hesitating, the figure looked around, but did not appear to see them; as the person considered the notes, they exclaimed: "Release!" Pulling the hood back at last, the wan face of Edgar Allan Poe was revealed.

Enid gasped in shock; Diane's fingers clutched the younger woman's arm in a vise-grip of fear and panic.

"Release!"

As the women watched, the spirit took the papers and fed them into the flame of the lantern. While they burned, the specter of Poe dissolved little by little into the shrouding mist, finally vanishing towards the heavens with the smoke from the letters...

Released at last. Forevermore.

+ · +

THE DROWNING CITY

by Loren Rhoads

Loren Rhoads says: "Poe's story *The Assignation*, which appears in *Tales of Mystery and Imagination*, begins with a gondola ride and a child falling into a canal. Poe's lovely description of the crumbling city compelled me to visit Venice. On my first day there, I discovered the Church of the Assumption, where Alondra hears the siren sing. Getting lost in the alleys that night led me to write *The Drowning City*."

❖ · ❖

THE WET WINTER AIR SWIRLED around Alondra DeCourval, slipping icicle fingers under her collar. As she walked back from the landing at the *Fondamenta Nuove*, her nose felt raw, her throat ached, and her head throbbed. It had been a long time since she'd gotten sick while traveling. At least the trip to Murano had been worth it. Her new glass beads were warm under her shearling coat.

Venice was a maze during the best of times, one she enjoyed unraveling on a sunny day. Tonight, with the fog hastening an already early twilight, she wanted only to curl up beneath the comforter at Giulietta's palazzo on the Grand Canal, sip *cioccolata calda*, and be swarmed by cats. Instead, she took a wrong turn and found herself in a little dead-end square dominated by a stone cistern and surrounded by 16th-century apartment buildings. Lost.

Alondra pulled off a wine-colored glove to wipe her nose. She felt nearly miserable enough to knock on a stranger's door for directions. Instead, she replaced the glove, wrapped the scarf tighter around her throat, and retraced her steps.

A brief meander brought her to a paved square ringed by a few sad olive trees in marble planters. The trees had been carted to the sinking city and left to fall to ruin. Alondra brushed droplets of fog from one's sagging leaves.

A Baroque church loomed over the square. Age stained its white marble façade to the color of spilt milk. Black lichen gnawed permanent shadows beneath the pediment. Above the gutters stood a row of saints on soapboxes, clutching the instruments of their martyrdoms.

Alondra had never grown entirely comfortable with churches. She no longer felt personally threatened by the survival of the institution that had tortured and killed her ancestors as witches. She didn't assume modern Christians were better behaved. It was a prejudice she'd inherited at her grandmother's knee, but she had not looked for a reason to challenge it. Let the Christians beseech their god to work his magic on their behalf and Alondra would work her own. The less contact between them, the better.

Be that as it may, the unnamed church was open and bright inside. Alondra had no better concept of the time than she did of the direction of the Grand Canal. She was sure, however, that it was Thursday night. Whatever was going on inside the church, she guessed it wouldn't be preaching. Rather than drift around in the cold any longer, she climbed the steps and entered the sanctuary.

To her continual surprise, she did not burst into flames as she crossed the threshold. The earth, even liquefied as it was in Venice, did not tremble. The Christian god never betrayed any displeasure when the witch set foot in his house.

Alondra's gaze went immediately to the chancel at the opposite end of the nave, but everything behind the choir rail was blacker than the night outside.

What a splendid building it was: the ceiling rose in a series of domes, every surface adorned in contrasting relief with urns or acanthus leaves or dentition. The columns that stood sentry around the chancel were inset with green stone that morphed and grew in kaleidoscopic horticultural patterns. Swaying dizzily, Alondra sank onto a vacant pew at the back of the room.

Perhaps a hundred people sat in clusters, chatting. Alondra studied the congregation, trying to define their commonality. She saw rough-looking fishermen in patched wool coats.

Unabashed society women in mink. A knot of too-handsome men with black eyes, laughing together. Teenaged girls watched them enviously, craving their attention.

Alondra heard nothing spoken but Italian. Apparently this was not a show church, drawing tourists to an evening concert. These parishioners felt as comfortable in their neighborhood basilica as they would at the local *ristorante*. Alondra wondered that they hadn't interrogated the outsider in their midst. Just as well. She had enough trouble gathering her thoughts. Conversing in Italian might be beyond her. She promised herself that she'd sit for another minute, then seek a teenaged girl — surely they'd learned English in school — and ask directions. She loathed being reduced to a tourist bumbling along in a single language.

A balcony attached to the marble wall on her left caught her eye. Alondra realized the damask drapery that flowed from its canopy and hung in graceful folds from the balcony's lip had been carved from white marble, inset with green. The dagged edge of the canopy's valance: stone. The large tassels hanging from the valance: stone. The fringe on the curtains: stone.

The exuberant detail slaved over by the stone carvers made her want to laugh. She wondered if their god took the same amusement in it.

She touched chilly fingertips to her forehead, suspecting she was feverish. Everything sounded out of focus, as if cotton wool wrapped her head. She had better get back to Giulietta's. She reached towards the girl across the aisle.

To the rattle of polite applause, someone cleared his throat. Alondra prepared to flee, rather than sit through a sermon. As she rewound her scarf, however, she realized that she'd blundered into a recital rather than a religious service.

It was difficult to make out the speaker's words as they bounced around the stone space. The congestion in her head didn't help. Still, Alondra understood "voice like an angel." That persuaded her to settle back in the pew.

A woman gestured grandly to the audience nestled inside their winter coats in the unheated church. She wore a spotless white gown that fell in a single shining piece. An ornate gold brooch accented the shoulder. Her bare arms were an olive tone that spoke of sun and summer and the warmth of islands farther south.

The singer turned to her accompanist, who lifted a flute to her lips and quietly began to play. Her smoky voice was deep enough to be masculine, dark and strong as espresso. Alondra struggled to follow the words, garbled by echoes from the uneven stone walls.

The emotions behind the song were clear. The singer held a deep reverence for something Alondra couldn't decipher, as well as pride in her talent.

The first aria finished to an enthusiastic ovation. Alondra joined in. The voice had been lovely, as far as she could tell, but not spectacular. Maybe the singer was one of the congregation's own.

The accompanist exchanged her flute for some kind of lute. The singer's voice entered the music with a sustained high note that soared through the church, silvery and radiant. The tone dove back down into the depths, then rose again like a dolphin playing in the waves.

Around Alondra, people chuckled and swayed, enjoying themselves immensely. She wished she could hear better. Obviously she was missing something remarkable.

Alondra had grown up listening to vocal music, attending operas with her guardian. Victor taught her to appreciate the nuances of tone and color in various voices, the ways different singers could flavor a familiar song. She pushed down a stab of grief, one in a long series, for the guardian she'd lost. She swore she would not cry in public.

The third piece changed mood again. This was some kind of threnody, for a love that was gone and would not — could not? — return. Alondra watched a tear roll off the nose of a weathered fisherman. Black-clad grandmothers dabbed their eyes with lace-edged handkerchiefs. Younger couples clung to each other and sobbed.

Alondra felt terribly out of place amidst the stricken crowd. What reduced these people to such a state? As the song built in intensity, so did the crowd's lamentation. One young woman flung herself to the travertine floor, screaming in distress that eerily paralleled the soprano's melody. Those around her nodded, unable to offer comfort through their own suffering.

Perhaps she'd misunderstood and the recital was really a memorial service. Whatever the case, Alondra felt she was intruding.

She gathered her gloves and crept out of the church.

❖ · ❖

The fever worsened as she staggered through the empty streets. Fog muffled every sound but the quiet lapping of water in the canals. The sound reverberated around her, confusing her sense of direction even more. The streetlights cast halos in the fog that hurt her eyes. Inside her shearling coat, her flesh felt clammy, but she was too chilled to open her collar or loosen her scarf. She vowed that if she ever saw another soul, she would beg him to escort her to Palazzo Schicchi.

But she'd never seen a Venetian night as uninhabited as this. It seemed every god-fearing citizen was tucked safely into bed, shades drawn, lights out.

Gooseflesh crept up Alondra's arms. *Something* walked the night, something ancient and malevolent. She hunched into her black coat and hid in the shadows. Tears prickled her eyes. She'd never felt so alone or so frightened in her life, so incapable of protecting herself.

She stumbled over a little bridge that arched like a cat's back, above a narrow canal cutting knife-like between the houses. Beneath her, black water flowed, not a sparkle of reflected light to break its inky surface.

Alondra leaned over the spiral pillars of the balustrade, willing her eyes to focus. There had to be *some* reflection. A white streetlight burned at either terminus of the bridge. The fog above her held in enough light that she could see even when streetlights were scarce. She should at least be able to see a shadow of her own reflection.

Her scarf uncoiled from her throat and dangled one fringed end toward the water. As Alondra reached out to wind it tight again, the scarf slipped from her shoulders and fluttered downward. She lunged after it, nearly losing her balance on the slick stones.

A pallid hand stretched out from beneath the bridge, fingers cupped around the black water in its palm. The hand was attached to a wrist in a shabby wool coat. Slowly, the corpse bobbed out of the shadows. Alondra recognized the crying fisherman.

His mouth gawped open. Several of his teeth were blackened and rotting.

Another body nudged his: the young woman who'd flung herself to the church's floor. Behind her drifted one of the handsome men Alondra had unconsciously labeled Gondoliers. With eyes closed, he seemed to be still listening to the angelic voice.

Alondra reeled to the other side of the bridge to gaze down on bodies glutting the narrow canal. They stretched back as far as she could see.

Slipping, falling, picking herself up, she ran.

The flight through the city evaporated instantly from her memory. Alondra remembered only the stitch in her side and the terror that stole the labored breath from her lungs. Finally she lurched through the courtyard of the correct palazzo and flung herself at the bell cord.

Giulietta Schicchi answered the door herself, a flannel robe thrown over her beribboned nightdress, silver hair loose around her shoulders. Alondra collapsed at her hostess' slippered feet.

Giulietta's knees snapped with a sound like breaking twigs as she knelt at Alondra's side. In English, she asked, "Oh, my dear one, what's happened?"

"They're dead!" Alondra whispered hoarsely. "They're all dead."

Giulietta touched fingers soft as wrinkled silk to Alondra's brow. "You burn," she said sympathetically. She looked up to where her two remaining servants stood on the stair. "Help her to bed, Cesare. Maria, call Dr. Serafin. Then bring us some tea and that *torta* from dinner. I'll sit up with her tonight."

✦ · ✦

Alondra woke with a sensation of water inside her head, like swimmer's ear. Tossing onto her side, she hoped the water would just drain out. With dazed affection, she noted Giulietta sleeping in the armchair beside the bed.

Instead of draining from her ear, the infection festered. The pain in her head flickered so vividly she could almost see it as golden, like standing too close to amplified trumpets. Alondra writhed beneath the duvet, disturbing the cats, unable to find comfort.

In the back of her mind, she heard the melody sung at the fantastical church. She picked at the song, trying to learn its tune, anything to distract herself from the swollen burning ache inside her head.

Dawn painted streaks of rose outside the window as bubbles crackled like fireworks behind Alondra's eardrum. The pain crescendoed, nearly unbearable, before liquid dribbled from her ear. She fainted.

When she woke again, watery blood streaked her pillowcase. Giulietta had gone from the chair and the cats guarding her had changed. Pain ramped up in her left ear, so Alondra flung herself onto that side and implored her eardrum to rupture already.

+ · +

Alondra bolted awake, disoriented and dizzy. As Giulietta spoke, her words seemed to come from a great distance. "This is Dr. Serafin. He will help."

The doctor had striking black eyes, fringed with velvet lashes. He set an old-fashioned black bag down on the armchair where Giulietta had spent the night. Alondra whispered, "*Buongiorno*." Her voice sounded loud inside her skull.

"*Buongiorno*," the doctor replied.

"I can't really hear you," Alondra said. "I think my eardrums burst. But I can read lips."

He rubbed his hands together, warming his fingers before he touched her forehead.

"The fever has not broken. I will give you something to bring it down."

He squatted down to insert an instrument into her right ear. Alondra appreciated that he didn't make her sit up. Even lying still gave her vertigo.

He touched her face gently so she would watch his lips. He spoke slowly so she could understand. "I see small punctures in your eardrums. They allow the fluid to drain. This used to happen all the time before antibiotics." He smiled reassuringly. "Allow Giulietta to fuss over you and take the pills I give you. You will be well soon."

As the doctor repacked his bag, Alondra asked, "The bodies...?"

His head snapped toward her. "What did you say?"

"Last night I saw ... perhaps I hallucinated ... a canal full of bodies. As if a hundred people drowned."

He took her hand. "This is true. This was why I couldn't come to you sooner. Rio di Santa Caterina was choked with corpses."

Alondra shuddered. "How did they die?"

"Drowning," the doctor said. "We don't know why."

The doctor touched her face again so she would look up. "Do not to worry about this. Sleep, get well, and try to erase this horror from your mind."

+ · +

Giulietta roused her to drink some broth and take her pills. Congestion prevented Alondra from guessing the broth's flavor. Her hearing had become entirely internal. Every swallow was full of gurgling like the tide going out.

Drinking the broth exhausted Alondra. She curled up and surrendered to sleep again.

The siren's lament wove through her dreams. *The others were gone. The others were at peace now.* Why hadn't she gone with them? Tears welled under her closed lids.

Alondra wrenched herself awake. Ringing filled her head, different pitches in each ear.

She tottered to the window, praying that the view would distract her. On the Grand Canal below stretched a parade of gondolas. Each shiny black boat held a long wooden box.

Seagulls wheeled above the procession. Alondra could not hear their screams.

The gondoliers must be ferrying the siren's victims to San Michele in Isola, the island where Venice buried all of its dead.

So many caskets floated by. Alondra didn't count them. She stood witness, a pallid spirit in a white nightdress at the Gothic window of a 15th-century palazzo.

She had no tears left for the unknown dead. They were beyond her help now. Even if she had her full strength, she wouldn't dare go to the graveyard and ask the ghosts what she might do for them. The weight of all that pain, grief, and hunger would blow her out like a candle.

After *vaporettos* full of mourners passed, reflections danced on the wavelets, colors muted by the mist curtaining the sun.

Alondra returned to bed.

What could she do? Something evil had happened, something she'd accidentally observed. However the singer caused the audience's despair, whatever magic had been in her song, Alondra had escaped. She wondered if she was the only survivor.

She tried to envision the congregation leaving the church. They must have come out soon after she fled. Had they taken their leave of each other, kissed one another goodbye? Or had they simply filed to the canal and flung themselves into the gelid water?

Where was the Christian god to prevent the suicides? Why had he allowed the siren to sing in his house? Why hadn't he intervened?

Alondra shivered under the duvet, tossing so fitfully that the cats sought peace elsewhere. The soprano stalked her dreams. Alondra remembered the shining white garment she wore, like a goddess on a Roman urn. Had she seen Alondra leave the church? Would she come after her, after Giulietta? Alondra was so weak now; it would be better to capitulate than to fight.

✦ · ✦

Giulietta brought a tray of tea and toast. Alondra ate dutifully, but the sound her teeth made as she crunched the toast filled her head with ominous rumbling.

"Do they know why they died?" she asked.

Giulietta examined Alondra's face, gauging what she was strong enough to hear. "No," the old woman said at last. "There were people from every walk of life: shopkeepers, charity wives, fishermen… They had nothing in common."

"They were all at a church somewhere in the Cannaregio, the night I got sick. It had a balcony with stone drapery. There was a woman … a creature … who sang to them."

"You were there?"

"This infection," — Alondra waved toward one ear — "I think it saved my life."

"Then let us count your blessings," Giulietta said. "I have heard of these things, these women who sing people to their deaths."

"This has happened before?"

"Oh, yes. Three times that I know. When I was a little girl, at the end of World War I, the authorities said it was the flu that killed them, but it was not. Years later, they blamed a bomb, then invisible gas… Each time there were rumors of a woman in a shining white dress with a golden ornament upon her shoulder. *La Sirena.*"

"What is she?" Alondra asked.

"That would have been a question for your guardian," Giulietta said, gently patting Alondra's hand. "Victor would have consulted his books and found the answer and discovered how to fight it. We are left with guesswork and rumors. If it's the same woman, she must be immortal. Or else there are several women, one a generation, trained to lead people to take their own lives."

"But why?" Alondra whispered, sinking back to the bed. "There were children in that church, widows… What could anyone have against them?"

"Perhaps simply that they were Venetian. Perhaps the vendetta is against the city itself."

Giulietta smoothed tangled flame-orange hair back from Alondra's eyes. "You must not worry about this. There are some evils in the world that are too ancient to fight. To them we are candle flames — *phfft* — too easy to blow out. You must do what you can do; this is what Victor taught you. Save your strength for the battles you must fight, fight with all your mind and all your heart... but you cannot win every battle. In the end, you must not mourn those you cannot save."

After the old woman had gone, Alondra considered Giulietta's final words. Alondra had been mourning Victor, dead now six weeks. She'd done everything in the world that she could think of to save his life, made every bargain, cast every spell, but in the end — in pain, exhausted — he'd crossed the threshold with a smile on his face, anticipating those he loved awaiting him.

She'd spent all her strength battling Death for him, then she'd spent the last six weeks mourning her failure. Victor was certain he'd gone to a better place. And she, however miserable she made herself, could not throw her life away just to join him. If nothing else, he hadn't invited her to.

Alondra rolled onto her left side and stared at what she could see of the sky. The fog swirled and eddied, a vortex that drew her out of herself, out of her sick weak body and into her stubborn, determined center where she could puzzle over the Siren without distraction.

Sirens were first mentioned in Homer's *Odyssey*. The sorceress Circe warned Odysseus to stop up the ears of his men with beeswax, lest the sirens seduce the sailors to their deaths. Odysseus directed his men to bind him to the mast so he could listen to the sirens' song, knowing that it would suck the joy from his life, that he had "no prospect of coming home and delighting his wife and children."

In some tales, after Odysseus and his men escaped them, the sirens flung themselves into the sea and drowned in a fit of pique. That implied that the sirens were mortal and could be outwitted. Stopped. Perhaps, as Giulietta suggested, there was not a single woman, but a chain of them, taking revenge slowly on the city that had wronged them.

Odysseus' advantage was that he knew the sirens' isle lay ahead. He could protect his men. Maybe, Alondra thought sleepily, that was her role in this tale: to be the Circe who warned the next generation of Venetians before the vendetta came due once more. Perhaps she could end it forever. Maybe she had a purpose here after all.

+ · +

A generation later, the train no longer ran out to the historic part of Venice. Its causeway lay submerged beneath the surface of the lagoon, a hazard to navigation. The Venetians-in-exile refused to demolish it, to concede that *la Serenissima* would not be stolen back from the sea. Paolo, whose father — God rest him — had been a gondolier in Alondra's youth, pointed the tracks out to her as they followed them in his little motorboat.

The city still rose out of the lagoon like something from a dream. Most of it lay abandoned, inhabited only during the day by tourists. Life in the crumbling buildings had been challenging before, but now, with the lowest floor of every building under a foot or more of saltwater, living quarters were accessible only by partially-submerged staircases. Most residents that stayed slept on yachts moored to their ancient palazzos.

Water filled the city streets so that there were few places boatmen could not go. Only the highest bridges rose above the waterline, islands in themselves, bridging nothing. Paolo handed over his handkerchief with a complicated smile. Alondra wiped tears from her cheeks.

She had an appointment with Casio, a mad musical genius who recorded the creaks and gasps of Venice in its death throes. She'd heard his music via the internet, told him what she needed, and he promised to be ready. Based on the timing of the previous attacks, Alondra figured they had three days.

She recalled her last visit with Giulietta, more than two decades ago, so soon after Victor's death. Stumbling upon the Siren's concert had changed Alondra's life. She thought back over the adventures she'd had, the wonders she'd seen, the creatures she had come to fight because of the monster in the Cannaregio. The Siren had inadvertently given Alondra's life purpose: to protect as many people as she could from creatures they could not defend themselves against. She had inspired Alondra to become a champion.

+ · +

While Paolo spread word of the recital to the remaining denizens of the city, Alondra and Casio rappelled from inside St. Mark's, mounting public address speakers to the bases of the domes. They built a small stage from scavenged lumber in front of the chancel. Casio had Alondra stand upon it, singing pop songs and anything else that came into her head as he learned the acoustics of the cathedral.

Alondra careened between worry that her calculations had been wrong and the Siren would not come, and dread that she had been right and was luring all who remained in Venice to their deaths.

As late afternoon fog swallowed Venice, Alondra assumed her place in the rickety gallery above the flooded sanctuary. Casio played one of his compositions while Venetians arrived in little motorboats, rowboats, kayaks, and a pair of scuffed gondolas. Each boat brought a pitch-soaked torch to light the cathedral, sparking the 13th-century mosaics to life.

If *La Sirena* harbored any suspicions about having been led to St. Mark's Basilica, they didn't ruffle her serene exterior as she ascended the makeshift stage. Alondra marveled again at the shining white garment that accented the creature's curves, giving grandeur and mystery to her body. She did indeed look like a goddess of antiquity.

The accompanist was a hunched crone now. Still, she somehow summoned enough wind to play her flute. The recital soared, even lovelier than Alondra remembered. With clearer hearing, she appreciated the crystalline purity of the Siren's high notes, the controlled depth of her lows. The voice spanned four octaves effortlessly, no seams between the registers.

The Venetians appreciated the performance, too. They cheered, encouraging, enthusiastic, but not with the hysteria that Alondra had witnessed so many years ago. Casio's sonic magic was working.

Alondra didn't understand the finer points of the electronics, beyond that Casio's recorder analyzed the frequencies of the vocal performance, graphing them as it committed them to memory. Simultaneously, his sound generator flipped the frequencies and broadcast their inverse through the public address system.

The audience could hear the Siren's voice, lovely as it was, but the extra-auditory control frequencies — the tones beyond hearing she used to manipulate her listeners to despair and suicide — were canceled out. Alondra could not have been more pleased. She'd staked too many lives, her own included, on the recording engineer's skill.

Alondra lifted her opera glasses to study the siren's gold brooch. As she'd suspected, the tightly coiled spiral unraveled to reveal a mermaid with a sinuous tail. And the Siren was the exact same woman Alondra had seen twenty-five years ago: un-aged, undiminished, her hair as luxuriant and black.

The Siren lifted her gaze. A smile flickered across that cold, self-assured face. Alondra nodded, acknowledging the recognition.

The Siren sang the same program as before. The audience grew increasingly impressed, although without histrionics. Amused, the Siren added extra flourishes, additional arpeggios. In contrast, her accompanist struggled and sweated, pressed to the limits of her skill to keep up.

At last the performance ended. The Venetians' ovation thundered back from the domes. *La Sirena* inclined her head and did not move from the stage. When it became clear she would grant no encore, the Venetians turned their boats and filed out through the basilica's doors, taking their torches with them into the deep black night.

Alondra ignited her flashlight and crept carefully down the stone stair from the women's gallery. Paolo's boat was not waiting at the foot. She sat on the steps, unconcerned. He and Casio probably had equipment to pack up.

The ancient basilica reverberated with the lapping of tiny wavelets against its marble-faced walls. Alondra had the sense that something moved in the night, but it was not the malevolence she remembered. This was melancholy embodied. Snuffing her light, she crab-walked back up the stair, out of reach of the water.

"I'm the last of my kind," the Siren said from somewhere below, her Italian strangely accented. "You have murdered me." She sounded perversely glad.

"I don't require you to follow the ancient ways," Alondra told the darkness. "All I ask is that you cease your vendetta against the people of *la Serenissima*."

Something large splashed in the cavernous basilica. The echoes took forever to subside.

Moonlight filtered through the windows in the domes, reflecting cold radiance from the spectacular golden ceiling. Alondra shivered in the damp old church, which — though it appeared to be vacant — was not quite empty.

The long cold night gave Alondra plenty of time to think. Over the years, she had set foot inside many churches. She'd dealt with a spectrum of Christians, even loved a few. Their faith told them that sometimes a witch could work God's will. She had seen nothing to disprove that, but she wasn't comfortable being used by anyone, even a god.

When dawn finally came, Alondra found four bodies floating in the hip-deep water inside the nave. The Siren and her accompanist she expected. Casio did not surprise her— listening to the recording had been too much of a temptation for the engineer. Unfortunately, Alondra had needed him too much to tie him to the mast.

Paolo's death saddened her, though. He still wore the headphones Casio lent him, plugged into the recorder. Like Odysseus, Paolo chose to hear the Siren's voice unmasked. Knowing what she was, what she wanted, hadn't protected him.

Four dead, rather than 100, and these would be the last: that counted as a triumph.

Alondra waded through the chilly waters, careful not to slip on the submerged floor. She fumbled the Siren's corpse into Paolo's little motorboat.

As she motored back to the mainland, Alondra weighted the Siren's corpse with Casio's electronics and dumped the creature into the lagoon. The others would be discovered by the police on their daily patrols.

She would probably never know the source of the vendetta.

✦ · ✦

Inside a crumbling palazzo in the drowning city, a solar-powered hard drive went to sleep.

✦ · ✦

THE ORANGE CAT

by Kelley Armstrong

Kelley Armstrong says: *"The Orange Cat* is my riff on Poe's *The Black Cat*. I wanted to take the same basic plot-line and give it a modern twist, as a case being investigated by the male lead of my Cainsville series. Gabriel Walsh is an unconventional Chicago defense attorney who has some experience with the preternatural, which makes him perfectly suited to tackle the case of a man who really wants his cat dead— and a cat that refuses to comply."

◆ · ◆

"THE KILLING OF THE CAT was unimportant, though not inconsequential," Gabriel said as his aunt walked into the parlor with a pot of tea in one hand and a plate of cookies in the other.

"You'd better not say that in front of a jury."

"That I believe the cat's death played a role in the later crime?" He took a cookie. "Yes, I'm still deciding how to frame that in the defense. It *is* an important factor, yet it may be difficult to explain."

"I meant calling the death of a cat unimportant."

"My client is hardly on trial for killing an animal. I could bargain that down to a misdemeanor. This is felony murder. But it started with the cat."

"Such things often do."

Gabriel sipped his tea. "It's not that sort of crime, where one begins with small animals, and moves up the food chain. That's a natural progression. The cat? Nothing about the beast was natural."

While she waited for him to continue, he took his time eating his cookie. She glowered. Then he said, "It began two weeks ago..."

+ · +

As Gabriel walked into the office at eight Tuesday morning, he hung out his shingle. That was the common phrase for it, derived from the Old West, when lawyers and doctors would use shingles as business signs. Of course, in 2007 one didn't hang out a real shingle. One put a brass plate on the door or a discreet sign in the lobby. Unless one was a new lawyer who time-shared the space and literally had to hang out his sign when he started work for the day.

Gabriel Walsh had passed the bar two years ago. To have his own office already did not speak of a brilliant career. It spoke of failure, of being unable to find a position in a law firm and hanging out a shingle in hopes of bringing in clients foolish enough to hire a twenty-five-year-old barrister. Or it did if one actually wanted a position in a firm. Gabriel did not. When he'd finished interning for Mike Quinlan, the man *had* offered him a job. And had breathed an undisguised sigh of relief when Gabriel refused.

"I had to ask," Quinlan said. "You're fucking brilliant, and I'd be a fool not to try. But..."

He didn't need to finish that sentence. Gabriel knew what he was. Cold, ruthless and unscrupulous. Also driven, tireless and ambitious. That made him an exemplary defense attorney. It did not make him someone even Mike Quinlan wanted on staff. What Gabriel wanted was Quinlan's title: Most Notorious Defense Attorney in Chicago. And most successful.

Step one toward achieving that goal was hanging out his shingle in this rented office. Step two would be getting his *own* office. He could afford one. He'd put himself through law school running a gambling ring, where he'd played all the roles, from bookie to loan shark to enforcer— Gabriel did not work well with others. It'd been far more profitable than law, meaning he could easily find the money to rent an office. Yet he'd set his sights on purchasing one of the historic greystones on this very street. The neighborhood was safe and quiet and within a short walk of the Cook County Jail. Until he could justify such a purchase to the IRS, he would share this office. The rent was cheap, which could be explained primarily by the faint chemical smell wafting up from the basement. Gabriel pretended not to notice, promised he would never be in the office between sundown and sunrise, and offered pro bono legal advice to the owner, all of which resulted in a very low monthly rent.

Gabriel had just settled at his desk when a man walked in. Mid-forties. Average height. Above-average weight. Balding. Dressed in a department store suit. In other words, strikingly ordinary.

Seeing Gabriel, the man stepped back out the still-open door and checked the sign.

"Uh, you're… waiting for Mr. Walsh?" he asked Gabriel.

"I *am* Mr. Walsh."

Gabriel rose and the man's gaze rose with him. Then the man stepped back again. At six-four, Gabriel wasn't simply tall— he was big. Not overweight, though it was easy to slide in that direction if he paid too little attention to his diet and exercise.

"Ben said you were, uh, young. Just caught me off guard there." A slightly nervous laugh. "He's the one who recommended you. Benjamin Hall. You helped him out with a problem last year."

By *helped out with a problem,* he meant *got him off on a DUI charge that put a woman in a wheelchair.* It'd been one of Gabriel's finer moments. Not setting free a drunk who'd permanently disabled a mother of four— that was nothing to be proud of. But the case had been turned down by Quinlan himself, who'd deemed it unwinnable. Yet Gabriel had won, which got him his first front-page story, his first hate mail and his first full roster of clients.

"Yes, of course," Gabriel said. Then added, a little belatedly, "How is he?"

He didn't listen to the answer. He didn't care, but this was the expected response, so he made it.

"Now I have a problem," the man continued. "And I'm hoping you can help."

Gabriel waved him to a chair. He did not offer refreshments. There was a difference between civility and servitude.

"It's about a cat," the man said. "I think I might need to kill it."

"I would advise against that." *That'll be one hundred dollars, please, and the door is behind you.*

"*Strongly* advise against it?"

Gabriel considered. While he understood that he shouldn't need to, what he thought was very different, because emotion had no place here. He was a lawyer, not a priest.

"Is the cat a nuisance?"

The man shifted in his seat. "Kind of."

"That is the crux of the matter," Gabriel said. "If the animal is a danger to you or your children or your own pets, then you could argue it is a nuisance animal. The first step, however, would be to contact animal control. I presume it's a stray?"

"No, it's mine."

"Oh. That, I'm afraid, is a whole different matter, falling under the animal cruelty laws. In that case, I would even more strongly suggest animal control."

"I've taken him to the shelter twice. He comes back."

"Ah." Gabriel tapped his pen against his legal pad. "I'm going to need more information then. Why do you wish to get rid of the cat? Is it a health issue? Allergies? Or a financial one, such as medical needs you cannot fulfill?"

"I... just want to get rid of it."

Gabriel waited for a better answer. The man squirmed, then said, "It's bothering me."

"Attacking you? Being abnormally noisy?"

"No, it just... stares at me. I know that sounds..." The man pushed to his feet, and began to pace. "It sounds crazy. But you don't understand. It just sits there and it stares and it stares. One yellow eye, staring at me all the time."

"One?"

The man ran a hand through his hair, upsetting the fine balance of his comb over. "It was a mistake."

"A mistake? You mean the loss of the other eye? You blinded—"

"*Half* blinded. The cat can still see perfectly well. It's not a big deal."

Gabriel was not particularly empathetic. All right, not one bit empathetic. But when the man said that, with a plaintive whine in his voice, it was all Gabriel could do not to say, *And if I blinded you in one eye? Would you consider it 'not a big deal'?* He decided then that he did not like the man. Which had absolutely no bearing on the case— or on his ability to defend him. If it did, Gabriel would have no business at all.

"I was drunk," the man said. "I came home and it was screeching at me, and I get enough of that from my wife. So I had this penknife in my pocket—"

"I understand," Gabriel said, which was not true, but comprehending the reasons for a client's behavior was as unnecessary — and improbable — as liking him. "So you half-blinded the cat and now it follows you about and stares at you accusingly."

"Not *accusingly*," the man said. "It's a cat. It doesn't think that way."

"So after half-blinding it, it randomly follows you about. I can see where that would be disconcerting." *And I don't blame the cat one bit.* "If you wish my legal advice…"

"I do."

Gabriel scratched numbers on his pad and then turned it toward the man. "That would be my fee for the advice. Any further consultations would be an additional charge."

The man hesitated at the amount and then said, "That's fine."

"First, you will provide me with the name of the shelter that took the cat. I will obtain confirmation that you did in fact deliver the animal and that it escaped. In the meantime, you will take the cat to a different shelter, for one last attempt to divest yourself of it." Gabriel hated to make the next suggestion but saw no other reasonable alternative. "If that fails you will do what a shelter would have done if unable to find a home for it— have the animal euthanized by a licensed veterinarian. There is no legal issue with euthanizing a healthy cat, but in the event of any such claim, you have proof of your attempts to get it adopted." While Gabriel could not imagine any legal grounds for complaint, suggesting otherwise would have halved his fee. "Does that sound reasonable?"

"My wife won't like me putting the cat down."

"Then I would suggest you don't tell her." Gabriel took out his writing pad. "Now, if you could provide your personal details and the name of that shelter…"

❖ ∙ ❖

Gabriel made the phone call as soon as the shelter opened for the day. Naturally, the woman who answered did not wish to admit they'd lost the cat— twice. She insisted that the man had been playing some sort of game with them.

"He must have come in and taken the cat out," she said.

"Is that possible? Anyone can simply wander in and open the cages?"

"Of course not, but we're a shelter, not a jail. All I know is that the cat was there when we closed for the night and gone when we opened and Mr. Patton insisted it was on his door-step. Which means not only did it need to open a cage and two locked doors, but it traveled clear across the city in a matter of hours. That is not possible. He must have taken it."

＋ · ＋

The next morning, Gabriel's phone rang almost before he had time to put down his briefcase.

"It came back," Patton said by way of greeting. "I took it all the way out of the damned county and it still came back."

Which was, Gabriel had to admit, odd. Not entirely impossible, despite what the woman from the shelter had said. Still, very improbable.

"You suggested your wife is fond of the cat. Could she be retrieving it from the shelter?"

"I didn't tell her where I was going."

Which did not mean she didn't know, but Gabriel said, "Then do what you must. Just do it properly, at the appropriate facility, and be sure it's documented."

＋ · ＋

Gabriel thought no more of the cat that day. The matter had been dealt with. Naturally, he'd have preferred a conclusion that did not involve the death of an innocent beast. Even more, he'd have preferred a conclusion that didn't involve the death of a wronged beast, since the blinding of the cat gave it every reason to torment Patton. But more desirable steps had failed, and it came to a choice between a painless death and a more terrible conclusion, with Patton losing his temper, as he had that night with the penknife.

Gabriel arrived at the office the second morning after Patton's initial visit to hear the phone ringing. As he unlocked the door, it went to voice mail. Then, as he was removing his jacket, it began to ring again.

Gabriel answered. The voice on the other end rattled off an address. Then, "Get here. Now."

Gabriel recognized Patton more by the home address than his voice, which was thick with rage.

"What has—?"

"I'll pay double your rate. Just get over here, Walsh. Now."

＋ · ＋

Gabriel was not in the habit of taking orders from clients. Of course they tried to give them, as if he was the hired help. Which he was, technically, but the balance of power in any relationship was critical. Being young and inexperienced already tilted it out of his favor. He'd wrench it back any way he could, including ignoring such a summons... unless the client offered him double his rate and he didn't actually have an appointment for three hours.

He arrived at Patton's home, a tiny house in a working-class neighborhood. When he rapped on the front door, Patton called, "Come in!" and Gabriel entered a dark and empty front hall.

"In here!" Patton's voice came from an adjoining room.

Gabriel paused. He did not carry a weapon. He had many — relics of his youth — but they were in his apartment, security talismans, their existence quite humiliating enough. He'd certainly never carry one. His size usually kept him safe and when it didn't? Spending one's teen years living on the streets of Chicago meant one didn't require weapons to fend off a threat.

He still paused, and when he walked into that room, he angled his entry so he would see Patton before he stepped through the doorway. The man sat on a recliner and stared at the coffee table. And on the table? A huge orange cat. With one good eye.

"Explain this." Patton jabbed a finger at the feline and then glowered at Gabriel, as if he'd resurrected the creature himself.

"Are you certain it was euthanized?"

"I stood there while she did it." Patton yanked a paper from his pocket and held it out. "Here's the bill. Euthanization and proper disposal. This" — he waved at the cat — "is not proper disposal."

"Hmm."

"That's your answer?" Patton's voice rose. "My dead cat has come back."

"Yes, that's very odd."

"Odd?"

Patton started raving, spitting and snarling about how 'odd' didn't quite seem adequate to the situation. Gabriel ignored him and walked to the beast. It sat still as a gargoyle, staring at Patton. Gabriel lowered himself to a crouch in front of the animal and it deigned to look at him, yellow eye meeting his and blinking once, as if to say, *Yes, I'm alive.* Then it returned its accusing stare to its owner.

Gabriel reached out carefully, being sure the cat could see his hand moving. He touched the back of its neck. The cat shifted, but didn't otherwise move, too intent on the target of its silent outrage. Gabriel rubbed the cat's neck, feeling the warmth and the pulse of life there.

"Yes, it's clearly alive."

"No fucking kidding it's alive! What did you think it was, a zombie?"

Gabriel had never encountered a zombie, but he did not believe in ruling out any possibility. As for the fact of the cat's return, to Gabriel it was simply a puzzle. There was most likely a logical explanation, and one ought always to consider logic and simplicity first. Yet he would not discount the possibility of a less-than-natural cause either.

The second sight ran in his family— his aunt Rose had it, indubitably. And she lived in a town where gargoyles appeared and disappeared, depending on the weather, the time of day, even the time of year. The world had its mysteries. He accepted that as readily as he accepted the existence of bacteria. He could not see either, but he did see both in action, and that was enough.

"I'm going to kill it," Patton said.

"You already did that. I hardly see the point in repeating the process." Gabriel stood and looked about. "Do you have a carrier of some sort?"

* · *

Gabriel took the orange cat to Cainsville. He'd hoped to speak to his aunt about it. Beyond having the second sight, she was also an expert in matters of folklore and magic. Her car was gone, which meant she'd gone out of town— there was no place within town that required a vehicle. Still, he took the cat to the door and knocked. No one answered. He was putting the carrier back in his car when a voice called from across the road.

"What are doing with that?"

He turned to see Grace perched on the front porch of her three-floor walkup. He did not use the word 'perched' facetiously. Old, wizened and permanently scowling, Grace reminded Gabriel of the town's gargoyles, hunkered down on her stoop, watching for trouble, and never so delighted as when she found it.

"It's a cat," he said.

"I can see that. What are you doing with a cat?"

He took it over to her, primarily to avoid shouting across the roadway.

"Please tell me you aren't giving your aunt a cat," Grace said. "She has about as much use for one as I do. Or you, for that matter. What—?" She peered at the beast in the carrier. "Something's wrong with it."

"Yes, it's missing an eye."

She rolled hers at him. "Obviously. I mean something else."

"Apparently, as of yesterday, it was dead. Then it came back."

"Huh."

"That's what I said. It's somewhat troubling."

Her thin shoulders lifted in a shrug and she said, "It happens." Gabriel couldn't tell if she was joking but decided it best not to pursue an answer.

"What are you going to do with it?"

"Find a place for it, I suppose. It keeps returning to its owner. I thought perhaps if I left it here, in Cainsville, and it appeared in Chicago again, I could be certain unnatural forces were at work."

"Because returning from the dead isn't proof enough?"

"I didn't actually witness the death."

"Well, give it to me, then. Patrick's been looking for a cat. I'll drop it at his place." She smiled. It was not a pleasant smile, and he was quite certain the young local writer had no need of a cat, but if it took the beast off his hands...

He set down the carrier. "And in return?"

Her smile then was genuine. In other places, one might take offense at the suggestion that a favor was not given freely. Cainsville was different. "Two scones and a coffee," she said, and Gabriel nodded and headed off to the diner.

✦ · ✦

When the phone rang at two the next morning, Gabriel was expecting it. Indeed, that's why he'd given Patton his cell number. If the cat returned, Patton was to contact him immediately and Gabriel would be there in twenty minutes, regardless of the time of day or night. Because while Gabriel could tell himself that he simply wanted to know if the cat returned, that promise suggested that, perhaps, he had developed a certain respect for the feline. Far more than he had for Patton. The man was a bully and a coward. There had been plenty of those in Gabriel's life. The cat, however? It was a survivor, and that was to be admired. Despite the possible inconvenience of the hour, Gabriel would intervene to ensure it did not suffer further at Patton's hands.

Then he answered the phone... and discovered there was, perhaps, even more to worry about than the life of a cat.

＋ · ＋

Gabriel arrived at Patton's house twenty minutes later. He sat in his car and watched the crime scene technicians coming and going. Then he climbed out and headed for the front door.

He stepped over the yellow tape and continued up the walk. One young rookie looked over, but made no move to stop Gabriel. If he acted as if he belonged, he was rarely questioned.

He climbed the steps and went into the house. He found a crime scene tech — a girl no older than him — and said, "Gabriel Walsh. I'll be handling the case. Can you tell me what happened here?"

The woman nodded, presuming he meant he was with the State's Attorney's Office. Not a lie. Simply misdirection.

"Vic was found over there." She pointed at the blood spray on the sofa. "And the other vic was supposedly there." She waved below a dent in the wall.

"The second victim being the cat, I presume."

"Yeah. The perp woke up with the cat sitting on his head-board, staring down at him. He said some nonsense about the cat being dead or in some other town. I don't know. Anyway, he chases the cat out, saying he's going to kill it. Wife goes after him. She sees him throw the poor thing against the wall and totally freaks. Then he goes ballistic on her. Killed her with a penknife. A *penknife*. Can you believe it? Coroner lost count of the stab wounds."

She shook her head. Gabriel walked to the dent in the wall. He could see orange fur embedded in it. He bent and noted the dark stains on the carpet.

"And the cat?"

"Well, he swore the poor thing was dead. Said its head was all bashed in. Hell, he said he stomped on it, just to be sure. Sick son of a bitch."

"Did someone take the cat's body?"

"Wasn't one to take. By the time we got here, it was gone. Apparently, the crushed kitty got up and walked away."

＋ · ＋

The orange cat was on the back porch. It sat there, patiently waiting for the people inside to leave and for its target to return.

Gabriel crouched in front of the beast. Its jaw seemed off-kilter, as if it had been broken and healed badly. When Gabriel put out his hand, the cat let him rub its neck and he verified it was, indeed, warm and breathing.

"You know he isn't coming back," Gabriel said.

The cat gave him a level look, as if it realized that was the theory, but was not yet convinced it was necessarily fact.

Gabriel shook his head, rose and headed back to his car.

＋ · ＋

"Your client is crazy, Walsh," Assistant State's Attorney Pena said as they left the prison two days later.

"Would you care to state that opinion for the record?"

Pena snorted. "It wouldn't matter if I did, considering he's refusing to cooperate with a psych eval." They walked from the building. "If you can't get him to bargain, he's screwed. You know that, right?"

Unfortunately, Gabriel did know that. Patton may have hired him as his counsel, but he wasn't actually taking counsel. He refused to plead diminished capacity. He refused to consider a plea bargain. He insisted on being tried by a jury of his peers, convinced they would understand.

"I'll speak to him," Gabriel said.

＋ · ＋

First, Gabriel had to bribe the guards. That was easy enough. It wasn't as if he was trying to smuggle in an automatic weapon. They'd rolled their eyes, said "Whatever," and held out their hands. Bribery was usually a simple matter. The tricky part was figuring out how to include the expense on a client's bill.

Gabriel sat across the table from Patton after the guards bought him in. He laid out the terms of the plea bargain— what the State's Attorney's Office offered and what Gabriel thought he could negotiate down to from there.

"You're wasting your breath, Walsh," Patton said. "I'm going to a jury. They'll understand. I killed that cat because—"

Gabriel put the pet carrier on the table. The orange cat peered through the wires at Patton, who backed up fast, chair legs screeching across the floor. The guards made no move to interfere. They'd been well compensated for their inattention.

"You did not kill the cat," Gabriel said.

"Th-then this seals it, right? I can show them the cat and prove that—"

"That it came back from the dead? No. There's no way to prove this is the cat you allegedly killed, and the SA would simply accuse me of a very poor trick." Gabriel adjusted the carrier so the cat could better see its quarry. "Do you know where I found it? At your home. Waiting for you." Gabriel looked at Patton. "Would you like me to try for bail again?"

"What?"

"Pursuing your bail request. Would you like me—"

"You said the cat was at my house. Not here."

"Of course. It can hardly come in here. Security would remove it. It will be at your house, waiting for you. Not that I'd suggest you allow that to influence your decision. It is, after all, simply a cat."

Patton glowered at him for at least a full minute. Then he unhinged his jaw just enough to say, "What was the deal again?"

✦ · ✦

Later that day, Gabriel returned the cat to Patton's house. He opened the carrier on the front porch. The cat came out, sniffed and planted itself in front of the door.

"He's not coming back," Gabriel said. "He took the plea bargain. He'll be in jail for a very long time."

The cat looked at him.

"You don't need to wait."

The cat seemed to consider. Then it rose, stretched and trotted down the steps onto the sidewalk. It took one last look at the house, head tilted, as if committing it to memory, planning to return when the time came. Then it headed off down the street and disappeared.

✦ · ✦

"I would have made more if it had gone to trial," Gabriel said, with deep regret, as he took a bite of his second cookie. "But I couldn't have won the case, and I decided my reputation was better served with a decent plea bargain."

"It is justice," Rose said. "For his wife... and for the cat."

"Hmm." That was, of course the least of his concerns. He was simply glad he'd insisted Patton wire him the money before sealing the plea bargain. The man had not been otherwise inclined to pay his bill.

"Do you think the cat's gone for good, then?"

"I doubt it." He took the last cookie from the plate. "It's a very patient cat."

+ · +

THE INHERITANCE

by Jane Petersen Burfield

Jane Petersen Burfield says: "The raven of the poem, with his raspy, sonorous voice cawing *nevermore*, has both fascinated and terrified me since I first read it in grade school. Poe led me into reading horror stories which was not helpful when I tried to get to sleep. I felt haunted in my grandparents' house, — like my protagonist — and lived there in fear of the dark. Writing a contemporary story that referred back to the darkness and magic of Poe captures my personal experience."

＋ · ＋

"ARE YOU ALRIGHT, MADAM?"
Slowly I opened my eyes, squinting against the shards of light. "What happened?"

"I heard a thump as I was passing the library and saw you lying on the floor. Can you get up?"

I tried to nod my head and winced. "Just give me a minute." When I opened my eyes again his sharp-nosed face hung over mine, anchored to a black tailcoat.

I was surrounded by piles of books, and above me faded leather spines showed along the shelves. Corbett hauled me up, showing surprising strength for such an old man, and guided me to the high-backed wing chair beside the window and then opened the velvet curtains. My shoulder hurt like hell but I leaned back and hoped the pain would ease.

"Shall I call the doctor, Madam?"

"No thanks, Corbett. I'm fine. And you've known me all my life. You don't need to keep calling me madam."

"I have always called my employer 'Madam'. Shall I get you some tea?"

"Thank you."

Corbett was old school and believed that tea fixed everything from broken bones to brain tumors. Aunt Eleanor believed that too.

He disappeared out the door, the dusty black of his clothes following him like a shadow.

What had happened? I reached for a book and turned abruptly at the noise— that same ominous tapping and scraping I remembered from my childhood visits. The noise that screeched into my nightmares. But I had always heard the frightening sounds after sunset, never in daylight. What really chilled me was that no one else ever heard them, not my mother, and certainly not my detestable cousins who teased me mercilessly about my night terrors. "It's such an old house," Aunt Eleanor said once, stroking my hair. And here I was, back again in the old family home, sorting out her estate. With the too-familiar terror stalking me in the library.

How I yearned for my best friend Liz to arrive, bringing her robust laughter, her practicality, her quiet understanding. I didn't want to be alone here with just Corbett, who lived in his quarters off the kitchen. Maybe taking this on had been a horrible mistake.

A few minutes later, I heard tapping coming up the hall. I tensed, but it was only Corbett bringing the tea, his cane hitting the wooden planks rhythmically. I wondered how old he was. Would he retire, now that he had a legacy from Aunt Eleanor? Her Will specified that he could stay until he moved out, or was carried out feet first. Of course it was his decision but I wasn't sure how I could deal with this old place without him.

I sipped my tea and after he left resumed sorting. I couldn't resist leafing through a few pages and my vision blurred with tears as I recognized my aunt's bold rounded handwriting in the margins of her favorite poetry selections. Shoved at the back of one shelf I found a slim leather journal with a note in a jagged script quite unlike hers. The page was ink-stained and difficult to read, but I could make out the words: '*I shall hide the remains of my precious treasure... a pearl beyond price!...*'
And written quite clearly at the bottom and underlined twice:
Unkindness will not go unpunished!

As children, my cousins and I had heard the adults talk about hidden treasure here at Mooreland. We spent hours hunting for pirates' gold, digging holes in the ground, climbing up into the dusty attics. I was twelve when Aunt Eleanor took me aside and told me that not all treasures are of gold. She showed me a miniature of Edgar Allan Poe with his signature scrawled at the bottom. "He's a distant cousin, you know, and he visited here one summer, about 1830, if I recall correctly. The story goes, he left behind a leather-bound journal, but no one has ever found it. Can't you just imagine him sitting there at Great Great Grandfather's old desk, scratching away by candlelight?" I could imagine it all too well. I had always felt a darkness in this room.

I stood, stretched, and walked to the casement window. Dark birds were circling above the old graveyard behind the spiked iron fence on the west side of the house. They were probably ravens. My birdwatcher father told me this was not their natural territory but he believed they had migrated here in the first half of the nineteenth century. My father told me many things, most of which belonged more to the realms of dreams than reality.

After a day among the dusty shelves, I was relieved to get back to my room. Even the simple dinner served by Corbett in the shadowed dining room was not exactly relaxing. I wanted desperately to talk to Lizzie. I curled up on the old sleigh bed and dialed her number.

"How's the decluttering going?" Her cheerful voice made me feel better immediately.

"So many memories, Liz. When will you get here?"

"Hopefully, Thursday. Getting this rambunctious brood settled takes some doing, you know, and Andy hates it when I go away. You okay?"

"I will be when you get here."

"How were your nasty cousins at the funeral?"

"They are horrible, greedy vultures!" I burst out, making her laugh. "They didn't even bother coming to the church but they showed up for the reading of the Will. You should have seen them when the lawyer read out the bequests. And I thought they would explode when he explained about the living legacy for Corbett."

"What happened when they heard you inherited the house?"

"Oh Lizzie, it was awful! Although in a way it was glorious seeing them so worked up. The Unbearable Twins actually accused me of manipulating Aunt Eleanor into changing her Will. As if I would put in that bit about having to live here for three years, like some pathetic woman in a Victorian novel, complete with a butler right out of Masterpiece Theatre! They kept saying she had *promised*, sounding like two year olds. Anyway, they assured me they'd contest the Will and by the time it was over they were looking daggers at me. I don't know why Aunt Eleanor would leave all this to me."

"She probably thought you were special, Ellie."

"Yeah. So special I'm broke and unemployed!"

"Well, you've got a full time job now! See you Thursday."

⁜ · ⁜

I stood at the bedroom window shivering as I closed the curtains against the encroaching darkness. At night the trees seemed to crawl across the rolling lawns, edging closer and closer to the house. I slipped into one of the flannelette nighties I'd brought along to ward off the draughts of the house, and then climbed into bed, only to realize I had nothing to read. *Just a quick trip down the hall to the library*, I told myself, *pick a book and back to bed. Nothing to it!* If I was going to live here for three years I had better get over my childish fears.

I opened my door to find Corbett going up the hall. I jumped back inside and waited for the tapping of his cane to be muffled by the worn carpet on the stair treads. The light died and in another half minute I figured he was back in his own quarters.

The hall was deep in shadows but ambient light from the bright moon shone through the window at the far end. The house felt colder in the dark and I hurried along the runner to the library and switched on the light. The wall sconces glowed but barely penetrated the overriding gloom. Across the room above the fireplace, a gilt mirror reflected the feeble illumination, throwing back the wavering image of a pale oval face with long dark hair straggling over narrow shoulders. I stifled a cry, then instantly realized it was *my* face. *Grab a book and go!* I told myself severely.

This was not the time to be picky. As I snatched a well-read volume of Jules Verne's *Journey to the Center of the Earth*, I heard it. Cold fear paralyzed me and I dropped the book. Panicked, my eyes scanned for the source as the scraping raised goose-bumps on my arms. "No!" I stumbled to the door, wrenched it open and ran right into Corbett.

"Madam? Is anything wrong?" he asked, steadying me.

"I... no... Yes! I heard a noise. Did you hear anything?"

"Nothing, Madam." He stepped back, leaving me to stand on my own.

"I'm sorry, Corbett. I thought I heard that scraping noise that used to scare me when I was a child."

"Never mind, Miss Ellie. I'll walk you to your room."

As I climbed into bed and pulled the duvet around me pro-tectively, I wondered what was waiting for me in the library. Something dark flickered in my memory, and then was gone. I closed my eyes and prayed for sleep.

＊ · ＊

The next day the library was filled with sunshine. Exhausted from a sleepless night, I went back to sorting, cataloguing and re-shelving.

It was nearly noon when Corbett appeared. "Peter Moore called earlier, Madam. He and his brother wish to visit this afternoon, if that would be convenient."

The Unbearables! I didn't want to see them on the best of days and this was not my best day. "Please tell them I'm not available."

Corbett cocked his head to one side and gave me an intense stare. "Very well, Madam."

Around 4:00 pm I heard the deep chime of the front door, followed by Peter's loud, bullying voice demanding to see me. Then Jake, equally aggressive but speaking with a higher pitch that set my teeth on edge said, "Get out of the way, old man! We have a right to come in!"

"I think not, sir." Corbett's voice, cold as an Arctic breeze. But seriously, what could he do if they pushed past him?

I grabbed my cell phone and headed into the hallway. Suddenly, what sounded like a loud blast of wind welled from the front hall, rising in pitch until I wanted to cover my ears. I peered over the banister and saw my red-faced cousins back-ing out the door, Corbett nowhere in sight. I rushed to the window in time to see their green Porsche speeding down the long driveway leaving a cloud of dust behind. Suddenly from the trees a swarm of ravens swooped down and followed the car, as if chasing after it.

+ · +

The following morning the aroma of bacon beckoned me to the kitchen. Hot coffee dripped through the coffeemaker and Corbett was slicing a grapefruit in half. I welcomed this touch of normalcy.

But could I live in this mausoleum for three whole years? Could I endure constant bullying from the Unbearables for money they neither needed nor deserved? And more, could I stay sane amidst the terrifying sounds that only I could hear? And what would I do with myself when I'd finished with the library? I seriously doubted there would be work available in the small village for a librarian. The lawyer said it would take a few months to sort through my aunt's various investments so I wouldn't know the exact size of my inheritance for awhile.

After breakfast, I took my coffee and my worries upstairs and sat down at the old desk in the library. The fold-down desk top hid pigeon holes, small drawers and narrow recesses crammed with documents and old correspondence. There were more drawers under the desk top. And, the family rumor had it, a hidden compartment, though I couldn't find it.

I started sorting letters, cards, bills, receipts, some going back many decades. It was easy to get sidetracked by details, like finding the hand-written survey of the land dated 1802, and the plans for the conservatory addition which I was sure was even earlier, but there was no date. There was an old newspaper article cut from the *Village Bugler* newspaper about local birds and legends. *Crows and Ravens were known in this area in the early days, when the land was settled, but had abandoned the region by the turn of the previous century,* I read. *It is rumored they reclaimed their territory sometime around the 1830s...* So my father had been right. I wished he was still with us so I could show him the article.

That afternoon, the appraiser came by, but he was unimpressed with most of the furniture or paintings, apart from the Poe miniature. He mentioned a dip in the silver market, and swore that in the current economy it would be difficult to find a buyer for the Regency dueling pistols. But he gleefully announced that the desk in the library was a real treasure.

'Mid-eighteenth century Chippendale,' he claimed, beaming. I could hear Aunt Eleanor: *Can't you just imagine Mr. Poe sitting at this desk, his quill scratching by candlelight...*

After the appraiser left, the sun came out again, pushing back the shadows, and I worked through the rest of the day. By the time Corbett announced dinner, I felt as if I was finally getting a handle on things.

✦ · ✦

That night I awoke from a troubled sleep to the familiar scratching that left me cold with fear. I climbed out of bed, wrapped myself in the duvet and crept into the hall. Light seeped from under the library door. Strangely, this gave me courage. I tip-toed closer. Rustling noises came from inside, almost overpowered by the keening only I could hear. I flung the door open. The Unbearable Twins, dressed like ninjas in black clothing, leapt away from the desk, startled. Peter clutched something dark in his hand.

"What the hell are you doing here?" I shouted.

Peter straightened to his full height and squared his shoulders. "Who do you think you are, shutting us out of our inheritance!"

"How dare you! You're breaking into *my* house! How did you get in, anyway?"

"Wouldn't you like to know," sneered Jake.

"Get out!"

"Not without what we came for. We want the Will."

"Yeah, the *real* one," Jake added, "that spells out what *we're owed*."

"Get out before I call the police!"

"Go ahead," Peter said. He flicked his hand in dismissal in my direction and two black feathers sailed towards me.

I screamed and jumped back.

The room shimmered and tilted, the light graying. A huge ornate bird cage with the door hanging open appeared...

"Annabel!" I cried.

Great Aunt Ida had raised that raven with the damaged wing from babyhood, keeping it in the Victorian cage. And I had been given the hateful task of looking after the creature with midnight wings one summer. I was afraid of birds, and this one was smart and had grown large. It seemed to take pleasure in frightening me with sudden weird caws. But I carried out my duties... until that day...

A grey shadow… Annabel, at the window… black feathers insanely beating the glass… talons scratching… caws like shrieks… the air flecked with crimson…

I screamed again and the world snapped back into the present. To the laughter of my cousins.

"You!" I shouted, pointing at the twins. "You killed Annabel!" I picked up the two black feathers that must have been hidden all this time in a secret drawer of the old desk.

"You're crazy!" Peter took two steps towards me, then paused. Corbett was at my side.

"Shall I call the police, Madam?" Corbett held up an old flip phone enquiringly.

The two brushed past him, down the stairs and out the front door.

"How do you think they got in?" I asked Corbett.

"They looked rather dusty, Madam. I suspect they came down the coal chute, as they used to as boys. I shall see to it the chute is blocked."

"Thanks. Corbett. By the way, do you remember Annabel?"

"That was a most unhappy incident a long time ago. I will see you to your room, Madam."

I suddenly felt very childish as I walked beside him the few steps back to my room. The coal chute. The nerve of those two! I sat down by the window. The trees kept their distance tonight, but the moon was bright. A dark shape caught my eye. It glided from the side yard and soared around the house. My father told me that most birds don't fly at night, just owls and nighthawks. This looked like neither and was too large to be a bat. By now it was gone anyway. How odd.

Seconds later I heard the front door slam shut, the series of locks clicking into place.

❖ · ❖

The next morning I prepared the second bed in my room for Lizzie. I'd been longing to see her but, to my surprise, wasn't as desperate as I'd been a few days earlier.

Liz arrived just before five. As we were having a drink before dinner, I told her about the latest escapade of the Unbearables, omitting my visions of Annabel.

"Surprisingly daring for those two cowards," she remarked. "Anyway I'm here now. They'd better not try anything like that again."

"My tough bff!"
"Damn right!"

✦ · ✦

Later on as we lay in bed, Liz was filled with all sorts of practi-
cal ideas about what I could do with the house if I insisted on
staying: conference center for small groups; Bed and Breakfast;
historical house and garden tours— once I'd restored the place
to its former glory.

She was gently snoring when I heard a ragged cawing. I got
up to look out the window; dark birds that I felt certain were
ravens wheeled overhead in the moonlight. I heard the front
door open and shut and watched Corbett walk across the lawn
to stand in the deep shadow of the tree at the cemetery gate
until he seemed to fade into the darkness. I was fascinated as the
birds swooped over the rooftop then back over the graveyard in
acrobatic flight, seeming to dance together, following the alpha.

For the first time I felt comforted by birds. I sensed that they
were protecting the house, and the graveyard. I glanced at the
two black feathers lying on my dressing table. Quietly, I slipped
on my robe and slippers and picked up the feathers, then headed
down the stairs and outside.

Shrubs and gravestones formed distorted shadows in the
moonlit cemetery. A subtle hint of decaying vegetation scented
the air. The mound of Aunt Eleanor's grave, beside her parents'
graves, was still high, raw earth and dead flowers. Around her
lay sisters and brothers, aunts and one uncle. Farther back grandparents, great-grandparents, and here and there, a child's grave
marked by a grieving stone cherub. I knelt beside Aunt Eleanor's
headstone and touched it. "I think I know why you left me this
place. You want to force me to face my fears, to remember and
understand. I'm getting there, Auntie. Thanks." I laid the two
feathers amongst the flowers and moved away.

I heard a rustling of leaves and stepped into the deeper shadow
where I froze behind an oak trunk, hoping I couldn't be seen.

Corbett emerged into the moonlight and moved to Aunt
Eleanor's grave. He reached down and picked up the feathers,
then turned and walked along the narrow path farthest from the
gate and stopped in front of Great Aunt Ida's grave. There, he
crouched down and buried the feathers in the leaves and dirt.

I turned away, embarrassed to be spying on him. Of course the feathers belonged to Great Aunt Ida! She had loved Annabel. When I looked again, Corbett was gone.

I shivered, my feet cold, my arms covered in goosebumps. I ran back into the house, up the stairs, and... there was Corbett, coming out of the library, smoothing his butler's coat!

"Corbett! You startled me. I thought I saw you outside just now."

"How could I be outside, Madam? I was closing the library window."

I went to my room and opened the door quietly, but Liz stirred. "Everything alright?" she asked sleepily.

"Fine. Just fine."

＊ · ＊

My dreams that night were intense but when I finally woke, all I remembered was a sense of motion, the rising and falling sound of the wind wailing like sirens in the distance.

I let Liz sleep in, dressed quickly and then joined Corbett in the kitchen. After an initial greeting, he said, "I take it, Madam, you have not yet read the *Village Bugle* this morning," handing over the paper.

"Not yet," I said. I took the paper and saw the startling headline. Peter and Jake had been killed in a car accident on the main road near the house.

"Perhaps you heard the sirens last night," Corbett said.

"No. No, I didn't." I put down the paper with its scant details. "Do you know what happened? Were they drunk?"

"According to the villagers I spoke with earlier this morning, I don't believe they were. It's speculated that their vehicle encountered a large flock of birds— because of the black feathers found on and around the car. The driver must have lost control, and they careened into a tree; the two were not wearing seatbelts."

He said more, but I didn't hear. In my mind I saw that horrifying scene I had repressed for so long: *the terrified Annabel, slamming her shiny midnight wings against the window pane, her talons scratching the glass frantically, desperate to escape the claws and teeth of the feral grey cat that snarled and leapt and... And while I screamed, two unbearable boys hid in the dark shadows and laughed...*

＊ · ＊

SYMPATHETIC IMPULSES

by David McDonald

David McDonald says: "Poe casts a long shadow across
a number of genres, from mystery to horror. But, it was
always his more Gothic tales that captured my imagination, and it was to those that I turned to for inspiration.
Many of his stories deal with helplessness in the face of
greater forces, or consequences catching up with someone, and this story attempts to blend those aspects."

＊・＊

GARIEN'S SHOULDERS TWITCHED as an icy rivulet of
water ran down his back, adding to his already foul mood.
The vaulted limestone ceilings of the tunnels under the Keep
of Truth constantly sweated moisture, dripping into pools that
soaked the hem of his scarlet Inquisitor's cloak and seeping into
the tooled, black leather of his knee high boots. The damp air
also played havoc with the lungs of the prisoners who called
the dungeons these tunnels led to their home, leaving them
susceptible to often fatal disease. The healing spells that Garien
and his men possessed could prolong the prisoners' stay in the
hell of the dungeons as long as required, but even the most
skilled adepts could not resurrect a prisoner found dead in
the morning.

The guards at the first gate were already unlocking the
intricate mechanism that secured the iron portcullis by the
time Garien reached them. They knew better than to keep him
waiting. So did his second in command, Jon, who hurried out
through the second gate to meet him. He was wearing the same
scarlet cloak as Garien, but his black tunic bore only a single
garnet brooch rather than the twin rubies of his commander's.

"High Inquisitor Garien! I didn't expect you here until the third bell," he said.

"I received a summons from the Grand Inquisitor," Garien said. "He is most insistent that we will solve the mystery of our special guest. And when the Grand Inquisitor insists on something, we must leap to obey."

Jon paled. "Yes, indeed, sir. I am afraid that I have little progress to report."

Garien sighed. "I feared as much. Never mind, I am determined we will extract the secrets we require."

He followed Jon through the second gate, ignoring the guards who stiffened to attention as he walked past. They turned down a narrow passageway that opened into a large room, ten yards across and at least three high, with a domed roof. Smokeless, alchemical torches hanging on the walls illuminated the slab of stone in the middle of the room, and the man bound to it. Looming over him were two muscular men in black, unadorned tunics. One held a curved knife with a wickedly serrated blade, the other a metal bar that glowed incandescently hot at one end.

"Acolytes!"

The men froze at the sound of Garien's voice.

"You may leave," he said. "Now."

The two men hurriedly exited the room. Garien walked to the bench and examined the equipment. Laid out in neat array was an assortment of blades, pincers and hooks. He nodded approvingly, each tool spotlessly clean and perfectly maintained. He was intimately familiar with every tool, and knew the exact way each could be best used to inflict pain. He had started out as an acolyte and clawed his way up the slippery ladder of the Keep's hierarchy, and now stood within an unfortunate accident's reach of the highest position he could hold. Until then he was still bound to serve the pleasures of the Grand Inquisitor, and the source of his superior's current displeasure was lying on this slab.

The prisoner was in the prime of his life, and in the shape of a man used to action. There was little fat on him, and his muscles bulged in stark relief, much like the statues that stood watch in the courtyard of the Keep. Every inch of him was marked in some way, with red patches where the skin had painstakingly been peeled from his weeping flesh, and scorch marks where red metal had been applied. All the wounds had minor enchantments laid on them to prevent infection, but other than that had been left untreated. By rights the man should have been a quivering, trembling mess, begging to tell Garien everything he knew. Instead, he turned his head — the only movement that his bonds allowed — and was regarding Garien with a sardonic smile.

Garien loomed over the prisoner and said, "So, this is our mystery?"

Jon nodded. "Yes, sir. I have tried all the techniques that you recommended but he will not break."

"Everyone breaks in the end," Garien said, letting his disapproval come through. "Even you or I. All that's required is finding the right lever."

The prisoner's grin grew wider. If it weren't for the fact that their spells would prevent it, Garien might have thought that his ordeal had unhinged the man's mind.

"What is your name?" he asked, "or is that information a secret, too?"

"You can call me Karl if that suits," the prisoner replied.

"Karl, why must you make this so difficult for us all? We both know eventually you will break, and tell us everything you know. There is no need for more unpleasantness."

Karl laughed. "Oh, but you are wrong. I won't break, no matter what you do."

Garien shook his head sadly. "There *you* are wrong, Karl. You will. My superior has tasked me with extracting certain information from you, and I never fail him."

He gestured to Jon, who moved up beside him.

"Pass me the glass rod."

Silently, Jon handed it to him. Karl's eyes were fixed on Garien's as the Inquisitor began to work

"Now, Karl, if I slide this rod in here, it is meant to be very uncomfortable. But, it doesn't seem to be bothering you," Garien said. "But if I do this apparently the pain is simply exquisite."

There was a sharp crack as the glass rod snapped into jagged fragments, but Karl didn't react, his gaze unwavering.

"You see, this is what my superior wishes to know. How is it that you are able to withstand such pain? If you were the only one with such an ability we might think you some sort of aberration, a freak of nature. But there have been other spies we have captured who have shown the same quality. Even our most talented Adepts have been unable to discover any sort of enchantment that might be protecting them, or you. If they had, they would have dispelled it. Wouldn't that be terrible, Karl? All that accumulated pain rushing through you at once."

If Karl was alarmed by the thought, he showed no sign of it. Garien kept up his conversation, occasionally gesturing to Jon for another implement.

"This war of ours, it has gone on for almost half a century. I am a realistic man, I feel no need for the base jingoism of many of my fellow inquisitors, I know that neither side has the advantage, that the balance shifts back and forth from time to time but always returns to that uneasy equilibrium. Pliers, please, Jon. No, the thicker, blunt tipped ones."

He held them in his hand, idly turning them over as he spoke.

"It's not so much that we need to find out what secrets you might have discovered, though we will certainly ask that once you are broken. But, we must know how you thwart our ministrations. The idea of spies immune to torture gives my superiors nightmares, because such immunity takes away our chief deterrent. If spies don't have to worry about the consequences of being caught, then we will soon be swarming with them. And we can't have that, can we, Karl?"

"Of course not," Karl said, smirking even more. "But, you will have to learn to deal with it, I'm afraid."

"I think not," Garien said. "I will have your secrets."

He leant forward and returned to work. Karl's eyes never left his, and the smirk remained.

◆ · ◆

Garien dried himself briskly with a thick towel and then pulled on his sleeping robe before sliding beneath his silken sheets. He had soaked in the steaming bath for almost an hour, trying to ease the tension in his aching muscles. He had worked on the prisoner for most of the night, bringing every technique in his arsenal to bear, and then inventing new ways of coaxing agony form his subject, but nothing he had done had smashed through that mocking exterior.

Finally, Garien had reached the limits of his body's endurance, and fatigue made him sloppy. Knowing an hour or two of sleep would do him wonders, he had instructed an Adept to clean up the mess and heal the prisoner enough to keep him alive, then he had left for his chambers in the heights of the Keep. He would sleep, and then he could return to the dungeon and continue his work, bring fresh eyes and a fresh mind to bear. Already, merely from the time spent relaxing in the bath, he had a few faint glimmerings of ideas; one involving scorpions and a ball of twine seemed particularly promising.

Garien laid back and waved his hand, the globes around the wall going out, leaving the room dark. He closed his eyes, and tried to sleep. Just as he began to drift off there was the clangor of bells urgently echoing through the rock walls of the Keep and sending Garien scrambling to his feet before his fatigue-addled brain even knew what he was doing. These were not the hourly bells that chimed softly enough to sleep through, but the harsh-sounding tones of the alarm bells. Garien had not heard them for years and it took him a moment to work out what this particular combination signified. He gasped as the realization sank in. Enemies within the Keep!

"No, it's not possible," he muttered.

In the almost fifty years of war, no one had ever breached the walls through force of arms, and even the occasional spy who penetrated their defenses had been apprehended before completing their mission. The enemy within the walls was simply inconceivable, and Garien wondered if the alarm was simply an elaborate drill.

Hurriedly he began to dress. He was reaching for his sword when the door to his chambers burst inwards in an explosion of splinters and intruders swarmed into the room. They were all dressed in black as if they had used the cover of night to infiltrate the Keep and they carried short swords with blackened edges as to not glimmer in the light.

The half dozen men were on Garien before he could grasp his weapon, and two men, one on each side, pinned his arms behind him. He opened his mouth to cry out, but all that emerged was a strangled gasp as one of the intruders drove a mailed fist into his midriff.

Garien doubled over in pain. Still trying to catch his breath, a silken hood was pulled over his head. A small part of Garien's mind was able to appreciate the neatness and professionalism, but most of his attention was given over to the struggle to breathe.

The men holding his arms half dragged, half walked him to the door. In the distance Garien heard the clash of blades and screams of agony. He was forced down flights of stairs and through corridors that should have seemed familiar but now echoed strangely and reeked of his fear. A change in the air told him that he was outside. He heard the soft whicker of a horse just before he was thrust into a carriage. The crack of a whip and he lurched as the carriage moved, then, as it moved faster, he was jostled with every bump. None of his captors had uttered a word, and every time Garien tried to speak, he was silenced by a stinging slap or a blow to the head.

The next few days passed in a blur of pain and humiliation. Every few hours he would be dragged from the carriage and given a drink, and then allowed to relieve himself. Completely disoriented, Garien had no sense of the direction they were heading and only a rough estimate of the time that had passed. He knew the nationality his captors must be, but he did not know whether he was being held by their army, or by one of their more secret forces. As a man of authority he might be able to hope for a ransom if he had been captured by one of their regular units. But he shuddered to think what might happen if his kidnappers were one of the enemy's secret spy rings. He could end being handed over to their equivalent of Garien's own role, and he had no illusions about his ability to withstand pain.

Finally the hellish journey came to an end. Garien was pulled from the carriage and into a building. After taking almost as many flights of stairs down as he had been forced up at the Keep, Garien was roughly stripped — save for his hood — and doused with buckets of icy water. Shivering and naked, he stood waiting, until he was taken to another room. The door slammed behind him and he was roughly forced down into a hard, wooden chair. Exhausted and aching from the beatings he had endured, Garien slumped gratefully against its stiff back. He fought hard to maintain consciousness, knowing he would need to keep his wits about him if he were to escape.

He heard a door open and close, and braced himself as he sensed someone move towards him. There was no blow, only an uncomfortable brightness that left him blinking and trying to focus, as the hood was pulled from his head.

For a moment the table and the figure seated across from him were blurred. As his eyes focused, he let out a strangled sob.

"Hello, Grand Inquisitor," Karl said. "So nice to see you again."

Karl's smirk was the last thing Garien saw before darkness crashed down and he fainted.

✦ · ✦

When Garien awoke, he was washed and his wounds had been cleaned and bound. He was lying on a soft, comfortable bed in a neat and well appointed, if slightly austere, room. He was dressed in a white tunic and breeches, both made of expensive cloth that belied their plain design and modest cut.

Karl sat in a chair watching him. Heart hammering, Garien bolted upright with a jerk, groaning as the throbbing in his head threatened to split his skull open.

"Relax, Garien," Karl said. "I may call you Garien?"

He nodded warily.

"Excellent," Karl said. "Just because we are on opposing sides of a vicious and ongoing war doesn't mean we can't be polite, does it?"

Garien didn't reply, merely moved so that he was sitting on the edge of the bed, muscles tensed in readiness.

"Oh, there is no escape for you, Garien, but please try to relax. You will not be harmed."

"After what I did to you? Were our positions reversed, you would already be screaming."

"I hold no grudge. I was a captured spy, and you were doing your job. Besides, as you can see, our Adepts have healed all my injuries." The mocking grin that Garien remembered from the dungeon was splayed across Karl's face. "And, it is not as though you were able to actually hurt me."

Their Adepts had done a remarkable job. When Garien had last seen the other man he had been battered and bleeding, and missing several unessential appendages. The man before him looked like he had never known suffering. His arms, neck, face and chest did not present a single blemish, and he had all of his teeth, and both eyes.

"You expect me to believe that you will not hurt me?" Garien asked, not daring to let himself hope.

"We are both nobles, Garien. Such methods are for common men. You will live out the rest of the war, or until the next Exchange Day when you will be ransomed back — whichever

comes first — in as much comfort and luxury as we can provide," Karl said. He must have seen the doubt in Garien's eyes,
because he continued. "I swear by the Three on pain of death
that not a drop of your blood will be spilt, or a bone of yours
broken, or any of your body disfigured, through any action
or choice of mine or my countrymen."

He sat on the ground to seal his oath, and Garien relaxed,
the tension running from his shoulders. Such oaths were more
than mere words. The Three had ways of showing their displeasure for the breaking of oaths in their name that made
Garien's methods seem merciful.

"Thank you," he said. "That is highly honorable of you."

Karl smiled, some of the mocking edge gone. "Well, there is
the fact of honor. But, we also know that you are not privy to
the sort of information we require. You are no spy or general.
You may be very good at your job, but that is of no use to us."

Garien felt the last of his doubts fade away in the face of
Karl's pragmatism.

"Well then, I seem to have no choice but to accept your
hospitality," Garien said.

"Excellent!" Karl leapt to his feet. "Before I get you settled
in, I want to share something with you. I have been waiting
for someone who can appreciate the true genius of it, and
something tells me you are that man."

Garien's wariness returned. "And what would that be?"

"You so desperately wanted to know the secret of how we
are able to withstand so much pain. Well, I am going to show
you."

"Why would you do that?" Garien said, trying not to let his
fear show. "Why would you let someone who might one day
return to his own people have such knowledge? You swore
an oath not to harm me!"

"Please, Garien, calm yourself," Karl said. "It doesn't matter
if you have this information, it is not something that any of your
Adepts will be able to combat. It will do no harm me showing you, in fact it may convince you that perhaps you should
join the side of the inevitable victors. Come along with me."

He gestured at the door, and followed Garien out into the
corridor. As they walked, Karl pointed out the features of the
castle, making sure that Garien was very aware of the number
of guards that stood at attention at every corner. There would

be no easy escape and, for now, all he could do was bide his time and humor Karl.

They arrived at a huge double door, oak and bound with iron, twice the height of a tall man. At a command from Karl, the two guards standing either side rushed to open it. Garien followed Karl into the chamber and then froze in his tracks, looking about in astonishment. The chamber was enormous, easily a hundred yards from side to side, forming a rough square. At least one hundred stone slabs dotted the room, and on each lay a bound body. Leather restraints at wrists and ankles held down arms and legs. Most were gagged with thick pieces of leather between their teeth. Servants moved around the slabs, taking out a gag here or there to spoon feed gruel, or give a mouthful of water.

"What is this?" Garien whispered.

"Our answer to the question of pain," Karl said, leading Garien to one of the captives.

Garien looked down at the young man who might have been handsome if it weren't for the complete vacancy behind his eyes. His idiot's stare passed through the two men as if they were not there. Drool trickled down either side of his mouth, pooling on the smooth, stone beneath him, and occasionally he moaned softly.

"I don't understand," Garien said.

Karl smiled. "Do you understand the basic principles of magic, Garien?"

"Of course I do, I am not an idiot," he snapped.

"And what is the Second Principle?"

"That nothing can be created or destroyed, only transformed."

"That's right, that's why magic always has a cost. The energy has to come from somewhere, either the wielder or a sacrifice. Or it has to go somewhere. I knew a Adept who tried to put out a fire by magic but didn't have anywhere to transfer the heat; the flames burnt him up from the inside out. Took us weeks to get the smell out of his chamber."

Garien grimaced. "But what does that have to do with pain?"

"Every spy runs the risk of capture and torture. Injuries can be healed easily enough, it is not that which breaks a man. Even when you know it is not a permanent thing, the pain still has be endured," Karl said. "Our Adepts were given the task of creating a magic that would stop a man from feeling pain."

"That's impossible!" Garien said. "At least for more than a few minutes."

"So we thought, and so it seemed for a while. But pain is like any other energy, it has to go somewhere. Attempts to block it, to suppress, just leads to paying a larger price later. A number of slaves died in an agony more incredible than you can imagine. Then one of the Adepts came up with the idea of transferring the pain."

"That is genius," Garien said. "Evil, twisted, but genius."

"Yes," Karl said. "It is. Each of these slaves is linked to one of our captured spies. Whatever pain our men feel is channeled here through bonds of sympathetic magic. Unbreakable and undetectable."

He reached down and caressed the captive's face.

"Markus was my surrogate. The whole time you were torturing me, he was feeling my pain. Every cut, every burn, every mutilation. I have to give you credit, you are a craftsman. You broke him over and over again."

Garien started as strong hands grabbed his arms. Two guards had come up alongside him as he had listened, and now held him fast.

"I gave you my word that neither a drop of your blood will be spilt, nor a bone of yours broken, or any of your body disfigured. And I will keep my word. But, my wounds were extreme and I need a new body to bear my pain. You broke my captive Markus; you owe me a new surrogate."

Garien screamed, but not for the last time.

✦ · ✦

ASYLUM

by Colleen Anderson

Colleen Anderson says: "Our everyday language is peppered with idioms that we don't always realize were due to the influence of such writers as Shakespeare, Dickens and Poe. 'Oh he must have a picture hanging in the closet' references Oscar Wilde's *The Picture of Dorian Gray*. And 'The lunatics are running the asylum,' comes directly from Poe's *The System of Doctor Tarr and Professor Fether*. That story is considered one of his comedic works and is definitely satirical. I added a darker vein."

❖ · ❖

THE LABYRINTHINE COUNTRY ROADS, land as flat as an old politician's speech, made a GPS useless near the Dewdney Trunk Road. It twines several cities, running the perimeter and weaving the farmlands together. The daylong search led me to think that Professor Fayther's directions had steered me wrong. So odd a duck was he, I had never been sure what constituted alcohol-conjured ramblings and what a small distillation of truth. Perhaps it was a wild goose chase and there was no asylum. Yes, asylum. Such a quaint word conjuring images of madmen and Gothic edifices, which was what I hungered to find. My stomach growled and I peered at the scrawled directions again. Every road looked the same, leading nowhere but to another field, or an abandoned, ramshackle house. Harvest season had ended; the sun now hunkered pallid in the leeched sky, the fields wasting to yellow.

I drove on as my need grew. Except for the tongues of pavement, I could have been transported back in time. The professor had assured me that this last relic to an archaic institution for the mentally ill still existed. Beyond the government's eye, the rich sent their embarrassments there, away from public scrutiny.

The sun was a bleary orb by the time I spied a structure in the distance. The first unusual sign in the Fraser Valley countryside was a rusted iron fence with fang-sharp spikes piercing the low lying clouds that cloaked the evening sky. Lonely birch and oak trees worked at carpeting the road with an enticement of leaves. I wanted *Gothic*, praying that the inhabitants were mad as loons and that the madhouse was decrepit, ghastly and forgotten. I was far from the nearest town. Should I have to stay the night I would find somewhere to sleep, even if it was on an old couch.

The road curved gently, revealing the peeling facade of what once would have been a mansion, one turret and three gables visible. I parked in a yard devoid of any cars and walked up to a sturdy wooden door. My keys went into one pocket of my jacket and I patted the other, making sure all my tools were there. I could find no buzzer, not even a knocker. I looked around, noting the tarnished doorknob, the damp smell of mold that permeated the autumn air, the reluctance of the dwindling light to touch the wood. Eventually I discovered a rotting cord and, fearing it would break in my hand, pulled it. I expected a delay at best, or no answer at worst, but the door swung open immediately.

A grinning woman with frizzled blonde hair and tattoos of feathers and waves down her bare arm greeted me. "Yes, ma'am. How can I help you?"

Her retro tortoiseshell, horn rim glasses surprised me as did her nurse's scrubs, and I took a step back. "Is this the Rockyview? I'm looking for Dr. Canard."

She smiled again and beckoned me into a bright butter-yellow corridor with warm fluorescent lighting. I frowned at the boring moderness, and then watched a man approach. He was tall, bearded, with a long moustache pointed on both ends, and beautiful eyes like green glass. He looked like a hipster or someone affecting steampunk fashion, wearing a pocket watch tethered to a burgundy collared vest, a white shirt with an ascot, and slim pants. "Dr. Canard," I questioned, reaching out to shake his hand.

He stepped back from my touch, opening his arms wide. "Welcome. You must be Felicia Jones that Professor Fayther sent. You are interested in our asylum, yes?"

I licked my lips, trying to savor the atmosphere. "Yes, I'm working on my PhD in psychology, and my thesis is comparing different modes of rehabilitation used in institutions, and their effectiveness in integrating patients back into society."

In truth, I cared less about the modes and more about madness, eagerly anticipating a diet of lunatics, and their absolute lack of inhibitions regarding social conventions. What can one gain by cracking the walnut and tasting the furrows of the meat? It was into such minds that I hoped to delve, to satiate my constant hunger. I queried about a tour and meeting some of the inhabitants.

"Of course," replied Dr. Canard, "but we were about to eat. Join us — it's communal — and I can give you a tour after, yes?"

I smiled at him. "All right, I am hungry… for information as well."

The nurse grinned widely, as if I'd just accepted an invitation to a ball, and led the way, her floral tunic like a small garden. Dr. Canard brought up the rear. He chattered as we moved down the hall, his voice drifting airily behind me. "We've been trying a new way of rehabilitating our patients. We have two areas, as you will see, and they can choose in which area they spend their time. Only those with the more excitable conditions are kept confined."

We passed what could be considered a living room with a big screen TV, several computers on tables against one wall, a collection of books, and various board games. People were engaged in assorted activities and dressed in T-shirts, jeans, skirts. It completely contradicted the outer facade. I was disappointed by such ordinary attire, and I was famished. I sniffed the air, sifting the stale odors of bacon, sweat, tobacco and onions. There was the underlying tang — a frisson of copper and blood and charcoal — that told me madness lived here.

"Why does the Rockyview look so old on the outside and so very modern inside?"

There was a pause, and I looked back. Dr. Canard wore a thunderous frown, but he smiled when he noted me watching. "We use the facade to keep the curious at bay. They are less likely to… interfere."

But as we moved farther into the asylum's interior, the hallway narrowed and the color slowly changed so that when I noted the drab institutional green and the grey and white linoleum beneath my feet I blinked, wondering if I'd only imagined the brighter corridor.

The building went deeper than I had surmised and we entered what must have been the original structure. Dr. Canard flickered into my peripheral vision and I turned. He seemed pale, as if recovering from an illness. He gestured right, toward a large room with wooden tables and simple utility chairs. "That's where our clients eat. And through here…" He now moved into the lead as the nurse who had followed us went off calling others to dinner. "…is where we eat."

The ornate room was ribbed in dark wood. Several Tiffany lamps painted rainbows on Persian carpets, and numerous candlesticks adorned a plethora of cabinets and side hutches. An oval mahogany table was at the heart of the room, with seating for twenty. People entered from several doorways, some dressed in scrubs, others in street wear. As they sat, tureens and platters of food were brought in. Someone pulled a chair out for the doctor and he gingerly sat on the edge of the seat; his overly-stiff posture made it look as if he would take flight at any moment.

He smiled at me and nodded. "Go ahead, we don't stand on form here."

The food was peculiar: peaches on mashed potatoes, carrots mixed with grapes, and a whole roasted animal carcass, disturbingly the size and shape of a skinned cat, including a long tail, withered little ears, and the feline face with remnants of claws on each foot. The deep red meat was displayed on platters heaped high with a sprinkling of colored marshmallows. I scooped a bit of the tamer food onto my plate. I nibbled a carrot but tasted only copper. I tried a slice of safer looking meat, most likely ham, and tasted charcoal.

Putting my fork down, I asked, "Does your staff stay through the night?"

The doctor nodded. "They do, but not all. They have to eat after all, and someone must bring in supplies."

Several of the staff nodded. "Eat," one small woman said.

"Yes," smirked a hawk-nosed man. "Eat."

They started to laugh. "Eat. Heh heh. Oh that's good. Eat!"

The room rumbled with laughter and the nurses and aides pointed forks of food at each other and screamed "Eat!" They laughed and guffawed until they were nearly falling from their chairs, tears streaming down their cheeks, food spraying from their mouths.

"Enough!" shouted Dr. Canard, and immediately they all fell silent. The overhead lights flickered and dimmed, the glow of the candles adding to the ethereal glare.

I looked at the doctor but he glowered down the table, his food untouched.

I quivered. The energy that seemed to infect the staff ran through me as if a lightning storm were near.

"You've barely touched your food, Miss Jones."

I stared at the bizarre concoctions and watched a woman with freckles nearly the color of the carrots shovel marshmallows and meat into her mouth, barely stopping to swallow. "I'm just not that hungry."

Which was a lie. I was famished, and had been hunting a long time for just such a place as this. Out of the way, forgotten, filled with the delectable strangeness of those who untether their minds from reality's shores.

I looked up at Dr. Canard and again noticed flickering. But it wasn't the lights. I likened it more to bringing an image into focus, one that had faded over time. "You're not eating either."

His smile creased his face. "I don't often. That is, I take my meals later."

A food fight began at the other end of the table until he cleared his throat.

"Tell me," I asked, trying to ignore the strange food orgy. "What is your success rate for returning your patients to normal society?"

"Alas," he sighed. "What is normal? You see, our guests are of an unusual disposition. They will maintain to their last breath that they are fine, and refuse to see their behavioral flaws. The worst of these must be confined so that they do no damage to themselves or us."

"Indeed," called out the hawk-nosed man. "They walk like a chicken," and he jumped up and strutted around the table with his hands tucked into his armpits. "And talk like a chicken." He crowed and clucked until Canard yelled, "Silence! You give me no rest. My only boon is that you'll die or move on, and leave me in peace."

The dining room doors slammed shut. I was as much amazed by this display as I was by the doctor's outburst. In all other institutions quiet and behind-the-scenes reprimands would have happened. This was as refreshing as it was unorthodox. I couldn't help but inhale deeply, my tongue tasting the air.

A plump little woman to my right laughed. "That's nothing. Mere pranks and antics. Why, a more absurd and disturbing sort was the woman who howled and snarled and thought herself a werewolf."

I reached for a bun, thinking it the safer sort of meal from the menagerie of food, and she growled. I snatched my hand back and she lunged towards me, jaws snapping, and then leaped onto the table on all fours and howled.

I couldn't completely stifle my smile. The lunatics were running the asylum but it mattered not to me. "Dr. Canard!" I spoke loudly for the raucous staff was gaining in volume as they indulged in the one-upmanship game. "Do I take it that you have no criminally insane here?"

He steepled his fingers, glaring across them at his unruly personnel. "Oh very few, Miss Jones, very few. We have a few personalities that could be dangerous, but we take care of them."

"Might it be possible to get that tour before it gets much later? It's a long drive back from here."

I noticed he had not touched his food at all. That tang of madness was becoming thick enough that I thought I would be able to sip it straight from the air.

"All right. I think you are ready, yes?"

Just then someone shrieked and the cacophony continued. As I turned back to Dr. Canard, I blinked. Did his hand just pass through the chair?

"All right, everyone! Dinner's over. Clean up the mess, please."

As we turned away, there was little to indicate the nurses and orderlies were different from children at a birthday party.

Canard moved into the hallway and away from the brighter rooms, explaining, "These next suites, isolated from the others, offer a more sedate environment." The air felt weighted as if it hadn't moved in years.

Canard's white shirt seemed to stand out wraithlike as the shadows absorbed the color from his clothing. He never stopped to turn on a light; in fact there seemed to be no switches, just lit sconces along the walls.

"We like to keep this institution private, with little interference from the outside world."

As he prattled on, I had to clasp my hands to keep from fidgeting, my need growing greater, almost unquenchable. "Where do you keep those with the more excitable conditions? I'd like to examine them."

Canard grew silent. I followed behind his ghostly figure that seemed to fade into the ever-darkening hallway. I had to reach out, feeling my way along the walls. A door creaked open ahead and he replied, "They're down here. You might want to grab a lantern."

"Where?" I asked, unable to locate the door he had opened. A lantern? Gone were the last vestiges of modern conveniences.

I bumped into a hall table. Barely able to see in the murky corridor, I patted along the surface until I felt the base of a small metal lamp, and next to it a box of small wooden matches. I fumbled one match out and struck it, causing shadows to caper up the wall.

I thought it unusual that he didn't help me and that no other staff were present. I turned the knob of the antique glass chimney, adjusting the flame, and it settled into an amber glow. Turning toward the door, Dr. Canard seemed to materialize in the light. "After you, Miss Jones."

A cool breeze wafted up from the dark mouth of the door's interior, causing the light to dance. With it came a complex odor.

I hesitated but moved toward the doorway, inky shadows dancing before me. The dark maw led down steep stairs to an underground chamber. The smell of rotting socks and something sharp and stinging assaulted my nose. I licked my lips and ran my tongue over my teeth.

The air was different than that above, more copper, less charcoal, as if down here madness grew in its embryonic stage. Edging down the steps, the light crawled over shapes behind rustic bars. A grubby hand reached through. "Please, help us. We don't belong here."

"Why not?" I asked, holding the lamp high, trying to get a view of the incarcerated.

"We're not mad!" A woman's voice whispered.

The basement cells were stone walls and floors, with the fourth wall nothing more than sturdy metal bars. There were four cells in all, two on each side of the wide central area, much like a prison. Each 'room' held four cots.

I set the lamp on the floor so that I could examine the lock plates set in the inch-thick bars. I ran my fingers over the metal, granular with rust. The cells must have been here a long time.

I could make out the dim shapes of three inmates, each in his or her own cell. The cloying odor of shit and sweat swirled and mixed with the copper scent.

Another, a gravelly male voice, cried out, "We were the staff here! They've imprisoned us. Please, call the police!"

It was at this that Dr. Canard spoke up. "You see, they have the worst delusions, believing they are sane."

"I see. Well, perhaps you can show me some of the others upstairs now." I turned toward Dr. Canard and he wavered into view. Of his ethereal nature, I no longer had doubt.

"I don't think so," he said. "You see, Miss Jones, you suffer the same malady, yes? This belief in being sane, of being above those you call insane and would study. It is here you'll reside for awhile until we know you are cured."

"But I'm not ill, Dr. Canard. And while you cannot leave this place there is no reason I should not."

He smiled and it was a terrible sight to see in the dim lighting. People moaned behind me. Soft weeping began. "But you shall not."

He raised his arms, pale and translucent, the weak light casting no shadow behind him. Yet for all his ephemeral nature, a ghostly wind blew dirt and debris into a dervish. My hair whipped about me and as I strove to see in the sputtering illumination, I was knocked off my feet and slammed into one of the cell doors behind me.

The gate crashed open, I fell in, then the door shut, the lock snickering closed. Beyond, Canard floated in the corridor, spinning slowly as he looked at each of us.

Wiping grit from my eyes, I called out, "You can't do this! Professor Fayther will notice when I don't return. He'll alert the authorities."

Canard laughed as he drifted up the stairs, leaving the light where I had placed it on the floor. "I think not, for you see, Miss Jones, he is my jailer as I am yours. He sends me tidbits from time to time to amuse me, for my... experiments."

With that, the upper door slammed shut and I was left to view what I could of my dim surroundings. My hunger was all-consuming as I turned to survey my fellow inmates.

I had searched for years for that right blend — like sugar and spice, like sweet and savory — and it had been in madness where I found my tastes best fit. Now Canard thought he could keep me in this place that time forgot. Like him, I didn't want the authorities snooping. In the past I'd had to take pains to make my intentions circumspect, moving on from time to time. But here we would see who would be the keeper.

Two women and a man, bedraggled in rumpled and smelly clothing stared at me, their eyes deadened with hopelessness. "We were hoping you could save us," said the skinny balding man. "But you're one of us, one of us… n-now."

"Oh I won't save you," I said as I moved closer to examine him. In fact, I was exactly where I wanted to be. The feeding ground was ripe. They had stewed in madness long enough that it would add texture and sustenance for me. There was ample food in this building.

I would have to feed carefully but one would keep me sated for a good long while. I pulled my toolkit from my dress pocket and just laid it near the lock— first, I had other needs. I reached through the bars and caressed the man's leathery cheek. "I won't save you but I can release you."

I pulled his head close to the bars and kissed him, pushing my tongue between his lips to open him up. Then I began to suck the charcoal and copper and blood that swirled in his essence. At first he was pliant, possibly surprised by my youthful exuberance and unexpected passion. But then as I siphoned the redolent vapors and he felt his essence draining he struggled and flapped beneath my grip like a dying fish.

It took some time to drain him. As his struggles lessened, I felt my strength growing, my skin plumping to full youthfulness. I should have gone slower but it had been so long, and I greedily sucked down his soul. As his body emptied, he grew lighter in my arms, skin shrinking, desiccating. I released him and his mummified body clattered to the stone floor. I barely heard the screams of the others as I fed on the madness.

I had sought asylum, and had found it!

❖ · ❖

THE RETURN OF BERENICE

by Tanith Lee

Tanith Lee says: "Since my early teens, I was interested in Poe. At sixteen, a friend lent me a huge Collected Works. In this was *Berenice*. I read the story and couldn't understand the basic, if horrifying, scenario. One night I read it again and thought, with darkest horror, so that's it! My friend, an intelligent young woman, hadn't got it at all. I've been haunted by the tale for years."

✦ · ✦

Proprium humani ingenil est odisse quem laeseris.
It is part of human nature to abhor the one you harm.
— *Tacitus*

ONLY SOME WHILE AFTER the events I shall recount, did I learn of them, and only then, too, was I told — in that kind of secrecy, the seal of which demands, finally, to be broken — of the concluding scenes of the tragedy of the man known solely to me as Egaeus, and his cousin Berenice.

The Family was immensely rich, and not, in itself, unpowerful. But for their male relative, Egaeus, he was a scholar and a recluse. He had no interest, it seemed, in outer things. He dwelled within the House, among his books and personal fascinations. Something of an invalid, he appeared himself to have confessed that his observation and character were actually obsessive perhaps to the point of slight mania. An eccentric, then, yet he did no harm and caused his Family neither distress nor shame. Until, alas, the last acts of his life.

The Family records have it that some while before that time, he had become engaged to marry his cousin, who also lived in the House. Initially the arrangement had seemed to be completely to her liking, and to his, although his generally remote manner did not evince an especially passionate delight. She was however, a lovely young woman, gently vivacious, slender, pale and clear as a lily, seeming ideal in all forms. What else could such a sensitive aficionado of the Fine, indeed the *Perfect*, as Egaeus, tolerate. Dynastically, and in other ways, their match suited their House exactly.

Most unfortunately nevertheless, and with no warning, a malady of incalculable proportions then struck down Berenice, she who had been the hale and able-bodied partner of the cousins. Far more ill than Egaeus the misfortuned girl became, shocking all, and her ailment, both mysterious and intransigent, had, it turned out, no negotiable cure.

While Egaeus reportedly declared: "I knew her not— or knew her no longer as Berenice."

The disease involved, additionally, a form of what is detailed as epilepsy, whose fits could induce a death-like trance. Although her recoveries from these attacks were 'startlingly abrupt.'

Perhaps it might go without saying, in the atmosphere of this, Egaeus's own sickness grew worse. Which brought on additionally an increase in his *morbid* exaggeration of attention to the most ordinary matters and objects. He would lose himself nights long in staring at the flame of a lamp, or whole days lost in the scent of some plant. He considered these obsessions 'frivolous.'

Naturally, one may not be amazed by any of that, given what had fallen on Berenice.

Yet while feeling perhaps mostly aesthetic distress for his cousin, he began to be obsessive over the physical changes he noted in her—

Let it be said too, rather repellently, he now admitted to never having loved her, and indeed that he had already come to regret the inevitable tradition of marriage that would normally join them forever, and was like a shackle to him.

There arrived instead a period, then, during which, perhaps predictably, he saw Berenice in a fresh and feverishly repulsive light. It seemed to him her dark hair had gone yellow; *had* it so? Her unlustred eyes had lost both *pupils* and color. Last of all, he noted the *teeth* of Berenice. They, unlike the remainder of her vanquished frame, looked to have grown uniquely and flawlessly long, white and obdurate.

He dwelled then upon them, both when viewing them, and in subsequent reverie. They represented to him now a separate Power, and a very strong one, where Berenice was no longer humanly vital in the least. They seemed to him, as it were, independent beings in their own adamantine right.

Not so long after the revelation of her teeth to him, his cousin abruptly died, amid a terrible outcry that shook the House like an earthquake.

Her own destiny, her destination now, could only be the doors of the grave, and presently the burial was performed in the grounds of the House, and the doors of the Sarcophagus shut fast as the frozen lids of two dead eyes. Following which all else too certainly might have been expected desolately to calm and to decay.

But, for Egaeus at least, it did not.

❖ · ❖

On the exact evening of her interment, he awakened in the library, where he sat so very often.

He afterwards alluded to feelings both of wild excitement and vague horror. But he could, apparently, make nothing comprehensive of his own mood. Yet he seemed, even so, to hear the shrieking of a female voice on and on in his head. He had, he thought, 'done a deed' — but what?

A small box lay on the table by him, rather oddly, and it made him shudder, if again in utter ignorance as to why.

This blissful ignorance was not to linger.

In another while, a servant crept into the room. The man was plainly in an agony of fear. It seemed a shrieking had indeed occurred, cracking wide the vaulted silence of the night. This had sent the entire Household, (aside, evidently, from the self-locked Egaeus himself) in the direction of the unholy noise: which, it transpired, was the now-violated tomb of Berenice.

The servant next, shivering and wan, pointed out to Egaeus that Egaeus's clothes were filthy with damp earth and soil, and — far worse — thick with blood. The servant in sequence indicated a muddied spade left leaning on the library wall. Only at this did Egaeus reach out and grasp the strange little box on the table, then uncontrollably dropped it at once. Thus he beheld how it broke in bits. And from it, with a rattling note, there flew out the brutal and cruel instruments of dental surgery. Plus thirty-two 'small, white and ivory-looking sub-stances' that were cast all about the floor.

It would appear that even at such a juncture, Egaeus did not immediately identify them as teeth; the perfect and vital teeth of his dead cousin, Berenice.

+ · +

I have to confide here that what amazed me when initially informed of all this, was Egaeus's total and continuing, likely genuine, unawareness and misunderstanding of what he had actually done— which was, evidently, to break into his cousin's Sarcophagus and rip and cut, by means of the dental imple-ments he had somehow acquired, every exquisite, long, white tooth from her head. He appeared to persist in believing he had effected this admittedly, at least, in a sort of trance, surely one as intense as any of her own during her sickness, solely because of his insane obsession with minute details. But it goes really without saying, does it not, why he was driven to carry out so vile and disgusting a deed? He had plainly become aware, in some annex even of his convoluted mind, that Berenice had become, although by what means he did not know, nor do any, it seems, a vampire. And in order to save others, not to mention the denizens of his ancestral House, he had gone at once to deprive her of her major weapon, her piercing fangs. That he brought them back with him, perhaps, is in itself curious and disturbing. But then, he would, that way, have them with him, a proof of her disarming. If any further proof of the fact — and the efficacy — of the action is demanded, the awful shrieking that resulted in the tomb unarguably furnished it. The truly dead do not shriek. That are dead. But Egaeus's cousin was Un-dead. And by his peculiar and frankly alarming single-mindedness, he rendered, or attempted to, a great service to the rest of the area.

The history of this, then might end here. But it does not. For subsequent occurrences take the dreadful affair farther, unless one does not at all in any way credit the rest of the report which was rendered me. We are all the judges and arbitrators of our own opinions, or we should be. Each then must draw his conclusion, as it seems apt to him.

+ · +

The House did not expose Egaeus to any external or public justice. They did not desire, no doubt, such an exposure themselves. Instead they kept him, as ever, a rare and useless flower, in his tropic case, and in addition, their own unofficial prisoner now. He kept his few favorite rooms and was denied meanwhile any access to the outer environs, including the remainder of the Mansion. Let alone did he retain any social unity with members of his Family Tribe. Servants, choicelessly selected, two particular men, exclusively waited on him, servitors and jailers. They seldom spoke to him beyond the barest phrase. Very likely he would not have minded this at all. He had never been garrulous, nor desirous of intimacy, when in the mode of his original life. He was fed, kept in clean linen, awarded minor comforts and all necessities. He was 'forgotten', erased from thought.

Some months passed through various dismal seasons towards a sunless summer. Beyond the gracious windows of the blinded, shadowy building, the park of trees hung thickly massed with heavy and leaden leaves, as if packs of whispering creatures had gathered on their boughs, to watch and monitor, savagely and mockingly, the goings on of human things.

Apparently it was a nocturnal of full moon, white rifts of glare flung like bolts of bleached flame across and over the grounds and the House, making distorted patchwork most deceptive to the clearest eye.

As usual, Egaeus was not abed, although it was well past the second hour of the morning. In the library he sat. At that same table. The spade and the fatal box, with its contents, had, naturally, seasons before, been removed. There was by then no physical clue to history, even for him.

✦ · ✦

In what he expressed later, it seems he said, first and foremost: "It was as formerly. Without preface or omen, she appeared again before me, in vacillating and indistinct outline. And, exactly as before, if now with entire astonishment, a freezing chill ran through me, sole to crown."

The old 'consuming curiosity' he at once felt also, seemingly, if one would say most strangely, given such circumstances.

A vast exaggeration, nevertheless, had been added to the vision. If when yet, previously, she lived, the emaciation of her ruined body had attained for him so extreme and livid a pitch, she had at the time stayed as some vestige still of Berenice. Now not so. She was currently most like a skeleton, and clad only in part-translucent flakes of her shroud, and the thinnest, least textural gauze of a partly transparent skin. Through this inadequate veil her bones themselves, it seemed to him this night, or so he averred, were themselves half transparent, thin as milky and discolored water.

Her eyes, he said, were now as well *entirely* empty of any ocular feature. They were quite white, lacking, it would seem, all ability to see. And yet she did, for she advanced towards him, weightlessly as something blown, and stood on the opposite side of the table on which, so much earlier, her severed teeth had sat bleeding in their tiny prison-box.

Before, of course, he had noted primarily the *presence* of those teeth in her mouth. Now, in a ghastly parody of remembrance, Berenice, or whatever remnant of Berenice here remained, opened wide her colorless lips to reveal the colorless and shriveled vacant gums. Not one fang had been left embedded there. He had been scrupulous, after all.

And then, he said, and those that later wrote down his trembling and enfeebled words, agreed that he seemed to faint even as he voiced them, "And then my cousin spoke to me."

She spoke some while. He made no try, during his recital, to describe her voice. Conceivably her vocality was now quite beyond analysis, or connection. She did not at first, nor at any point in her monologue, which I was not surprised he made no attempt to interrupt, either for a question or a mere exclamation, to outline how she had come to her vampiric Fate. Instead she set upon Egaeus, at once and completely, the razor edges of an awful and diabolically resentful wrath.

"I had loved you," it seems she said. "You were to be my husband and my lord. For this I had waited patiently and for so very long. But when events befell me, you treated me with such an evil and Satanically indifferent cruelty, that I cannot comprehend it. Nor can or could I ever forgive it."

Berenice told Egaeus that what he had done to her, in the matter of her dentition, was nothing less than the most sordid and granite-hearted injustice he might have coined. For, having become what then she was, how else was she to sustain her altered 'life' — it would seem too, that 'life' was how she referred to the Un-dead fix in which she had found herself.

Dependent on her teeth, Egaeus had robbed her of them, and so left her in an abyss of remedyless pain and despair. This then, the final gift of her reluctant husband. Thereafter, toothless, she had persisted in a limbo of wilting, writhing desuetude, unable either to maintain herself or to cease to be. Dead, she could not die. She languished in Hell, in extremes of torture, those physical enough still, and highly cognitive, aside, of course, from her rage and suffering at his ineffable and indifferent malice and 'spite'.

After these stanzas, a silence fell in the library, or so Egaeus afterwards recalled. He lay back, he said, barely conscious in his chair. But in those moments, once more startling and terrifying him, her skeletal wraith slid lightly up onto the table-top, with the ease of a swimming imp.

He found then, to his utmost dread, this too astounding him— since he thought he had reached the limit of his responsive endurance, she leaned forward to him, closer and ever closer, until her vile and barely viewable face had slipped near enough he feared indeed that she might place her shriveled lifeless lips on his. But no doing that, she arched up her frightful neck, like that of a grayish snake. And from this neck, once lovely and now outside every boundary of both the real and the describable, a phalanx of what appeared to him to be, for several frenzied nightmare moments, long, spiny *teeth* protruded after all, not from her lips, but out of her very *throat*.

Before he could do anything, even to cry aloud in terror, these fang-like protuberances elongated further, and with vast ease, or so it looked to him, in a moment or so more, they had gained and *touched* his own throat, and its vital vein.

He was aware instantly of a drawing, which he had, now and then previously experienced on being medically bled by a physician. But all about, the darkling room dimmed suddenly, as would a window in the stormy curtain-fall of deepest night. The very last words she spoke to him, or so he believed, were these: "But for my kind, dear husband, there *are* other ways. What an obscure slow numbskull you always were, and have remained."

After which Egaeus knew no more, until he woke, late the morning after. By then it transpired, he was dying. He had been leached of most of his blood.

Through some massive intransigence of will, which very seldom before had he demonstrated, save maybe on the night he unwittingly drew the fangs of Berenice, he gave his final statements and avowals to the two cold, unwilling and, by now, frenziedly revolted servants. Others also, however, witnessed the testament. It is their report which has come into my possession.

Egaeus died writhing with an icy fever, screaming sometimes, not more than five hours following this. He left an ultimate menu of instructions, which one at least faithfully, or perhaps merely in pure fearfulness, had also, and conceivably inaccurately, written down. This read, when translated from the jumble of the dying, wrecked mind: "When deceased, every tooth in my head, every bone in my frame, must be smashed like broken bottle-glass. My heart must be pierced, my head, perhaps, disassociated from my neck. I must be burned, and the ashes interred in some deep vault." There was no more after this, *nor perhaps was any needed.*

＊ · ＊

As I have stated, you, or any other, will believe my account, or not. For myself, I am uncertain even as to what, thereafter, was finally concluded upon by the great Family. Let alone any alternative authority. Besides, could any creature rest, if ever so dealt with?

The House has long since fallen, stone on stone. The trees are dead and lie in ranks. Those Sarcophagae remaining in the grounds have also lost their shape and meaning. Maybe, whatever Power may briefly oust him, and itself drive the chariot of poor, helpless Man, when once it lets go, this is always ultimately the result. Creatures of air and wind, we: vehicles, playthings of the gods.

＊ · ＊

THE EYE OF HEAVEN

by Margaret Atwood

Margaret Atwood says: "I'm pleased to be taking part in this tribute to Edgar Allen Poe, one of the greatest, as well as one of the most original and peculiar and influential writers of nineteenth century America.

"My contribution is not a new one, however. It's approximately sixty years old, was written in longhand with a cherished fountain pen, the kind you filled with a plunger, and dates from my very early writing time as a sixteen-year-old high school student.

"Anyone reading this little story can tell at once that it was heavily influenced by Poe— most notably by his tales of obsession, such as *The Telltale Heart* and *Berenice*. I'd read the Collected Works some years before, as a pre-adolescent; in fact, I'd devoured them, then gone back and read them all again, many times. I'm sure I was also learning from them: from the poems, much about meter and stanzas and internal rhyme; from the stories, much about atmosphere, unity of effect, and melodramatic climax, and, of course, gore. And tombs; lots of tombs. Not all of those things were directly useful to me later on, but I could never again be a person who did not know about gore and tombs. I even read the criticism. I didn't understand it much, but it was the first time I'd encountered someone writing about writing as if it was a serious thing to be doing.

"Who had seen fit to put *Poe's Collected Works* into the children's section in the library? Someone who must have thought that the dividing line between child and adult was Sex, so it was all right to expose us kids to a man who comes out of a hypnotic trance and dissolves into a puddle of decomposing goo, or the heart of a murder victim beating under the floorboards, or a man digging up the prematurely-buried object of his love and pulling out all her teeth. Such details stuck with me, as they tend to do.

"Why is it that teenagers take so naturally to horror? And especially to Poe's various brands of horror, in which Eternal Love is strongly connected with death, or death is strongly connected with revenge and justice? Possibly because they're so newly conscious of bodies, of their possibilities and limitations and mortality; possibly because they're more ruthless than adults are, and thus understand vengeance and justice in their pure forms, devoid of any mitigating second thoughts.

"It interests me to note that I chose a male narrator as my crazed, obsessive killer. I wonder why? Possibly because all such narrators in Poe's work are men, and who was I to quarrel with tradition? In the event, it's curious to look back through time and to catch myself in the act of becoming a writer. "The Eye of Heaven" might not be very good, though it's good enough for a sixteen-year-old. But at least I finished it, and that — when you're starting out as a writer — is a large part of the battle."

＊ · ＊

ALL I EVER WANTED WAS PEACE. When I lived on the farm, I could have it whenever I felt the irritation rising in me: when my mother's strident voice rasped my nerves, or my father's after-dinner snoring was too loud. I could take my rod and lose myself along the stream in the wood-lot. No matter if I caught nothing.

As I grew up, the stream seemed to shrink. It was no longer mysterious and hidden, but a well-known friend. We had no secrets. I still spent hours on the damp cedar-grown banks. "They" said I kept too much to myself; they were strangers to me, and had no right to judge. It was at this time that I noticed the first eye: the eye of a trout I was about to kill. It looked at me with an expression of such terror, and, somehow, of accusation, that I let it fall to the ground. I felt cold. The fish made an instinctive flop towards the water— only a fish after all, I thought, and caught it just in time, and slid my hunting knife quickly through its brain. The eye became glassed in death; but I remembered.

When I was sixteen, they sent me to the city. They said it was to give me a better education, but I knew that they wanted to be rid of me. They feared me. I said goodbye at the station and forgot them almost immediately. My hunting knife was in my pocket; I grabbed the handle during the whole trip. It symbolized the stream.

The clock at the city station was watching me. I was to board with my aunt. She came to meet me; when I saw her, my heart stilled— I was horrified. For her eyes were the eyes of the fish I had killed— the same fearful, accusing, translucent stare from behind her glasses. Her hat had a red flower on it. I thought of the blood of the fish, and shriveled. As we left the station I could feel the cold gaze of the clock drilling through my back.

My aunt was a nervous woman who moved in little jerks, like a hen. Her voice was like a hen's too. The house was small, cramped; the district would be a slum in ten years. My aunt seemed perpetually with me when I was inside. She feared and mistrusted me, and wanted to watch me and keep track of my every move. She was forever questioning, questioning. When she asked me, on the first Sunday, to go to church with her, I refused sharply and watched the fear increase. Churches made me even more restless.

I hated the city: the dirty streets, the smoke, the little patchy lawns and the garbage cans; I hated school. As my marks were high, the teachers could not complain, but I sensed their apprehension. I made no friends. Only once was I approached by another student: the captain wanted me to join the football team. I am very strong. But I walked away; I hated talking to people. I walked to the tiny park near the school to regain my composure. It had no stream and no cedars — only a few motley maples and some bare spots on the grass — a poor substitute. I sat on the wooden bench, took out my hunting knife and sharpened it. The handle was loose but the blade was bright. I stabbed it into the ground, to kill the city.

The park became my refuge. In November I spent one whole day there, instead of going to school, immobile, looking at the ground. I returned to my aunt's in the evening, late for supper. The radio was on— it was always on. I went into the kitchen.

Then my aunt was screaming at me; I had never heard her scream before. Even her scream was hen-like. But her eyes... out of her eyes beamed the hate, the fear, the outrage, of all the animals that I had ever killed. I glanced down... there was mud on my shoes. My aunt was tidy. I drew my hunting knife, and killed my aunt. I feared for an instant that she would not die, but it was just as easy as killing the fish. Her eyes stared at me out of the blood as I left the room.

I should've closed the eyes. That was my mistake. I took the northbound train, using my Christmas-holidays ticket; I had to leave... they would not understand about the eye. Now that my aunt is dead, I thought, it will not bother me; but I should have closed the eyes, for it was worse.

Everything now... everything. The headlights of cars, the pine-knots in the wood of the windowsill, the clocks, the bald head of the man in front of me. I would not be safe at the farm; I would have to steal money and go farther north. I held my knife in my pocket and dug it into my thumb every time I remembered so the pain could drive away the eyes. People looked at me — I must have been pale — but I pretended to be oblivious. I got off the train; I could feel the blood against the skin of my thigh, seeping through the pocket.

They were surprised to see me. I went upstairs keeping my hand in my pocket; I knew where the money was. I climbed out through the window and took a train north. It was almost dawn when I left the train and snuck into the bush. The cold was biting; the snow was deep. I had forgotten that there would be this much snow. There was none in the city.

The eyes were left behind. I was at peace, at peace. They would never find me. I was free.

The sun rose out of the rough pines. I watched it gloatingly. I was safe at last from the eyes. The sun was warming... and then, suddenly, it blinked in blazing accusation.

I fell...

❖ · ❖

THE OPIUM-EATER

By David Morrell

David Morrell says: "Thomas De Quincey — the main character of my Victorian mystery/thrillers, *Murder as a Fine Art* and *Inspector of the Dead* — was one of the most sensational and inventive English authors of the 1800s. He anticipated Freud's psychoanalytic theories by more than half a century. In his 1854 blood-soaked postscript to "On Murder Considered as One of the Fine Arts," he described England's first media-sensation mass murders, the Ratcliffe Highway killings, with such vivid detail that he invented the true-crime genre. He was a major influence on Edgar Allan Poe. In this story, based on actual events, De Quincey tells the heartbreaking tale of how he became known as the Opium-Eater."

◆ · ◆

LONDON, 1855

The stranger stepped from the storm-ravaged street, dripping rain onto the sand-covered floor.

"I'm told that the Opium-Eater is here." Thunder rumbled as he pushed the door shut against a strong wind.

"Aye. A lot of other people heard the same," the tavern's owner replied, wiping a cloth across a counter. "He's in the back. Thanks to him, even with the foul weather, business is good tonight."

The stranger approached a crowd at the rear of the tavern. Everyone was strangely silent. Dressed in cheap, loose-fitting garments that identified them as laborers, men held glasses of ale and cocked their heads, listening to faint words through an open doorway.

"Murder as a fine art? Not *this* time," a voice said, its tone suggesting a man of advanced years. "There aren't any killings in *this* story."

From the back room, murmurs of disappointment drifted out toward the crowd.

"But there are several deaths," the voice continued.

Now the murmurs indicated anticipation.

"Father, you don't need to do this," a young woman's voice objected.

"This man asked me a question."

"Which you aren't obliged to answer."

"But on this particular night, I do feel obliged," the voice insisted. "There's no such thing as forgetting, but perhaps I can force wretched memories into submission if I confront them."

Recognizing the voices, the stranger touched two men at the edge of the crowd. "Pardon me. I need to move past you."

"Hey, the rest of us want to go in there too. Who appointed *you* lord and master?"

"I'm a Scotland Yard detective inspector."

"Ha. That's a good one. Tell me another."

"Better do it," a man cautioned. "His name's Ryan, and he is in fact a detective inspector. I saw him at the Old Bailey last week, testifying against my brother."

Grudgingly, the crowd parted.

Detective Inspector Ryan squeezed his way into a congested room that was thick with the odor of pipe smoke and ale. People sat at tables or else stood along the age-darkened walls, their attention focused on an elderly man seated in front of an iron-lined fireplace.

The man was Thomas De Quincey. More than forty years earlier, in 1821, he'd become notorious for writing the first book about drug addiction, *Confessions of an English Opium-Eater*. The nickname had followed him ever since. De Quincey's troubled opium nightmares, in which all of history marched before him and the ghosts of loved ones haunted him, made him conclude that the mind was filled with chasms and sunless abysses, layer upon layer. Writing about this unsuspected subconscious world, the Opium-Eater had established a reputation as one of the most controversial and brilliant literary personalities of the era.

Because of De Quincey's notoriety, people often expected to see someone larger than life. To the contrary, he was slight, so short that his boots didn't reach the bottom of his chair. From a distance, he might have been mistaken for a youth, but when seen this close, his wrinkled face conveyed a lifetime of sadness. His melancholy blue eyes had a dry glitter, as if years of sorrow and regret had exhausted his capacity for tears.

Next to him stood an attractive young woman whose blue eyes resembled his. Her name was Emily, and Ryan's gaze shifted toward her as quickly as it had toward De Quincey— perhaps even quicker, because in the months that Ryan had known her, his impatience about the way she spoke her mind and exerted her independence had turned to respect and indeed much more than that.

Emily's clothing was an example of that independence. If she'd been wearing a fashionable hooped skirt, the immense space it consumed would have prevented her from fitting into the packed room. Instead, her skirt hung freely, with a hint of female trousers beneath them, a style that the newspapers sneeringly called "bloomers," an insult to which Emily paid no attention.

Worry strained her features as she tugged at her father's frayed coat, urging him to leave.

Beside her, a tall, burly man wore shapeless street clothes similar to Ryan's. His name was Becker. In his mid-twenties, he had a scar on his chin suggesting that he was the kind of man whom Ryan customarily arrested, although in fact he, too, was a police detective.

Both he and Emily looked relieved when they saw Ryan enter the room.

"I began searching as soon as I learned that he'd gone missing," Ryan told them. "Finally a constable mentioned a little man walking along this street muttering to himself, and a woman and a detective sergeant asking about him."

"It took us hours to find him," Emily said, sounding exhausted. "For the past week, Father wouldn't stop brooding about this date. When he disappeared, I was afraid that he might have done something to hurt himself."

"The nineteenth of March?" a man in the crowd asked, puzzled. "What's so special about tonight?"

Ryan ignored the question. "I'll find a cab," he told Emily. "We'll take him back to Lord Palmerston's house."

The reference to the most powerful politician in the land made the crowd lean forward with even greater interest.

"Please come with us, Father," Emily implored. She increased her effort to raise him from the chair.

"But I haven't answered this man's question— about how I became an opium-eater."

"It's none of his business," Ryan said.

"All I wanted to know was whether his obsession with murders gave him nightmares that led to *this*," a man protested, pointing at a glass of ruby-colored liquid on the table in front of De Quincey.

The liquid appeared to be wine, but Ryan had no doubt that it was laudanum. The skull-and-crossbones warning on bottles of the opium/alcohol mixture — legally, cheaply, and easily purchased from druggists and even grocers — was normally sufficient to discourage anyone from swallowing more than a teaspoon of the pain reliever. In contrast, De Quincey's tolerance was such that he sometimes drank sixteen ounces of the opium mixture per day.

"After I read his essay about the Ratcliffe Highway murders, all I dreamed about were bodies and blood," the man in the crowd continued. "He was starting to tell us if *he* suffered the same nightmares from writing about so much killing, but then these two" — he indicated Emily and Becker — "and *you*" — he indicated Ryan — "barged in and interrupted him."

"Bodies, yes," De Quincey agreed, staring at the glass of laudanum. "Terrible deaths. But if they were murders, God is the one who committed them."

"Father!" Emily said in shock.

"Perhaps the happiest day of my life was when I met William Wordsworth," De Quincey said.

"What does Wordsworth have to do with this?" someone complained. "The opium makes his mind jump around."

"Not at all," Emily corrected the man, giving him an annoyed look. "It's just that other minds aren't quick enough to follow my father's."

"Wordsworth? Who's *he*?" a shabbily dressed customer wanted to know.

"Didn't you learn to read?" a better-dressed man asked. "William Wordsworth was one of our great poets."

"Who cares about a poet? I thought this was a story about a murderer."

"That's not what he said."

"I loaned Coleridge three hundred pounds," De Quincey said.

"Another great poet," the better-dressed man explained, but he looked worried that De Quincey's mind was indeed jumping around.

"Neither man was considered great at the time." De Quincey kept staring at the ruby-colored liquid before him. "I was twenty-two. In those long-ago years, hardly anyone knew about Wordsworth, but I admired his verses to the point of obsession. I loaned his friend Coleridge three hundred pounds from an inheritance I received, hoping to gain his favor so that he'd introduce me to Wordsworth. Mind you, it wasn't my first attempt to meet Wordsworth. Twice before, I'd made my way to Grasmere."

"You talk too fast about too many things. Grasmere? Where's *that*?"

"The Lake District," De Quincey replied. "It's a village that Wordsworth called 'the loveliest spot that man hath ever found.' Twice before, I'd traveled there to pay my respects to him, but each time, I'd felt so nervous that I stayed in a village in a neighboring valley. Twice, with a volume of Wordsworth's poetry in my coat, I climbed to the ridge that looked down on Grasmere's lake and a particular white cottage gleaming among trees. Twice, my courage failed me, and I retreated.

"But this time, I wasn't an intruder, for Coleridge had asked me to escort his wife and children to his home near Grasmere. This time, my nerves didn't falter as our carriage stopped before that white cottage. I hurried through a little gate. I heard a step, a voice, and like a flash of lightning, a tall man emerged. He held out his hand and greeted me with the warmest welcome that it's possible to imagine. The week in which I enjoyed Wordsworth's hospitality was the happiest time of my life. But such is the wheel of fortune that only a few months later, a catastrophe plunged me into the *worst* time of my life."

"Is this where the murders come in?" someone asked.

"Pay attention. He said *terrible deaths*, not *murders*," the better-dressed man objected.

De Quincey gripped the glass of ruby liquid, raised it to his lips, and took several swallows. The crowd gasped. For an average person, that quantity of laudanum would have been lethal.

Ryan gave Emily a troubled look.

"Today, Wordsworth's fame brings many visitors to the Lake District," De Quincey explained. "But a half century ago, the Grasmere valley was as unknown as his poetry. Fewer than three hundred people lived in the area. Above the lake, only five or six cottages were scattered among the woods and meadows on the rugged mountains."

The rain lashed harder against the room's window.

"The solitude was so extreme that the few families who found shelter on those mountains waited eagerly for the rare social events that occurred in Grasmere and the scarce other villages. These events were usually auctions of cattle, sheep, wood, and such. To attract buyers, the auctioneers provided refreshments — biscuits, tea, and even brandy — to make the atmosphere resemble a party. It was during one of those occasions, on March the nineteenth, forty-seven years ago tonight, that George and Sarah Green descended from their cottage in a remote upper valley."

De Quincey shuddered.

He pointed as though the mountains loomed before him. "Looking up from Grasmere, you can't see any indication of that valley. Hovering mists conceal it. A rough path was the only approach. After ascending through dense woods and difficult ridges, the path crossed a wooden bridge with a gap in the middle. Great care was required to avoid falling through the hole and into the force."

"The force?" someone asked. "The force of what?"

"The Lake District has a private language. A raging stream is called a force. From that seclusion, George and Sarah Green set out for an auction that was eight miles away in a village called Langdale. In that direction, there wasn't even a path."

"Father, I beg you not to upset yourself. Please, let's go," Emily urged.

But De Quincey persisted. "The auction involved furniture. Two elderly parents were disposing of their household goods, preparing to spend their remaining years with a married son and his family. But it wouldn't have mattered to Sarah Green *what* type of auction it was. She and her husband were too poor to buy even the smallest object. As the auctioneer made jokes and attempted to raise the bids on the various items of furniture, Sarah's fervent purpose was to obtain a future for her eldest daughter. In her youth, Sarah had fallen prey to a man whose intentions were base. Her first daughter had been the result, burdened with the stigma of being illegitimate. Sarah's unfortunate history was familiar to everyone in the area. That George Green, whom she'd met later, had offered to marry her made people think of him as compassionate. Perhaps her past was the reason that she and her husband lived in that remote valley. Perhaps it pained Sarah to mingle among townspeople and know that they still whispered about her.

"But on this day, Sarah didn't care what people whispered. Her out-of-wedlock daughter was grown, and Sarah had come to Langdale to beg various people of means to provide a position for her. Perhaps the girl could work in a shop, or she could learn to be a cook in a great house, or she could feed and dress children at a manor. Sarah's hope was that her daughter would meet families who offered opportunities, and perhaps one day the daughter would find a suitor who didn't care about her origins. The alternative was that the daughter, who now worked in a tavern, might succumb to the peril of that environment and suffer the same misfortune that Sarah had."

Everyone looked at Emily to see how she responded to this immodest topic. But if they'd expected her cheeks to redden with embarrassment, they were disappointed. She displayed no reaction, accustomed to hearing her father speak of matters that were far more indelicate than illegitimacy.

"Try as Sarah might, rushing from group to group with increasing urgency, she couldn't persuade anyone to consider her petition," De Quincey said. "People later remembered the earnestness with which she approached them and the regret with which they declined her pleas. Then, all they cared about was the auction. They had a vague recollection that she and her husband departed just before sunset. Voices were heard hours afterward, from high in the mountains— perhaps shouts of alarm, but more likely the echoes of jovial partyers going home. No one paid attention."

De Quincey stared at the glass of ruby liquid before him.

"As the sun descended, snow fell in the mountains. From the front door of a distant stone cottage, an eleven-year-old girl, Agnes, watched the flakes accumulate. In the gathering silence, she strained to hear sounds that might indicate the approach of her parents. She closed the door and looked at her five younger brothers and sisters.

"Little Agnes studied an old clock on the mantel, one of the few items of worth that the Green family owned. Her parents had told her that they would try to return by seven, but that hour was long past. The children had already eaten the simple meal that their mother had laid out before departing. Agnes assured the children that their parents would arrive soon, that there wasn't anything to worry about. When the clock's hands showed eleven, she finally made the children wash their faces and get into their sleeping clothes, all the while promising that their mother and father would be in the kitchen to greet them when they wakened in the morning. Agnes led the children in their evening prayers and put them to bed. She sang a lullaby to the very youngest. Then she looked out the window in the direction from which her mother and father would approach, but the blowing snow prevented her from seeing anything.

"George and Sarah Green were not in the cottage when the children wakened. Agnes told her brothers and sisters that their parents, seeing the foul weather, had decided to remain in Langdale and would set out in the morning. 'They'll be here before noon,' the little girl predicted, looking at the hands on the clock, which were now only three hours away from the promised time. Feeling a jolt, she remembered that the clock needed to be wound.

"The fire was fueled with peat. During the night, Agnes's uneasy mind had wakened her several times, prompting her to put more peat on the flames. The family's tinderbox was broken, and if the fire went out, there wouldn't be any way to restart it— she and the other children would freeze to death. To give her younger brothers something to occupy them, she put on their coats and made them follow her outside to a shed where the peat was stored.

"As the snow fell harder, they went back and forth, piling a large stack of peat in a corner of the kitchen, lest the snow become so deep that reaching the shed would be difficult. 'Perhaps Mama and Papa won't come back to us today,' Agnes told her brothers and sisters. 'Because of the snow, they might not be able to set out from Langdale until tomorrow. We'll show them how grown up we are.'

"Agnes examined the almost empty cupboard and made porridge, conserving what she had, giving small portions to every child, with a little extra for the two youngest. 'Until Mama and Papa bring the oatmeal that they planned to buy in Langdale,' she said. Then the cries of the cow in the barn warned her about other duties. Again, Agnes went outside, where the snow was even deeper. Holding her often-mended coat tightly around her, she reached the barn and climbed to the loft, where she pushed hay down to the animal. The bundle was almost too heavy for so tiny a girl. Then she milked the cow, but the animal was so aged that it provided less than a pint.

"There was other milk in the house, a small quantity of skimmed milk, of little value, purchased cheaply the last time her father had journeyed down to Grasmere. Agnes worried that it might spoil, even though it was kept near a cold wall. She remembered her mother telling her that a way to stop milk from turning sour was to scald it, so Agnes put the old milk in a pan and boiled it. When the skin on it cooled and thickened, she divided the milk among the children, providing their midday meal.

"She kept peering out the window but still detected no sign of her parents. When the wind slanted the falling snow toward the cottage, she assigned the children the task of stuffing rags beneath the windows and the door to keep drifts from blowing under. She went to a corner of the kitchen where potatoes were stored in a bin, but as it was near the end of winter, few remained. She chose the two that were least spoiled, cut off the bad parts, and boiled them, providing supper. She dressed the children for bed. She led them in their prayers. She drowsed near the fire, taking care to add more peat whenever she snapped awake."

"I feel cold," someone murmured.

Others in the tavern hugged their arms and nodded their agreement.

"On the second morning, the snowfall continued. Normally, the children might have been able to walk the several miles to Grasmere, with Agnes carrying the youngest, but the weather made that impossible. The force was too wide for them to leap over, and the narrow wooden bridge could not be crossed, as the deep snow concealed where the treacherous hole in its timbers was located. A false step would drop them into the raging, ice-cold water.

"Agnes assured her brothers and sisters, 'As soon as the snow stops, Mama and Papa will come back to take care of us.' She wound the clock. She put more peat on the fire. She boiled the last of the oatmeal, of which there was so little that when she discovered a small quantity of flour, she added water and baked tiny cakes on the hearth. She persuaded the smallest children, who didn't realize the danger, that they were having a party. Agnes even made tea, although the family was so poor and the leaves had been boiled so often that there was almost no taste."

"You're making my hungry," someone in the tavern told De Quincey.

"After milking the cow, which gave even less than on the previous day, eleven-year-old Agnes discovered that the water in the cow's trough was frozen. In the house, she boiled snow and carried a pail of the steaming water to the barn. She did this several times until the gathering darkness felt so rife with threats that she ran through the drifts back to the cottage, afraid that she would lose her way. She prepared the last two potatoes for supper. She put the children in their nightclothes. She led them in prayers. She went to sleep."

"Pray God that she didn't let the fire go out," someone said.

"Indeed she did not," De Quincey assured the crowd. "Not Agnes. She slept upright in a chair. Whenever her head jerked, she opened her weary eyes and made sure that the fire had more fuel."

"I knew it!" the man exclaimed.

"The third day brought a gleam of hope," De Quincey told them.

Everyone straightened with excitement— except Ryan, Emily, and Becker, who knew the harrowing direction that the story was about to take.

"The wind changed, shifting the drifts so that portions of the ground were exposed," De Quincey resumed. "Agnes put on her coat and hurried to the bridge, but it remained blocked, the hole in it still hidden. Farther along the force, a wall had been exposed. Agnes rushed to the house and brought her younger brothers. The wall was made from rocks that weighed upon one another without the need for cement. In the chilling wind, Agnes and her brothers pushed the rocks away until the wall was low enough for them to climb over. They picked up the rocks and threw them into the water, ignoring how difficult the labor was, until they had created a small island. Agnes's brothers watched in dread as she leaped onto it and then to the opposite bank, the cascading water splashing on her. She waved good-bye, then raced from one bare patch of ground to the next, disappearing into the snowfall. The brothers hurried back to the cottage and prayed for her.

"The difficult route to Grasmere took Agnes over ridges and through dense trees. Sometimes she had to wade through hip-deep snow. But other times, she reached wind-cleared ground and rushed onward in her desperate mission. Cold gusts numbed her cheeks. Her hands and feet lost sensation. Exhaustion made her plod. At last, the odor of smoke pinched her nostrils and directed her toward a screen of trees, where she found a house.

"With senseless hands, she pounded on the door. The woman who opened it looked surprised that anyone would come visiting on so hostile a day, especially a little girl. The woman smiled in welcome, then opened her mouth in horror as Agnes screamed, 'Help us!'

"'Is that Agnes Green?' the woman asked. 'Good heavens, child, come in where it's warm! What happened?'

"'Mama and Papa didn't come home!' Agnes cried.

"'From the auction at Langdale? But that was three days ago!'

"As the woman warmed Agnes by the fire, her husband quickly dressed and braved the storm. When he finally reached Grasmere, he banged on the rectory at St. Oswald's Church. He and the minister took turns ringing the church's bell, sounding the alarm.

"Perhaps only sixty families lived in the village. Meeting at the church, the men of those families made their plans. One group would climb to the Greens' farmhouse and rescue the children. The rest would proceed over the ridges toward Langdale. There was still a possibility that the Greens had stayed with a family in that village, and there was also a chance that they'd found shelter in a shed along the way, although without a hearth and a fire, a shed would offer little protection from the cold."

The crowd squirmed nervously.

"Each group of searchers carried a bell so that they could signal to the others if they found something or if they themselves were suddenly in need of rescue," De Quincey told them. "Indeed, the dangers of the expedition were considerable, and the women of Grasmere didn't relax until night brought their men back unharmed.

"George and Sarah Green hadn't been found, but at least their children were now safe. As various families sheltered them, the village learned what Agnes and her brothers and sisters had endured, how brave the children had been, and how heroically Agnes had acted. The village also learned how truly impoverished the Greens were. Whenever they'd come to town, they'd worn their least-mended clothes, never letting anyone see the tattered garments that they were reduced to in their cottage. Only the most meager of furniture remained, everything else having been sold to buy food, of which there was now virtually none.

"The next day and the day after that, the search teams pursued their desperate mission, never giving a thought to the risk. Every half hour of daylight was made use of. No man came back to eat and rest until long after dark.

"On the fourth night, Wordsworth's sister, Dorothy, asked a neighbor — a young shoemaker — what he intended to do the next morning.

"'I'll go up again, of course,' the young man replied.

"'But what if tomorrow should turn out like all the rest of the days?' Miss Wordsworth asked.

"The young man told her, 'Then I'll go up with greater determination on the *next* day.'

"It became evident that George and Sarah Green must have veered off the direct route from Langdale, if *direct route* can be used to describe the uneven landscape that they needed to climb and descend to reach their cottage. Falling snow can cause a person to wander off course without knowing it, possibly moving in a circle, becoming hopelessly lost.

"Finally, dogs were added to the search, in the hope that the animals might hear faint cries for help that the searchers couldn't. Few men said out loud what everyone was thinking— that the dogs might also detect the odor of corpses, even if the cold kept the bodies from deteriorating.

"Around noon on the fifth day of the search, the clanging of a bell echoed throughout the mountains. A shout from a misty ridge produced other shouts that spread with what we would now call telegraphic speed from group to group. The Greens had been found."

"*Alive?*" a man asked breathlessly.

"George Green lay at the bottom of a precipice," De Quincey answered.

"No," someone murmured.

"The severe damage to his body indicated that he had fallen. The precipice was in the opposite direction from the Greens' house, which showed how severely he'd become disoriented in the blowing snow.

"Sarah Green's body was at the top of the cliff. Trying to establish what had happened, the searchers concluded that husband and wife had stopped in confusion. Sarah wore her husband's greatcoat. Perhaps George Green had gone forward, hoping to catch a glimpse of a ridge or a peat field that he might recognize. The precipice from which he had fallen was only a few yards from where Sarah's body was found.

"It was later decided that the mountain voices heard in Langdale on the night of the auction were in fact only one voice, Sarah Green's, first calling to her husband and then, when she didn't receive an answer to her repeated calls, shrieking. Perhaps she had stepped forward to do her best to help her husband, but when she realized how close she was to falling, she lurched back. One of her shoes was found at the edge of the precipice, as if she had recoiled so violently that the motion caused her to lose the shoe.

"Her body was on an outcrop of the precipice, with steep drops on three sides. Wanting to find a way to reach her husband, but with danger seemingly at every turn, she must have remained in place in the darkness, hugging his greatcoat around herself as numbness crept up through her shoeless foot and invaded her body. She was found covered with snow in a seated position, as if she had succumbed to exhaustion or as if she had never stopped waiting, convinced that her husband would somehow return. She probably died dreaming of the warm fire in her house and of the darling faces of her little children whom she would never see again.

"The funeral took place eight days later in the graveyard at Grasmere's church. The weather provided a perfect contrast to the conditions that had killed George and Sarah Green. Although snow remained here and there on the ground, the azure sky was unstained by a cloud, and golden sunlight warmed the hills over which they had struggled. What had been a howling wilderness was now a green lawn in the lower regions and a glittering expanse of easily crossed snow on the higher bluffs. Wordsworth himself read a memorial poem, referring to the 'sacred marriage-bed of death / That keeps them side by side / In bond of peace, in bond of love / That may not be untied.'"

"What happened to the children?" someone quickly asked.

"In a letter, Wordsworth's sister told me that the grief of Sarah Green's illegitimate daughter was the most overwhelming she had ever witnessed. Throughout the valley, people volunteered to take the children. Even the poorest families put in a claim. But it was decided that none of the children should be entrusted to those who, because of slender means or old age, might need to surrender the obligation they had asked to assume. Two of the orphans were twins and stayed together with a childless couple who took them in. The others were dispersed, but into such kindhearted, attentive families that there were constant opportunities for the children to meet one another on errands, or at church, or — ironically — at auctions.

"Thus, in the brief period of a fortnight, a family that, by the humility of poverty and the simplicity of their lives seemed sheltered from all attacks, came to be utterly broken up. George and Sarah Green slept in a single grave in Grasmere's churchyard, never to want for anything again. Their children were scattered among guardians who offered opportunities that never would have been available to them otherwise.

"Meanwhile, the Wordsworths applied themselves to raising funds for the children's education. Wordsworth's sister circulated an account of the terrible deaths, prompting people to offer what they could, sometimes only sixpence and sometimes several pounds. I was a student at Oxford during that fateful March, and if Wordsworth's reputation had been what it is now, I would have had no difficulty collecting a large sum from my classmates. But given the low esteem with which his poetry was then regarded, no Oxford contributions were forthcoming. When the royal family heard about the children's plight, however, they sent a generous donation. In the end, more than one thousand pounds were collected, enough to ensure the children's welfare."

"What happened to Sarah Green's illegitimate daughter?" a man asked.

"She was rescued from working at the tavern where Sarah Green had feared that the girl's reputation would be destroyed. A better position was found for her. As for Agnes, the brave little girl grew up to have a happy marriage with a loving husband and many sons and daughters."

"So the story had a satisfactory end. Although the parents died, the children triumphed," the better-dressed man decided.

"But that wasn't the end."

"Father, please don't take your mind in this direction. I beg you to go away with us," Emily said.

But De Quincey seemed not to have heard. "Consider the perfect symmetry of these events. A desperate woman leaves her six children at home while she and her husband journey down to an auction so that the woman can attempt to protect another of her children, one who seems destined to repeat her mother's misfortune. Sarah Green fails in her frantic appeals. Despondent, she and her husband return to the mountains and die miserably in their effort to reach their farmhouse, where their other children wait for them. But the deaths of Sarah and George Green result in every success that Sarah Green wished for her children. Without knowing it, by dying she achieved her desperate goal. I could never hope to invent a story that contains such geometric proportions. Even the family's last name, Green, is perfectly apt, suggestive of springtime, new life, and new hope. If I put that name in a story, readers would accuse me of being too obvious. But in life, we say 'How appropriate that the family was named Green.'"

De Quincey picked up the glass of ruby-colored liquid.

"Only God can create a story like that," he said, his voice edged with anger.

He swallowed the rest of the laudanum.

The crowd gasped as they had earlier, only this time louder. The shocked expressions on their faces made clear that they didn't understand why so much opium didn't put De Quincey to sleep or into a coma. For him, the drug wasn't a sedative but a stimulant. As he had told the story, his voice had become faster, energized by anguish.

"Father, it's time to leave," Emily insisted.

"Indeed," Ryan said, he and Becker stepping forward. Ryan knew where the story was going, and he feared that De Quincey's attempt to confront the harrowing memory wouldn't restrain it but would only make it worse.

De Quincey resisted. "We say that what happened to George and Sarah Green was a terrible accident," he said. "But if we look closely, we realize that it wasn't an accident at all. It was the unavoidable result of a series of events that began years earlier when a young man convinced Sarah to succumb to his faithless charms. Everything followed from that. If not for the illegitimate daughter, Sarah Green would never have gone to that auction. She and her husband would never have died. The children would never have enjoyed a future free of poverty. The faithless suitor began the decades-long sequence that led Sarah Green to be accepted into the Wordsworth household."

"Your mind's jumping around again!" someone objected. "You said that Sarah Green died in a mountain storm."

"But one of the rescued children, nine years of age, was also named Sarah— after her mother," De Quincey said, "and *that* Sarah Green..."

"Please," Ryan urged, trying to raise him from the chair. "Don't take this any farther. We should have left a long time ago."

Despite being a little man, De Quincey squirmed from Ryan's hands, telling the crowd, "In October of 1809, eighteen months after George and Sarah Green died in that winter storm whose anniversary is tonight, I moved to Grasmere. I established residence in Dove Cottage, the humble white dwelling where Wordsworth had lived until his growing family required him to move to larger accommodations. Wordsworth's new residence wasn't far from Dove Cottage. I often walked there to visit him, hardly able to believe that only two years earlier I had finally met my idol and that I now lived in the cottage where we had first shaken hands.

"Wordsworth's younger daughter, Catherine, was then an infant. A more adorable child was never seen. I made faces to her or ducked below her cradle and popped up waving, making her giggle. She enjoyed my company more than that of any other person except her mother. In April of 1810, more than two years after the Greens died, the Wordsworths assigned young Sarah, now eleven, to watch over her, but this Sarah Green was list- less and inattentive, as far removed from the energy and duty of her mother and of heroic Agnes as it's possible to imagine.

"Coleridge told me of the morning when, as Wordsworth's guest, he came down to the kitchen and found young Sarah Green feeding uncooked carrots to infant Catherine. Coleridge warned Sarah that raw carrots were an indigestible substance for an infant and might cause her to choke. But this warning went unheeded, and a short time later, Catherine was seized with strong vomiting. I was shocked to find her convulsing when I arrived that afternoon. By sunset, the convulsions finally stopped, but the fit affected Catherine's brain, and from that time onward, her left arm and left leg drooped, capable of only limited motion. Perhaps because of little Catherine's pathetic affliction — or perhaps because of my dead sisters — I became more devoted to her."

"Your dead sisters?" a man asked.

De Quincey drew a long breath.

"Please don't Father," Emily said.

"My younger sister Jane died when I was four and she was three. When a strange fever struck her, she was taken to a sickroom from which she never emerged alive. A servant — annoyed by the constant vomit that needed to be cleaned — struck her in exasperation. That was my first experience with evil.

"My sister Elizabeth was the next to die. I was six, and she was nine, my constant playmate, the joy of my life. She, too, experienced a strange fever. After she died, I snuck into her room and stared at her corpse. She had an unusually large head. A physician theorized that perhaps water on her brain had caused Elizabeth's death. I found out later that before she was buried, a surgeon sawed into her skull and declared that her brain was the finest he had ever examined.

"Catherine Wordsworth's head was large also. Perhaps that's why I was reminded of Elizabeth and why the affection for my sisters was transferred to Catherine. As one year and another passed, I often visited Wordsworth's house to see Catherine. Frequently she came to Dove Cottage and spent the day with me. When she napped, I sat next to her, gazing at her innocent face. She had a spirit of joyousness that made me feel as if my sisters had been reincarnated.

"In June of 1812, I was in London. I received a letter from Wordsworth's sister. It had a seal of black wax, and I can never forget the words. 'My dear friend, I am grieved to the heart when I write to you— but you must hear the sad tidings. Our sweet little Catherine was seized with convulsions last night. The fits continued until after five in the morning when she breathed her last. She never forgot you, De Quincey.'"

He paused, trying to steady his voice. "Catherine had difficulty saying 'De Quincey' and called me 'Kinsey.' The Wordsworths told me that when I was traveling, she used to search their house to try to find me. She was only three years old, the same age as my sister Jane when *she* died. But never, not even when Jane and

Elizabeth died, did I feel so fierce a grief as that which struck me when I learned of dear little Catherine's passing.

"I hurried back to Grasmere as swiftly as I could. I went to Catherine's grave in the churchyard at St. Oswald's, and I found the thought of being away from her so unbearable that every night for the next two months, I stretched upon that tiny resting place and clawed at the earth. People later told me that in the darkness they heard me moaning there. When I wasn't in the graveyard, I took long agonizing walks through the valley. On the opposite side of every field, Catherine and my sisters materialized. They each carried a wicker basket filled with flowers. They walked toward me, their short legs moving in the long grass, but they never gained any distance."

De Quincey picked up his glass and studied the ruby-colored remnant.

"I first became acquainted with opium when I was nineteen. A toothache led me to a chemist's shop where, for only pennies, I made my first purchase of laudanum. In an hour, oh, heavens, what a lifting of my inner spirit. That my pain vanished was a trifle compared to the immensity of pleasure that opened before me. This was an abyss of divine enjoyment, a panacea for all human woes. Paradise! Or so I mistakenly believed. For the next eight years, I indulged in opium on an occasional basis, foolishly convinced that I was stronger than it until, by the time I was twenty-seven, it got the better of me, torturing me when I tried to stop, forcing me to ingest ever greater quantities merely to feel reprieved from hell.

"Catherine Wordsworth's death tipped the balance. Throughout the last of June and then all of July and August, my frenzy of grief persisted until, at the end of that summer, having relied on opium in a desperate attempt to relieve my sorrow, I was doomed."

De Quincey looked at the man who had asked the question that began it all.

"When I first came in here, you saw me pour laudanum into this glass and wanted to know why I became an opium-eater— or, in this case, an opium-*drinker*. Was Catherine Wordsworth's death to blame? Was Sarah Green's daughter to blame for feeding Catherine uncooked carrots and causing the convulsions that crippled the darling little girl and permanently damaged her health? Were the deaths of George and Sarah Green to blame, flooding the Grasmere valley with tears, prompting villagers, including the Wordsworths, to take the children into their households? Was the long-ago faithless suitor to blame for tricking Sarah into surrendering her virtue and conceiving an illegitimate daughter, the fate of which so worried Sarah that she and her husband descended into Langdale forty-seven years ago today and then returned without hope, dying in the mountains?

"The string of causes and effects is overwhelming. Suppose my sisters hadn't died as they did. Suppose a sudden storm hadn't trapped George and Sarah Green. Suppose they were able to arrive home when they'd promised they would. Suppose another of the Green children, and not young Sarah, had joined Wordsworth's household. Suppose I hadn't idolized Wordsworth and lent Coleridge three hundred pounds so that Coleridge would favor me enough to arrange for me to meet my idol. Remove any one of these elements, and the chain is broken. I wouldn't be sitting here tonight holding this empty glass."

De Quincey peered up at Emily, tears trickling down his face, tears that Ryan would have thought impossible an hour earlier when he'd noted that De Quincey's melancholy eyes had a dry glitter, as if years of sorrow and regret had exhausted his capacity for tears.

"I weep for the George and Sarah Green. I weep for Catherine Wordsworth. I weep for my weakness," De Quincey told his daughter.

Emily hugged him tightly. "And I weep for you, Father. Please, will you go with us now?"

This time, Ryan and Becker didn't need to try to raise him. He set down the glass and slowly stood. Emily led the way, the crowd silently parting for them.

✦ · ✦

Contributors' Bios

Writers

COLLEEN ANDERSON has published nearly 200 pieces of fiction and poetry in such places as *Chilling Tales, Evolve, Horror Library* and *Cemetery Dance*. She has been poetry editor for the *Chizine*, host of the Vancouver ChiSeries, co-editor for *Tessearcts Seventeen* and *The Playground of Lost Toys*, as well as a freelance copyeditor. She has been twice nominated for the Aurora Award, received honorable mentions in the *Year's Best* anthologies and been reprinted in *Imaginarium* and *Best of Horror Library*. New works for 2015 are in *Nameless, Second Contact, Our World of Horror, OnSpec* and *Exile Book of New Canadian Noir*.

◆ · ◆

KELLEY ARMSTRONG is the author of the *Cainsville* modern gothic series and the *Age of Legends* YA fantasy trilogy. Past works include *Otherworld* urban fantasy series, the *Darkest Powers & Darkness Rising* teen paranormal trilogies and the *Nadia Stafford* crime trilogy. She also co-writes the *Blackwell Pages* middle-grade fantasy trilogy as K. L. Armstrong with M. A. Marr. Armstrong lives in southwestern Ontario with her family.

◆ · ◆

MARGARET ATWOOD is the author of more than forty books of fiction, poetry, and critical essays. Her latest book of short stories is *Stone Mattress: Nine Tales* (2014). Her *MaddAddam* trilogy — the Giller and Booker prize-nominated *Oryx and Crake* (2003), *The Year of the Flood* (2009), and *MaddAddam* (2013) — is currently being adapted for HBO. *The Door* is her latest volume of poetry (2007). Her most recent non-fiction books are *Payback: Debt and the Shadow Side of Wealth* (2008) and *In Other Worlds:*

SF and the Human Imagination (2011). Her novels include *The Blind Assassin,* winner of the Booker Prize; *Alias Grace*, which won the Giller Prize in Canada and the Premio Mondello in Italy; and *The Robber Bride, Cat's Eye, The Handmaid's Tale,* and *The Penelopiad.* Her new novel, *The Heart Goes Last*, will be published in September 2015. Margaret Atwood lives in Toronto with writer Graeme Gibson.

✦ · ✦

ROBERT BOSE grew up on a farm in southern Alberta reading the Hardy Boys and making up stories that only entertained his mother, himself, and maybe his dog. He still loves spinning yarns and can clear any room by starting a conversation with 'Remember the time...' Robert is working on a novel about the modern world after an all too real Ragnarök while annoying his wife, raising three troublesome children, and working as the Director of Innovation for a small Calgary software company.

✦ · ✦

Double Bram Stoker Award-nominee **JASON V. BROCK** is a writer, editor, filmmaker, composer, and artist, widely-published online, in comic books, magazines, and anthologies, including *Qualia Nous, Disorders of Magnitude* (nonfiction collection), *Simulacrum and Other Possible Realities* (fiction/poetry collection), *Fungi, Weird Fiction Review, Fangoria,* S. T. Joshi's *Black Wings* series, and others. He was Art Director/Managing Editor for *Dark Discoveries* magazine for four years, and publishes a pro journal called *[NameL3ss].* He and his wife, Sunni, run Cycatrix Press (publishing the anthologies *A Darke Phantastique, The Bleeding Edge,* and others), and run a technology consulting business. As a filmmaker, his work includes the critically-acclaimed documentaries *Charles Beaumont: The Life of Twilight Zone's Magic Man; The AckerMonster Chronicles!* (winner of the 2014 Rondo Hatton Award for Best Documentary); *Image, Reflection, Shadow: Artists of the Fantastic.* He is the primary composer and instrumentalist/singer for his band, ChiaroscurO.

✦ · ✦

SUNNI K. BROCK has been involved in digital creations since the late 1980s. She has consulted for Microsoft, Adobe, and Sonic Solutions. In spite of her strong background in Computer

Science, she's not just a geek: Sunni is also a published poet, writer, and talented vegetarian cook. She enjoys spending her days working alongside her husband, author/filmmaker Jason V Brock, tending to their pet reptiles, and aggravating friends on Facebook.

❖ · ❖

JANE PETERSEN BURFIELD still lives in her hometown of Toronto. She has explored widely in career, education, and travel throughout her life. Three careers, in journalism, teaching and business, led her to writing crime stories. With her first short story, Jane won the Bony Pete Prize at Bloody Words 2001. She has stories in these anthologies: *Bloody Words, The Anthology*, Baskerville Books, 2003; *Blood on the Holly*, Baskerville Books, 2007; *Thirteen, The Mesdames of Mayhem*, Carrick Publishing, 2013; and *World Enough and Crime*, Carrick Publishing, 2014.

❖ · ❖

RICK CHIANTARETTO is the author of the *Crossing Death* series, *Façade of Shadows,* and *Tailored for the King* (included in *Twice Upon a Time*). His novels have appeared on ReadFree. ly's Top 50 List of 2013 and 2014.

❖ · ❖

J. MADISON DAVIS is the former president of the International Association of Crime Writers and Professor Emeritus at the University of Oklahoma, where he taught fiction writing and screen writing. His first novel, *The Murder of Frau Schütz,* was nominated for the 'Best First' Edgar. Seven other novels followed, including *The Vertigo Murders; Law and Order: Deadline;* and *The Van Gogh Conspiracy.* He has also published many nonfiction books, including *The Novelist's Essential Guide to Creating Plot; Stanislaw Lem; The Shakespeare Name Dictionary* (with A. Daniel Frankforter); and the anthologies *Murderous Schemes* (with Donald Westlake); and *Conversations with Robertson Davies.* His short stories have appeared in publications from *Mississippi Review* to *Zürich, Ausfahrt Mord.* He is currently working on a novel— he is always working on a novel.

❖ · ❖

BARBARA FRADKIN is a retired psychologist with a fascination for why we turn bad. She is best known for her easy-read novellas and her gritty, psychological detective novels featuring the exasperating, quixotic Ottawa Police Inspector Michael Green, two of which have won the *Arthur Ellis Best Novel Award*. However, she has also written more than two dozen dark, compelling short stories that haunt numerous magazines and anthologies. She loves the short story format for allowing her to explore the extremes of storytelling, even to the edges of the supernatural.

✦ · ✦

NANCY HOLDER is the *New York Times* bestselling author of over 80 novels and 200 short stories, essays, and articles. She has received five Bram Stoker Awards, among others, and is the current vice president of the Horror Writers Association. She has written material for *Buffy the Vampire Slayer; Beauty and the Beast; Teen Wolf; Smallville; Kolchak the Night Stalker; Sherlock Holmes*; the *Domino Lady*, and others, and edits comic books and graphic novels for Moonstone Books. She teaches in the Stonecoast MFA Creative Writing Program through the University of Southern Maine. She lives in San Diego, California.

✦ · ✦

MICHAEL JECKS is the author of thirty-five novels published by Headline, HarperCollins and Simon & Schuster; he has been writing for twenty years. A past chairman of the Crime Writer's Association, he was also a founder of the Historical Writers' Association and created Medieval Murderers— a performance group of historical crime writers. In quieter moments he has written short stories and novellas for anthologies, and a modern spy ebook, *Act of Vengeance*. His books are translated and published all over the world.

✦ · ✦

MICHAEL KELLY is the Series Editor for the *Year's Best Weird Fiction*. He has been a finalist for the Shirley Jackson Award and the British Fantasy Society Award. His fiction has appeared in *Black Static, The Mammoth Book of Best New Horror, Supernatural Tales, Postscripts, Weird Fiction Review*, and has been collected in *Scratching the Surface*, and *Undertow & Other Laments*.

✦ · ✦

TANITH LEE was born in London, England in 1947 and began to write at age 9. After a variety of occupations, in 1975 she was liberated when DAW Books USA published her 3 Fantasy/SF novels The *Birthgrave, Don't Bite the Sun* and *The Storm Lord*, followed by many more. She has written by now almost 100 novels and collections (including Fantasy, SF, Horror, Childrens, Young Adult, Steam Punk, Historical, Detective, Dark Contemporary), almost 350 short stories, 4 BBC radio plays and 2 TV scripts (Blake's 7). She has also been honoured with several awards, including the August Derleth for *Death's Master*. In 2008 she was made a Grand Master of Horror, and in 2013 given the Life Achievement Award. She is married to the writer/artist John Kaiine.

+ · +

ROBERT LOPRESTI is the author of two novels, including *Greenfellas* (Oak Tree Press, 2015). His short stories have appeared in most of the mystery magazines and won the Derringer (twice) and Black Orchid Novella Awards. He blogs regularly at *SleuthSayers, Little Big Crimes*, and *Today* in *Mystery History* (where Poe comes up pretty regularly). He is a librarian in the Pacific Northwest.

+ · +

RICHARD CHRISTIAN MATHESON is an acclaimed best-selling author and screenwriter/executive producer for television and film. He has worked with Steven Spielberg, Stephen King, Dean Koontz, Bryan Singer and many others on Emmy winning miniseries, feature films and hit series. His critically-hailed, dark psychological fiction has appeared in 125 major anthologies including many Years' Best volumes. 60 stories are collected in *Scars and Other Distinguishing Marks* and the #1 Bestseller *Dystopia*. Matheson's terror novel *Created By* is a scathing glimpse of network television and his mystery novella *The Ritual of Illusion* is a sinister love letter to the movies. His latest story collection, Zoopraxis, will be published in 2015. A professional drummer, he studied with legendary *Cream* drummer Ginger Baker. He is president of *Matheson Entertainment*.

+ · +

DAVID McDONALD is a mild mannered reporter and editor by day, and a wild-eyed writer by night. Based in Melbourne, Australia, he is the editor of a fortnightly magazine for an international welfare organization. In 2013 he won the Ditmar Award for Best New Talent, and in 2014 won the William J. Atheling Jr. Award for Criticism or Review and was shortlisted for the WSFA Small Press Award. David is a member of the Horror Writers Association, the International Association of Media Tie-In Writers, and of the Melbourne, Australia based writers group, SuperNOVA.

+ · +

DAVID MORRELL created Rambo in his award-winning novel, *First Blood*. His numerous *New York Times* bestsellers include the classic spy novel, *The Brotherhood of the Rose* (the basis for the only television mini-series to be broadcast after a Super Bowl). An Edgar and Anthony finalist, a Nero and Macavity winner, Morrell is a recipient of three Bram Stoker awards and the Thriller Master award from the International Thriller Writers organization. His other Thomas De Quincey works include *Murder as a Fine Art* and *Inspector of the Dead*.

+ · +

LISA MORTON is a screenwriter, author of non-fiction books, award-winning prose writer, and Halloween expert whose work was described by the American Library Association's *Readers' Advisory Guide to Horro*r as "consistently dark, unsettling, and frightening". Her most recent releases include the novella *The Devil's Birthday* and the novel *Zombie Apocalypse: Washington Deceased*, and coming this fall (from Reaktion Books) is *Ghosts: A Cultural History*. She lives in the San Fernando Valley.

+ · +

WILLIAM F. NOLAN writes mostly in the science fiction, fantasy, and horror genres. Though best known for coauthoring the acclaimed dystopian science fiction novel *Logan's Run* with George Clayton Johnson, he is the author of more than 2000 pieces of fiction and nonfiction, over 80 books, and has edited twenty-six anthologies in his fifty-plus year career. Of his numerous awards, there are a few of which he is most proud: being voted a Living Legend in Dark Fantasy by the

International Horror Guild in 2002; twice winning the Edgar Allan Poe Award from the Mystery Writers of America; being awarded the honorary title of Author Emeritus by the Science Fiction and Fantasy Writers of America, Inc. in 2006; receiving the Lifetime Achievement Award from the Horror Writers Association in 2010; and recipient of the 2013 World Fantasy Convention Award along with Brian W. Aldiss, and being named World Horror Society Grand Master in 2015. A vegetarian, Nolan resides in Vancouver, WA.

+ · +

LOREN RHOADS discovered *Tales of Mystery and Imagination* as a child, thanks to the Alan Parsons Project album of the same name. She's visited Poe's dorm room at the University of Virginia and the Poe Museum in Richmond, but regrets that she hasn't been to his grave. She is the author of *The Dangerous Type, Kill By Numbers*, and *No More Heroes*, to be published by Night Shade Books in 2015.

+ · +

CHRISTOPHER RICE published four *New York Times* bestselling suspense novels before the age of thirty. His supernatural thrillers, *The Heavens Rise* and *The Vines*, were both finalists for the Bram Stoker Award. He has also published several works of erotic romance in his series, The Desire Exchange. He is the co-host and executive producer of the irreverent Internet radio program, *The Dinner Party Show with Christopher Rice and Eric Shaw Quinn*.

+ · +

THOMAS S. ROCHE's first novel, the paramilitary zombie crime thriller *The Panama Laugh*, was a finalist for the Bram Stoker Award. He has published more than 300 stories, mostly in the horror and erotica genres, with occasional forays into crime fiction, fantasy, and science fiction. Among Roche's editing projects are the crime-erotica series *Noirotica*, vampire anthologies *Sons of Darkness* and *Brothers of the Night*, and two volumes of dark fantasy co-edited with Nancy Kilpatrick: *In the Shadow of the Gargoyle* and *Graven Images*. Roche's early stories are gathered in the e-book collection *Dark Matter*.

+ · +

UWE SOMMERLAD has over the years published many reviews, articles and essays in many periodicals, and a few books in Germany, but his work also appears in English language magazines. He has also worked as an actor on stage and on television in Germany. He was once invited by the University of Siegen to portray Edgar Allan Poe, reading some of Poe's stories and, in character, answering questions from the audience. His afterword to the German edition of Basil Copper's *The Vampire in Legend and Fact*, covering the thirty years since the book's original publication, was nominated for a Nyctalus Award. He lives in Frankfurt am Main, Germany.

✦ · ✦

CAROL WEEKES has been writing and publishing fiction, mainly in the horror field, since 1995. Short stories have appeared in myriad magazines and anthologies, including Don Hutchison's *Northern Frights* series, *Space & Time, The Dalhousie Review*; novels include *Walter's Crossing, Ouroboros* (co-written with Michael Kelly), *Terribilis*, and the short story collections *Dead Reflections* and *The Color of Bone*. Carol continues in the dark fiction and screenplays genres, writing amid her muses: one dog, four cats and two rats, who watch over every word.

✦ · ✦

CHELSEA QUINN YARBRO has been an award-winning professional writer for forty-seven years, has sold more than ninety books in a variety of genres and more than ninety works of short fiction, essays, and reviews; she also composes serious music. Her novel *Hotel Transylvania* was among six nominated for the Horror Writers Association one-time Bram Stoker award for the Most Significant Vampire Novel of the (20th) Century. She lives in the San Francisco East Bay Area.

✦ · ✦

Editors

NANCY KILPATRICK is a writer and editor with 18 novels and over 225 short stories in print. In her editorial capacity, *nEvermore!* is her 15th anthology. She enjoys wearing two hats and exploring both hemispheres of her brain. She won the Arthur Ellis Award for Best Mystery Story, and several awards for her dark fantasy writing and editing, including the Paris Book Festival's Best Anthology of the Year for *Danse Macabre*.

✦ · ✦

CARO SOLES is the founder of *Bloody Words*, Canada's biggest annual mystery convention, which finally closed its doors in 2014 after a long and successful run. Her work includes mysteries, erotica, gay lit and science fiction. She has been published in many anthologies and has edited quite a few herself. She received the Derrick Murdoch Award from the Crime Writers of Canada for her work in the mystery field and was short listed for the Lambda Literary Award. She is looking for time to work on an historical novel.

✦ · ✦

ACKNOWLEDGMENTS

The editors wish to thank the many people who helped make this project a reality, including: Adrienne Soles, Alice Basrzotti, Alison Graham, Amanda Gordon-Young, Amelita Flores, Andre Wahner, Angela Bell, Angela Larson, Ann Boivin, Annette Rudy, Barbara Gordon, Bill Zaget, Briana Fowler, Carol Smith, Cathy Astolfo, Charles Karotseris, Cheryl Freedman, Christian Saucier, Colleen Anderson, Constance Prokop, Dan Martin, Danielle Rose, Dave Beynon, David Lott, David Perlmutter, Debbie Currie, Dennis Lowery, Derrick Burton, Don Kinney, Doug Shearer, Eady Mays, Ed Washburn, Erin Underwood, Francesca Gale, Gloria Ferris, Hugues Leblanc, Ilse and Gary Sullivan, J. Madison Davis, Jan Archibald, Jane Petersen Burfield, Jane McDowell, Jason Stuckless, Jayne Barnard, Judith Ransome, Kari Maaren, Kate Davis, Katharine Burfield, Kelsey Attard, Kevin Wilson, Kieron O'Conner, Kristi Petersen, Linda Addison, Linda Cahill, Linda Disbrowe, Linda Simser, Lisa De Likolits, Loren Rhoads, Lucas K. Law, Lucy Taylor, Lynne Jamneck, Malte S. Sembten, Mari Anne Werier, Marisa Iacobucci, Mark Martin, Mary Hall, Matthew Rogers, Meghan Schuler, Meila and David Mesner, Michael Sheffield, Michael Stewart, Mike Kilpatrick, Nancy Baker, Nika Rylski, Pat Flewwelling, Paul Murphy, Peggy Perdue, Plexor Property Management, Rebecca Senese, Renee S. De Camillis, Rick Chiantaretto, Robert P. Bose, Robyn MacGarva, Rose Eisenger, Sandrine Scialdone, Scott Barnes, Shawn Geauvreau, Stephanie Cardwell-Clitheroe, Stephanie Schmitz, Stephen Volk, Susan Pieters, Suzanne Rozon, Sylvain Drasse, Sylvie Dubois, Terry Tweed, Tina Rath, Trent Walters, Uwe Sommerlad, Jason and Sunni Brock, Mitchell D. Krol, and to those who wished to remain anonymous; and these companies:

www.masochisticreligion.com/full_band_bio.htmwww.etsy.com/shop/GirlyGeekChic
www.etsy.com/shop/hellostrangermx?ref=custom_order_convo
www.etsy.com/shop/AhtheMacabre www.ebay.com/usr/magic7608?_trksid=p2047675.l2559

www.etsy.com/shop/goddessglass10359?ref=custom_order_convo
www.etsy.com/shop/NorthofSalem?ref=custom_order_convo
www.poepuppet.com/aboutfilm.htm
www.octobereffigies.com/finalmain.html
www.etsy.com/shop/NGArtPrints
www.etsy.com/shops/5ChicsAndAPendant

We also thank Brian Hades of EDGE Science Fiction and Fantasy Publishing for partnering with us in a venture entirely new to him, and to Janice Shoults at EDGE for her hard work promoting this book. And most of all we are overwhelmed by the generous and enthusiastic response from our contributors who love Edgar Allan Poe as much as we do! Your stories are indeed an homage to this unique writer who changed the literary landscape.

Our titles are available at major book stores
and local independent resellers who support
Science Fiction and Fantasy readers like you.

EDGE Science Fiction
and Fantasy Publishing

www.edgewebsite.com

Our titles are available at major book stores and local independent resellers who support Science Fiction and Fantasy readers like you.

Evolve: Vampire Stories of the New Undead edited by Nancy Kilpatrick (tp)
- ISBN: 978-1-894063-33-3
Evolve Two: Vampire Stories of the Future Undead edited by Nancy Kilpatrick (tp)
-ISBN: 978-1-894063-62-3
Expiration Date edited by Nancy Kilpatrick (tp) - ISBN: 978-1-77053-062-1

Fires of the Kindred by Robin Skelton (tp) - ISBN: 978-0-88878-271-7
Forbidden Cargo by Rebecca Rowe (tp) - ISBN: 978-1-894063-16-6

Game of Perfection, A (Part 2 of Tyranaël) by Élisabeth Vonarburg (tp) - ISBN:
978-1-894063-32-6
Gaslight Arcanum: Uncanny Tales of Sherlock Holmes edited by Jeff Campbell &
Charles Prepolec (tp) - ISBN: 978-1-8964063-60-9
Gaslight Grimoire: Fantastic Tales of Sherlock Holmes edited by Jeff Campbell &
Charles Prepolec (tp) - ISBN: 978-1-8964063-17-3
Gaslight Grotesque: Nightmare Tales of Sherlock Holmes edited by Jeff Campbell
& Charles Prepolec (tp) - ISBN: 978-1-8964063-31-9
Green Music by Ursula Pflug (tp) - ISBN: 978-1-895836-75-2
   Green Music by Ursula Pflug (hb) - ISBN: 978-1-895836-77-6

Healer, The (Children of the Panther Part One) by Amber Hayward (tp)
- ISBN: 978-1-895836-89-9
   Healer, The (Children of the Panther Part One) by Amber Hayward (hb)
- ISBN: 978-1-895836-91-2
Hell Can Wait by Theodore Judson (tp) - ISBN: 978-1-978-1-894063-23-4
Hounds of Ash and other tales of Fool Wolf, The by Greg Keyes (tp)
- ISBN: 978-1-894063-09-8
Hydrogen Steel by K. A. Bedford (tp) - ISBN: 978-1-894063-20-3

i-ROBOT Poetry by Jason Christie (tp) - ISBN: 978-1-894063-24-1
Immortal Quest by Alexandra MacKenzie (tp) - ISBN: 978-1-894063-46-3

Jackal Bird by Michael Barley (pb) - ISBN: 978-1-895836-07-3
   Jackal Bird by Michael Barley (hb) - ISBN: 978-1-895836-11-0
JEMMA7729 by Phoebe Wray (tp) - ISBN: 978-1-894063-40-1

Keaen by Till Noever (tp) - ISBN: 978-1-894063-08-1
Keeper's Child by Leslie Davis (tp) - ISBN: 978-1-894063-01-2

Land/Space edited by Candas Jane Dorsey and Judy McCrosky (tp)
- ISBN: 978-1-895836-90-5
   Land/Space edited by Candas Jane Dorsey and Judy McCrosky (hb)
- ISBN: 978-1-895836-92-9
Lyskarion: The Song of the Wind (Part One of The Chronicles of the Karionin) by
J.A. Cullum (tp) - ISBN: 978-1-894063-02-9

Machine Sex and other stories by Candas Jane Dorsey (tp)
- ISBN: 978-0-88878-278-6
Maërlande Chronicles, The by Élisabeth Vonarburg (pb) - ISBN: 978-0-88878-294-6
Milkman, The by Michael J. Martineck (tp) - ISBN: 978-1-77053-060-7
Moonfall by Heather Spears (pb) - ISBN: 978-0-88878-306-6

Necromancer Candle, The by Randy McCharles (tp) - ISBN: 978-1-77053-066-9
nEvermore: Tales of Murder, Mystery and the Macabre
   edited by Nancy Kilpatrick and Caro Soles (tp) - ISBN: 978-1-77053-085-0

Occasional Diamond Thief, The by J. A. McLachlan (tp) - ISBN: 978-1-77053-075-1
Of Wind and Sand by Sylvie Bérard (translated by Sheryl Curtis) (tp)
   - ISBN: 978-1-894063-19-7
On Spec: The First Five Years edited by On Spec (pb) - ISBN: 978-1-895836-08-0
   On Spec: The First Five Years edited by On Spec (hb)
   - ISBN: 978-1-895836-12-7
Orbital Burn by K. A. Bedford (tp) - ISBN: 978-1-894063-10-4
   Orbital Burn by K. A. Bedford (hb) - ISBN: 978-1-894063-12-8

Pallahaxi Tide by Michael Coney (pb) - ISBN: 978-0-88878-293-9
Paradox Resolution by K. A. Bedford (tp) - ISBN:978-1-894063-88-3
Passion Play by Sean Stewart (pb) - ISBN: 978-0-88878-314-1
Professor Challenger: New Worlds, Lost Places edited by Jeff Campbell &
   Charles Prepolec (tp) - ISBN: 978-1-77053-052-2
Plague Saint, The by Rita Donovan (tp) - ISBN: 978-1-895836-28-8
   Plague Saint, The by Rita Donovan (hb) - ISBN: 978-1-895836-29-5
Pock's World by Dave Duncan (tp) - ISBN: 978-1-894063-47-0
Puzzle Box, The by The Apocalyptic Four (tp) - ISBN: 978-1-77053-040-9

Reluctant Voyagers by Élisabeth Vonarburg (pb) - ISBN: 978-1-895836-09-7
   Reluctant Voyagers by Élisabeth Vonarburg (hb) - ISBN: 978-1-895836-15-8
Resisting Adonis by Timothy J. Anderson (tp) - ISBN: 978-1-895836-84-4
   Resisting Adonis by Timothy J. Anderson (hb) - ISBN: 978-1-895836-83-7
Rigor Amortis edited by Jaym Gates and Erika Holt (tp)
   - ISBN: 978-1-894063-63-0

Shadow Academy, The by Adrian Cole (tp) - ISBN: 978-1-77053-064-5
Silent City, The by Élisabeth Vonarburg (tp) - ISBN: 978-1-894063-07-4
Slow Engines of Time, The by Élisabeth Vonarburg (tp) - ISBN: 978-1-895836-30-1
   Slow Engines of Time, The by Élisabeth Vonarburg (hb)
   - ISBN: 978-1-895836-31-8
Stealing Magic by Tanya Huff (tp) - ISBN: 978-1-894063-34-0
Stolen Children (Children of the Panther Part Three) by Amber Hayward (tp)
   - ISBN: 978-1-894063-66-1
Strange Attractors by Tom Henighan (pb) - ISBN: 978-0-88878-312-7

Taming, The by Heather Spears (pb) - ISBN: 978-1-895836-23-3
Taming, The by Heather Spears (hb) - ISBN: 978-1-895836-24-0
Technicolor Ultra Mall by Ryan Oakley (tp) - ISBN: 978-1-894063-54-8
Ten Monkeys, Ten Minutes by Peter Watts (tp) - ISBN: 978-1-895836-74-5
   Ten Monkeys, Ten Minutes by Peter Watts (hb) - ISBN: 978-1-895836-76-9
Tesseracts 1 edited by Judith Merril (pb) - ISBN: 978-0-88878-279-3
Tesseracts 2 edited by Phyllis Gotlieb & Douglas Barbour (pb)
   - ISBN: 978-0-88878-270-0
Tesseracts 3 edited by Candas Jane Dorsey & Gerry Truscott (pb)
   - ISBN: 978-0-88878-290-8
Tesseracts 4 edited by Lorna Toolis & Michael Skeet (pb)
   - ISBN: 978-0-88878-322-6
Tesseracts 5 edited by Robert Runté & Yves Maynard (pb)
   - ISBN: 978-1-895836-25-7

Tesseracts 5 edited by Robert Runté & Yves Maynard (hb)
- ISBN: 978-1-895836-26-4

Tesseracts 6 edited by Robert J. Sawyer & Carolyn Clink (pb)
- ISBN: 978-1-895836-32-5

Tesseracts 6 edited by Robert J. Sawyer & Carolyn Clink (hb)
- ISBN: 978-1-895836-33-2

Tesseracts 7 edited by Paula Johanson & Jean-Louis Trudel (tp)
- ISBN: 978-1-895836-58-5

Tesseracts 7 edited by Paula Johanson & Jean-Louis Trudel (hb)
- ISBN: 978-1-895836-59-2

Tesseracts 8 edited by John Clute & Candas Jane Dorsey (tp)
- ISBN: 978-1-895836-61-5

Tesseracts 8 edited by John Clute & Candas Jane Dorsey (hb)
- ISBN: 978-1-895836-62-2

Tesseracts Nine edited by Nalo Hopkinson and Geoff Ryman (tp)
- ISBN: 978-1-894063-26-5

Tesseracts Ten: A Celebration of New Canadian Specuative Fiction
edited by R.C. Wilson and E. van Belkom (tp)
- ISBN: 978-1-894063-36-4

Tesseracts Eleven: Amazing Canadian Speulative Fiction
edited by Cory Doctorow and Holly Phillips (tp)
- ISBN: 978-1-894063-03-6

Tesseracts Twelve: New Novellas of Canadian Fantastic Fiction
edited by Claude Lalumière (tp)
- ISBN: 978-1-894063-15-9

Tesseracts Thirteen: Chilling Tales from the Great White North
edited by Nancy Kilpatrick and David Morrell (tp)
- ISBN: 978-1-894063-25-8

Tesseracts 14: Strange Canadian Stories
edited by John Robert Colombo and Brett Alexander Savory (tp)
- ISBN: 978-1-894063-37-1

Tesseracts Fifteen: A Case of Quite Curious Tales
edited by Julie Czerneda and Susan MacGregor (tp)
- ISBN: 978-1-894063-58-6

Tesseracts Sixteen: Parnassus Unbound edited by Mark Leslie (tp)
- ISBN: 978-1-894063-92-0

Tesseracts Seventeen: Speculating Canada from Coast to Coast to Coast
edited by C. Anderson and S. Vernon (tp)
-ISBN: 978-1-77053-044-7

Tesseracts Eighteen: Wrestling With Gods
edited by Liana Kerzner and Jerome Stueart (tp)
- ISBN: 978-1-77053-068-3

Tesseracts Nineteen: Superhero Universe
edited by edited by Claude Lalumière & Mark Shainblum (tp)
- ISBN: 978-1-770530-87-4

Tesseracts Q edited by Élisabeth Vonarburg and Jane Brierley (pb)
- ISBN: 978-1-895836-21-9

Tesseracts Q edited by Élisabeth Vonarburg and Jane Brierley (hb)
- ISBN: 978-1-895836-22-6

Those Who Fight Monsters: Tales of Occult Detectives
edited by Justin Gustainis (pb) - ISBN: 978-1-894063-48-7

Time Machines Repaired Whie-U-Wait by K. A. Bedford (tp)
- ISBN: 978-1-894063-42-5

Trillionist, The by Sagan Jeffries (tp) - ISBN: 978-1-894063-98-2

Urban Green Man edited by Adria Laycraft and Janice Blaine (tp)
  - ISBN: 978-1-77053-038-6

Vampyric Variations by Nancy Kilpatrick (tp) - ISBN: 978-1-894063-94-4
Vyrkarion: The Talisman of Anor (Part Three of The Chronicles of the Karionin)
  by J. A. Cullum (tp) - ISBN: 978-1-77053-028-7

Warriors by Barbara Galler-Smith and Josh Langston (tp)
  - ISBN: 978-1-77053-030-0
Wildcatter by Dave Duncan (tp) - ISBN: 978-1-894063-90-6